A Beckoning War

Matthew Murphy

ISBN: 1493714880
ISBN 13: 9781493714889

Author's Note

The following work is a work of fiction. Though the story takes place during a real military campaign, the Allied advance through the Gothic Line in northern Italy in September 1944, the names of military units directly concerning the main actions of the novel have been changed to allow for some poetic license in terms of character development. All characters in the novel are entirely fictional, and small differences in local features have been implemented (such as the fictional hamlet of San Mateo) to accommodate the actions of the characters. Any misrepresentations or errors are mine and mine alone.

Dedication

For Lia

I

Thump!

A jolt, accompanied by a breeze, stirring delirium.

Bump!

His mother, wearing her apron and pouring tea for him at the kitchen table, dissolves in his mind in a scramble of fragmentary impressions, the dissipation of dream. Damn it to hell! His eyes squint open into narrow gun slits in the fading evening light and he finds himself very much in the world of the moment. His shallow, bowl-shaped helmet has been knocked askew by the last bump and he straightens it out with sleepy annoyance. His neck is kinked from his head lolling to the side, and his back is stiff against the seat from the ride. He pulls a Player's cigarette from a silver case in his breast pocket, puts it in his mouth, and lights it. A quick glance around informs him of his surroundings and his place in them as they scroll by.

It is early September 1944, north of the Foglia River in Italy. The jeep in which he rides bounces over the Italian country road, surrounded by the rolling green and gold pastures and grain plots of the Apennine foothills in the early dusk. It is part of a long convoy of trucks, carriers, jeeps and Sherman tanks, which together rumble and kick up a fog of dust. Artillery thunders in the distance. Moving opposite, toward the rear of the column, is an equally long line of bedraggled, grim-looking Italian civilians, possessions hung under their arms, slung over their backs. Husbands, wives, children and the elderly, some with sackcloth for shoes. A few drive beat up old cars, a few others ride bicycles, yet others ride mules or in carts and buggies; but most walk, walk in a slow, defeated and exhausted rhythm, the rhythm of the uprooted and uncertain. Some manage a smile and a wave to the passing Canadians, knowing that the farther north the Allies move, however destructive their guns and planes, the shorter this war will be. Towers of smoke curl into the sky far behind and around and in front of the train of vehicles, signifying a recent sacrifice, a large battle. From everywhere, all directions, the sweet stink of death and decay, mingled with the acrid smells of smoke and fire and cordite, invades everyone's nostrils—dead soldiers, dead civilians, dead livestock. Everywhere, it seems to those accustomed to such destruction, dead everything.

In the passenger seat of the jeep, Captain Jim McFarlane of the Canadian 5th Armoured Division sits, taking this all in, smoking his cigarette. It is grey and cloudy, an atmosphere befitting carnage and decay. His ears ring and his eyes squint: he is exhausted. He looks around at the passing scenery. A roofless stone house, shelled hollow. A broken cart, a dead ox, several dead German soldiers lying twisted and grey, blasted trees, a burned-out German Tiger tank—and off in the distance, a smashed and abandoned howitzer, ringed by spent shell-casings, flipped from the explosion that wrecked it. All around him he sees the destruction of an era and the encroachment of a new one, tracked and printed and pitted into the earth. Flicking his cigarette butt amongst the passing detritus of war, Jim grunts, looks away, and closes his eyes.

"Hey Captain," bellows Corporal Cooley, driving. "You're about to fall asleep again." Cooley is young and beefy and given to undue jolliness.

"Huh? Uh, yeah. Yes, Corporal. You just continue driving, alright?" Cooley glances over at the captain, uneasy. "Yessir." Ah, Cooley. Too observant for his own peace of mind. It is not good to see your exhausted commander doze on duty. Jim blinks and is once again taken by the beckoning whispers of his exhausted mind. Tired, so very tired, this last campaign … by God we won the day didn't we, didn't we? I think I've finally proven my worth at this. Marianne, see? I made the right decision, yes, but I just feel tired—THUMP!

Dozing again. The jeep's bump jars Jim awake. What a long, long couple weeks it has been. The Gothic Line was broken by the Allies in a horrendous maelstrom of murder. The soldiers of the Eighth Army have been pressing northward through the layers of German defences toward their distant objective, the seaside city of Rimini, a dozen long miles away. Given the determination of the Germans to hold, it might as well be a thousand miles away. Between the Apennines and the sea, an opening only a few miles wide, the infantry and tanks and engineers push under curtains and carpets of artillery. Day after day they have been shoved into battle after battle, through massive and well-prepared German fortifications, through broken towns, through minefields and across riverbeds, into the rough and hilly countryside, and over finger-like Apennine ridges sloping downward from the mountains in the west to the Adriatic sea in the east that impede the slow, grinding advance northward, exposing the attackers to the steel and fire of the tired and bitter enemy. Into well-laid ambushes launched from under the false Edens of orchard and vineyard canopies, from fortified villas and farmhouses, from behind stone walls separating farmers' orchards and grain plots, from hilltop villages turned into citadels, from hastily dug front lines of slit trenches and sandbags. And to add to it all, they're not getting much press anymore, not since the gigantic Allied invasion of France several months earlier, the storied 'Second Front' that the Italian Campaign never quite was, and now, with the Allied armies fully engaged in Northwest Europe, never will be. They are now fighting to stall as many German divisions as they can from heading west to impede the advance in France, or from heading east to impede the advance of the Red Army. They know this, that they have been reduced to a bloody diversion, that the headlines and newsreels and radio broadcasts have for the most part moved elsewhere, that they are now forgotten men fighting on a forgotten front.

Each day, it seems, has added a new crease to Captain Jim McFarlane's exhausted war-leathered face. He pulls another cigarette from the silver cigarette case, liberated from the body of a German major last spring, and lights it. He offers one to Cooley, who gratefully accepts.

"Thank you SIR! I'm fuelled on small pleasures."

"So's your mistress too, I'll bet."

"Ouch." Cowed, Cooley lights his smoke and continues driving. He further attempts to converse with the captain, and glances at him as he drives. "Sir, you're lucky. Who sends you so many good smokes that you can have 'em one after the other and hand 'em out like Yanks handing out Hershey bars?"

"A disapproving mother," is Jim's distracted and uninterested answer.

Cooley is about to reply, but opts to shut up as he realizes the curmudgeonly captain is not in a talking mood. Jim draws on his cigarette and thinks back, the last year rolling into focus like a personal newsreel. Steaming on an American troopship, part of the convoy conveying the Canadian 5th Armoured Division to reinforce the Eighth Army in the eternally escalating and perpetually bogged-down Italian front, when suddenly it was attacked by German planes in the dead of night in the Mediterranean. He had heard the distant thuds of an escort ship's depth charges against a phantom German U-boat while en route to England aboard a troopship, he had heard and seen German bombs go off in the distance before while in England, and he had seen planes shot out of the sky, but never before had he been part of an intended target. The air crashed with the cataclysmic fury of bombs and gunfire. The staccato rhythm of machine guns, the deep thudding ack-ack-ack of anti-aircraft turrets, the ear-splitting blasts of bombs and torpedoes that hit their marks. The sky flashed and flickered, silhouetting the besieged ships into brief photo-negatives of sheer overwhelming spectacle. Jim, huddling unwisely on the open deck to catch a view, was suddenly and briefly paralyzed with both excitement and terror, his body seized up and his mind racing—this is war this is it this is the real thing, Jesus Christ what have I gotten into now? But he collected himself, and was filled with a resolve to terrorize the Germans in return. Like everyone else on his ship, he was now chafing against events larger than he, being honed and defined by the very edges of experience. Being reforged through fire and fury.

Days later, landing in Naples under the brooding gaze of Mount Vesuvius, the harbour slicked with the rainbow hues of oil and gasoline and littered with the half-sunk carcasses of scuttled ships in the wake of the retreated Germans. A postcard of war, an image captured in the faces of people and the façades of buildings wearing the same scars, dragged down by the same wearying gravity of privation and violence. Then, bloodshed in the snowy, frozen, broken winter landscape of the Arielli Line in the Ortona Salient. Holding the line under shellfire through the cold months in sleet-glazed slit trenches chopped from frozen mud. Perilous, and some would say often useless, patrols in the dead of night behind the lines of a ferocious, determined and hardened enemy. Why so many bloody patrols? So that the generals could say they had done something that day?

"All you have to do," said the colonel with a wink of good cheer the day before one particularly bad one, "is cross over their lines, kill the sentries, and nail those snipers 'D' Company spotted. It's all there, marked out on the map." A clap on the back for confidence. Followed by a tot of rum on the colonel's tab, numbing his tongue, warming through his wintry constricted veins, dulling his nervous mind.

"Yes, sir. Thank you for the rum, sir." Aye, sir. Anything for the king. I am but a servant of a larger cause. A low rung on a very high ladder. I understand my place in this machine the army. Sneaking out with three other men, their faces so clearly visible in his recollection that his pupils widen and adjust to the reimagined darkness in order to see them better: Private Clarke (later killed in the Liri Valley), Private Pitwanikwat (still the battalion's premier sniper and scout), and Sergeant Stringer, still miraculously the second in command of No. 9 Platoon despite his monthly penchant for being wounded. An arm, a leg, and his chest so far. Nearly lost an eye in that training accident, didn't he? Stalking out on their own into No Man's Land, resembling somewhat the moonscapes of the Great War, a cratered scar born of stalemate stretching between the two opposing forces, into the territory of the enemy to play a deadly game of hide and seek. Hide and seek: that's how he'd thought of it to keep himself cool and to try desperately to inject a sense of fun into such missions. The jagged ground ahead, in its hillocks of upturned earth, reminded him of a mountain chain, which reminds him in his reminiscence of the mountains of Cassino seen months later, the craggy ridges overlooking the bombed-out remnants of the town, they once again holding the line under shellfire. Here, once again conducting dangerous patrols behind the enemy's lines and responding to the enemy's own. More than once, running the gauntlet in a jeep or carrier along a mountainside road, exposed to German observation, ducking from mortar rounds as they burst behind and above. They always missed, thank God. I'll bet I was the subject of a bet, too, a few bored Germans with a pair of binoculars and a mortar commanding the heights: "A bottle of Schnapps says you can't nail that jeep." Intercontinental poker, with stakes as high as an elephant's eye, and no one bluffing. And the Germans have had all the Aces until the last year or so. Elephant's eye—where's that from, he wonders to himself in a lazy tangent of recollection. Oh, yes. That new Broadway album of the colonel's. Oklahoma! Where the wind comes—creeping, is it? Down the plain. Sweeping, that's it.

And the Road to Rome, the Liri Valley drive of the spring, crossing and holding the Melfa. Ten days of intense and furious combat. Tanks covered in foliage, snarling out of the woods at them. Walking into minefields and ambushes. And now, after much of a summer held in reserve, occupied with training exercises, tedious waiting and the occasional bout of sightseeing and revelry, a rough reacquaintance with battle. Against all reason, once again charging headlong into shrieking hurricanes of fire and smoke and steel, through rivers soaked with blood, over shattered grounds and through shattered towns tangled with the twisted figures and broken futures of the dead. He begins to think of his friends, men who have become old friends in a matter of minutes in the moment-to-moment life of wartime. And more scenes bubble up, scenes that haunt him every day, and especially overnight on the rare occasions he is allowed to sleep.

Lying with his platoon in the littered brick- and glass-laden junkyard of a street in Ceprano, behind the burned-out crust of a German halftrack, bullets pelting and whistling. A machine gun sputtered from down the street, pinning them down. He could see the Sherman tank, their trusted cover lumbering ahead and BOOM! It burst into flames, victim of a rocket fired from a window. At this, Big John Peltier, the "Chief", an Ojibwe and the most honour-bound of soldiers and friends, dashed out into the storm of metal to save the commander, who was desperately shrieking and clawing to free himself from the top hatch.

"Cover him!" screamed Jim. A Bren machine gun and two dozen rifles stuttered to the rescue, firing up at the sniper's storefront. John raced through the rubble, pressed flat with tank ruts. He dashed up onto the blazing wreck, tugged the screaming man, hoisted him over his shoulder ... and dropped him. The tankman had just been shot dead. Big John yelled in childish impotent rage and then snapped around in a half turn, clutched his gut and fell to his knees. He too was hit. He crawled back to his position, bullets snapping past him and a tight wide-eyed grimace of pain pressed to his face. He took another in the foot and winced. A big machine-gunner, Lemuellen, and a young rifleman named Cook pulled him by the collar behind the wrecked halftrack. Big John, victor of a thousand arm wrestles and as strong and silent as the cliché implies, whimpered and screeched and bled from his mouth and his stomach and his foot. He died with a gurgle and with shit in his pants.

Then there was Captain Bly, whose very name conjured up jokes of company mutiny; however, he was much more respected and liked than his namesake. His death by a mine during the Liri Valley campaign in the spring gave Jim his promotion from lieutenant to captain—a bitter reason for an extra shoulder star. And Doc Leprenniere, the tireless regimental medical officer; his was one of the most meaningless deaths Jim had witnessed. He died behind the lines during the Melfa River action the spring in a makeshift aid post in a villa, transfusing a moaning young man from Toronto who looked to Jim like raw hamburger. Jim was waiting for his arm to be patched, one of many lined up against the wall or lying on the floor. Those who could, smoked or sipped water or rum. Then, with a sharp suddenness that nearly collapsed his eardrums and loosed his bowels, the air exploded with the fury of shellfire. A bombardment. Jim clutched his ears and prayed fiercely and fast. Leprenniere cursed, "Goddamnit!" and kept at his work, teeth clenched. So admirable and courageous. The window blew inward. The blood bag burst into a crimson shower of wasted charity. Leprenniere was flayed by flying glass and shrapnel. So much blood for one afternoon's suffering.

And now, with the war working its way into his subconscious, his dreams, the very core of his being, it has become part of him, a shadow hanging over his inner world, fuelling nightmares. He has at least one a week now, assuming he is resting behind the lines and is thus able to sleep at all. He can see in the faces of the padres, of the visiting army psychiatrists, that such shock and exhaustion is ubiquitous. That behind the veneer of most of the fighting men, even those who never seem to show fear, is a psychic landscape fractured with war's heave and strain, reflecting the destruction and ruin with which their eyes paint their minds. Yet, in a curious way, he has never been happier. He is forced to think within the narrow confines of his orders and is entrusted to carry out those orders with a body of men under his command. He likes the responsibility of leadership, the fact that he is trusted and that so far, by a hair's breadth, his nerves have not failed him. He is happy that he is in a situation where he can test himself to his physical, mental, emotional and spiritual limits, even if he does not always like what he learns about himself. That combat has rendered him a nervous chain-smoker with yellow-stained fingertips. That it has turned him to drink. That drink in turn has made him do things that he regrets. That he is not nearly as brave as he thought he was when he joined up, his guts churning and his muscles flexed every time he is preparing to carry out an attack. That he is prone to lose focus suddenly under moments of intense pressure, his lieutenants and sergeants looking intently at him for their next cue. This self-knowledge he values because it is true, and because it is true it makes him happy that at least he knows the man that he is. He feels secure with the men in his battalion and has experienced a depth of comradeship with them that he never dreamed possible in civilian life. Indeed, he has felt closer to some of his fellow officers and soldiers than to anyone else he has ever met, excluding Marianne. But now Marianne was half a world away, and worlds apart in experience—war has made Jim a different, harder man.

The two grubby soldiers finish their cigarettes at the same time, and Jim immediately lights up again. He proffers another to the always grateful Corporal Cooley. Jim has strayed into the black and miserable introspection of war: the dead friends of battles past and the gnawing, corrosive dread of battles yet to be. Pull yourself together, man, he thinks. Pull yourself together or you'll be behind a desk in London. Or back home. Or jittering and rocking yourself on a hospital bed, courtesy of the army shrink.

"You know, Corporal?" he suddenly muses. Cooley seems surprised at Jim's sudden talkativeness. "This whole bloody place has me beat. I feel like a bootprint in a shellhole." The two men laugh. He continues: "I think when I get out of here, I'm going to become a monk and whip myself continually for joining the army. Flagellate myself for not knowing any better."

"You won't be the only one, sir," Cooley adds, agreeing in the manner of an upstart subordinate. "But hey, ain't you married, Captain? Monks are celibate."

"Hell, yes. I'll just have to take a leave of absence. She'll understand." These words are followed by the truth in his mind: I've already left her and I'm not sure she understands.

"Yeah," Cooley says. He is dreamy, likely thinking of the possibility of leave in the near future, or at least a day held back in reserve. A small, tantalizing taste of peace and freedom. "I'm just lookin' to get laid with some Italian whore in Rome one of these days."

"Rome? Christ, Corporal, we're not going to Rome!" Jim snickers and draws on his cigarette. "Reserve time is over. There won't be much sightseeing for a long time. Besides, that's a Yankee playground. Why, they own that place right now, armed to the teeth with more perfume, stockings, cigarettes and Hershey bars than any of you horny little bastards can offer to the ladies. They beat us there, remember? The closest we'll ever get to that carnival again is probably seeing some snaps from some returning Americans or some goddamn prewar postcards that we'll find in some ruined farmhouse we're ducking out in. We can just stew about outside of town and listen to those American bastards whoop it up. Maybe steal some chickens, too, on the sly."

"You mean *wop* it up. That's a Canadian reward for a job well done—bargain for basement wine and scrounge for chickens and eggs." They both snicker knowingly. "And whistle at toothless old mamma-mia types. Eh, Captain?"

"Yes," answers Jim, who has suddenly lost the appetite for soldierly humour. He thinks instead of Marianne. Marianne, whose letters come less and less frequently. Her father, who had lost an eye, who was partially deaf and half mad due to the First World War, should have served as a warning. Jim's nerves are already wounded, together a collective casualty paining him from within. And his ears ring, ring with a vengeance that reverberates into his soul, shaking up his dreams. He is exhausted. But he cannot stop now, cannot even think about it.

"Look at us," Jim says. "Just look at us: volunteers in a volunteer army. What fucking fun! As volunteers, we should be singing as we ride. A good ol' marching song."

"Not I, sir. I was drafted."

"You? You were drafted? Of all people, you were drafted?" Jim looks at him incredulously. "You never told me that."

"Yessir. I was drafted and put on guard duty. Then I figured, if you're gonna put me in the army, you might as well send me all the way. That, and I was tired of all the active guys on leave calling me a Zombie."

"A Zombie," Jim muses. "Any regrets about going active?"

"No sir, not at all. I always wanted to travel, and the Germans make it interesting. Beats baling hay on the farm in Markham, that's what I say."

"True, I suppose." Jim changes the subject. "We're a little uncelebrated here, aren't we? These locals should be more thankful."

"Yes, sir! There should be exuberant Eyeties at every turn, giving us a ticker tape parade, even while we're fighting. Like sports fans for morale!"

"You have it, Corporal. Why, in our volunteer army, the bloody Italians should roll out the red carpets everywhere we march, drive, crawl and dash for cover! And you know what, Cooley? They should be lighting our cigarettes for us in the heat of battle, and ladle our soup for us in our slit trenches while we're being shelled."

"They, or those bloody POWs. Don't they get a free and easy ride," grumbles Cooley.

"You'd count that as a blessing if you ever got captured. Do unto others as you would have done to you. *Comprenez-vous?*"

"True enough sir. True enough. I was just jealous. When they give up, they get to sit it out."

II

Directed by a signalling, whistle-blowing provost ahead, Corporal Cooley turns onto a detour road, an equally bouncy Italian country track heading north. Three large trucks and one small, open, tracked carrier turn with him, all being with the same company. The rest of the convoy keeps moving down the same road as they were. Jim's entourage drives toward the shattered ruins of an Italian village, perched atop and on the slopes of a recently taken ridge that was captured by an advance Canadian patrol in the last several hours. They pass a battery of 25-pounders dug in on either side of the road, the guns obscured somewhat amid tattered foliage and underneath camouflaged netting, the noses of the howitzers snubbed squatly and arrogantly upward at high angles, the men fixing, or joking, or sleeping. A man at the gun nearest them waves, shirtless, his helmet cocked sideways as he brews up tea in a bucket in a hole where a small gasoline fire burns, dark heavy orange, just outside the crew's truck and just far enough out of the way of the attached ammunition trailer to not be dangerous. His five compatriots smoke cigarettes while engaged in a craps game under netting in the shallow pit they have dug just behind the howitzer. Jim and Cooley wave back. A comforting sight, men making do amid mayhem. Like the birds singing anyway on the stumps of amputated limbs of blasted trees. They pass the battery, which has just moved upward in the wake of the day's advance, leaving behind them a train of white dust and the grumbly echo of passing vehicles. The vehicles park at the base of a low hill just past a hastily hammered-in road sign that yells in its stencilled block capital print, "DANGER!

YOU ARE NOW AT THE FRONT LINES. DISMOUNT FROM YOUR VEHICLES AND SPREAD OUT IN YOUR MOVEMENTS." Jim stands up in his seat and orders the rest of the company to stop behind him.

"Okay, dismount!" he shouts, and the infantrymen grab their gear, leave their vehicles and form up in their squads with their corporals. To his sergeant major, he says, "Lead them into the nearest orchard. The moment nightfall comes, we move right in and relieve the Sydneys at my signal." The sergeant major, Warrant Officer Witchewski, barks corresponding orders to his men, and the men of Jim's company form into their respective squads and march further up the road for about half a minute, and then gather under and around the gnarled oaks and cypress pines and weeping willow trees that grow in clusters in the field just beyond the weedy roadside ditches. The vehicles depart. A light evening breeze plays the leaves and the grasses in a slow rhythm, underneath a subtle and loose melody of birdsong. Breaks form in the clouds, and the leaves catch the last dying rays of the sun as it sinks in the west beyond the near but unseen sea. Behind them is heard the rumble of trucks as support troops of the battalion decamp into their positions. In perhaps two hours Able Company will move into town and once again be on the tip of the sharp end. After that, the night will become alive with flares and rockets, and the sounds of tanks moving forward into hidden attack positions, into tree stands, behind barns, under carefully assembled foliage and camouflaged nets, hidden from German view. The cat and mouse and hide and seek games of a night at the front.

"Able Company, dig in!" Jim yells amid the clusters of trees, some of which have been blasted to ragged stumps and split kindling. Witchewski looks at Jim and says, "I'll get them digging." Witchewski is fortyish, with dark hair, broad shoulders and dumpling cheeks. There is a bandage wrapped round his head from where he has been slightly wounded. He turns to the main body of men and bellows, "Waste no time and dig in deep! I want real slit trenches this time, not the shitty shellscrapes you guys are accustomed to digging! C'mon Davis, throw yer shoulders into it, damn it! That's it Keating, dig like yer diggin' for treasure! For Chrissakes Lucas, earn your keep around here and hoof into it! I got more results from blind-drunk rotgutted work camp hoboes in the goddamn Depression!" The other sergeants and corporals follow his cue and bark at their platoons and sections of men. The soldiers pierce and hack at the earth with their spades, grunting and sweating under the crepuscular light that drips balefully between the pineneedle netting. Sweat beads on Jim's brow and runs in rivulets down his face like rainwater, and it soaks his armpits and itches under his pack as he digs himself a shallow shellscrape with his own spade. As he shifts his weight a slight breeze makes its way through the opened flue between pack and arched back, shivering through him and cooling the sweat on his skin and soaked in his shirt, making him feel wet and dirty. There is a momentary lull in the distant shelling, all is quiet. He reaches into his webbing and pulls out his canteen, sweat pouring from his brow, his scalp sweating and itching under his helmet, and he stands amid the huff and puff of men, the clenched swearing, the chink of spades against the hard unyielding earth, the clump of discarded shovelfuls of dirt. A drop of sweat drips off his lashes and into his eye and his world goes swimmy in amoeboid distention, and he blinks to clear his eye and a curious relaxation takes hold—you took your objectives with aplomb today Jim, good work, this Gothic Line is nothing really if you just move order by order and don't think too much on it. He looks down and ruminates a discarded German helmet, punctured by a bullet, missing its body now; an artifact, yes, an artifact layered on top of others, on muskets and spears, on top of the helmets of Malatesta nobles and Roman centurions and Carthaginian mercenaries and Greek hoplites; and he pours the water into his mouth and it is as though the cells in his mouth drink in the water, soak in the water before he can swallow, such is the relief of his thirst, and he lifts the canteen high in the air above him, leaning back to a skyward vista of cypress pines, his lips pressed to the rim in refreshing receipt of—

A blast of shellfire, off to the side. Face hugging the dirt, shovel to his side. Jesus Christ. His canteen is still clamped tight in his hands, and he raises it to his lips and takes the sip he was denied by the volley of shells. All is silent again, and the men finish digging their holes.

Jim settles into his shallow trench and waits. Waiting, waiting. This is very much a war of waiting, he thinks. It is in the waiting that his nerves are in danger of frazzling altogether, keying up for danger for hours or days on end at a time. It is in waiting that he and the others have discovered depths of boredom and frustration they never knew were possible. His battalion waited for over two years in Canada after he joined, before the gung-ho and tally-ho Lieutenant Colonel Hobson replaced the lazy and complacent Lieutenant Colonel Brophy and sent the unit to England. Two and a half years of exercises, moves, recruitment tours, more exercises, coastal guard duties, here, there, everywhere, everywhere but where their presence mattered. The Exhibition grounds in Toronto, converted into an army camp of huts, with marches through the streets of Toronto, sporrans flopping against their orange kilts to the pipes and drums of "Garry Owen" and "Endearing Young Charms." Camp Borden, north of Toronto, a sea of white pointed soldiers' tents that resembled a field sown with dragons' teeth. Ski training in the north of Alberta, the smooth slide of skis through the snow amid the night quiet of the pines on either side. Stew cooked in the open, warming frozen bodies before sleep time in snow dugouts. Then, recruitment marches through Quebec, where they were oft hated, where in some towns and villages they were taken to be supreme examples of *Les maudits anglais* in their kilts and pom-pommed cobeens, where the men thus frequently found themselves fighting with the locals in pool halls and dance clubs. Guard duties in Halifax, a navy town if there ever was one, which led to inevitable brawls with sailors, and where Jim first caught an orange-hued glimpse of war in the glow of a torpedoed tanker burning outside the harbour at night. Then, England, stationed in Aldershot southwest of London, where they conducted further exercises on the Salisbury plain, drank in pubs and saloons, toured when possible, and took frequent trips to sample the London nightlife. And where they waited, waited, waited to be sent into action, reading and listening to reports of the fighting in Sicily, and then later, mainland Italy, longing to be a part of it. All this waiting fomented the whispering of rumours. Every day there was a new one. We're going to fight the Japanese. We're going to North Africa. While ski training in Alberta: We must be going to Finland to fight the Russians! All this while, waiting, waiting, now waiting in this orchard, this time tempered with the experience of combat in its ugly actualities, waiting tinged by fear and knowing rather than by boyish excitement.

"Sir?"

"Yes?" Jim looks up and sees Cooley standing over him. "Would you like me to start scrounging up dinner, sir?"

"Not yet. I'll bet you can find better stuff in the town. Take a moment and rest a little. We don't have to do anything till nightfall. Consider it a temporary leave pass."

"Yes, sir." Cooley stalks away to join a poker game that has just begun among a gaggle of soldiers from both his headquarters section and No. 8 Platoon. He is the perfect batman, Jim thinks. If it weren't for him I'd be confined to eating army grub all the time. Such food at the worst of times is wont to make men want to walk toward the enemy with their hands in the air, begging to be shot. With reviled amusement he recalls the first time he ate British military food aboard the Queen Mary, stripped of its décor and turned into a troopship. Lifeless kippers staring deadeyed at him from his breakfast plate, indifferent in their inertness at their fate of being eaten. Sludgy lamb stew for dinner and cold meats for supper. Leathery and chewy cold roast beef, and Spam and Klik and Spork, soft and pink and malleable and shaped to the tins in which they were served. He thinks of a marching song sung in the barracks during training:

There is bread, bread, heavy as lumps of lead,
In the stores, in the stores,
There are rats, rats, big as alley cats,
In the quartermaster's stores.

Such wretched food so poorly prepared could only be transformed into the most halfhearted fighting energy. One cannot properly march into danger when made of kippers 'n Klik. All spiced with saltpeter of course. Welcome to the army, where instead of black pepper they put gunpowder in your food.

My cock is limp, I cannot fuck,
The nitrate it has changed my luck.

Ha! He thinks. Saltpeter has salted our peters and withered them as though they were leaches. The saving grace in officially issued rations and shipboard meals is the tea menu, with its cucumber sandwiches and biscuits and crackers and other nibbles and finger foods.

These thoughts of food bubble up in gurgles of agitated stomach acid, the oasis dreams of a growling and hungry body and mind. No wonder he has suddenly awoken and is feverish with an exhausted and borrowed sort of energy—he is starving. My, he thinks, I'm so hungry I could eat my rations. Sitting here waiting makes him jumpy. For God's sake, let night fall so I can move up. Even the front line is better than this bloody waiting for our cue. The only thing scarier than battle is waiting for it. Waiting for battle, wading into battle from behind the lines. The ominous signs that sober those marching or riding forward with a grave clarity. The sight and stink of shallow temporary graves and their wooden crosses, capped crookedly by the empty helmets of the fallen, standing in rows along the roadsides. Like scarecrows. The tree stumps. The burned-out smell of ruin. The sporadic fall of nearby shells that say in their shrieks, you are not safe beyond this point. Here, you are at the mercy of a casual and impersonal interplay of politically sponsored mathematics, of trajectories, the calculated collision of bodies. Beyond this point it's us or them. At any cost.

Jim unfurls a map of the village, with the positions of the Sydney Highlanders company currently occupying it hastily scrawled in. He studies the positions and figures out where he wants his platoons to be stationed. He then looks at his watch: 2000 hours. Time for orders. He yells, "Company 'O' Group, form here by me!" thereby summoning his lieutenants for their orders. Lieutenants Doyle, Olczyk and Therrien, the Company Orders Group, assemble around Jim. Missing is Major

Goldberg, wounded leading the company in his first day in action in an attack at the beginning of this offensive and leaving Jim for a time the sole commander of Able.

"Good evening gentlemen: orders." He shoots them together a brief glance. "I have here a map of San Mateo. When we relieve the Sydneys, we're going to take whatever positions they have made for us. We're covering the division's western flank, and our company is covering the battalion's own flank. Therrien, I want you where their No. 18 Platoon is. Right here." He gestures with his finger. Most of the houses there, I'm told, are completely destroyed. You may want to really dig in there, if the Sydneys haven't already."

"Yes, sir." Therrien pensively studies the map.

"Olczyk, you are moving to the south side. Again, the houses there are apparently utterly wrecked. So you'll want to dig in if the Sydneys haven't. We may be moving tomorrow, we may stay a couple days. I don't know. So you'll want adequate cover. Both of you," Jim continues, looking them both in their careful, studying eyes, "make sure your machine guns facing centre interlock. Set up a good enfilade. Also, watch your flanks with your outward-facing machine guns. I don't want any patrols sneaking in. Doyle, you have the centre. Again, dig in."

"Yes, sir." All three look at Jim, waiting for further cues. For a moment, Jim draws a blank. He stands outside of the moment, viewing himself from outside himself, his thoughts fogged in fatigue and shaken in a tremor of nerves. Get it together. This is not the time. He focuses on the map and centres himself, draws himself back into the requirements of the moment. Responsibility looks him in the face through three pairs of expectant and perceptive eyes. Therrien blinks.

"As well," continues Jim, "at some point in the night, we're getting three 6-pounders from the AT platoon. They'll set up in case of German armour. Keep your PIATS at the ready for tanks, too. Staff Sergeant Nichols is seeing to it we have plenty of ammo. Also, a battery of 25-pounders is deploying to support any possible advance we may be ordered to make, between you, Olczyk, and 'B' Company, just behind. We're going to have noisy neighbours. Tanks from the Hussars will be moving into hidden jump-off positions as well, just behind us, to support the brigade should we get any orders to move out and cross the Marano. They will also be giving us fire support while we wait. The colonel will set up Tactical HQ just north of us on a promontory where he will face the river and determine when we advance. The other companies will move into the line beside us when he arrives. Any questions so far?" He surveys his lieutenants. There are no questions.

"There is more. At about 2400 I want you, Olczyk, to lead a contact patrol to their lines in the valley to test the flank." Olczyk winces.

"Yes, sir," he says, unhappy with this task.

"I know that's a joyless task, but Colonel Hobson wants patrols, and it falls on us and 'B' Company. He wants to know exactly who we're up against. I'll leave it up to you to select a party. No more than five. If it makes you feel any better, HQ and Charlie are sending out their own patrols to test the approach to the river."

Addressing the group as a whole again, Jim advises them, "Study this map for a minute and familiarize yourselves with it. When we're ready, I'm going to dispatch the company." The lieutenants pore over the map.

"One other thing; for your pickets and sentries, tonight's call sign is 'Il Duce', and the countersign is 'Dupe.' Got it?" They answer with nods. "Next 'O' Group assembly is after supper once we're settled. Meet me in my HQ for supper, and I'll brief you of any developments. I'll let you know where exactly my HQ is before that, of course. Probably the church in the centre of town. It has a good vantage point. We move at 2100 hours." He observes them a moment as they examine their maps. He adds, "I know five hours behind the line wasn't much of a rest, but here we are again. Sorry."

Doyle looks up at him and winks. "No problem sir. No rest for the wicked, eh?" He returns to his map reading.

"No, no rest. It looks like we'll be on the line longer than anticipated. C'est la vie, such is our lot." After a minute, Jim dismisses them. Jim trails off into lazy thoughts again for a brief time. Waiting, waiting. Wading in and out of consciousness.

From behind there is an explosion as though someone threw a keg of gunpowder on a fire. Jim is startled into hugging the dirt.

"What the Christ?" he yells, looking backward. A flame shaped like an arrowhead shoots skyward like that from a lighter, followed by another, similar concussion. Now that it is darkening, the crews of the battery they passed are opening fire, sending their shells into the German positions. "You'd think they could warn us or something!" He looks above and sees shells sparkling overhead between the netting of branches and leaves like manmade meteorites, trailing their whistles and screams, divorcing themselves from sound and leaving it shrieking in their wake. A minute later there is an explosion nearby, about two hundred yards distant, as the Germans return fire. There is another, a clutch of artillery shells landing in rapid succession in a wave of overlapping blasts. Jim yells out to his resting company: "Able Company, dig in deeper!" The men hack into the earth with their spades in tactile response to his order, shovelling as the sky explodes above them, and Jim leads by example, heaving out great clots of earth from the haphazard hole which he dug for himself earlier. After a time waiting out the bombardment, the shelling abates enough for them to move. He yells to his men over the sporadic crash of nearby artillery, his words ringing out between blasts: "Attention! Form into your sections! We are moving into the town!"

Able Company assembles into squads, abandoning card games and small talk. Jim moves to near the front of the line as the company forms up and marches single file down the dirt-track road, cloaked in the protective layer of the night, a silent march, the soft crunch of boots in the dust. They snake their way toward the village, spaced out in the darkness to limit possible casualties, the desultory flash and flicker of the guns and the sporadic return fire of the Germans throwing into moments of reddened relief the skeletal trunks and branches of trees, the silhouettes of farmhouses and barns, and the backs and helmets or balaclavas of men laden with packs, spades clanking against their other supplies, rifles slung over shoulders, and in the case of a few, bulkier machine guns. For well over a mile they march, sullen and silent, tramp, tramp, tramp, crunch, crunch, crunch, squelch, squelch, squelch, through puddles left behind from rain earlier that day, their boots against stones eroding only a cosmic fraction of the forces of wind and water, the patient arsenal of time.

As they march up toward the slope of a ridge, the men of Jim's company file section by section into the ruins. The town, Jim can see from where he stands, consists mainly of a few dirt lanes, and a handful of stone houses and a church. Much of it is damaged or destroyed. Outlined against the night, the jagged ruins of the town fang the horizon of the front line. Here, in the village, the homey smells of olive oil, of garlic, of fish, and of wine are apparent, duelling for supremacy with the rank stench of war. Jim strolls up to a tired officer of the Sydneys' pioneer platoon, who is resting with one of his corporals at the entrance to the hamlet. Jim perks up and asks, "Is it clear?"

"As clear as we can make it," responds the engineer in a slight Cape Breton brogue. "But keep an eye out—be really careful. Y'know how they mine just about anything. There's bound to be a few of those *schu* mines lurking about. There's a lotta rubble to hide boobytraps in this village, so watch out. We nailed them hard on the way in, so I'm sure they left some calling cards. I'm leaving a couple sappers with you guys, so you're in good hands."

"Thank you. Could you tell me where the CO here is right now? We're relieving the garrison."

"Yes, sir. In the general store in the piazza, just down the street. Ask for Major Rankin."

"Thought so. Just making sure. Thanks and good luck, Lieutenant."

"And to you." With that, Jim's entourage enter the village proper. Jim yells, "This is it! We're here! Go to your assigned destinations and dig in for the night!" 'Here' is roughly a thousand yards from the first known German positions of the newly reconfigured lines. Troops of Able Company quickly begin making the village theirs as the holding platoon from the Sydney Highlanders files out, relieved in more ways than one. He finds the commanding officer, a Major Rankin, headquartered in the ruins of the general store. The floor is jumbled in household goods and broken shelves, and other remnants of civility. Rankin is squat, strongly built, red-haired and unshaven, every bit the burly Highland Scot. His company radio set pops and hisses and screeches from the headphones, and a young signalman is bent over it in concentration.

"I'm Captain McFarlane, 'A' Company, 1st Irish, and I'm here to relieve you, sir," Jim says upon a mutual exchange of salutes.

"Major Tom Rankin, 'D' Company, 1st Sydneys," replies Rankin, who has returned to gathering up his things. "Pleased to meet you. She's all yours, what's left of 'er. I'm not sure how our ordnance fares on German targets, but it's all too effective on Italian scenery, is it not?"

"Yes, sir."

"They've been shelling the crap out of us on and off all day since we took the place. Had to fend off two counterattacks. You'll notice the wrecked Panzer IV just outside the town. Taken out by one of our own earlier. I had sixteen casualties just taking this shithole, and another twelve holding out. You may want to take that church from the priest there. It's obvious, but it's strong. I never took it out of the kindness of my heart to the priest there, but you'll want something resembling a bunker here, and that's the closest you'll get. You'll want to dig into the leeward slopes mostly during the day—they'll shell the shit out of you. We're taking a shitload of fire from the next ridge—looks like the British attack there failed. Well, let's take our leave of one another before they find out two officers are chatting here and level the goddamn building. Good luck, Captain," he says on the way out.

"Good luck to you, too, Major."

The passing troops exchange glances that both size up their regimental rivals and acknowledge their mutual prowess. Jim surveys the town surrounding him. The northernmost reaches of the village are a jagged topography of rubble, a mountain chain arisen from the seismic forces of modern combat, obliterated, Jim was told before moving in to occupy the village, by RAF fighter-bombers that had dropped their bombs just short of approaching German reinforcements while confused in a morning fog. Jim looks about and eyes the small Romanesque stone church, with its arches and its steeple pointed hopefully to heaven, though smashed by shellfire in the damnation of war. There are several large holes in the roof and in the walls, but on the whole it is standing and Jim immediately decides it is a good place to make his company headquarters at the moment. The priest, an old man with wild white hair, emerges from the church to greet the troops at the front door. He exudes exuberance to the liberators and shouts happily at them in Italian. He runs up to Jim and shakes his hand.

"*Accocliere cordialmente San Mateo, Capitano,*' he says, noting Jim's captain's stars as he squints in the darkness. Jim smiles and says, "*Buona sera, Padre. Parla inglese?*"

The priest shakes his head, and says in a thick accent, "*Non inglese, non inglese.*" He eyes the soldiers somewhat suspiciously, likely knowing that he is going to lose something by their being there.

"I doubt he's going to like this," Jim predicts. He turns to Witchewski. "Can you get a translator? My tourist Italian isn't good enough for this. We need to make this prettier."

"Sure. Fratini can do it." Fratini is an Italian soldier posted to the battalion as a guide and translator. Witchewski summons a runner, Private Lafontaine, to get him. "I doubt he'll surrender this church to be a barracks," says Witchewski of the priest, arms folded. "If the last guys in here didn't take it, obviously he doesn't want us to take it."

"We'll tell him we're the Forces of Goodness here to combat the Nazi Devil. Angels in khaki. Heh, heh." After a couple minutes, Lafontaine returns with Fratini. Fratini is tall, dark, chiselled, and wearing a beret. He and Jim salute each other and Jim tells him, "Tell him we have to take over his church."

Fratini smiles a wide Italian smile and says, "I'll try," in a somewhat muted accent. He talks to the priest in Italian, gesturing to the troops and to the church.

The priest shakes his head. "*Non non non!*" He shouts animatedly. "*Nessuno soldatos in mio chiesa!*" He looks toward Jim and Witchewski and yells at them, "*Andate via!*" Fratini continues bargaining and cajoling with him. Finally he caves in with an angry and mournful "*Non il mio chiesa!*" He saunters off, muttering, "*I Canadesi, i canadesi,*" in a tone salted with disgust. Heading out of town the way Able Company arrived, he is likely to go and complain to deaf ears at Brigade Headquarters.

"*Grazie*, Fratini," says Jim, and he tips his helmet to him in gratitude.

"*Prego, Capitano.* It was my pleasure."

"What did you tell him, anyway?"

"I tella him his church has been bombed anyway, what difference is it to have Allied soldiers in it? He says it was the Allies who-a-blasted his church. And then I tell him if Allied soldiers a-move into your church, the Allies won't bomb it anymore. Ha!" Jim and Witchewski laugh. Fratini goes his own way, heading toward Battalion Headquarters. Witchewski turns to Jim and says, "Let's just hope Father Macaroni there isn't some Fascist informer. This far north—you gotta watch 'em."

Pointing to the church, Jim shouts in the style of the moment, "*Avanti i miei compagni!*" and the men move in with aplomb.

III

Night-cloaked, the men begin to make themselves at home, billeting themselves in and fortifying houses for the night in this small village, under the supervision of their sergeants and corporals. Some dig slit trenches between houses, others occupy and improve upon those abandoned by the Sydneys. Defensive positions are set up and manned in the dark, and machine guns and mortars are put at the ready at various points. A map is spread out on the altar in the broken interior of the church, where a crucifix of Christ stares down in fixed agony on the officers and men of Jim's headquarters, one stone arm sheared off from an explosion. Several of the soldiers raid the wine cellars of the houses they have occupied, making the most of their spartan quarters and miserable conditions.

"Tell the men not to get too pissed tonight," says Jim, absently looking at a map spread on the altar of the church. "We're too close to Jerry for comfort."

"That's easier said than done," Witchewski answers.

"Although, let them have a few, it's been a rough show. Ration whatever they find. I don't want them firing in the wrong direction." As he finishes his sentence, he produces a metal flask from his web-gear, unscrews the lid and takes a sharp, numbing swig of rye whiskey. He offers some to Witchewski. "Have some."

"Aye aye, Captain. Orders is orders." He, too, takes a large, pungent, comforting slug of booze.

"Is the company kitchen behind up and running?" Jim inquires.

"Well, if it's up, it's running behind," quips Witchewski.

"To hell with that overdue 'victory' gruel." He makes a Churchillian victory 'V' with his hand. "'V' for vile. Cooley!"

"Yessir!" Cooley snaps to attention.

"Cut the parade drill crap. You have an important mission, code-named Dinner. Take Briggs and Lafontaine with you."

"Yessir." He salutes knowingly and with a slight grin. "We'll scrounge up a banquet." He rounds up the two soldiers detailed as company runners, Briggs abandoning the short range No. 38 radio set he has just been testing, and the three move out into the night to scrounge up food.

"There's not much for me to do now," Jim says to Witchewski. "Go oversee the fortification. I'll be off in a corner on my own for a bit if I'm needed."

"Sure, sir." Witchewski looks at him and notes in his expression Jim's dogfaced weariness. The captain, the emblem of the company, is also the emblem of their fatigue and their torment.

"Tell me when the chow's ready," he says to no one in particular as he goes to the back of the broken church, dusts chips of fallen masonry and plaster off a pew, and sits. He lights a couple candles stuck in old bottles of Italian wine the men have brought in from the village as makeshift candleholders. Under the candlelight he sits and reflects. From his pocket he produces a sheet of YMCA-issued notepaper and a pen. Time to squeeze out a couple letters home. Yesterday it was his father. Tonight it will be his mother and Marianne.

He twirls the pen in the air pensively as he gazes at the blank sheet of paper resting on a clipboard on his lap. What to write? he thinks. What this time? Jesus Christ, after the last few weeks, what do I write? Death. Stormed a pillbox yesterday Mom, killed a few German boys with a grenade. Whew! You should have seen the mess! I watched a guy turn into a geyser of blood the other day when he tripped a mine! He was seventeen! He was under my command! And to top it off, I'm going deaf! I smoke too much and get the shakes! Such sardonic thoughts crowd his mind. He closes his eyes, inhales slowly and deeply and then exhales, and thinks, peace. Peace, that's right, peace, home, peace. He puts his pen to paper. He starts with a scribbled letterhead:

—Somewhere in Italy—

Dear Mother,

I miss you too. I got your last letter when you told me about your trip to Muskoka. It sounded fun. I miss simple pleasures like that. I especially miss the lakes in Canada. What these Europeans call lakes are more like puddles. A trip anywhere not here sounds pleasant. When we're told we're going on a trip somewhere we get nervous and load our weapons. Still, there is always leave, and we have had some great times in Naples and Jesi. Rome is a bit harder to get to; you have to curry favours to get there. Usually a bottle of booze can buy you a ride from thirsty Americans. We'll see if the censors let that bit through! All in all, this really is a beautiful country in the summertime, the cypress trees in full splendour, the mountains, the orchards, and especially the art and the architecture. At least the architecture that hasn't been destroyed. The black and white postcards I've sent you of Naples and Jesi don't really do this place justice, though the ones I sent you of England last year are spot-on, at least for the winter months. The sense of history is palpable, too, everywhere you look or step. Pompeii really rammed that home. A perfectly preserved day in the life of the Roman Empire. There was even preserved graffiti from the time! A meal set out, reduced to stone. I wonder if the marks we're making here will be the subject of a guided tour two thousand years from now. I do get the feeling that I am a part of history, if only an infinitesimally small part of it being carried along in the tide.

Once again he twirls the pen as his mind draws a blank. He feels a dull ache in his head and takes a gulp of whiskey from his flask. Much better, he thinks. Again, he puts the pen to the paper.

Right now I am in a church that we soldiers have taken over. A bit of sacrilegious sanctuary I guess you could say. Being in here reminds me of Pompeii—in a way, we're like the eruption of the volcano, ending one era and beginning another. And wrecking everything around us. I should have been a philosopher! I am safe right now so you don't really have to worry too much about me. I take care of myself and I take care of my men. It can get hard here and when it does I do nothing but think of home. But still this is where I belong now. This war is important. It's hard but it's the right thing to do. And if I ever stop thinking that, I have no business leading men into combat. There is no way I'd make it out of my trench. I think Marianne's starting to come around and see it that way. When the guns open up and we hit the dirt, you have to rationalize it—this is the right thing to do, because if I were to die here, I would at least think there was some meaning to it. But, I don't want you worrying, because I am competent and confident in my abilities. If I were not, they would never have made me a captain. You and Dad raised a strong son. Take pride in that.

For a moment he pauses in search of the right words. He continues. He thinks to himself. Tell about the battle. About the smell. Jesus. Across the room is a stone Jesus. Stone Savior. Stoned by pieces of lead. Martyred Marble. Mangled Messiah. Ha! He clears his mind of babble, and writes again.

Overall I am fine. Give Dad my best. Love you always,

Jim

He folds the letter, puts it in an envelope, and takes out another sheet of notepaper. Again, he writes 'Somewhere in Italy' at the top of the paper. He continues—

Dear Marianne,

I know I haven't written you for a bit, but things have been hectic here. Heavy fighting and not much sleep. I have a little bit of a break here, a lull in the action and a chance to collect my thoughts. I just finished writing a letter to my mother, as I owed her one. Nobody frets and worries like a soldier's mother, and if you miss a week, she would assume the worst. I couldn't let poor Mom go through that! Mind you, I did miss a week, and that's why I wrote to her first.

In the dim flicker of the candlelight, he ponders, once again pirouetting his pen in the air with his hand. In the distance, he hears the dull crump of artillery. Outside the window he can see the flicker of distant gunfire. Closer, he can hear the manoeuvring of men and vehicles moving in the darkness. Up above is the drone of unseen planes, likely British bombers heading north on a night raid. So much commotion.

"Chow's ready!" shouts Witchewski when Cooley and Lafontaine and Briggs arrive with some food and wine scrounged from nearby locals.

"I'll be there in a minute," responds Jim, exhausted. He adds to his letter.

I know what me coming here has done to you, but I want to tell you, I'm fine. We all take care of each other here so we can all go home. We recently fought a series of major battles that have had an effect on our campaign here. It's rewarding to think that there is a flip side to all this suffering and that we are gaining ground, and that we are fighting for something. As our lieutenant colonel likes to say, with us on the job, the Third Reich's entered its third act.

This experience is important to me. I had never taken many risks until I did this. It's important to learn your strengths and take your licks. Doing this tells you exactly what kind of a man you are. There is no ambiguity. That said, everyone has his limits, and you have to keep yourself sane to avoid being stretched past yours. I have seen more than a few men invalided out of here without a visible scratch, but their minds shattered.

He stops and thinks. Thinks of home. Thinks of coming home after a day's work to his wife. Thinks of her wrapping his arms around him, thinks of her smell, a clean, inviting, warm, womanly smell. His heart quickens, and he begins to write at a feverish pitch—

I miss your meals. I miss your beauty. I miss your smell, your perfume. I miss your love. I miss everything about you. I will come home. I assure you. And when I come home, I won't leave again. Ever again. I'll stay with you. I will have had enough adventure for one lifetime, I think. Forgive me for leaving—you know I had to—if you saw what this enemy does, you'd understand why it is we're here. But I promise you—I promise you—when I come home I will never leave you again. I should go for now, I'm about to eat dinner and I'm starving, I can hardly think straight and write. I'll write you again very soon. I love you more than ever—

Jim XXOO

Hands jittering from this tremor of emotion, he folds this letter as well and puts it in an envelope. He joins members of his headquarters section and his fellow officers. There are Cooley, Briggs and Lafontaine, as well as Private Thibeault, the company signaller. And there are Lieutenants Doyle and Olczyk. They are young, younger than Jim, and an epoch younger than Witchewski, who is forty and a career soldier. Doyle and Olczyk are replacements. Doyle of Lieutenant Barry, killed by mortar fire while manning the Cassino line in April, and Olczyk of Jim's friend Lieutenant Barrett, wounded in the leg during the Liri Valley offensive a month later and since sent home. Therrien has opted to eat in his position in the dark, and has sent his new second in command, Sergeant Webster, to dine in his place. Other than Therrien, Jim hasn't really bothered to get to know any of them yet. Witchewski sits among them, and together they eat unleavened Romagnola *piadina* bread with salty Parma ham and drink rich Sangiovese red wine. Cooley has once again proven his worth as a scrounger. They are bolstered by this, and by their field rations, bully beef and hardtack and other such soldiers' fare. They eat, they make small talk, they smoke a cigarette, they consult over orders. Then, they retire to their duties, or if they can, a few minutes or maybe even an hour of sleep. Under a pew surrounded by broken masonry, Jim crashes, his boots still on, his Browning automatic pistol still at his side, and sleeps, sleeps for a half hour on the cold flagstones, an unexpected and overdue luxury. This time there is no nightmare.

IV

"Is there anyone sitting here?" he asked in the crowded aisle, light suitcase and cap in hand, after she caught his eye, curved into her window seat, wearing a royal blue cotton summer dress, culminating downward in white leather sandals, one foot crossed over the other, top foot pointed down, a confident and refined womanly poise evident from head to toe and back again. She was reading a paperback novel and was utterly and soberly immersed, eyes half shut and brow rippled in concentration, her fine-featured face framed by tresses of dark curly hair. He was seized by this presentation of beauty. After a moment, the spell was broken. She looked up slowly, and with a warm smile that set his stomach aflutter, answered, "No, go on ahead, feel free." At this, her eyes and her attention went back to her book, her face utterly, wonderfully serious again as she engrossed herself back in her reading. His heart pounding, he opened his suitcase and rummaged for the *Canadian Forum* magazine he'd been reading, found it, and placed the suitcase on the overhead rack before sinking into the seat beside her before pretending to read, or rather, reading the same two sentences over and over again without at all interpreting their meaning, the fine black print defamiliarized into hieroglyphs. As the train lurched into motion, screeching over the track and settling into a soporific rhythm, his eyes scanned the article in the magazine, and he frantically tried to think of a way to start a conversation with her. Beside him, she yawned, and her hands slid down to her lap, her book still open, and she shut her eyes and dozed, buying him time as he nervously fidgeted his way into making a move of some kind. He didn't. After awhile she woke up, and her heavy-lidded eyes met his. She smiled and yawned, blocking her mouth as she did so with the palm of her hand.

"Enjoying your magazine?" she asked.

"Uh, yeah. I'm reading an article by Arthur Lismer, about the relationship of art and intelligence. It's quite interesting."

"Sounds like it. He's the nature artist, right?"

"Yes, he is, with the Group of Seven. Are you enjoying your book?"

"Oh, it's alright, I guess. Passes the time, anyway."

"You seemed to be really into it. What's it about?"

"Oh, it's just a romance novel, kind of silly and all that; it's about a woman schoolteacher who falls for a man in a small town where she moves to in order to escape the memories of a failed love affair in her past. You know, it's one of those stories." She smiled a smile of unabashed glee at enjoying a tale constructed of such clichés, of relishing such a guilty pleasure. Jim immediately fell in love with her.

"Well," he said, hesitant and momentarily unsure about the wisdom of what was about to come out of his mouth, "this reminds me of another story." He flashed a grin.

"And what story would that be, exactly?" she responded, playing along, adding a dimension of loaded expectance into the air.

"It might be a bit of a cliché, but ... did you ever read the one about a man and a woman who meet on a train to Ottawa? The man is a schoolteacher on his way to a new job, and ... I'm not exactly sure about the woman, but I do know this ... " A nervous, excited thrill coursed through him and his heart jumped a bit, and he felt himself flush about the face, " ... that the man finds the woman utterly attractive, and asks her to have dinner with him. I don't remember if she says yes; I think I only read that far."

Taken aback, she uttered a surprised giggle, embarrassed and flattered all at once, looking away from him and at the situation itself, eyes wide and eyebrows raised, incredulous at what the moment brought. "Oh, my. I wasn't expecting that." Turning to him and looking into his eyes, she continued after a moment: "And I suppose you would like us to continue the story by my saying yes, am I correct in assuming?"

"Indeed you are correct. But whatever your answer, please accept what I said as an honest compliment. It would have been criminal had I not even tried." He smiled, and she beamed in response.

She turned serious. "Well, I think I could be persuaded, but—"

"But what?" His tone was light, but nonetheless he felt himself backsliding into failure after such a promising start.

"But I don't even know your name. You have to let me know who you are before you can treat me to dinner, Mr. Stranger on a Train."

He blushed at his mistake, and relief washed over him when he realized his small oversight. "Oh, I'm sorry. James McFarlane. You can call me Jim." He held out his hand. She took his hand. "Marianne Temple. You can call me Marianne. Pleased to meet you, Jim McFarlane."

"And you too, Marianne. Stranger on a Train. Strangers on a Train. That would be a good name for the story, wouldn't it?"

"I agree. It has that novel feel: *Strangers on a Train*, by James McFarlane. Sounds like a bestseller." Jim was uncertain if he was being mocked or flattered. "And a bit of a cliché." She rolled her eyes as she said this. Now he was certain. "Well, that was an awfully dashing way for you to ask me out, if I must say, but, well, I don't know if I can take you up on your offer." She was aware that she was in control of the situation, was having a little fun with his insecurity.

"Why is that?" Jim was suddenly crestfallen.

"You have to prove something to me." Her voice had a playful, mock-serious timbre.

"And what do I have to prove, exactly?" Jim was smiling, up for this game, heartened by her tone.

"You have to prove to me that you really want to be with me. Can you go a month without seeing me?"

Jim sighed, a shadow of defeat settling over his features. "I suppose so."

"Good, because I am going to visit my cousins in Montreal after you disembark. I will be there for almost a month. When I return to Ottawa, I would love for you to treat me to dinner." Jim felt a tide of relief topped by a giddy lightness. Outside, a line of telephone poles whooshed by one by one by one, framing the farmers' fields like the rolling of a film reel, the film adaptation of *Strangers on a Train.* Filmed in Technicolor, starring promising newcomers James McFarlane and Marianne Temple in their first leading roles.

"Do you live in Ottawa?" he asked.

"Yes, I do. I was just visiting my sister in Toronto. I live in Sandy Hill, not too far from the Market. My parents own a furniture store nearby, Temple Furniture. I help them out; earn my keep, if you will. Learning the trade from the table legs up. I like working there, but I want a little more. I was thinking of taking some clerical courses and working in an office." She paused a moment, thoughtfully. "If ever there is work to be found."

"I will be teaching at Ashton College. I have a boardinghouse arranged already nearby. It's a pretty good position, I should think, great considering the lack of jobs around."

"Well, Jim, I will definitely take you up on your offer when I'm back. We'll go have dinner, and perhaps we can see a film."

"I'm sure it can be arranged." And so they talked, and talked, and talked, all the way to Ottawa, talked of their families, their upbringing, their interests, the train clickety clacking its way down the track, by the deep rippled blue expanse of Lake Ontario, by the fields, by the forests, by the stacks and steeples and through the whistle stops of small towns, the countryside rolling by in all its myriad majesty.

The ensuing courtship was immediately fruitful. He received a telegram from Western Union two days later:

HEY YOU STOP LOOKING FORWARD TO DINNER STOP WITH CHARMING STRANGER ON A TRAIN STOP TAKE CARE AND SEE YOU SOON.

He could barely contain himself, and wrote a letter in his lonely room in his Elgin Street boardinghouse, surrounded by semi-unpacked luggage—

Dear Marianne,

Thank you very much for the telegram. It really lifted my spirits when I got here. You know, I came here and realized with some dismay that I don't really know anyone yet in these parts. Such is life. Still, I think I am settling in as well as I can, considering how short a time I've been here. My experiences so far have included being defecated on by a pigeon and nearly getting run over by a streetcar. There is, thus, only one way to look at my future here, and that is up: it can only get better, as it certainly will when I see you again—

How is life in Montreal? By all accounts, it is a beautiful city. I wouldn't know, I've never been there. I've been in the U.S. before, but until now, I'd never been east of Toronto or North Bay. I went north to saw wood for a year to build some character and muscles, but that's about it ... It's time to broaden the old horizons, take the bull by the horns. Well, take care and I'll see you when you get back—

Sincerely Yours,

Jim

V

Sunbeams through the August window touch his face. The floral-patterned curtain flaps in the teasing morning breeze in the absence of glass or screen. A stir, a murmur, the light fanning of sheets as he awakens. Beside him, she sleeps, Marianne, his wife. He kisses her gently on the cheek and she smiles softly in her slumber. Ssssssshhhhh … Let her sleep. I've been here before. I think. Never mind. Look out the window. He parts the curtain and looks out over a jagged sea of faded terra cotta roofs and chimneys and steeples into the piazza in the early dawn. Beyond the cobblestoned piazza and its fountain, through the downward curve of a narrow street between the pastel façades of buildings strung lazily together by lines of drying laundry is the sun, gilding the waters that lap molten at the beach as it rises from the horizon of the sea. He looks back down into the piazza. The Neo-Classical post office is colonnaded with marble columns that remind him of the legacy of the Romans. There is no one in the street. The world belongs to him and Marianne. She has come all this way—I can't believe she made it! Must've bribed her way over here! He whistles to himself at his good fortune. He crawls back into bed, careful not to awaken her. He fingers a tendril of her dark, soft corkscrew curls spilled about the pillow and tickling his shoulder. She sleep-sighs and stirs slightly in an expression of utter contentment. The earth quakes underneath his feet and the sky goes black with ash as with a deafening, volcanic roar the air is sucked from his lungs in a Vesuvian—

Up with a start to a thundering jolt. He bashes his head on something hard above him upon coming to. "Marianne," he mouths, but no sound comes out. Dream flickers dissipate like smoke. The church trembles and Jim immediately covers his head with his hands, a well-practised attempt to duck from danger. His forehead throbs from its contact with the underside of the pew.

"Shit!" he can hear someone shout in the commotion. He looks about in the darkened interior of the church amid the scurrying silhouettes of men dropping their playing cards and their books and their letters, and hitting the floor. Outside, a massive shell has burst, rattling everyone and everything in the town.

"That's a 150!" Witchewski yells. Jim is still in an addled blear, not fully responsive to the alarmed commotion about him. He shakes his head and comes somewhat to his senses. Clarity asserts itself. He briefly thinks, is there a moment's respite?

"What was hit?" Jim asks.

"Dunno yet," Witchewski answers. Lieutenant Doyle of No. 7 Platoon rushes into the church from a brief inspection of defensive positions around the church and says, "Hit the outskirts of the village. Shook our forward-most positions but did no real damage. They're stonking us."

"The usual," grumbles Jim. "Hold onto your tin hats, gentlemen." There is a whoosh akin to a freight train racing overhead, followed by another jarring bang. He hears another whoosh, heading the opposite way. The German guns are being answered by the Canadian and British guns in the rear.

"This is our castle and to hell with anyone that gets in our way!" Jim shouts, boosting the men in his ramshackle headquarters. There is a loud, fists-in-the-air cheer. From further behind the lines arrive two artillery spotters with their scopes and their radio, looking to set up in the steeple of the church. For the love of God, thinks Jim. Not there! Now we're toast! He runs up to one of them, the Forward Observation Officer, a lean young man with a long and sharp nose and sandy curls of hair protruding from below his skewed beret, and addresses him with a smart salute.

"Captain McFarlane, 'A' Company, 1st Irish."

The FOO returns his salute, his binocular telescope clanking against his shoulders as he does so. The other, a stout signalman with black hair, a large flat nose and wide football shoulders, is encumbered with a radio set and headphones. "Lieutenant Blake, 18th Field Artillery. At your service, Captain." He flashes a cocky grin. "This is Private Cole. We were sent ahead to set up an observation post. We were just about to check out the steeple here."

Before Jim can further address Blake, Witchewski blusters his way into the conversation: "You must be brand-spanking new around here if you think you can camp out in what's left of that steeple. Much of it's been blown away already, and you may notice the bell is on the floor. A hell of a clang that must've made. Pardon my French, sir, but to occupy a steeple in a church on a patch of high ground in front of a battle-hardened enemy holding the higher ground is a wet-behind-the-ears dumb shit kinda thing to do." A medium-sized shell hits the roof and they duck instinctively at this unintended exclamation mark to Witchewski's tirade. They all lift their heads after a moment.

Jim interjects before Witchewski can continue. "Meet Warrant Officer Witchewski, my CSM," he introduces in a genial tone, gesturing to Witchewski. "Don't mind him, he's an old grouch. Anyway, if Jerry sees your scope, and your German counterpart is trying to do just that, they'll flatten this church and destroy my company. *Comprenez-vous?*"

"Yes, sir." Blake is slightly crestfallen, put in his place and embarrassed to be so rebuked in front of his signalman by a leathery non-commissioned officer. An NCO, for crying out loud! Jim imagines him thinking in undermined incredulity.

"Sorry son, this old Polack's seen many things, and among them many greenies getting hurt or killed doing something stupid in their first days on the line," adds Witchewski in a manner of fatherly advice. "Mind the veterans around you; watch and learn, and you'll find your way fast around here."

"Thank you, Sergeant Major," says Jim in an attempt to reassert the observance of the chain of command. "You are dismissed." They exchange salutes, and Witchewski withdraws into the jumbled

Guernican shadows from which he emerged. Jim takes Blake and Cole aside to a corner as the church palsies under yet another impact. Dust rains from the ceiling. He produces his map and spreads it on the dusty floor. "Your best vantage point may be just ahead in one of these houses with one of my forward platoons. I have two fanned out in front here." He points to an area on the precisely lined and arrowed topographical map with his index finger. "Go to Lieutenant Therrien here, about a hundred yards southwest of here, and he'll set you up in a room with a view. Or a one-star slit trench. I can get you a field telephone wired up once the rest of the battalion's in place. Tell him Captain McFarlane sent you."

"Yes, sir, thank you." Blake seems quietly grateful for Jim's gentlemanly consultation.

"First day up front?"

"I've been in Italy for two months, but I didn't get moved up until last week when another officer got it. I've taken artillery fire but this is my first actual mission. Say, where're you from, sir?"

"I'm from Canada, just like you." A 150 millimetre shell quakes the church in its reverberations as it gouges a crater into the rubble-strewn street outside and renders the existing debris into deadly missiles. Bricks and splinters and dirt and glass pelt and ring and crunch against the walls of the church. Jim and Blake both find themselves lying instinctively prostrate. They pick themselves up. "And meet—" head ringing, thoughts scattered, "And meet our neighbours from Germany. Now you'd best get moving." Jim shouts into the interior of the church, to shadow soldiers in corners and under pews. "Cooley!"

"Yes, sir!" Cooley's voice is curiously muffled.

"Escort these two gentlemen to Therrien's positions, will you?" He can't help but notice a slight waver in his voice, the seismic upheaval of the shell still vibrating through the strained fibres of his nerves.

"Yes, sir!" Cooley crawls out from under a pew, pulling his helmet up back on top of his head from its position on his face.

"Lieutenant Blake and Private Cole, meet my batman, Corporal Cooley." There is the customary exchange of salutes.

"A pleasure to meet you both," Cooley says in disarming salutation, sold with a smile. "Now follow me, if you will." He leads them out the door into the man-made storm outside and they dash through the moan, crash and flicker of San Mateo.

Following this, the colonel appears with his entourage from Battalion HQ. When Lieutenant Colonel Hobson appears at the door, Jim jumps up from a pew on which he sits and stomps his right foot at attention, salutes and lowers his arms rigidly at his side.

"Sir!" Jim barks.

"At ease, Captain," responds Colonel Hobson, returning the salute. "This is quite the setup you have here. I'm impressed. This is a nice church you've found for yourself. A good vantage point from which to pray for victory, is it not?" Lieutenant Colonel Hobson is a tall man of about forty, with broad shoulders and a smart, British-style officer's moustache. Hobson, his green-plumed cobeen (a hat ridiculed in other regiments as being just a backwards beret) propped jauntily upon his head, is the emblem of the regiment, in terms of both leadership and attitude. He is both proud and droll in his bearing, unshakeable under fire, with an offensive attitude on the field that Jim has tried to copy. He's the man. I'd follow him anywhere, Jim thinks. I've followed him to hell more than once. And I think I'm about to again.

"Sitrep?" asks the colonel in military shorthand.

"FUBAR," responds Jim. He shrugs: there is laughter from the soldiers listening. Colonel Hobson breaks into an amused grin.

"All fucked up indeed, I could not agree more. Did the arty reps come by?"

"Yes, sir. I sent them out to a better vantage point. Didn't want their telescope to catch the view of Jerry. The officer was as green as the grass, and was heading up to assess the steeple. After what we did to that steeple in Pesaro, I thought better of allowing it."

"Good choice. Well, you seem to be well set up in here. I'm going to move to my new HQ. Gordon has it up. Jerry may think this is our HQ, and they'll send you more parcels than they send me. Much to your discomfort. It'll give me some time to concentrate on our next attack." He winks a grey eye at Jim.

"It would be an honour sir, a real honour."

"Anyway, carry on as you were, Captain."

"Yessir." Into the shadows Hobson moves, addressing men, sharing compliments, jokes, words of encouragement, before making his way to his own headquarters down the road where he will enjoy a clear northward view of the river valley through which the battalion is soon expected to advance.

VI

News from the patrols sent out is not good—resistance is stiff, and men from the patrols are wounded in firefights with German infantry dug into valley positions and by artillery called in from the looming heights. For the rest of the night the men are kept awake much against their wills by the sporadic scream and thunder of the barrage. A few clutch rosaries, some crouch and play cards, some try to sleep but are constantly jolted awake from their semi-conscious reveries by the noise of the bombardment, some chat and joke quietly as if nothing was going on, and some, like Jim, skulk quietly in corners and under pews to themselves, smoking silently away, sitting still or rocking themselves into makeshift comfort. Every now and then someone makes a joke out loud to all in the church, and everyone erupts into laughter, taut nerves slackened suddenly in a momentary release of comic catharsis. Inside the darkened church, it smells of smoke and sweat and cigarettes. Outside, the shells burst. No less than five hit the church itself. One explodes in a confession booth after whistling through a ragged hole in the roof made earlier by Allied shells when the Canadians took the village, daggering the air with wood splinters. Three of Doyle's boys are wounded and are carried out by stretcher-bearers. The church is choked with smoke and dust, and the stunned men cough and sneeze. Another explosion tears the main door off its hinges and wounds another one of Doyle's soldiers. The other platoons take casualties as well in their slit trenches, windows and cellars. Stretcher-bearers scurry about and around the ruins and the slopes in the haphazard hailstorm of shrapnel and splinters, to and fro, conveying the wounded to the rear where they will be patched up in the nearby aid post and the clearing stations on their way to the field hospitals much further away.

Jim observes, with slight relief, that the Germans don't quite seem to know where specific Canadian positions are yet, only that there are Canadians on the hill and in the village. Thank God they haven't utterly bullseyed this church yet. They get a bead on me and they'll level this place like a wrecking ball. For us this is a natural fortress. To them it's a natural target. A perfect equation in the mathematics of conflict. The highest reason, the most precise measurements, applied to the most savage of aims. As the church shudders under another blast, Jim hits the ground and scuttles back under the pew from which he was awoken hours ago as though he were a panicked cockroach. Others shimmy under the cover of the pews, leaving no one in the open expanse of the room. He lies on his back and puts his helmet over his face, heart thudding and fists balled, and sweats to the howling of the shells. His mouth is a desert. A soft undertone of chatter whispers from corners and under pews and accompanies the barrage, audible only between shrieks and blasts.

Lying, sweating, shaking. Oh, fuck. Please not now. Hold it. Don't come apart, you've been through this before. Play a game. Guess the calibres. Those were 105s. That was a 100. A line of dull thuds, less sharp and thunderous than the big guns—mortars. A reminder of how close the Germans really are. Another volley of 105s. This is like standing on the highway and guessing what kind of vehicle is going to run you over. Marianne. Marianne, I miss you, I love you. Nostrils tickle to a remembered redolence of perfume and potpourri. A powdery, flowery smell, reminiscent of rose. Nowhere to run but the past, nowhere to run but into the arms of the woman he loves, to a warm flicker of home carried within.

Potpourri, papery in the hand. Scented with the spirit of dead flowers haunting their own desiccated remains. Pheromones, pleasure, olfactory enchantment in the crumple of leaf and petal, scenting his fingers as he reaches around her and rubs his finger in a dish of potpourri on the windowsill. A release of the spirit. He runs his hand gently along her upper lip, under her nostrils, trailing the perfume of dried flowers. With a sniff she ingests its essence. Into her blood goes the spirit of the flower, and now the flower is she, and she is the flower in the rubbing of skin on stem, dermal residue on rose. An exchange of smells. His briefcase on the floor, hands soft and warm and now wrapped about her waist as she stands over the sink, her welcoming sigh soft on his ears, a tickle in his loins, the waft of breeze-blown potpourri on the windowsill beside the silky efflorescence of African violets in a green flowerpot, and rubbed onto his fingers. Hands moving upward, cupping her breasts, bra-held and ripe in his hands; another sigh, a moan, a turn of the head and a placid smile below eyes half closed in domestic calm, the eye of the storm, the centre of tranquility. Hands moving upward, up the soft nape of her neck and over her button chin, his fingers over her lips, a soft kiss puckering underneath them and tickling him as they move up and tease her nose with the essence of flowers. She turns around and fills his embrace, presses her lips to his … To have that again, to have that again, oh to have that again.

"I love you, I love you so much," he says into the soft warmth of her shoulder as she combs her fingers through the oily tendrils of his unwashed hair.

"You look so tired and dirty. Come, let's get you cleaned up," and she leads him by the hand.

"Okay, dear." He can't think of anything better to say amid the distraction of destruction and he can't imagine a response. This cursory retreat home fades as the flicker of sanctuary is snuffed out in the displacement of passing shells. He surrenders to the moment, trapped upon the pinnacle of the present, where the lightning strikes again and again and again with a calculated coldness, trying to hit him. The fatalism of the veteran soldier overtakes him, and he waits for his, the one you don't hear coming as they say, as they said to him when he arrived, the 1st Division vets, as he imagines everyone else under their pews is doing, each trying to keep from going mad from musing on mortality as mortality asserts itself with each concussive crash. Mortality—began thinking of that in church, didn't I? When Mom would take us on Sunday mornings. Dad preferring a lie-in. The dreary sermons, endless in a child's perception of time; the mysterious rituals, the Latin prayers, the sombre hymns, the Halleluiah refrains.

Curled up with Ma in church, huddled up to the floral prints on her Sunday dress, up against the warm musky leather of her purse, clasped onto her arm as Father Russo ruminated on mortality and eternity, which stretched his boyhood mind to its very limits. Forever. Forever and ever. Forever and ever, forever and ever ringing in eternal reverberations. Foreverandeverring. Forever: the ring of eternity in that word, R's curving inward into a loop which offers no escape, a vortex. Turning forever in his mind, forever turning his mind. How can you live forever? The thought made him dizzy. He couldn't think. The word forever surpassed his powers of definition, he couldn't stretch its words and syllables over such an expanse of time. Even time eluded him in this context. Eternal life? How could time go on forever? Trapped in a world framed by beginnings and ends, looped in cycles, circles. He thought of seeing his grandparents again after their deaths, bathed in an ethereal light, in a flowered meadow scented by the wave of daisies in the breeze, among thousands of other people, all with an angelic glow about them, clad in white robes, milling about, smiling kindly at one another, meeting again, talking together, walking together, holding hands, arm in arm in eternal picnic, eternally strolling, forever and ever. He nestled into his mother's arm deeper and she ruffled his hair with her fingers as he listened and daydreamed in a childhood depiction of eternity which offset his fidgeting boredom at the length of the Mass, the prayers, the hymns, the sermons, the invocations, the standing, the sitting, the kneeling on the hard wooden retractable kneeling bench.

Crying later that night in his bed, thinking of his grandparents—they will die, won't they? Death. The monosyllabic certainty of that word. Finality. The door creaking open, the baleful glow of the hall light trickling in, the twin pillars of shadowy legs on the floor, the elongated torso and head preceding on the floor and walls the figure of his mother standing at the door. Mother coming to him, sitting down on the edge of his bed, soothing him, caressing him softly with hands and words: "Don't worry, Jimmy, they're going to heaven when they die."

"But how long will they live?" he sobbed.

"Oh, a while yet. For years. Don't you worry so much." She smiled at him, reassuring him in maternal warmth of voice and gesture. "Don't you worry so much sweetheart, you little sweetie pie, if you worry too much you won't ever enjoy the here and now, what's happening in front of you." She continued stroking his hair as he fell into a contemplative mood.

"Will they live forever after they die?" He looked up at her from his contemplation as he asked this. She chuckled, taken aback at his precocious earnestness. "The priest said that we'll all live forever in heaven after they die. Is that true?"

"Yes honey, it's true."

"Okay. Goodnight Mum."

"Good night to you too. I love you, my little worry wart." A soft kiss on the cheek.

"I love you too." They hugged and he returned her kiss. She got up off his bed and the springs groaned in relief as she floated up to the door in her nightgown in the midnight-shadowed semi-dark, and said, "So no more worrying, okay? I want to see you wake up with a smile. You have something to look forward to. You're going tobogganing tomorrow with the Fitzsimmons, remember? Sleep tight, and don't let those nasty little bedbugs bite!"

"Okay." With that, she shut the door, closing off the nightlight glow from the hall in which his bedroom had bathed, and left him to his thoughts of eternity, forever and ever and evering their way into his mind, stumping it, challenging it, teasing it.

Forever and ever. From here in the here and now he is taunted by that phrase, perched upon a precipice overlooking the very vortex that phrase attempts to define. The here and now. His mother's phrase turns in his mind, the loops, curves and masts of letters glinting off the light of sleepy contemplation like a mobile as he settled into the cozy nest of his covers, a crisp sheet and puffy quilt topped by the soft fuzzy weave of a mohair blanket. The here and now, impeded by the eternal advance of forever and ever, always making its way.

He opens and closes his eyes to little difference in the dark under his helmet. Eyelashes brush gently against unseen bonds of oilcloth and rubber. Here and now. The worn rubbery smell of the underside of his tin hat, infused with that of the oil and sweat of his own dirty hair, fills his world as his world contracts to the limits of its thin protection over his face and to the olfactory memories of months of wear, and he can hear the wheeze of his shallow nervous breaths against the concave dome of padding and metal against which his nose is lightly pressed. Its feeling of protection is enhanced slightly by the lived-in odour, a time signature of experience, the added dimension of trust, that he has worn this helmet on and off for months during moments such as this. That it has seen him through eight and a half months on and off the battle lines. Scratched and dinged, pinged and knocked about, it is a material diary etched and inscribed by shot and shell, fire and brimstone. He runs his hand over its convex exterior. A slight dent from a pebble cast by an artillery blast. From his first battle, the diversionary attack on the Arielli Line in the Rapido River valley last winter, launched on a clear, cold morning from the hard mud of icy slit trenches. Exhilarating and terrifying—grimacing as hundreds of guns opened up at once and plumed the German positions ahead in eruptive geysers of smoke and dirt; pound, pound, pound, fifteen minutes of relentless thunderous sky-splitting clamour, a sonic dominion of devastation absolute in its rule of the senses, followed by sudden silence, the cue for the assault companies to dash out of their slit trenches. Ragged grey shrouds of smoke hung and slowly unthreaded themselves in the air after the guns stopped. Another bombardment, this time of smoke shells to obscure the Germans' view of their own lines and the cratered earth ahead of them in a thick fog of eye-stinging smoke, to hide the attackers. He was situated above and behind the battle line, in immediate reserve to exploit whatever gains the first wave might make, his platoon along with the others offering machine-gun and mortar support from the top of a gentle incline overlooking the front line proper, about two hundred yards behind. He peered over the sandbagged lip of his narrow and confining slit trench through his field glasses as squads of infantrymen, hunched over and running to their objectives, were suddenly clearcut in a serrated staccato of machine-gun bullets and rifle fire, crackling hollow against the hillsides, and blasted by mortars and artillery. Return fire began crashing into the reserve positions, and into the artillery emplacements behind. PING! A pebble dashed off his helmet from a nearby shellburst. He maintained his composure and was proud of it. You have a cool head under pressure he said to himself, and felt proud. He heard an unearthly metallic wail, approaching from ahead and above, increasing in volume.

"Fire in the hole! Fire in the hole!" he yelled, and hit the floor of his trench. The world of his impressions was concussed into fragments by a series of deafening bangs. The ground spasmed with each and he was jarred up from the protesting earth. The air above whirred and rippled with molten shrapnel and stones and splinters and clots of mud. The last in this series of blasts was right beside his hole and he was partly buried in an avalanche of dirt. His ears rang like the echo of a gong. Get used to this, he remembers thinking, get used to this. This is only the first day.

Here and now. Stay in the here and now. He draws air deeply into his lungs to offset the febrile conjurations of the past that have plagued him all day. The reverberating ringing of the past, from ever, forever. He hears a likeness of Lieutenant Colonel Hobson bark in his ears as though he has stuck his head under the pew to give him a good pasting: "Goddamnit, McFarlane! You're a captain! Now get a hold of yourself and start acting like one before you're sent back to Civvy Street!"

He runs his hand over his helmet again and traces over a dented ripple in the rim, a distracting imperfection in the cold lip of metal that feels to the tip of his finger like the edge of a warped cymbal. One well-percussed in war's cacophonous rhythm, in this case during the battle for Montecchio only a week ago in the fortified hills overlooking the Gothic Line, and he begins to lapse into another memory, of a relentless bombardment while digging into the slopes of Point 111—

"Sir?" His shoulder is being ruffled. "Sir, you alright?" His eyes flutter open. He looks to his side to see Cooley's face peering down in the space between pew and floor. The floor ripples as a shell bursts nearby. "You just yelled out really loudly. Scared the shit out of me." He chuckles.

Jim looks at Cooley and smiles. "Yes, I'm okay Cooley, I just had a charleyhorse. It's all cramped up down here, and I'm stiff and kinked." His hands and face are cold and sweaty. There is a mixture of concern and suspicion on Cooley's face, a sadness in his eyes coupled with a close and clinical examination, a sense of responsibility to always assess those around him. A lingering gaze. He blinks. A lingering gaze through my malingering ways.

"Yes sir, I understand." In the wavery lanternlight Cooley's face is spectral, lit softly like a gibbous moon hovering in the dusty darkness. I'm sure he didn't buy that. He knows I've been shot before, and I never as hell screamed then. Didn't even hurt till Charbonneau pointed out to me that I'd been shot. Then, did it ever hurt. A slight wave of dizziness washes over him, and the wound in his arm throbs in cutaneous remembrance. Quit dwelling on the past, don't get eaten by your demons, don't fall into the snapping, hungry mouths of the crocodiles in the swamps below. The sweat on his hands cools in the shellshaken darkness. He realizes he is breathing shallowly, tugging at the air in an arrhythmia of rising panic. He attempts to collect himself. Breathe in, breathe out, breathe in, breathe out—his breathing becomes more relaxed, more deep and restful, and he falls into a meditation of sorts as the world shakes around him, under him and over him, as he breathes himself into a trance in which it does not shake within him. He closes his eyes and keeps them closed.

VII

The summer of 1940 had passed so far with a monotony incongruous with the fact that a war was apparently raging overseas. That is, for James McFarlane. War, for Jim, was nothing but some frantic headlines and grainy pictures, and radio broadcasts with the muted, staticky wails of air-raid sirens in far-off, fabled London. Those sirens may have alerted Londoners to the peril of incoming German bombers, but to Jim, they were a call to arms, much more exciting than the summer evening vocational school classes he'd been teaching lately. Marianne, his wife, was not impressed. During the past few months, the tension in their home began to reach a boil. At the breakfast table amid coffee, sausages and eggs one Saturday morning, they argued.

"Hmm. Look at this," he said, intent behind the sanctuary of the front page. And now, the statement that would light the fuse of battle: "You know, I do think I should join."

According to the paper, German bombers were now hitting central London. He sipped his coffee.

"Jim, you're twenty-nine years old. Even if you did join, do you really think you'd actually fight? You have a home, you have a job, and you have me." Her eyes were pleading pools of nervousness. And annoyance.

"Well, they need everyone they can get." He looked so important, so knowledgeable, wielding the morning paper. "My brother, he's in the service and he's doing fine."

"Your brother is single and can do whatever he wants." His brother was currently training in the RCAF at the air force base in Trenton. His letters were enthusiastic, the kind of letters that a little brother sends his big brother, wide-eyed about airplanes and women, complete with humorous caricatures of his commanding officers.

Jim was pensive for a moment. Then, he tried a new approach in a careful, understanding voice: "Look, I'm married to you because I love you. I want to be married to you. I—"

"But to get married to me and then run off to the army within a year? That's like *leaving* me Jim, really leaving me. You have to understand how that makes me feel."

"I'm not leaving you if I join. And if I do join, remember that I wouldn't be anywhere near the action for a long time. I'd be training here for quite some time, and I know for a fact we'd get to see each other. I'd get leave money. I can always catch a train if I'm posted elsewhere."

"How about all the footage from the last war? Mud and blood. You've seen what it did to my father. It's scary." She looked more worried than angry. The Great War had billed her father for his left eye, most of his hearing, and much of his wits.

"Well," he said slowly and thoughtfully. He peered out from behind the paper. "Look at it this way. If I join the army, I could be making more than I am now. Much more. I think I could make officer. I'm fit and strong. I'm a little older than most recruits, I have more life experience, and as a teacher I'm in a position of authority. Of some sort. But the fact is, I know I could do it. And they'd look at all this when I've applied." He bit into a sausage, chewed, and then continued. "And, by the way, you know there's more than just infantry. So if that's your worst nightmare, me in a muddy trench, it may not come true. In fact, it's not even likely. For every guy up front, there are a few more keeping him fed, armed, whatever."

"But why the army?"

"Well, you know I'd never, never make the air force. Not any of the good jobs, anyway. Do you think I could fly a fighter or a bomber? I'd wind up tightening bolts on grounded shitboxes in northern Alberta or something like that. And I'm too much of a puker to join the navy.

I get seasick in the bath. I'd be too bloody green to do anything but lie in my hammock."

Marianne was attentive but unconvinced.

"Look, I know this is important. I'm not stupid. I read about it too. I listen to the reports with you. I'm aware of things that happen in the world. It's scary. But I don't think it's for you. It's not for *us*. We've just been married, and we're going to move into a new house, and—"

"But what the hell am I doing here?" he interjected. "Not much. I'm a teacher in a school full of kids eager to get in the action. Christ, a few of the boys quit and joined the service before the end of the spring term." He looked thoughtful, gesturing to the air. "The only thing going strong right now is the military and everything that feeds it. I might as well get in on it." The eager look in his eyes betrayed his pragmatic reasoning. Marianne sighed. This was going to be tough, tough, tough. "Also, we have no kids. Yet. It's not like I'd be abandoning young children that need me there, all the time."

"Look," she commanded, getting up and pacing. "There must be some sort of civilian job you can do, one that's connected to the war somehow. Then you could still contribute, and yet, you'd still be here, out of danger."

"No. I don't want to work in any mine, or in any factory."

"Why not? The pay's good, and they're essential to the war effort."

"Too dangerous," he said with a grin. Marianne rolled her eyes with exasperation.

"You're impossible."

"Let me just say it: I want to go to war. It's what I feel I have to do. Now if you excuse me, I'm going to go out for awhile." He got up.

"Where? Where the hell are you going to go now? I don't suppose you'd like to tell me," she demanded.

"Out," was his answer, followed by his proud, defiant exit.

Out into the streets he went, his mind awash with anger and excitement, his body with adrenaline. He glanced back at the house, an imposing white Colonial partly hidden behind a bushy stockade of poplars and an enormous and gnarly crabapple tree. It was a rental, owned by a doctor currently living in New York, a friend of his father's from the University of Toronto medical school. In a few more months, they would be making a down payment on a house of their own not too far away, a smaller one, albeit comfortable in its unassuming modesty. Connections got him this house, and they got him his teaching job, connections binding him to a world of quiet complacency. This sense of permanence frightened him, framed in the new house in its plain respectability. For Christ's sake, Mark had joined the air force, and being the family darling, became the family toast as well. Jim was the older one, left now with something to prove. From his pocket he produced a packet of Wrigley's gum, unwrapping the foil covering of a piece, unleashing a cool wintry zing of peppermint as he did so, and popped the pliable rectangular stick of gum into his mouth. He looked about as he walked. It was a sunny day, the sun peaking through the leaves along the oak-lined Glebe street and twinkling between the penumbral shadow branches on the grass. A young boy cycled by. An older man in a crooked straw hat and dungarees was mowing his lawn, pushing the wheel mower in rows, the turning blades chewing and shearing the grass, the man lost in a reverie of pastoral toil. Birds chirped. It was idyllic. One would never imagine the world was embroiled in war. On he walked, thinking: What the hell did I just do? He had just walked out on Marianne. Not permanently, of course. But he'd walked out on her just the same.

He walked and walked, around the town, tipping his hat and saying hello whenever appropriate, thinking all the while. He passed St. James's Church. A somewhat religious man, Jim remarked to himself that perhaps he should chat with Father Dave about all this. Father Dave would have the answer: or would he? Jim had been full of religious doubt recently, had been since the end of high school in fact. Would Father Dave recommend going to war? He might, having been a chaplain in the last one. Or he might not, having been a chaplain in the last one. The recruiting office was just a half-hour walk away, at the Cartier parade square. Tempting, very tempting. A halfhearted career as a teacher, a banshee wife, and a war that's just too good to miss, he thought crassly. Oh the thrill of such thoughts. On Jim walked, wasting much of the morning in his musings.

He ended up sitting on a bench alongside the Rideau Canal, under the protective canopy of an oak tree. A small sightseeing motor launch putt-putted by with its cargo of waving weekenders. He waved back. Here he spent half an hour listening to the bustle of the city during lunchtime, the whine of saws and drills of construction crews hurriedly erecting buildings for the burgeoning wartime civil service, the sounds of the engines of a wartime economy. His hometown of Sudbury, nestled in and perched upon the rocky crags of northern Ontario, was in the midst of a nickel boom, the mines operating around the clock, as in the dark and dripping tunnels lamp-helmeted miners set dynamite and fuse lines and blasted at veins of nickel like the congealed blood of ancient titans, necessary for the armour plating of the Allied engines of war. From the depths of the earth and from the violent hearts and scheming minds of men arose the fever shapes of aeroplanes and artillery and tanks and battleships and their murderous munitions. In the distance, the Parliament buildings loomed over Parliament Hill and Major's Hill, where on weekdays the cabinet sat and the prime minister engaged in arguments relating to such unusual Canadian topics as mobilization and conscription and munitions. Prime Minister Mackenzie King, potato-shaped, dour, elusive and enigmatic, and, since partway through the Depression that this war cured overnight, in absolute control of the country he had sent officially to war on the heels of Britain, ten days after the German invasion of Poland.

The war, he thought. How can I not do something about it and feel good about myself? He had helped run a scrap metal drive at school last winter, the students bringing in all manners of old junk—old cans, broken tools, dinged and dented shovels and hoes and shears, bicycles, bicycle and automobile wheels, a broken-down car, empty food tins, ancient fountain pens, a clanging clatter of old pots and pans, dull knives, bent forks and broken spoons. Ploughshares to swords. The moment the military began mustering, thousands of men lined up in long queues at armouries and recruiting centres all across the country, in every province, wrapping around city blocks, signing up for what was for many the first steady job in years or the first they'd ever had. At school, on the street, in the cafes and diners and beer parlours and clubs, it was war talk. I'm joining the air force; I've got 20/20 vision. I've always wanted to sail around the world—I'm joining the navy. My two brothers and I just joined the army together. I'm training to fire the big guns! He one day bumped into a young Ottawa valley farmer on his way to market who was sure that because of his experience driving tractors, he would get into the Tank Corps. Men and women in uniform everywhere—everywhere. All of this in a little less than a year. Marianne was now working for the civil service, typing reports for the Ministry of Transportation, in addition to working shifts at the failing family furniture store. She had been flirting with the idea of joining the Royal Canadian Women's Air Force to work in communications. She had even suggested that he enlist in a non-combat position if he desired to take part. But he was adamant all along about joining the overseas expeditionary force.

"If I'm going, I'm going," he said that evening in the parlour, after a frosty détente of several hours' duration that ensued after his return home, and the truth of his words and intentions registered in her eyes. She looked at him with the weight of inevitability in her eyes, if turning to when in the certainty of his tone.

"It's not that I don't understand why you want to go, or feel that you have to go," she reasoned through gathering disappointment and sadness, "It's that we are married. I couldn't bear for you to be away so long having grown together into marriage as we have these last months. Surely you understand that, don't you?"

"I do," he said in the flat tone of the obstinate and inconvincible. He said nothing further, there being nothing further to be said. He looked out the picture window, at the sun winking between the mesh of leaves and twigs of the droopy weeping willow that obscured the other side of the street. "Let's put on some music."

He put a record on the gramophone, a Louis Armstrong jazz album, something altogether different from the gloomy, though undeniably exciting, atmosphere of foreign war that could be found in the sober radio reports of sinkings, bombings, air battles and invasions, and now epitomized through the songs of Vera Lynn. The pops and beats and joyous trumpet and ancient bullfrog bass voice of Louis Armstrong filled the room, fogged somewhat by the static and the tinny nature of the recording:

... Oh when the saints
Go marching in
Oh when the saints go marching in ...

Dusty record, dull needle, minds tuned into other things. They each sat on different ends of the chesterfield. Jim turned his eyes to Marianne and asked, "Now how is that?" as he began snapping his fingers and tapping his toes in an attempt to lighten the mood. Her eyes met his.

"You're awfully good at changing the subject, aren't you?" She smiled a little and her eyes softened. "But I'm not so easily fooled, Jim McFarlane, not so easily fooled by a boy like you." She moved closer to him and poked him in the chest with her index finger. The effect was one of playfulness concealing admonishment.

"You were when we met on the train," he said with a warm, languid smile.

She ruffled his hair and spoke softly over him, to him, critiquing him and loving him, "You're such a boy, Jim McFarlane. It's part of why I married you. It's one thing I love about you. But I don't want your boyish whims to make you leave here." She stroked his temple and he purred gently in a natural reaction. "Or to get you killed. You should have thought of this before we were married. It is a bit irresponsible for a married man to run away from his wife and his responsibilities, is it not? You know, some of the men my father served with joined because they were fleeing their wives. Leaving your wife to put yourself in horrendous danger and discomfort seems a little insulting to me, when there are others who can and should do this."

He tilted his head back upward, his eyes meeting her face. "Baby, I'm not running away. I could never leave you. I could never truly leave you. Even if I go, I am still coming back, back to you. I mean, I know the risks, and they are real, but—" he searched for the right words, "But, I mean, there is a real threat here to the world, much greater I think than last time. I think as a strong and healthy young man of reasonable intelligence that it is my duty to do something about it. Also," he continued, turning his head to her, "there is the very real chance that it will end long before I am sent to any theatre of action." He did not believe these words as he said them, and he doubted she did either. The song ended, and with it, the record. They were silent awhile, languid, dreaming about the future, each other, themselves, she stroking his temples and he nesting his head in her lap.

As the sun set, Marianne asked in an entranced near whisper, "Shall we go upstairs?" He opened his eyes.

"I think we shall." They hooked hands, and without thinking got up from the chesterfield and made their way upstairs as the evening softened the edges of the furniture and rendered them into shadow. And amid the shadows of their bedroom, they kissed, they caressed, they made love, they knew they were parting. He kissed the hot flush of her face and the heartbeat marble of her palms, she ran her fingers up and down his back, the dark ivy tresses of her hair hanging in curls over him as they lay down, redolent of shampoo, he tented within the strands of her waving tresses. They rolled over, and he entered her with the full might of his being, the full love of his wife. She, convulsive with ecstasy, moaned and whimpered and kissed. He shivered at his climax and rolled to the side, staring into her eyes as he did so, hands in her slicked hair, remembering their wedding night, the consummation, the first time they were able to make love ... The wedding photograph, on the steps of Christ the King Church in Sudbury, he in his pale blue wool suit, she in her burgundy dress, beautiful, the photograph touched up with colour tints, making them feel slightly unreal, touched up in the Technicolor manner of film stars. Yes, film stars, the flash bulbs, the glamour, the drama, the taking on of new roles, those of husband and wife.

He looked over at her in silence. She had a thoughtful expression, a mirror of her own mother when she was uncertain, the corner of her mouth twisted downward, her jaw moving, biting her lower lip.

The silence was thick, heavy, scented with perfume and with the musky sharpness of their own bodies. The room was still with musing, their own thoughts drifting about the room like radio transmissions on different wavelengths, floating in an ether of unease.

"Honey?" Her voice was mixed with wisps of whisper, vulnerable.

"Yes?" Her eyes met his as he answered.

"When you join up, don't forget me, don't just disappear into your duties. I mean that. Join up and try to work here in Ottawa, please, for as long as you can before they send you somewhere else. Write to me and call me. Please do that for me." There was a plaintive waver in her voice. Her hand squeezed his. Her eyelashes fluttered. Her eyes glistened, wet. "And remember my father. Remember what happened to him during the last war." Jim remembered, remembered being jealous of such a robust life experience, despite the consequences.

He nodded thoughtfully, exhaling through his nose, running his fingers over hers. "I will do that. I'll do that. For you, for sure, I'll do that."

VIII

About an hour before dawn the German shelling seizes, but the Allied shelling continues unabated. Canadian and British shells scream, sizzle and whirr over the brightening sky into and beyond the front lines of the Germans. Men crawl out from corners and from under or on pews and stretch their legs in the dusty air. It's about time for goddamn leave, Jim thinks as he pulls himself out like an insect emerging from under a log, and he lies down on the dusty wood of the pew itself. He blinks, naps ten more minutes, ten minutes of blissful dreamless limbo, and awakens to the grumble of an arriving Bren carrier and the strong smell of coffee and the lighter aroma of brewing tea. Runners have arrived under the cover of darkness from behind with thermoses full of thick, strong, bitter coffee and tea, and tins of bacon, beans and tomato soup. He knows this instantly as the aroma meets his mind through the drawing of his breath. The essence of coffee and bacon brings a warm familiarity of hearth and home that for an instant is interwoven with a feeling of loss and longing and regret.

"Been a helluva run gettin' this chow to you boys!" one of the runners complains with a hint of good cheer upon entering the church.

"Too bad we don't tip!" answers Witchewski to a collective snicker. Soldiers surface from their shadowy corners and from under pews like insects from under rocks and help themselves to the food. Staff Sergeant Nichols, Company Quartermaster Sergeant, enters the church, the last of the three runners, a tall, muscular and older man with an intense gaze, who, like Witchewski, is a longstanding member of the regiment whose service predates the war. Slung over his shoulder is a burlap sack. His usually hard, intense, critical eyes twinkle with satisfaction as he surveys the scene in front of him.

"What a shambles," he grumbles with exaggerated anger, "This place most certainly does not pass inspection. With all due respect, Captain."

"Good morning, Nichols," greets Jim, dusting himself off and stretching. "What's in the bag?"

"A morning rum tot. A little extra I managed to wrangle from Riordan and Gibbs." Soldiers perk up at the mention of rum. As they approach with their cups eagerly held out, Nichols bellows, "For Christ's sake boys, back off! You know the order—by descending order of rank! You'll get your portions, trust me. That or it's a shot in the back for me when I least expect it. And now for you, Captain." He pours a generous splash into Jim's cup which Jim downs immediately without ceremony, the sweet syrupy sugar burn of the rum working its way down his gullet like a sizzling fuse. Next up is Doyle, and then so on as tot by tot all soldiers get their eagerly awaited share.

"Have you brought any other treats and treasures for us?" asks Jim, still savouring the waning burn of the rum tot as Nichols continues to portion out rum to thirsty soldiers. "We ate our way through what looks like the last of our compos last night for dinner."

"We have a ton of rations on hand, so don't worry about eating the rest of your compos. We've also brought back some spare PIAT and Bren ammo, as requested," Nichols answers as he pours the last ration into the last soldier's cup. "If we get marching orders, we have plenty of fireworks for the parade." As he says this his two assistants deposit boxes of spare ammunition and field rations on the floor of the church.

"Any mail?" Jim is aware of a faint desperation, a trembly weakness in the timbre of his voice as he asks this last question.

"No, not lately. I woulda brought it for you boys if I had received any."

"Understood. Good work, Nichols."

"Thank you. Sounds like you boys had a rough night here," Nichols observes.

"Yes, very heavy shelling. As you can still hear."

"And as we can no longer," says Witchewski, joining the conversation as he helps himself to breakfast beside them. "Those bastards have been pretty much emptying their arsenal on us."

"I don't doubt it. Well, I've got rum to distribute," says Nichols, pausing to take a slug of water from his canteen before heading out to deliver rum to those outside.

Jim grabs his mess tin from his pack on the floor and fills it with soup. He eats it ravenously and quickly, hunched on a pew. All the men eat ravenously, as if they haven't in days. The atmosphere is slick with the sounds of slurping. The iron tension and pure exhaustion in their bodies burn up their food as fast as they can eat it.

"Mmmm mmmmm," someone hums with approval. "Buonissimo!"

"Sounds like chow mein time at a Chinese restaurant," some wag observes, likely Witchewski. He is answered with a few nasally snorts of laughter from men whose mouths are filled with food. Jim is unable to fully distinguish the voice on account of the pealing ring resounding in his ears from the enormous shell that landed when he was sending Blake out the door.

Nichols reenters the church and announces that he is returning to the rear. Before he and the others depart, various soldiers, Jim included, saddle them with letters to be mailed. About ten minutes later, the phone rings.

"Captain!" shouts Private Thibeault, looking about the church for Jim amid the commotion of the soldiers eating their breakfast.

"Here!"

"Colonel Hobson's on the line."

"Right," he says, and he makes his way to Thibeault and takes from him the awaiting receiver. "McFarlane here."

"Good morning Jim: here are your orders. We're holding until we know when we are to advance. It could be days."

"Yes, sir."

"Hold on tight and expect to catch a lot more hell from the enemy artillery. If we do get the order to advance, I'll summon you and the others to TAC for an 'O' Group. Otherwise, sit tight. Got it?"

"Yes sir, got it. Thank you." He hangs up the phone and reflects. Overall, easy orders. Though, he steels himself against the prospect that he, along with the rest of the battalion, could suddenly be ordered to advance. To this end, he decides to survey what he might be up against. He makes his way toward the bottom of the bell tower, stepping around the fallen, broken bell, and he ascends the steep and winding stairs.

From the ragged yawn at top of the broken steeple, he can see over the village down the slope of his small ridge and into the valley beyond where the first rosy fingers of the dawn have yet to reach. He sweeps the view in front of him with his field glasses. In the distance, beyond the patchwork maze of farms and orchards, zig-zagged with dirt tracks and roads, impose the verdant slopes of Coriano Ridge, the latest obstacle to continued advance. Treed with the grey-green barrels of guns unseen among the tree stands and farmhouses, guns canopied in the leafy mesh of camouflaged netting, which along with the metallic stumps of mortars form an ironic approximation of pastoralism. Guns unseen over the lip of the horizon on top of the ridge, visible only in vibration. Guns that have been hammering his positions all night and will likely be doing so until he moves. And cresting the ridge at its steepest slope, about two thousand yards from his command post, the town of Coriano itself, a cluster of white and pastel houses and churches wreathed and nestled in trees and bushes and hedges. Were it not for the fact that this ridge has just failed to fall in a British assault, the battalion would be surging ahead on its northward course today, making for the low-lying flatlands of the Po Valley. He scans to the left. Aquarelled in a soft and milky blue upon the horizon in the morning haze are the rocky bluffs of more distant mountains inland. A misty merger of earth and sky, as if the waking world is still creating itself beyond the visible horizon. Hearing a cataclysm of fire to the southwest, where the British are assaulting Croce and Gemmano Ridge, Jim is delighted that he is not part of that. Not a pang of guilt courses through him. Sooner or later, we will get our turn, he muses. Sooner rather than later, I hope—the suspense is killing me.

This is a risk, he thinks. I chastised those two guys last night and here I am in the area they wanted to camp out in. Get moving. He steps back down the tight dollhouse stairs of the steeple, into the main body of the church. As the bombardment has ebbed somewhat for a time, Jim decides to step out for a moment. He exits the church and turns sharply to the right. He looks down a long road of ruin to the horizon, shakes his head and steps back inside into the sweat and cigarette gloom of the church's interior.

The dawning sunshine is short-lived, replaced by a dark conspiracy of clouds billowing from seaward, and by midmorning it is raining, and raining hard. It rains on and off all day, from drizzle to deluge to back again, rain pattering through holes in the roof of the church, plopping down onto and from beams and onto the cold stone floor and piles of broken masonry, streaking down the dusty pew backs and pooling on the benches, making mud of dust, pattering and dripping on helmets and shoulders in great dollops and splatters from beam and cornice; rain, rain, rain, at times torrential, beating down and building to a snare drum crescendo and then subsiding to a soft hissing drizzle, residual water drip-dropping hollowly through the shellholes and cracks during the lulls. Outside, the view is obscured at times by ghostly veils of fog. Entrenched soldiers find themselves shivering in the rain and bailing out their holes with cans and pots and helmets, digging into the sides of their narrow slit trenches for shelter, covered in the protection of their gas capes and rain sheets. Those in the church and in houses fare better, but not by much.

And still the shells fall, one here, one there, beating the drums of misery. For much of the day, they endure the rain and the shelling as best they can, with humour, with stoicism, with silent prayer. The hours bleed into one another, ticked and tolled by the bombardments that come and go like the desultory roll of thunder, the forming and raging and subsiding of storms.

Early that evening during a break in the rain Jim decides to do his rounds, to inspect his men about the hilltop ruins after they have crept forward into their night positions in the gathering dusk. He walks in a half crouch, stepping over the shattered stones of a ruined house, through a shattered lane lined by the façades and shells of houses resembling collapsing molars. The air is bitter with the smell of wet charring. Shards of glass chime feebly in the night breeze, a desultory melody of loss. He makes his way under awning and eave through this jagged forest of ruin to Therrien's position. He finds Therrien in the sandbagged basement of a house on the very edge of the ridge, just ahead of which is the downward slope into the valley. Manned slit trenches are dug around the house, helmets glinting in the flare of a nearby explosion. Therrien's stout farmer's face is a study of exhaustion, stubbly, scar running down his cheek, eyes set in rugose sacks of sagging purple.

"Good evening," is Jim's greeting.

"Good evening, sir."

He can't figure out what to say, can't quite get to know people anymore. "One helluva night, eh?"

"Yessir."

"How've you been managing?"

"Okay, I guess, considering everything dropped on us. We've dug in deep, good and proper, and saved ourselves a lot of additional casualties."

"Your positions look good." More awkward silence. "The church is a shambles. That's what happens when you take the biggest building in town." He laughs to himself at this. "Well, onward like the Christian soldier I am," he says as he salutes, turns around and leaves, whistling the melody to "Onward, Christian Soldiers." Field glasses dangling about his neck and bumping against his chest, Jim goes up to the blasted attic. Cole and Blake are perched under the sandbagged window there, their binocular telescope scanning the dusky horizon for what little detail can still be discerned. A volley of shells erupts beyond the perimeter of the village, in 'B' Company's zone. The desultory shelling is like the waxing and waning of the breeze, the changeable properties of weather.

"I wish those bastards would quit," Jim says wearily, as if it might persuade the Germans to stop firing. I never did like thunderstorms, he adds to himself.

"Don't worry sir, we're here to give them a headache of their own," says Blake, as he peers through his scope. Cole relays orders into the receiver of his field telephone, orders that will direct gunners to hit targets even they cannot see in this modern game of numbers, this Industrial Age duel of machinery.

Jim, surveying the view from the window, takes an evening swig of whiskey, a nip of liquid sanity, as he and Witchewski like to say. The whiskey courses down his throat like liquid sandpaper, an agreeable abrasion. With analgesic properties, Leprenniere might've added. Ah, Leprenniere ... "To my favourite anaesthetic," he toasted to the clink of glasses. An anaesthetic for the soul. We certainly killed that bottle that night yes we did, Christmas '43. "Bottoms up!"

"Drinkin' on the job, sir?" asks Blake with a wry hint of a grin.

"If you don't drink on the job here, you're mad. Things work backwards here."

"Yessir, true enough."

Don't wanna patrol. Don't want to fight. Want to go home. Take a walk. Smell the roses. Fuck my wife. Make looooooooove. Change my underwear (for a change). Ha! Eat some real food and—

"Sir?"

"Yes, Blake?"

"Division artillery's going to start really nailing Jerry gun positions beyond. We got a fix on some big, fat targets earlier. Jerry's on the run."

"No, he's not. He's inching backward bit by bloody little bit, and booby-trapping every step of the way. *Comprenez-vous?* I'd like to meet Field Marshal Kesselring, shake his hand and punch him in the face. Besides," he looks Blake in the eye, "Haven't all you gunners had enough fun already?" He laughs uncontrollably for no real reason. Blake and Cole exchange puzzled glances suggesting Jim is mad.

With some effort he recovers his composure. Twitches and snorts of laughter convulse within him and threaten to dissolve his stern demeanor once more. Breathe in, breathe out. "You'll pardon me, gentlemen, but I'm very tired from a night and a day of being shelled shitless. Maybe I should've given the order for everyone inside to kneel in prayer—maybe then we would've lowered casualties." He bites his cheeks as he feels his stomach muscles tense and his face muscles attempt to draw the corners of his mouth upward into a smile. He is aware that he is on the verge of slurring due to nervous exhaustion.

"Anyway, carry on, gentlemen, carry on." They salute one another and Jim leaves the house. He makes the rest of his rounds, from platoon to platoon in a delirious daze of details—machine-gun positions, daily standing orders, passwords, sentries, casualties, digging, whatnot. Over open ground along the slit trenches of soldiers he makes his way, over broken brick and beam, over shards of glass like pieces fallen from a fractured sky. The water in a rain-filled shellhole shines in a silvery red refraction in the light of a nearby flare. Moments later a volley of mortars bursts somewhere behind, out of sight if not out of mind. Chicken Little was right. The sky is falling down. And no one listened until too late.

IX

For another whole day they sit, both nervous and bored, holding the line, waiting for orders that may come at any time. The Germans resume shelling the ridge and with it, San Mateo and the men dug in and around its ruins. Charlie Company is forced to abandon its headquarters beyond the village along the ridgeline as it collapses into ruin under a weight of exploding ordnance, and the men are forced to retreat into slit trenches behind. There are more casualties in Jim's company, and in the others as well. In the early afternoon, one of Olczyk's boys, Private Kelly, is killed by a direct mortar hit on his slit trench. His helmet and head are found yards away, as if it were a soccer ball kicked by a wanton child. His trench is reduced to a hole full of guts and spilled sand from the torn sandbags abutting the rim. Olczyk himself is lightly wounded by flying splinters when a volley of 150s pummels his position, and he is treated at his post. Three in Doyle's platoon are wounded, one severely—Lance Corporal Fitzpatrick, in the stomach. Jim sees the stretcher-bearers scurry away out of the church with him writhing in a sweaty pallor, a scarlet bloom of blood efflorescing through the bandages and sheet in which he is swaddled—might as well be his burial shroud, or a sheet of butcher's paper. They load him into an awaiting unseen jeep. From out of view comes the rattle of an engine and the hurried squeal of departing tires as it races down the opposite side of the ridge to Major Henderson's regimental aid post, a few hundred metres away in a cinderblock farmhouse. He is unlikely to survive the day—from the RAP to RIP, as the medics say. Dog Company is ravaged when a large German shell explodes on one its platoons, killing one and wounding another seven. Dead is Lieutenant Briscoe, in since the Liri Valley, and whom Jim never bothered to get to know. Another statistic. Since the Liri Valley, Jim hasn't bothered to get to know new people for reasons of continued sanity and in the interest of keeping a cool head.

Radio waves bring reports of woe. Shells hit troops and vehicles behind, and the Canadian and British guns attempt to target and destroy the German ones by range-finding via the vibrations of gun blasts. The battle at Gemmano Ridge to the south proves to be a dirty hand-to-hand affair, and staticky reports of vicious, confused street-fighting crackle in on the company wireless between screeching episodes of German frequency jamming. Jim monitors these reports, does more rounds, naps under the pew, frets over his charges, daydreams about home, muses on the battle he knows is coming.

After a bland supper of compo rations, runners being unable to bring hot meals up front on account of the heavy shelling, he decides to write a letter. He pulls out his pen and produces another piece of paper from his pocket, and begins to write. Words scrawl across the top of the page, shaky and canted to the right:

—Somewhere in Italy—

Who should I write to this time? Dad. It shall be Dad, my dear old Dad, pater familias and dispenser of advice. Shellfire rumbles underfoot in a wave of molecular protest. Sounds like they're hitting 'B' Company now. Spreading their joy around to all of us in equal measure. Another display of Teutonic thoroughness. He slurps a scour of whiskey from his flask, warms his veins, and puts pen to paper:

Dear Dad,

I am suffering from the throes of dipsomania and what those in the trenches the first time around wisely called shellshock. I am currently under fire. I spent last night under a church pew while being shelled incessantly—the Germans have poor bedtime manners and are wont to make a racket at the worst possible times. I believe I've smoked 30 cigarettes already. I am also a little tipsy, but that's how you stay sane. I wrote Mom and Marianne recently, and now it's your turn to put up with me. Yesterday I had a laughing fit while doing my rounds to my various platoons, and the two artillery guys stationed with us looked at me like I was a grinning monkey. I had an 'O' Group assembly a couple nights ago, where I relayed orders from above to my lieutenants, and I drew a blank. I am losing it. I must now appeal to the doctor in you, if I may: I haven't had an erection in over two weeks—is this normal? Is it the fear, the lack of sleep, the guilt I feel surviving others, the booze, the saltpeter in my food, or some combination of all of the above? My penis lies limp in my unchanged undershorts, undershorts that itch and burn as the drawstring braids its pattern into the skin of my waist. I long for Marianne, but I cannot become hard. C'est la vie. Maybe my energy is employed elsewhere, in a constant state of anxiety. I suppose this is battle exhaustion. That's what they call shellshock this time around, by the way. If I tell this to the army doctors, I will be effectively removed from combat status. And what the hell will I amount to then? This is the path I chose, and I have to see it through. So, our little secret. How is life in Sudbury? How has fishing on the lake been this summer? Catch many pickerel? Are all the citizens still griping about rationing? Can everyone get on with a little cut in their sugar intake? Tell everyone that we on the front lines in this great struggle against tyranny shed tears in mind of the privation of the citizens at home, who must get by with less sugar for their tea, less butter for their bread and less meat for Sunday night roast beef dinner. Luxury goods—the most regrettable casualties of war. We at the front are on guard—En garde!—to rectify any and all such injustices. Can you read this? I doubt it; I'm a trembling wreck. My hand is like one of those seismographs that measure earthquakes and it's registering what's happening within me. Am I crazy or am I sane? I'm clearly one or the other.

He surveys what he has written and snickers in response. I can't possibly mail this home. Therapeutic, but not something I want the old man to read. He crumples the sheet up into a tight wad of paper and it crepitates, crackle crackle, squeezes it in his fist, wrings it tightly into a ball in his sweaty palms, squeezes it again in a compulsive attack of nerves, drops it on the wet and rubble-strewn floor, steps on it with his boot, smears it into the ground with his heal in search of some kind of catharsis. He is aware that he has rocked himself back and forth, back and forth through this nervous episode. He takes several deep breaths and looks about him. Men are napping under pews, or are clustered here and there at what amounts to their posts. The breeze moans through holes and windows, punctuated by the sporadic exclamations of shellfire. My morale is done. It's finished. I can't lead. And here I am awaiting orders to continue advancing once the way is opened. Dear God. And here I am doing what I wanted to be doing: showing my mettle as an infanteer. Sure as hell got what I asked for.

His mind harkens back to a propaganda poster back in Canada. A wild-eyed soldier-boy brandishing his bayonet-fixed rifle against a backdrop swirl of wind-flapped Union Jack bars and colours. Red, white and blue: the symbolic spectrum of freedom. Floppy blonde schoolboy hair sticking up in the breeze. Looking every bit like a member of the Hitler Youth. C'mon Canada! Lick 'Em Over There! Freedom unfurled, snapping in a bluster of patriotic rhetoric. Propaganda slogans from posters and newsreels shout for attention: Let's put the drip on the three droops! Loose lips sink ships! We caught hell out there—someone must have talked! Buy Victory Bonds Now! Save scrap iron for our men in the struggle against the fascists!

Cue jerky newsreel footage of convulsing cannons, speeding tanks covered in straw under the sun, men dashing forward under fire, hunched low, rifles clutched. With bayonets fixed, they mop up whatever resistance is left in this ruined Italian village after a merciless barrage, and escort columns of exhausted, bedraggled German prisoners, sullen and exhausted expressions on their faces, hands on their heads.

ANNOUNCER:

Canadian forces are on the move! These are OUR boys! Captain Jim McFarlane of the Canadian infantry tells us what it's like to fight the Germans on the broken back of their fallen ally, Italy—

Cut to scene of tired and dirty Canadian infantry captain facing the camera.

CAPTAIN MCFARLANE:

They are better at set-piece fighting, mass discipline and what have you, but we're much better in close quarters. I like to get my men in as close as I can!" (*Turning, facing the men.*) Don't shoot 'till you see the whites of their eyes!

ANNOUNCER:

The spine of Italy is not broken. The vertebraic Apennines are a defender's paradise. But nothing the combined Allied air forces and artillery cannot reduce to rubble, along with every church, cathedral, abbey, palace, castle, villa, village, farmhouse, barn, henhouse, toolshed, vineyard and orchard along the way. You can't make an omelette, they say, without breaking a few eggs. What eggs! What omelettes!

"Hey Captain, you're looking under the weather." He looks up to see his trusty batman, Corporal Cooley, looking at him, concern in his eyes.

"You're damn right I'm under the weather. It's raining lead outside, didn't you notice? The roof's leaky, too." He nods to a stain of blood on the floor from where a soldier wounded by a shell was whisked out of the church by stretcher-bearers, covered partly by sand from a slit sandbag, black like an oil stain, pattered by the rain that sprinkles in through the holes in the roof and the walls. Cooley flinches a little. Jim adjusts his tone in response to Cooley's unease. "Sorry Corporal, I'm just a little tired is all. Neither side lets us sleep with all that gunder."

"Yes, sir. Anything you need done?" Cooley looks earnest and concerned, as a batman ought to. Jim does not want to deny him his useful intentions. "Sure, some tea would be great. Brew up a pot for all of us, if you don't mind."

"Sure, sir. I'll get right on it." Cooley ventures off on his task. Now where was I? Jim wonders to himself, the sardonic mock newsreels of his mind vanished in a puff of dream smoke from Cooley's disturbance. You shouldn't idle so much, damnit, he scolds himself. He sits down to rest a moment just as the church shudders violently under a sudden pounding of artillery. He scurries under his pew, this time resting on a thin straw-filled mattress procured by Nichols on one of his supply runs. Above him the dull slate of varnished wood gleams along its edge from the pale light cast by an oil lantern that has been hung low along the wall between two of the shattered windows. The soft light wavers in lucent response to the stone-muffled crunch of shells, like circles of water rippling outward when a thrown stone breaks the surface of a lake. He reaches to his right and takes his flask from his webgear and pack, rumpled in front of the pew, unscrews it and takes a corrosive, warming pull of whiskey. It numbs its way down his throat, and as it does so, spreads a giddy warmth within his veins. With a tremendous crash, masonry and stones rain from the hollow of the steeple as it is bullseyed. The sound ravages his ears. Air is displaced, and this disturbance brings with it a tide of dust under his pew. His mouth is dried by this chalky infusion. He coughs and sneezes and spits a gob of dirty saliva, purging the taste of musty dirt and its caustic effects on his mouth and nostrils. The taste of the earth, kicked up, like the dust kicked up by soldiers' boots and military vehicles on winding summer roads. Spitting in church! Mom would not be pleased.

"Hell's Bells!" he hears someone holler from under another pew.

"Are there any casualties?" he shouts, sticking his head out into the dusty nave of the besieged church. "Anyone hurt?"

"Nah, everyone's fine!" someone answers in the dark. Thank God, he thinks, and he takes another sip of whiskey. Thank God I didn't let Blake and Cole set up shop in there.

As he waits out the shelling, there is an itch in the left arch of his foot, and it is impossible to scratch. His feet feel hot and sodden stuffed as they are into his boots. He decides to air them out. He unbuckles and unlaces his left boot, loosening it, feeling the quickened flow of blood and the liberation of compressed nerves in his ankle and foot as he does so. A moist waft of rot hazes outward from the maw of his boot as he pulls it off. The boot reluctantly releases its sodden grip with a faint sucking sound. Good God All Muddy. He pulls his wool sock off afterward, a soaked moldy rag enveloping his foot in the peaty bog of his foot's own laboured sogginess. The cool, sharp fresh air pins and needles against his newly naked foot. He scratches away the itch with the fingernails of his hand, sighing as he does so. He removes his other boot and sock to match. What relief. Perhaps not so for all the others in here with me.

"How 'bout a song?" he hears in the dark from under another pew. "Keep the old spirits up, what do you think about that?" It sounds like Lieutenant Doyle, though he can't be sure. "How about the 1st Canadian Cuckoldry?"

Jim suddenly gathers himself, having been usurped by a subordinate in attempting to raise morale. I should be keeping up morale here, for Christ's sake! Don't be upstaged by your callow young lieutenant! Get up, get with it!

"Sounds good," Jim pipes in from under his pew. "Though how it can bring anyone comfort is beyond me. For all who feel cheated up here, on the count of four—Let's go, one, two, three, four!"

From under pews and from covered corners comes a ragged chorus of men, some in tune, others not, the rusty voices of men accustomed to singing when drunk or on the march:

"Dear John, Dear Joe,
There is something here that you should know,
Here's a reason for your pride to show!
Here is the transfer that you've craved,
In return for all that you have braved!
For your service to the king,
I have here a reason for all to sing!

For your efforts overseas,
Welcome to the Cuckoldry,
The 1st Canadian Cuckoldry,
The 1st Canadian Cuckoldry—

Dear John, Dear Joe,
My how you have sunk so low!
You really have been struck a blow!
Take off your trusty old tin hat,
As now you won't be needing that!
Take it off and put on these horns
And stand ashamed and cheated and forlorn!

For your efforts overseas,
Welcome to the Cuckoldry,
The 1st Canadian Cuckoldry,
The 1st Canadian Cuckoldry—

Dear John, Dear Joe,
Let not your emotions show
As you take up your quarrel with your foe!
Let's march together on parade,
And watch behind your marriage fade,
Listen to the rumours spread,
As you charge into the storm of lead!

For your efforts overseas,
Welcome to the Cuckoldry,
The 1st Canadian Cuckoldry,
The 1st Canadian Cuckoldry, Hooray!"

Rueful laughter follows the final chorus, and for a few this laughter is likely tinged with a rueful knowingness. Other songs follow—a rousing version of "Fuck 'em all," a longing one of "White Cliffs of Dover," sung in swaying verses, in unison of shared experience if not always entirely of tone.

After the sing-song, he replaces his socks with another pair from his pack, dons his boots and once again he closes his eyes and drifts in and out of sleep and semi-conscious whimsy as the rest of the evening passes in a succession of tick-tock eternities.

X

Once again, he was out walking after a fight with Marianne. As if last week's argument had not been bad enough, this time they had descended to yelling at one another. He passed the lines of shop-fronts, seeing himself passing in the windows, walking under striped cloth awnings on the sidewalk alongside the honk and bustle of traffic, boxy cars and trucks stopped bumper to bumper as a policeman blew his whistle to allow the cross traffic to go. He walked amid the snort of vehicles and the squeal of metal streetcar wheels, and under the sky strung above with streetcar lines and telephone wires, the telephone lines suspended and sagging slightly between the wooden cross-framed telephone poles, buzzing and humming with all manners of communication urgent and not so urgent—how many secret codes, how many new war initiatives, how many encrypted messages from spies now vibrated through those conduits?

On and on he went, down this street and that, turning right at Wellington as ahead of him rose the Gothic revival Parliament Buildings behind the grille of a wrought-iron fence, the stone walls clad in hanging garlands of ivy and flowers, the clock-faced Peace Tower and the dome of the Library of Parliament both capped in a rusty green copper verdigris; the buildings together commemorating and enshrining the unlikely covenant of the Dominion of Canada, the leap of imagination in the unity of French and English. He walked onward, over a bridge spanning the Rideau Canal, past the turrets and spires of the palatial Chateau Laurier hotel, past the stately columns and grand façade of Union Station.

Left turn onto Sussex and then a right, into the barnyard world of the Byward Market, the low-lying market buildings and cattle sheds and shops and produce tents commanded by the promontory of Parliament Hill, the sweet earthy scent of manure tinging his nostrils. He walked along the wide streets crowded with people and lines of parked cars; by bins and baskets piled high with apples, tomatoes, silken-haired green ears of corn; by parked flatbed and pickup trucks, some laden with produce, heaped with baskets of onions, leeks, lettuce, cabbage. Men and women, Ottawa valley and nearby Quebec farmers and their families, called out to sell their wares: "Fresh tomatoes, ripe and red and ready to eat!" "Getcher cauliflower here, folks, getcher cauliflower here for yer salads!" "*Sirop d'érable, frais du Québec!*" Aproned apprentice boys were hanging smoked sides of meat on hooks in the windows of Jewish butcher shops and grocers. A discordant chorus of coos and clucks and squawks announced a parliament of fowls: caged chickens cocking glances and pecking at the floors of their cages, ruffling their feathers, hooking their dry, spindly and sharp curved claws into the wire mesh of their cage fronts; fatted turkeys gobbling, their hooked beaks and wrinkly heads bobbing atop their creased, elderly necks and sprouting from their plump, dusty feathery bodies that tapered into dry reptilian stalks of legs and gnarled dusty claws; mohawked pheasants cooing in confinement and ruffling their tailfeather bouquets.

And onward past the one-storey sheds, inside of which were more fowl and other animals: the snot-shine of wet-snouted pigs snorting and squealing in their pens, and horned cattle sweeping their tails from side to side, fluttering their ears at the buzzing irritation of flies, chewing slowly, methodically. The manure and earth smell from the sheds was rich, intoxicating, moistly suggestive of spring rain, summer sun and autumn harvest all at once. He wished as he walked he were a farmer, or at least something else than that which he was. He wished to be tilling the fields, wiping his brow with his sleeve, riding atop his new Massey-Harris farm tractor as it sputtered, puffs of smoke pushing up the lid of the little chimney on the hood on a day awash in yellow sunshine; a horizon of land, his land, before him, shaped and furrowed by him, seeded by him to grow into a bounteous harvest. He enjoyed the summers he spent doing work on his Uncle Gabe and Aunt Theresa's farm as a teenager, loved the work, baling the hay, feeding the pigs, driving the tractor, waking up with or before the sun, riding the natural wave of the day. He yearned for purpose, and saw and heard and smelled it in all that he walked by, all that was not his, all that he did not do. A teacher? How did I become a teacher? Because you got the job from your father. Because after you left university, your father felt he had to set you up, concerned for your future, as you in his eyes would not do so for yourself. He enjoyed the work, that was true, looked forward to it even, but he was living out his father's contingency plan for him, an interim life. And with it came Marianne, the best thing, the best person, who had ever happened to him. But his newfound domestic bliss was only a bubble born of his father's insistence that he do something, that he engage in a profession and rise through its hierarchy. Maybe, just maybe, he would be headmaster one day. On a boring day in the withered years of the autumn of his life, this bubble would burst. And with it, perhaps this life. What did that make Marianne? An interim wife? He was sickened by the thought of it, by the words that had formed in his mind. But if he was not careful, that moniker may bode true for her. Still, he yearned to be consequential, yearned for something to prove himself at once and for all, yearned for something chosen by him, yearned for a theatre in which he could demonstrate his abilities and put his convictions into action. The war was this opportunity. He hated the Nazis and feared the shadow they were casting over Europe, and very possibly, the world. He was a Canadian patriot, a loyal British subject. For freedom, for peace, order and good government, for the king, for his countrymen, onward ho to victory! Ready, aye, ready! He was going to consummate his restlessness, damn it all, he was going to consummate it and that was that, despite whatever consequences may befall him.

On the way back home, he made his way around to the shops and restaurants of Elgin Street. He popped into the King George V restaurant and sat down at a table by the window, ordering a clubhouse sandwich and a coffee, munching and sipping in silence and crumbing on the checked blue and white gingham tablecloth. After his pensive and somewhat messy meal, he made his way for home.

When he got home, Marianne was not there. There was a note on the kitchen table, and he sat down at his chair as he read it. After, he stepped out into the parlour and dialled Marianne's sister.

"Hello?"

"Hi, Rhonda. Is Marianne there?"

"Uh huh." She could not mask her displeasure. Moments later, Marianne picked up the telephone.

"Yes, Jim?"

"How long are you staying there?"

"Perhaps the night. I think we need to cool off for a day, you know." She sounded stern but caring. There was a moment of silence. In the silence of the moment, they both knew he was joining.

"Hmm. Alright, then. Um ... I'm going to do it."

"I know. I know you're going to do it. I can't stop you, Jim."

"Look ... I'm applying locally. At the Cartier Armoury. I won't be going anywhere for awhile yet, if they even send me overseas at all."

"Mm hmm."

"Marianne, I'm sorry."

"So am I, Jim. So am I." The image of her father in his armchair sipping rye, wearing an eye patch, looking hollow and lost, entered his mind. She's sorry indeed, he thought.

"Goodnight, Marianne." He fumbled a moment and added, "I love you."

"Goodnight Jim." She hung up with a click that to Jim resembled a slamming door. He hung up in turn. He felt so suddenly alone and so suddenly free, all at once. A strange elation filled him, and an electric tingle sizzled upward through his spine. He had made a decision.

Join he did, the following Monday, strolling up to the armoury wearing a light tan jacket, wool pants, green slouch cap and two-tone shoes, with a spring in his stride. He was weighed and fitted, given an eye test, made to sign some forms, and was inducted into the Cameron Highlanders regiment. He was now in the army.

XI

The next night, Major Gordon, the battalion's second in command, visits to relay the commands of Colonel Hobson, the colonel having departed to the rear to meet with his own superiors.

"Hello in here!" he shouts.

"Good evening, Major," someone answers in greeting. "Lovely night for a stroll, isn't it?"

"Why on earth you'd want to visit this shell magnet is beyond me," criticizes Jim with a cynical smile as he emerges from the shadows, the bouncing bead of his cigarette conducting his words in the dark in a pyrotechnic illumination of disdain. "Why didn't you just ring me up by field telephone? We've been hit more times than I have fingers and toes."

"And hello to you too McFarlane," is Gordon's rejoinder. He is wet and miserable; it has begun raining again. "I would have called you up, but the wire's been cut by an explosion. I bring you all good news. It looks like we will be moving, at last. The 5th Armoured is to punch through and seize the ridge."

"When?" Jim asks, incredulous that the battalion has finally received marching orders. "I was beginning to think we'd be stuck on this hill forever."

"The whole regiment moves in the next few nights, in the wee hours. We know this much from our intelligence, from prisoners and local informers—the local German commanders in this sector wonder why we have not bypassed the ridge to take Rimini by the coast. They probably think we're too petered out to go on now, that we need some time to lick our wounds. Or they expect us to bypass the ridge in order to capture Rimini at some point soon. Who knows? We get relieved tomorrow night and rest for two days."

Jim exhales a lungful of cigarette smoke, and answers with a tone of tired reluctance, "We do so need time. And the Germans are right—we are too petered out. Christ, we've had thirty casualties in my company in the last week alone. I'm leading a company that's about, oh, two-thirds strength. And we'll get no fuckin' reinforcements, because we're just a shadow now. Those boys up in France and Belgium get the resources."

"Every rifle company and every tank squadron and what have you in the Canadian Corps right now are exhausted. But we have to move forward. That's our orders and we have to follow them. We're in the middle of a major offensive, we can't stop now. It is not as if I make these decisions, you know."

"Our company can't put up with much more over the next bit," Jim states matter-of-factly. "Not without reinforcements. We're getting whittled down just sitting here."

"You will. After Coriano is taken, likely we'll get some from the holding units. We could even get some before that. And starting tomorrow we get a momentary reprieve."

"Uh huh. A reprieve? That can mean anything. I have one of those every time I take a leak." He smiles at this to try to show he's not demoralized.

"It's the best we can get. This is a big push we're on, and we have to be back in the game soon. Sorry." He looks at Jim intently for a moment, and adds with words chosen and enunciated carefully, "And McFarlane, remember for the moment that you are not the only company commander around here. The others all have the same manpower problems you do, have been in the same action you have, and yet you don't see them whinging for special treatment. And those boys in 1st Division and 1st Armoured Brigade, they get double our action. Do you see them screeching for a break?" Pardon me? He shoots Gordon a look from under a furrowed armour of brows. He relaxes before saying anything stupid.

Insufferable fusspot Gordon, with his martinet's moustache, all disapproving twitch and huff. Orange Order uppity bastard. Never got along with him much.

"Duly noted, sir."

"Yes, we'll just be going into reserve for a couple days. Most likely, I'm sorry, for one day. But who am I to know? Once we take the ridge, I think it is fairly obvious, and incumbent on the brass, to give us leave. That's how it always works."

"Huh. Still in artillery range. So in effect, no reprieve, because that's just the standard rotation of units. This is not because I feel under the weather, you know. I just realize that we can't keep carrying out these offensives without significant reinforcements."

"Understood. But there is little I can do about it. That, I am afraid, is the reality of a volunteer army. Reinforcements are thin, and every man must thereby do the job of two."

"True," Jim acknowledges thoughtfully. He shifts on his feet, coughs, and declares, "Well, I'm afraid I'll have to have a drink now." He slugs a large mouthful of whiskey, and offers some to Gordon. Gordon, however, is a Calvinist teetotaller and says, with a trace of disdain, "I'd sooner take one in the arm."

"I've already done that," retorts Jim, feeling the knotted dent of his healed arm wound from the Liri Valley battle, "and I'll tell you, I prefer booze, thank you very much." He notes on a glance that his wound resembles a closed sphincter.

"Damn you McFarlane, you're a smartass." Within his stance of supercilious disapproval can be detected a modicum of good-natured banter. At least he tries on occasion, Jim thinks, at least he tries. The whole church shakes violently under the impact of a shell. Everyone hits the floor. Dust and masonry crash from the ceiling and coat everyone and everything. Stunned, the soldiers pick themselves up.

"Everyone okay?" Jim calls out into the pall of smoke and dust, his voice shuddery. "Casualties?" There are none, this time. Jim holds out his flask to Gordon and asks him with a wry grin while waving it in his face, a wellspring of whiskey sloshing within, "Are you sure you wouldn't like a drink?" Gordon scowls, stung.

"Oh, can it, McFarlane. Just get back to your duties. The sooner you do so, the sooner we can end this conversation."

"The feeling is mutual, Major."

"I am out of here." With a nod and a salute. "Captain—"

"Major." Jim returns the salute. Gordon eyes him carefully a moment, officious doubt in his eyes. He does a smart about turn, stamps his right foot, and marches out of the church and into the rain in exemplary parade square fashion.

"Gentlemen!" Jim addresses the hollows of the ruined church with a stentorian echo. "We are being relieved in one day's time!" The men cheer.

"Briggs!" he shouts to one of his orderlies.

"Yessir!" answers Briggs from his card game in the corner with Cooley and Lafontaine.

"Go out and inform Olczyk and Therrien that we are pulling out tomorrow!"

"Yes, sir!" Briggs immediately drops his cards and excuses himself from his game, leaving through the main door.

As he exits the rain increases in intensity again and is soon cascading through the holes in the roof and slanting through the shattered windows. Artillery thuds in the distance. Jim moves to a dry alcove next to the altar where is set the company No. 18 wireless set and field telephone, Private Thibeault monitoring transmissions from his headphones as if divining ethereal messages from a deep and meditative trance.

"Anything new?"

"No, sir, other than Staff Sergeant Nichols wired in and asked how we are for fresh water."

"Tell him we're fine, as we're out of here tomorrow."

"Yes, sir."

As he turns around to face the door a fusillade of artillery bears down on their position in a terrific overlapping thunderclap. Everyone standing or sitting hits the floor for cover. Stones crash to the floor. Jim looks up from the floor and sees a flash beyond the door, the stunned silhouette of a soldier framed in its exposure. The soldier falls to his knees in the doorway and wobbles like a bowling pin before collapsing backwards. Cooley and Lafontaine and several soldiers from Doyle's platoon all run to the man in the doorway as outside the shells flash and flicker.

"It's Briggs!" shouts Cooley over his shoulder from a squatting position. He cradles Briggs, and Lafontaine joins him, and Briggs writhes in the hands of his comrades, face blackened, eyes white, shivering. Several soldiers crowd around in a protective hunch. There is a cluster of explosions outside the door in the distance that captures their faces in its staccato flicker like a great bursting of flashbulbs. Briggs' breathing is rapid, his hands are trembly, and his eyes shine wide with pain. But he scarcely whimpers, perhaps because of the morphine styrette with which Lafontaine has just pricked him in the thigh.

Cooley speaks softly to Briggs, soothing him as though he were his mother or his nurse as he applies the dressing, "It's okay there Briggs, you just hang in there buddy, you're gonna be okay, you just hold on tight and breathe, that's it, just breathe there buddy, in and out, that's it, okay, here you go, take a bit of water, you still gotta cash out that full house you were holding," and he dribbles water from his canteen into Briggs' mouth, the water splashing on his trembling chin, glistening in the flare of a bursting shell, "that's it, nice and easy, take it in, soak it up, that's a good sport there Briggsy—"

"My legs," Briggs interjects with a hint of rising panic, "My legs, they're bad, aren't they?" His pronunciation is off, his face taut and stiffened with pain, "They're really bad, aren't they?" At this Jim sees through the weave of supporting arms and hunched shoulders that Briggs is missing both legs at the knees. The stumps shine in the flare of an explosion.

"Jesus, get a shell dressing on there!" Jim shouts, and Lafontaine pulls one looped to his belt and unwinds the gauze. "Make a fucking tourniquet or something! Are there no medics in here? Goddamnit, where are the medics?"

"Stretcher-bearers! We need stretcher-bearers here on the double!" hollers Witchewski into the howling thunder night beyond the door.

"You're gonna be fine, Briggs," Jim says, joining in, "You'll be good as new, you get to spend some time with the nurses, you lucky bastard, it's off to Blighty for ya, and then you're homeward bound."

"No, I won't, I'm broken aren't I, I'm broken and all messed up and they won't be able to fix me right will they—" His voice is whimpery and swimmy with panic and pain and morphine. Cooley calms him, shushes him, speaks softly to him as he gently cradles him.

A pair of exhausted stretcher-bearers enter the church, having just tended to wounded from other nearby positions. Cooley and Lafontaine and Jim defer to the medics as they tie a tourniquet around Briggs' stumps, stemming the flow of blood that has soaked the bandages, and they jab him with more morphine and speak soothingly to him, "That's it buddy, hold on tight, we'll get you back to the aid post good as new there boy, don't you worry," patting his shoulders as he looks up and shakes and clenches his teeth. They slide him onto their well-used, bloodstained stretcher and hoist him up and carry him away into the night in a low hunch.

Another volley of shells bears down. A chunk of the roof collapses and lands just short of the altar with a weighted, crumbly crash, and Jim hits the stone floor again as a wash of dust rolls over all. The stones on which he lies turn in his gaze as he picks himself back up to his knees, the room turning in a daze as the crash of the explosion slowly dissipates. He turns around to see a pile of stones on the broken altar and a torrent of rain pouring down through the gaping hole in the ceiling.

"I think we should abandon this church before it falls on us, sir," says Doyle, crouched against a corner nearby, "I think we should've abandoned this fucking church yesterday."

"Good idea," says Jim, his heart racing, "good idea." He faces the rest of the men. "Form up and abandon this position! Onward and on the double! Move into the trenches on the reverse side and dig in! Decamp and let's move out!" The men set about gathering their kit, slinging packs and weapons, radio and telephone equipment, ammunition and ration boxes, and they head out as more artillery bears down, and Jim runs out into the lanes and shouts, "Able Company! Abandon your positions and fall back! Abandon your positions! Fall back!" He sees another shell hit the church and then another, and much of the rest of the pitted and broken roof caves in, leaving only a blasted, gutted shell of a building. They wend their way squad by squad through the mucky lanes to the reverse slope of the hill, and they leap into the trenches many would hold during the day, bailing them out, digging deeper, heaving clots of sodden muck with their spades. Jim oversees at a crouch, his fevered breath misting with each panicked exhalation in the driving rain, and he helps several soldiers with their digging and bailing, using his helmet to ladle muddy water from sodden slit trenches. He opts to use the crumbled ruin of a farmhouse at the very edge of the town as a headquarters, and he orders Witchewski, Cooley, Lafontaine and Thibeault to set up shop in there. He invites soldiers to come rest and dry themselves out in shifts, as the rain pours in sheets and the night is rent by the artillery that peals like thunder, and Jim lies on his thin mat in the corner while soldiers sit and huddle with their knees against the wall in the clutter of the broken house, waiting, waiting, waiting through the hours for relief. Waiting, Jim thinks, and helps himself to a pull of whiskey from his flask to steady his nerves for another day of holding the line. Sooner or later we have to wade in and fight the undertow.

XII

Able Company awaits relief. Rain patters on the roof of the house, drips through holes, lands in cold drops on the floor and on the soldiers seeking shelter from the guns. Two minutes after the supposed relief time, after a brief but intense German bombardment, they hear approaching footsteps, footsteps of a large body of men making their way to their new positions. A changing of the guard. A figure appears in shadow at the door, and is questioned by the sentry, Private Cook. After a quick exchange of muffled words, an officer appears, wearing his beret instead of a helmet, very young, narrow-faced, freshly shaved, with a thin black Clark Gable style officer's moustache that suggests an effort to impersonate a young Field Marshal Montgomery, like so many Canadian officers. Jim and the officer salute one another.

"Captain James McFarlane, Able Company, 1st Irish."

"Acting Captain Edward Simmonds, Charlie Company, West Novas."

"Welcome to my position. It's yours. We've taken a helluva beating these last few days, but this house should stand you through the worst of it. The platoons are dug in pretty well here but we've taken some casualties. We had to abandon most of the ruins up top as we took too much of a beating. I leave to you the scenic splendour of San Mateo, illuminated by the fireworks of our friends the Germans." There is some laughter from the men at this. "You may want to dig even deeper—they've really been pulverizing this place. I believe it's been all de-mined, but watch your steps nonetheless."

"Thanks for the advice."

"No problem. It's free of charge. Take care here, okay?"

"Okay, you too." They briefly meet eyes. Jim averts his after a moment.

Jim addresses the men in the house: "Gentlemen, in official military parlance: Let's get the hell out of here. *Avanti!*"

Under a flickering sky they wend their way out of the house and the slit trenches, and they form up in the rain with the other companies moving out of their adjacent positions. During the transfer, a shell lands on Baker, causing three casualties. Jim reverses the journey he took days ago with his compatriots, this time on foot, as his jeep has been taken back to the rear. The soldiers march single file in the night on a dirt track furrowed by the cartwheels of farmers, their feet squelching in the mud, rain beating on their helmets and beading on and running down their gas capes, their breaths smoking in the rain. They march to the piping of Sergeant Mullen, the battalion pipe major, as he skirls the strains of "Garry Owen" and "When Johnny Comes Marching" and "Tipperary"; this keeps them in step, miserable and tired though they are, as they pace their way through the muddy puddles as the gullies to the sides of them fill and flow with gurgling runoff.

Through a mucky depression in the road he marches. Squelch, squelch, squelch. The mud sucks at his boot with each lifting step in an attempt to claim him. In the end, the earth always gets its man. A clutch of German shells lands nearby in a tree stand, too far away to cause alarm, lighting up the night with streaking umbrellas of sparks. They march, tromp, tromp, tromp, until they make it to the rest village over the River Conca, the hilly outskirts of which are lined with stakes embroidered with the vines of grapes, and that Jim can see in the darkness has not been scarred by battle or bombardment. When they crossed the river before, it was a cracked shingle bed, scored and furrowed with canyons in the parched summer drought; now it is a torrent, filling with rain, heralding the arrival of autumn underneath their tramping footsteps on the Bailey bridge with the erosive certainty of water and the seasons. Over a humped stone bridge beneath which a rain-glutted creek gurgles, and under a gnarled reach of oak branches they make their way. Into the cobbled and lockstone winding streets they march, passing on either side of them rows of pastel townhouses with shuttered windows that reveal their colours in brief flashes of sheet lightning that crackle through the clouds—light Easter egg blue, earthy mustard yellow, pink, wedding cake off-white, light cinder grey. They pass ornate window enclosures and colonnaded windows fringed with flowerboxes and planted herbs and tomatoes. Under an arch they march into an expansive tiled piazza ringed by shopfronts enclosed in an arched yellow portico, and onto a side street, alongside rows of tree-lined cinderblock and stone houses with sloping terra cotta tiled roofs. Several army trucks grunt and lumber by, the canvas roofs over their cabs dating them as relics of the desert campaign two years ago, given to Canadian units by the British when their own transport was sunk by the German air raid in the Mediterranean back before Christmas. Rain-drenched canvas canopies stretch over the metal rib frames, giving the trucks the appearance of gaunt and starving animals. A woman waves from a dark window through open red wooden shutters. Jim waves back. Maybe a washerwoman in the employ of the Eighth Army. He is directed with his company down a street to a row of four large houses that have been assigned to his company, and along with the others, is given changes of clothes by the rear echelons. He goes through the motions mechanically, bone-tired, accepting his change of clothes and told to report to mess at 0900 sharp the following morning. His men dispatched en masse to their houses, he joins the other officers of the battalion as they make their way to their own adjoining billets. Some of them are in a small hotel owned and operated by Giovanni and Estella Ceci, who have gleefully attached themselves to the Eighth Army as helpers, and who smilingly await their guests at the front door framed by the red shutters of the hotel windows. Captain Alward of Charlie Company whistles with approval at the sight of the small hotel, and exclaims, "I was betting on a tent. This will more than do!" Mr. and Mrs. Ceci are in their fifties; he is balding and has a weathered face and black moustache, and she is smiling and plump. They usher in Doyle, Therrien and a Lieutenant Volpe before Jim.

"Come in, come in, you must be cold," Estella entreats in a thick Italian accent, waving him in beyond the whitewashed façade of the hotel with her fleshy arms, "We have beds a-ready for you, yes we do, just come with me." She is the very embodiment of effusive hospitality, much as the priest at the church was the opposite. Giovanni smiles and nods at him as he is led in by Estella, his hand enveloped by her meaty matronly paw. Jim is pleasantly overwhelmed by the fragrance of garlic and herbs as he enters their cluttered but tasteful hotel by way of the front room, pictures hanging from the wall, a table and sofa and chairs beside a fireplace full of old ashes. Beyond is a dining room and kitchen, and in front of him is a staircase leading up to the hotel's handful of rooms. There is a fumy, dusty air of mothballs and must. In the lobby stands Major Riordan, cobeen on head, cup of coffee in hand. He is a tall, weak-chinned man with a wide moustache and spectacles, with the air of an accountant—which, in fact, he was until the war.

"Pretty good find, eh, McFarlane?" he asks, proud. "We were among the first guys in here scouting. I saw it and right away chose it for us. Some of the Johnnies-come-lately will be stuck in sheds and pup tents and old Jerry trenches. This is Irish Avenue!"

"Good work, Major," agrees Jim, complimenting Riordan on his acquisitions. "Good work indeed. You did it again. Certainly beats the hell out of a pile of rubble or a musty tent." Mrs. Ceci ushers Captains Alward and Van Der Hecke into their rooms. She points to his room, and settles the other officers into their rooms as well; Jim opens the door and finds himself in a small but comfortable room with a double bed, a desk, a dresser, and a sink and washbasin. At the end of a hall is a shared washroom with a chain-flushed squat toilet embedded in the floor. He lights a couple candles that have been provided in honour of the general blackout. Pulling off his boots, he is acutely aware that his feet reek, his socks sopping wet.

The night thuds with distant shellfire, and a sharper crack of nearby thunder. He pulls off his khaki bush shirt and throws it to the floor. It settles with a faint whoomping sound, billowing out air through its sleeves and folds like a collapsing tent, and he sits on the bed, which has been stripped of its bedding by the Germans and covered with a crisp white army sheet and grey woollen army blanket, more than likely provided by the quartermasters, and lies down on the mattress, his sopping stockinged feet still on the floor, socks sagging and loose at the toes, pulling downward painfully on his leg hairs as they slouch and pile at his ankles. He removes them and savours the feeling of his feet airing out, the relief of itchiness. He leans over and reaches into the breast pocket of his khaki bush shirt lying rumpled in a grimy heap, and pulls out his silver cigarette case. He lights a cigarette and lies back on the mattress again, the springs groaning underneath, feet still planted on the floor, and inhales, eyes pointed up at the stucco ceiling. One good thing deserves another, he muses, one good thing deserves another and I deserve a drink, he thinks, yes I do, I deserve a drink, and he sits up again and reaches into his webbing for his flask, and he gulps down a slug of whiskey and it warms him, his temples hum and thrum, and a warm wave of relaxation washes over him coupled with the nervous solace of the cigarette.

From through the floorboards and echoing from the halls is the controlled, plaintive howl of a harmonica to the longing strains of "Baby, Won't You Please Come Home":

When you left, you broke my heart
That would never make us part
Every hour in the day, you will hear me say
"Baby, won't you please come home?"

He feels a sudden longing for Marianne, a sudden regret for this decision to be where he is, almost two years away from his wife, in a situation of danger as self-imposed as it is imposed upon the world. He ashes into an empty wine bottle standing beside his bed. Why the hell am I here? Because I wanted to be. I wanted to be here, so I came here. I came here to prove something to myself. How many others are like me? Everyone in this expeditionary force is a volunteer. Just like you told Cooley in the jeep. There are thousands of us, signed up for King and Country. Or pride. Or a thirst for adventure. Or to run away from something. To run away from something … What the hell did you run away from? Complacency? A good job? A beautiful and intelligent wife? He turns his head to a mirror on the empty dresser on the far side of the room, and he can see himself indented into the mattress, lazily smoking, looking back at himself. A nagging sense of failure? Inability to cut it in the regular world? What the hell, Jim, you can't even cut it here. You're not all that tough. Think of that letter you wrote to your dad and tossed out in the church. He rummages into his trouser pockets and pulls a picture from his brown leather wallet stuffed with military-issue lire banknotes, the wallet a gift from Marianne two years ago. From this sepia print, she smiles at him, her natural vivacity channelled through her luscious-lipped grin, her wavy black hair an exciting contrast to her lilywhite face, her lashes turned up coquettishly, her finely curved features given extra definition in soft black and white tempered with brown. I miss you so much and I long to return to you.

From the same pocket he pulls a worn, folded note. He slowly unfolds it and looks at it wistfully. His last letter from Marianne, received one month ago. One month. Surely, she's written since then. Anything can happen. Goddamn army postal service is a farce. Maybe the letter's been shot down or sunk en route. It's happened before. Aww, whatever.

He reads and drinks in solace from the words.

Dear Jim,

I hope this finds you well. I do miss you. Your last letter sounded so passionate, so intense. I hope you're holding up over there. I read the newspapers, I listen to the radio. Italy's really blown up again, hasn't it? But now with the invasion in France, that's about all you find in the news right now. Normandy's the 'big show' now. You guys in what you call the 'Spaghetti League' don't get enough credit anymore, but you're not totally forgotten.

Jim is physically warmed by the embroidery of written words on the note. He continues reading:

> *Mrs. Wright came by the other day to give me home-baked cookies and tea—how very sweet of her, she knows how lonely it can get. She's taken on a sort of surrogate mother role to me. Her sons are working in lumber camps up the Gatineau River and her husband has signed up for reserve duty to complement his job at the lumberyard. Over here it's all work, and when people aren't working, it's talk about which team's on top in hockey. The usual. Well, I could do without the rationing around here, we all complain about it, but don't worry, I don't get too carried away with it, because I think of you sweating it out in the battlefields, and I know you have more to complain about than we do when we're stuck eating thin pork chops and you have to duck bullets in the mud.*
>
> *Well, I'll leave you now. Take care over there, and take care of your charge.*
>
> *Love you and hold on tight—*
>
> *Marianne*

He looks a moment at the letter he has just read, tracing the ink river of thought and emotion with his eyes, and says to himself, what another world I'm in. What another man I am now. Kill, kill, kill my way back home. Just as most of them are just trying to kill their way back home. Locked into mutual murder, just to go home to escape it. Fight your way to peace. Kill your way back to life. Run madly for your sanity.

There is a knock at the door. "Come, come have drink of wine with us before bed, come down to dining room, yes?" It is the voice of Estella Ceci, brimming with a robust hospitality and an eagerness to share what few resources she has.

"Okay, just give me a moment," Jim responds in a rusty and exhausted voice. "Just allow me to ... " The world of his perceptions distorts like the reflections in a water drop, images and sounds stretching and blending together in liquid impressions, I'm so tired just let me sleep through Gemmano row by row row across the Styx fromeverandeveramen—

He opens his eyes and reemerges from the dreamy netherworld of gibberish into which he has plunged. "I'll be right there," he slurs. Words fit his mouth like mismatched puzzle pieces, tongue and teeth unable to conform to the contours of sound and syllable, his tongue thick and tired and dry and dumb and his brain unable to conjure up any conversation beyond vapid banalities slowed by want of sleep. "I'll be … "

XIII

"You are defined by your decisions. And your decisions define you." Wise words spoken by his father years ago and miles away in Sudbury, where he worked as a family doctor and as an anaesthetist at St. Joseph's Hospital. These words were uttered when Jim was only seven and had been caught stealing penny candies from the corner grocery. Mr. Logothetis, the Greek owner, grabbed him by the ear, shouted at him and forced him to call his father at home before sending him on his way.

"Do you know what that means, son?" His father's fine, expressive Scots-Irish features, mirrored in softer definition in his own boy's face, loomed down on him in studied disapproval and disappointment. "Do you know what this means?" Jim averted his eyes as they filled with water, and his skin reddened in a searing of shame. His queasy humiliation was electrified by the fear of a spanking, the usual punishment for any wrong done, especially when his father was tired after a long week of work.

"Uh huh." Fumbling and fidgeting, he looked reluctantly back up at his dad.

"Look at me, Jim. Look up at me. Don't hide your eyes from me. Real men look up and face the consequences." Real men, Jim thought, real men. Will I ever be as big as Dad? Will I ever be a real man? Johnny Bailey says I'm weak and will never grow up to be strong like him or his dad. Jim felt small and weak right now, caught stealing from a store, stealing on a dare from the same Johnny Bailey. Johnny Bailey, the biggest boy around. He can play hockey and score on anyone, even the older kids. His dad owns a mine. His uncle plays on the refinery baseball team. Mom calls Johnny a reprobate. He says Mom talks funny because she's from Ireland. She says "Em" instead of "Um." He thinks that's funny. Listen to Dad.

"When you make a decision and you act on it, son, then others look at you in terms of that decision. Do you understand me?"

"Yes."

"What does that mean?" Jim thought carefully a moment under the scrutiny of his father before answering. The air was oppressive, as though he could feel the roof and the skies above weighing down on him.

"Umm ..." he began, his words wavering with uncertainty. "It means, um, it means that if you do some*thing*, then people think of you doing that *thing*?" His words were uncertain, curled up into questions at the end.

"Exactly. You become your decisions. You become what you do. Now what do you think that you should do to make it up to Mr. Logothetis?" Jim squirmed under the humiliation of consequence.

"Umm ... maybe I could apologize to him?" Apologize—that's the fancy way of saying sorry. Miss Ukranec gave me a prize for spelling that at the spelling bee. Miss Ukranec—from Ukraine, just like her name.

"Yes, you can apologize to him, but I think you should do something more. I think you should go and apologize and help him clean his store or stock his shelves for the day."

"Yes, Dad." He hung his head low in dejection and skulked away from home on the long march back toward George's Grocer, his nerves queasing his stomach from fear, his face hot with shame. As he walked, as the snow softly pattered about him, and as he exhaled a crystalline smoke of frost, he thought of what his father had said. You make your decisions. And your decisions in turn make you. He turned these words over in his mind as he sat in his chair. He had made a decision; he had defined himself anew.

"Are you sure that's your choice?" Headmaster Harris' voice stirred the uncertainty of his own thoughts. From across the desk, one leg crossed over the other, hand musingly on chin, Jim thought a moment and answered, "Yes."

"You know, this is a prestigious school, and a very good position that you have here." He held one of the arms of his pair of glasses to his lips, his habit when in a thoughtful mood. His sunburned head shined under the office light, and his fringe of fine white hair was illuminated at the edges like the border of a cloud in the sun.

"I know that, sir. But I feel that this is what I should be doing, given all that is happening in the world right now."

"Not that it is any of my business, really," began Mr. Harris, setting up what was sure to be an uncomfortable question, "but you were married not so long ago. How is your wife with this decision?"

"She is fine with it, really," Jim lied, and not altogether convincingly. "You know, I will probably just end up serving here in Canada. After all, I joined locally, here, at the Cartier Armoury. I could just end up working in the area."

"Mmm hmm." Mr. Harris was audibly dubious at this assertion. "You could be transferred anywhere at a moment's notice, I'm sure. You know, you're quite a good teacher. Some of the students have commented on your classes—you got this job because of my connection with your father, but damned if I don't feel that you are a natural fit for this job anyway. I feel that maybe you are leaving your natural setting here, and I want you just to think about it carefully."

"Well, sir, I thank you for the compliments, but I think my calling is elsewhere, now. Besides, when all is said and done, I will have amassed a whole lot of experience worth imparting to the students of tomorrow, don't you think?"

A reluctant nod. "I suppose you're right on that one. You are leaving us?"

"Yes, I am afraid I am. As you know, I already joined up."

"Well, we will definitely try to hold a position for you should you wish to return when this war is over."

"Thank you, sir. It is much appreciated." They stood and shook hands. Mr. Harris tapped him on the shoulder with his palm, adding, "Good luck."

"Thank you. Take care."

The classroom beckoned him with the groaning of the opening door. He stepped into the interior, greeted by silence and a smell of polish. The sun slanted in from the row of high windows and shined its dust-trafficked rays up the rows of empty wooden desks. On the wall was a painted portrait of the king, a Red Ensign flag, and a poster from the war effort—Save Scrap Iron For Our Fight Against The Fascists! He slumped down in his chair, surveying the empty seats, hearing the voices of students, hearing himself speak, feeling the soreness of his arm as he chalked notes onto the board to the rapt attention of the students and their feverish note-taking.

"And this, students, represented what?" Hands up. He selected one eager student, an earnest and awkward young boy in a navy sweater and collared shirt and with side-parted hair. "Harold Young?"

"This represented that the British North American colonies could now rule themselves internally."

"Exactly. Good answer, Mr. Young, you must've been reading your Creighton. The implementation of the BNA Act gave Canada its first inkling of independence, binding the four colonies together as a sort of economic and political bulwark against … " And on and on and on. Well, he thought, it is now time to act upon Canada's history instead of merely teaching kids about it, as he opened his drawers and began emptying his desk and the shelves of all that was his: books, pens, papers, mementoes such as a trophy for coaching the soccer team to victory, and a yearbook signed by his last graduating class. Many of who were joining the services, and all of whom made an impression on him. "I'm joining the air force, sir. I'm going into the navy. I'm joining the army, just like my dad last time." He couldn't handle being upstaged in such a manner when he was just young enough to taste the excitement, just young enough to want to ride the wave of an era, however catastrophic it may be, however possible and even likely it was to be dashed against the rocks, to be broken and beaten into flotsam or washed up as wreckage with the oily tide of man's messy affairs. Over the past year he would often interrupt his own dusty lessons on history and economics and geography to broker class discussions about what was happening. He brought in newspapers about Poland and Phony War and France, about possible conscription, about manpower needs, about where the war might lead, about how the last war affected it, and he found himself becoming increasingly eager to join up, to walk away from the high school right to the armoury, to sign up, shape up and ship out.

He finished packing up his things and left the school by way of the gymnasium, pausing in its silent expanse to look one last time: at the benches to the side and the stands and railing overlooking the gym from above; at the high windows; at the skeletal gymnastic equipment against the wall, ropes, rope ladders, dangling rings, high and low beams; at the hanging banners of victory commemorating championships in football, basketball, hockey, track and field, soccer, baseball, one commemorating the senior boys' basketball team that he had coached on to numerous victories; and at the polished wooden gym floor with its striped court markings and the scuffmarks of shoes. He could still hear the full-stop squeak of shoes of players jostling for the ball, the hollow rubber bounce of the ball, could feel the thudding clamour of twenty feet bounding up the court as one player broke away for a clear shot at the other end of the court. The gym was alive with the ghosts of his experience, with the painful adolescent longings for accomplishment and approbation, of pain, of expectation and celebration. You made an impression here, he thought. You were really onto something here, even Dad began to no longer care that neither you nor Mark decided to follow his footsteps into medicine. You'd be a headmaster in no time. Hmmm. A moment's pause. Encumbered by boxes, he continued making his way out through the gym doors and through the courtyard to the car, an old black 1932 Ford Model 18, with a long, tapered snout and boxy cab, and a scuff in the side from a newsboy's bicycle that veered too close. The sun winked through the courtyard leaves above and dappled his face and his shoulders, and light skeletal shadows of branches brushed over him as he put the boxes in the passenger seat and then went around to the other side to get in; and he slammed the door and turned the key and left his comfortable teaching job and the mundane possibilities it connoted to him.

XIV

Eyes flutter open to the aural insult of reveille, bagpipes skirling up from the street below. He yawns, and props himself up upon his elbows and bumps his head. He wipes the crust of sleep from his eyes, the afterbirth of awakening. Goddamn reveille. Still, he feels much better, more well rested, the outlines of his thoughts more clearly defined and separated from the world about him, his grip on sanity momentarily more firm. But what the hell? Above him it is dark. He has bumped his head on a wooden beam, just like in that goddamned church. He realizes that he is under the bed. Must've crawled here in the middle of the night. Don't remember a damned thing. Must've heard thunder or something. Came close to losing it up there at the front, didn't you, he chastises himself, nearly blew it up there. What was with that letter you wrote to Dad? Better hope the shrinks or the padre or, God help me, Gordon, don't get their mittens on that. Crushed it up good and proper. What would the Jerries say if they got their hands on that in a counterattack? Probably that our morale is in the toilet. If I'm any indication, anyway. Jesus Christ man, keep it together, keep it together. He crawls out from under the bed into the bedroom. As he shimmies out from under the bed he catches a musky whiff of his own armpit, and he realizes that is still wearing his undershirt and his pants from the front. The candles are still burning. He gets up and flops back onto the bed he somnambulantly departed some hours ago. As he turns his hand, he catches a glint of reflected sunlight and glances at the twinkling object playing off the light of the eastern sun that slants through the slats of his shuttered window; it is his watch. He looks at it. It is well after dawn, 0805 to be precise. Well, we got our R and R. A day of this and I could be as good as new. Mamma mia, this truly is comfort next to the cold stone floor of that bloody godforsaken church. Or that house. The shudder of artillery reminds him that he is still near the battlefront. He draws in deeply the air, and a relaxed and contented thrill courses through him. He savours the feeling of the mattress, lumpy though it is, and even the spring in his back isn't so bad considering his last bed. It's like that dream the other night under the pew. Except, no Marianne. And no bloody volcano. Well, that's not entirely true, he adds in his mind to the thud of a faraway shell. This must be the six hundredth or so consecutive time that I've woken up alone. You made your bed—now you sleep in it, says the old adage. That I will. He dozes some more, moving in and out of sleep, dreaming trivial dreams, his mind and body at rest for the moment until 0830, when he finally rises. As he yawns upon rising, he feels the itch of the whiskers on his face. Have to shave. Only shaved once in the last five days. I'm starting to look like a hobo. Mother would not approve. Nor would Marianne. A fleeting image of Marianne rubbing her fingers over his bristly stubble and wrinkling her nose, an endearing gesture, a pang of longing in his heart. Gotta spit and polish myself to perfection—be a gentleman in the mud, keep up morale. He rummages through his pack, lying on the floor, and produces his rations. He opens a Hershey bar and sinks his teeth into the squares of waxy chocolate, his teeth twinging in satisfaction and in anticipation of another deep, sinking waxen bite. He makes quick work of the bar, and the influx of sugar and caffeine sharpens him up. There is a knock on the door.

"Yes?"

"Mess call in twenty. There are showers in the courtyard. Get yourself washed up!" It is the curt voice of Gordon.

Jim opens the door to see Gordon perfectly made up, shaved and showered and in uniform, knocking on adjoining doors, waking up exhausted officers.

"Here, have a shower, they're prepared for all of you already," Estella Ceci yells merrily from further out in the hallway beyond, cutting through the clutter and bustle of awakening men gathering and muttering in the hallway, her voice muffled and echoing about the walls. He shuts the door and proceeds to strip, peeling off his reeking undershirt and pants and his unchanged underwear, each pulled-off garment lessening the itch and irritation that have been building over the last number of days. His pores open in relief to the freshness of the air. He wraps himself in a white towel that has been provided by the quartermasters, and he makes his way in a line of officers clad in towels down the hall and down the stairs and out a secondary door into a central courtyard in which wooden portable shower stalls have been rigged underneath an awning. In the centre of the courtyard, along with an old oak tree, are several saggy green pup tents, temporary homes to some latecomers unlucky enough to be denied a bed. Ahead of him are Gordon, Olczyk, Riordan, and Lieutenant Wells. When it is his turn he pulls the curtain shut and with a pull of a chain releases a weak trickling tide of cold but refreshing water on him. He dips a bath brush into a large bowl full of hot water on the ground and sighs audibly as he brushes himself with it, the bristles scratching his back, his arms, his legs, his stomach, and he loosens the grime that has clung to him, glued to him by the sweat in which he has been slicked, with a bar of soap and a rough cake of pumice stone. The water pours over him, washes him of his experience, and he whistles the strains of "It's a Long Way to Tipperary" as he does so without realizing it, its plucky melody apt for the simple but morale-boosting ablution he is undergoing. It is not as good as the hot bath he got just after a rotation out of the line at Cassino provided by the nuns at a convent, steaming hot in a marble tub, or his last one in an abandoned mansion before marching up to assault the Gothic Line. No, the feeble trickle of water under which he stands now can but little conjure the experience of the few hot baths he's had in Italy, and the many before Italy in the eons before, but given the circumstances, it is far better than nothing at all. He leaves the shower, which is snapped up greedily by a Lieutenant Flaherty, and makes his way out of the courtyard back to his room, his towel tied about his waist, whistling, feeling happy for the first time in days, if only for the pleasure of a trickly one-minute shower in the courtyard of a dilapidated small hotel crowded with soldiers and nearly emptied of its comforts. He dresses in clean woollen battledress, his summer denim khaki uniform now to be washed and steamed and put away; and he relishes the clean, cool feeling of the pressed and steamed fabric of his uniform, and the soap scent that his movements release into the air rather than the grimy musk of his bodily reek, the redolence of the animal existence lived at the front.

A knock at the door.

"*Capitano,*" comes a woman's voice. "*Capitano, qui è un pò d'acqua per radersi.*" Huh?

Then, Lieutenant Doyle's voice. "Captain, there is hot water for shaving!" He opens the door. The chambermaid is a young, pretty woman with rosebud lips, blue eyes and wavy dark brown hair. She smiles warmly, revealing a gold-capped eye tooth, and hands Jim a bowl of steaming hot water.

"*Grazie,*" says Jim, accepting this battlefield luxury wearing his trousers with suspenders and an undershirt, pants hiked up to his navel, nodding and smiling as he does so, blushing and embarrassed of his unshaven and partially dressed state.

"Not bad room service, eh, sir?" Doyle smiles at him, his chin dimple pronounced with the creasing of his chin.

"No, not bad at all, Doyle. Not bad at all. Now, if you don't mind—" He shuts the door. With this water, he proceeds to his washbasin and faucet, mixing it with a dash of cold that comes sputtering out of the old faucet with a considerable amount of air. He opens his kit, containing a small shaving mirror, straight razor, bowl and stick of shaving soap, and tooth powder and a worn and frayed toothbrush. He lathers the soap with water taken from the washbasin, and he caresses his face with the foam. Be careful now, he thinks. Looking into the mirror, he puts the razor to his face and enjoys the satisfying light scrape and tickle of the blade as it cuts a swath through the crop of stubble, harvesting whiskers. With a controlled, deliberate relish he shaves his face in rows, listening to the ssshk ssshk ssshk sounds of the blade scraping along skin, shearing stubble, and he rinses afterward, once again renewed. He looks in his mirror. I look a year younger, he thinks. We'll see how I look tomorrow. The purple sacks weighing down his eyes recently are faded somewhat, reduced in their pull of gravity. A distant shell ripples the earth underneath his feet, an echo from the front, a sonic shadow of intended destruction. Like a drumbeat, thinks Jim as he now brushes his teeth with the aid of his washbasin. Keeping time, like this were a Big Band or a symphony of sorts. Played in a minor key, of course. Ha!

After brushing his teeth he makes his bed, tucking the sheet and blanket under the bare lumpy mattress, pulling it tight enough to bounce a coin off of it, as the saying goes, and as his training sergeant Sergeant Cobb did so many times, forcing him to make and remake his bed many a miserable morning.

"Goddamn you McFarlane, what's your problem? Didn't your mommy teach you how to make your bed? Didn't your mommy teach you anything? Drop and give me twenty and remake that goddamn bed NOW!" He can feel his beefy presence looming over him now, can see his droopy moustache and hard grey eyes, can hear him barking in his ears telling him, you're not good for much are you, McFarlane, not good for much at all, you're a sissy McFarlane, you're a damned sissy and you'll not make it through officer training. Sure showed that mouthy bag of wind didn't I, he mouths to himself as he folds his blanket.

After a stop at the hallway washroom, a hole in the floor and a tap and basin, he steps heavy-footed down the creaking stairs and makes his way down to the dining room, now appropriated as the officers' mess. He can hear the murmur and muttering of various officers before he gets there. In it, he sees seven officers thus far gathered: Major Gordon, Lieutenant Sachs, Lieutenant Muller, Therrien, Captain McCambridge, Lieutenant Wells, and Major Henderson, the MO. Giovanni Ceci is seated among them, reading an old newspaper.

"Good morning Captain," says Therrien, bored and tired and awaiting his breakfast. Jim returns the greeting and gives the others a perfunctory wave, and takes a seat beside Captain McCambridge and Mr. Ceci, getting a better look at the latter's newspaper. Though it is in Italian, he can see that the headlines refer to the Battle of Kursk in the Soviet Union, many months ago. Mr. Ceci's face is a burnt and weathered sienna, centred by a tuberous nose from which his mighty moustache ruffles. He looks up and greets Jim with a smile and "*Buongiorno, Capitano.*" He puts his paper down on a small table in front of him and the pages settle in a flutter.

"*Buongiorno,* Mr. Ceci. Please, call me Jim." Jim manages a relaxed and sleepy morning grin as he speaks, and his last word draws out and dies off in a yawn.

Mr. Ceci waves off Jim's suggestion of formality. "No, you are *Capitano* McFarlane. Be proud of your title. You are brave soldier. Come, have coffee with us, my wife, she is brewing up some coffee the Germans left, very kind of them." He winks at the end of his sentence.

"It smells delicious. The best thing that I've smelled in two weeks."

"Lazarus awakens! It is a miracle!" McCambridge exclaims humourously. "Four days up there in that shellstorm myself and I don't even know how I woke up."

"Good morning to you too, Fred." Jim yawns again. His eyes still feel swollen, the lids droopy as though he were a morning flower yet to face the rising of the sun. Captain Fred McCambridge of Baker Company, sipping espresso from a chipped cup, bleary but relaxed, is wearing only his khaki woollen pants, a white undershirt and his suspenders. McCambridge resembles Clark Kent with his square jaw, black hair (often slicked when behind the lines with a generous dollop of pomade) grey-green eyes and wide, nearly lipless mouth. Always smiling, I don't bloody know how he does it. He was more made for this sort of thing than I was, I think. Jim can hear the sizzle and smell the unctuous savour of frying from the kitchen. Giovanni Ceci seats himself with an air of gastronomical expectation.

"*Buongiorno*!" chirps Mrs. Ceci from the stove over which she is hunched. "Your coffee, it is a-ready!" She comes out and, holding a steaming metal pot, fills and refills various cups, including Jim's.

"And *buongiorno* to you too, Mrs. Ceci," he addresses her with a sleepy smile. She matches his, the lines in her face filling into an hospitable smile that she has worn many, many times throughout the years.

"These aren't such bad digs we ended up in, eh?"

"Well, it beats San Mateo, that's for sure." Jim notes a listlessness in his own voice.

"I know what you mean. I took ten hits on my position alone up there on the ridgeline."

"I took at least double that. I shouldn't've picked the big obvious church. There was a reason that the major I relieved was using the general store instead. We were one helluva thin red line up there, let me tell you. Stretched out on that ridge like that."

"Well, we passed it off on others—rest easy now." Artillery rumbles in the distance, its dense and sharp vibration dispersed and muffled by time and distance.

"I fully intend to. Let someone else deal with the gunder and fighting." He looks down into his cup of espresso, the coffee dark and lined with foam like volcanic mud. It gives off a sharp, roasted earthiness, a deep invigorating bitterness, utterly inviting in its quest for consummation with his mouth. He downs it in one go. "I fully intend to," he repeats, the last syllable slackening into a loose and wheezy yawn.

"I don't know how you can drink that Eyetie tar coffee. You must be even more exhausted than I am. As if that's possible."

"You two, you look like dead people," jokes Mr. Ceci, who has been observing them all the while. "Me, I was in trenches in the last war, fighting the Austrians. Every time I went behind the lines I sleep. All the thunder in the world, it couldn't wake me up."

McCambridge is fascinated by this revelation, and decides to pursue it further. "You were in the Great War? Wow, that must really have been something." He whistles through his teeth. "What did you do?"

"Me, I was medic. I am big man, no? I a-used these big arms to carry men out of the trenches. I was wounded at Caporetto. See?" It is only now that Jim realizes that Giovanni Ceci has only one hand. He brandishes a gleaming two-pronged metal prosthetic, festooned to the stump of his right wrist. "And these *Fascisti,* they send us right back in for another war. Look where it gets us. Italy, it is a ruin, now. These Germans, they come in and take the place over. Then Allies come and bomb our country into rubble. The Monastero di Monte Cassino, the

Americans bomb it into stones. And the Germans, they were not even in it I read." There is an uncomfortable silence. Jim and McCambridge exchange glances. Mr. Ceci continues: "But, that is war. I a-rather the Allies take over, then Italy is safe from *Fascisti* and Nazis. These *Fascisti*, these Nazis, they start wars, and everyone lose. We admire fighting men like you who come to kick them out. You are like our son."

"Your son is in the army? Fighting with the Eighth Army?" asks McCambridge, curious.

"No, he is with Garibaldi *partigiani*. Fighting the Germans behind their own lines. He was in army before Italy surrendered, captured by British in Libya. They released him after surrender. I worry for his safety, but he is brave and tough."

"Like his father," adds Mrs. Ceci over their shoulders as she refills coffee cups. By now the other officers have arrived, and some thirty-odd men are awaiting breakfast and sipping coffee and chatting together. Breakfast is served by the cooks; today it is sausages, pancakes, scrambled eggs, fruit salad and cereal. In addition there is slightly stale *piadina* bread offered by Mrs. Ceci. McCambridge places a sausage into a *piadina*, rolls it into an unleavened half moon and eats it with his hands.

"*Buonissimo*, Mrs. Ceci, *treo buonissimo!*" he acknowledges with a wink, his words muffled by a chewed wad of egg and bread. Estella Ceci winces at McCambridge's mangled Italian.

"I say, stick to English, mine is a-better than your Italian," she admonishes with a hint of humour, refilling the two officers' coffee cups. From his first cup, Jim can feel a caffeinated jolt and an edgy anticipation working its way from his gut upward.

"How did you learn to speak English so well?" asks McCambridge in an attempt to change the subject.

"For a time we work in New York, at hotel owned by a cousin. Then we come back here to run our own place. Stock market crash closed hotel and sent us back."

"I see."

"Excuse me, please," says Mr. Ceci, and he gets up to mingle with other officers. When he is served, Jim devours his breakfast with scarce attention to table manners. An officer and a gentleman, hunger and nerves have temporarily devalued the second half of that title in reference to his commission. He scoops up the leftover clots of egg with a *piadina* and shovels it in, food becoming him in instant absorption. He feels centred and clear now, as if his prior lack of food had dissipated the mass and gravity that held him together. He is turning on his axis now, pulled together, "good and proper," as Witchewski would say.

"Atten-SHUN!" Feet together, hands at sides, fists balled, eyes staring straight ahead out of stern poker faces. Now that Gordon has everyone's attention, he continues: "At ease." Everyone relaxes his stance. "Good morning, gentlemen," continues Gordon. "Lieutenant Colonel Hobson is attending an 'O' Group at Division regarding our upcoming part in the coming offensive. Suffice to say, we are going back into battle quite soon. You are all required to be here at precisely 1800 hours for an 'O' Group led by him in which he will outline the battle plan. In addition, all NCOs from sergeant upward must be present.

"As for me, I have here your orders for the day, which after our last assignment, are somewhat easier, I should think. In reference to a conversation I had with one of you in San Mateo recently—" At this, he shoots a glance at Jim: "I bear welcome news. After our losses over the past week and a half, we have reinforcements. We are being allotted seventy new soldiers to join our ranks."

McCambridge whistles through his teeth at this.

"NCOs are to report to the central piazza to sort out these new greenhorns and allot them into their respective companies and platoons after lunch. RSM Albert is briefing them to this end. See to it that you get your rosters updated. In addition to other ranks, we have with us two new officers, a Captain Riley and a Lieutenant Pruitt. And a welcome piece of news for all of you—though we never got mail at all over the last few days, fresh mail arrived last night. The roads have been clogged, I guess, what with all the action lately. Mail call will follow this meeting at the stores, and will be distributed by company." Following this, Gordon dispenses housekeeping orders, that officers and NCOs are to ensure that all weapons are cleaned and inspected, that there will be movies shown for rest and relaxation in the afternoon, and so on and so on.

Upon dismissal, Jim makes his way eagerly along with the others down the street for mail call. He waits his turn with other members of his company as the company clerk stands amidst the eager crowd, calling names and dispensing mail to soldiers starving for correspondence. His heart thuds in anticipation, an excited thrill courses upward through him. Marianne, oh Marianne, please let there be a letter from you, Marianne ...

"And for you, Captain McFarlane," begins the clerk, Private Glasser, young and bespectacled and looking very much like an accountant in uniform, looking down as he rummages through the sacks of parcels and letters, "we have ... these." He produces two letters and a parcel bound together with twine.

"Thank you, Private."

"My pleasure, sir. Next, Sergeant Whitmore!"

XV

Under the shade of a willow tree and partly hidden by an overgrown, untended hedge, Jim undoes the twine and looks at his mail. In the distance artillery rumbles, the weather of war over the horizon. A letter from his father. A letter from Barrett. No letter from Marianne. His heart sinks. He starts with the letter from his father, peeling away the lip of the envelope, tearing the paper as he does so. He reads hungrily:

Dear Jim,

I hope this finds you as well as you could be, given where you are. Once again, I can't tell you how proud I am that you are doing what you are doing. You always impressed me as you were growing up, the way you took your younger brother under your wing and guided him. Maybe I didn't always let you know how proud I was of you. I sometimes feel I missed out on this experience during the last war, hellacious though it was, but my bum knee kept me out. But if I did go, who knows? Maybe then I would not have raised a pair of fine sons that would serve their country later on.

Your poor mother is always worrying about you and wished you had stayed behind, but I understand the call of duty. Well, it looks like you guys are really pulling your weight over there. The Nazis are really on the run now, aren't they, caught in a vice between two huge armies. I wonder how we will get along with the Soviets once all this is said and done. We do make strange bedfellows.

I got a letter from an old medical school friend of mine the other day, Dr. Theodore Jenkins. He's with the Canadian Neurological Hospital now based in England. When we declared war, the whole staff volunteered as one and left Montreal to set up shop over there. He attends to head wounds from Allied soldiers, sailors and airmen. Especially airmen. I had a flash of your brother possibly being delivered into his care when I read the message. Those boys in Bomber Command, they really take a beating. Have you heard from Mark lately? I haven't, but I trust he's all right. As you know, I really got a kick out of hearing that you two met up a few times while you were stationed in England. It is really important to keep those family ties strong no matter how far apart we are, and especially when some of us have put ourselves in harm's way.

Well, as well you might know from my letters previously, I've certainly been paying attention to the Allied operations since you and Mark went overseas. I now have a map decorated with arrows and flags. I have to do something; you boys are so far away and doing this allows me to put it all in perspective. I particularly follow the Italian front and the air war, naturally. When you have a personal investment in something, you tend to pay more attention!

I have sent along with this letter some socks knit by your mother, along with some treats. Well, take care over there Son, keep your head down and your fists up, and come home in one piece—

Yours sincerely,

Dad

Just like Dad to talk about war. He'll probably want to take me out to dinner with me kilted and cobeened and with a chest of shining medals, too. "This is my officer son! Look, all! He saw quite a lot of action over there in Italy, he did. Didn't you, boy?" Have I heard from Mark recently? Not for a month, I'm assuming he's alright, always lucky, that one. He looks at the package sent along with his father's letter. Inside there are clumped four new pairs of socks, a tin of soft, sugarcoated peppermint candies, a new carton of Player's cigarettes, and a bottle of Canadian Club whiskey, which in its brown glass bottle looks like a bottle of cough syrup. Medicine for the soul.

The letter from Barrett is entirely different in character from his father's. He welcomes the sarcastic tone of his friend and wishes he were still here.

Dear Jim,

Well, well, well. There you are over there having all the fun while I'm stuck here with my bum leg and all, at home with the birds singing outside the kitchen window where I am writing to you this letter. War is hell. But home is so boring, it makes you yearn for a little (s)hellfire once in a while. I'd rather be in the news than reading it, you know? I've been here a month now, laid up and the like, scrunched back into my parents' place. It was great to visit, but I tell you, if it weren't for this damn leg of mine I'd be back in a shot. You know, I hated the war in so many ways once I experienced it, but I was at home with all you boys. People here, they whine about rationing and this and that and I just bite my lip and think: if only all you knew what we do over there. You can take your complaints and put them somewhere warm and dark and smelly.

Anyway, forgive me my grouchiness. My leg hurts, it will never quite be the same again, but slowly but surely, I will walk again in some capacity. At least, that's what the doctor says. It hurts a lot, especially at night. So does my abdomen, there is still a lot of metal in there, the doctors tell me. I could probably make a fortune if I sell mineral rights to the highest bidder and have it mined. I can't sleep at night. I'm always thinking about all you guys still sweating it over there you know, and I have memories of being there, and nightmares sometimes when I do sleep. Nightmares about the Melfa, about the Arielli, about patrols at Cassino, the food, the clap, you name it. Especially those last two items.

By the way, congratulations on your promotion. Maybe by war's end you'll be discussing the postwar organization of Europe with the Big Three, moving a country here, dividing another there, offering Churchill a cigar, or Roosevelt a hot stock tip, or Stalin a moustache trim. Or, maybe you'll make major, anyway. Maybe you can replace Gordon as 2IC, that humourless ass. Don't show him this letter! How's he holding up as the Big Number Two? He and Bly made such interesting counterparts when they commanded the company, didn't they? One with a sense of humour, one without.

Well, shit, all this writing and reminiscing is making me miss it over there even more. I guess I can brew up some more tea and listen to some stupid radio comedy show or the Farm Report. Though, I must vouch for the tea at home. It is usually better than the filmy roadside bucket-brewed crap we cooked up with gasoline over there. I'll bet you're still swilling that stuff while ducking the shells, no?

You know, I can't help forget that time back at Christmas when you and I and the good doctor put back all that scotch together. God, we were so drunk, weren't we? I remember we couldn't even walk, the three of us swaying and staggering back home from the party, trying to slur some Louis Armstrong song together. The one you told me that you once made love to your wife to: you were a fountain of information that night. And of vomit. I remember I just about had his voice, because of all the cigarettes I'd smoked that evening. What a mess.

Anyhow, keep up with the correspondence. I am bored, bored, bored here. By the way, before I forget, let me remind you of our little deal. At war's end I'll meet you under the clock in the foyer of the Royal York for some drinks in the hotel saloon. We have plenty of remembering to do, and the booze will help us forget! Take care, old man—

Yours elliptically,

Lt. John Barrett (Ret.)

His stomach is sore from laughing, memories flooding his mind. His eyes are welled up with tears from both the humourous tone of the letter and the melancholy of having a friend so far away. He sniffles, and his eyes water and burn. He looks at the bottle of whiskey. He unscrews the cap and releases crisp and pungent fumes of distillation into the air. What the hell, he thinks as he takes a gulp, swishing it about his mouth, numbing his tongue. It burns its way down his throat and lights a fire in his belly before subsiding. He is overtaken by a pleasing dizziness, a relaxed euphoria, a convivial glow, which complements Barrett's memories of drinking in England. Many a night of drinking in British pubs and saloons and clubs are contained in that flavour, in that feeling. Long sudsy evenings of cards with Barrett and Leprenniere and Bly and Lieutenant Wole, and with British officers, with obliging locals, full many a midnight wobble back to barracks and billets, stumbling through the streets of Aldershot, London, Brighton, singing and swaying and hanging onto each other in hoarse-voiced hilarity.

The memories. Barrett, I miss you, I can't talk to many of these people anymore and I think I'm shellshocked. After stopping back at his room to drop off his bottle of liquor, he goes toward the quartermasters' stores, held in and around several large cinderblock houses and a large yard down the street, surrounded by army trucks, the front yards lined with the manicured cones of cypress trees. Inside the houses are piled stacks of kitbags in rumpled pyramids; as well, a small pavilion tent in the yard contains more. Private Breen, a doughy young man given to fits of temper and sweating, is sitting at a table sipping tea and smoking a pungent, cheap cigar as soldiers come and go on their various errands.

"Good morning, sir," is his greeting, as he stands up, stamps his right foot and salutes.

"Good morning, Private. As you were. Big plans for the day?"

"Oh, gonna head up to the mess to play some craps and poker with some of the boys there after weapons inspection. Got a new stash of stuff to sweeten the pot, sir." He leans into Jim as he says this, lifting his brows and creasing his forehead in emphasis.

"Huh?" Jim doesn't understand. Breen looks at him for a moment, expecting him to pick up on his innuendo. "Oh. Oh, my God, yes."

"Hey, sir, it all gets wasted if we don't do something with this stuff. They'd want it this way, wouldn't they?"

"Yes, I suppose they would. I suppose they would." Jim feels slightly nauseous. He would've found this exchange funny months ago, but he finds it funny no longer, he is no longer desensitized to the violence of the war in which he has opted to play a part. He plays along. "What do you have now?"

"Well, two cartons of cigarettes bound for Lance Corporal Fitzpatrick by way of his brother, a bottle of scotch bound for Lieutenant Briscoe from his uncle, a lemon cake all wrapped up really nice sent by Private Kelly's wife, a pair of German boots taken by Private Redding at Pesaro. They're no good for him now, either, unfortunately. That's the tally for San Mateo, sir."

"So Fitzpatrick never made it after all." A thoughtful pause. Fitzpatrick's feverish pallor and afflicted wince as the stretcher-bearers whisked him out by the church, mortality ascertained in the fleeting meeting of their eyes. He can smell the charred odour of ruin, hear the shriek of falling shells. Vertigo. He feels his stomach lurch. A new addition to his hyper-real flashbacks of his experience.

"And these cigars here, one of which I'm enjoying now. From an arty guy stationed up front."

A lightheaded chill courses through him, a shiver of nervous expectance. "An arty guy? What was his name?"

"Lieutenant Blake, I think. His radioman's pretty badly wounded, too. Cole, I think I heard his name is. Are you okay, sir? You look pale. Did you know him?"

"Blake ... Blake ... ah, fuck, Blake." He scarcely realizes he is speaking aloud until the end of the sentence. He is overtaken by remorse. "So, he's dead, then, is he?" Jim looks at Breen, who speaks his death through silence. "How the fuck did I not know he was killed? He was stationed with us, for Christ's sake. I kicked him out of the church because he wanted to use the steeple and then he gets it where I sent him! Jesus Christ." He is assailed by pointed, panicky thoughts. How could that escape my notice? Where was I? Did I black out? How could I not know, not remember this? Breen looks very awkward, ill-at-ease with Jim's emoting. "And why didn't anyone tell me?" There is a moment of silence. Jim's heart is thumping, his breathing is rapid, his fists are balled. How did I miss this? I must be losing it. Losing it. He inhales deeply, exhales slowly, and calms down somewhat. "You know, Breen, you might want to consider just putting some of that stuff for sale in the canteen rather than just putting it in circulation for gambling. Equal up the opportunities." On the other hand, he thinks, this is more of a mirror of real life, isn't it? At least for what we're doing here. Wager your life, lose, and your possessions become fair game, circulating about the table. His cigarette case, liberated from the body of a German major, reminds him of this. Should he die, it will likely be picked from his body.

"Well, that happens sometimes too, sir."

"You and Riordan run one hell of a racket here, let me tell you."

"Sir?"

"Trading in dead men's belongings—that's a bit sick, don't you think? Don't you?" Jim has a flash of grabbing him by the throat, of pinning him to the wall as his chair falls out from underneath him and clatters to the floor, of punching him in the face till his nose explodes and blood pours down his chin. He exhales, easing out the pressure.

"It's just—" Breen can't quite find the words. He looks at Jim in defensive astonishment, aware he's getting a tongue-lashing from an officer, but incredulous that it should be for something generally accepted among the men. "It's just that this is the case in every battalion, sir. We make do. This stuff comes anyway; we might as well let some people enjoy the benefits. You know what I mean, sir?"

"You guys are sick. This whole fucking place is sick." The last sentence attenuates into a grumbly whisper, directed in impotent frustration to the world at large. "Never mind, Breen, just never mind for Christ's sake. I'm sorry I've bothered you. I'm just going to my kitbag, if you don't mind."

"Yes, sir ... " Breen's eyes follow him as he goes to his kitbag, and an uncomfortable and loaded silence falls over the place. Jim finds his among his company's kit, a large green rough cloth bag stuffed with supplies, letters, souvenirs, clothing. Jim grabs it, stuffed and lumpy with a heavy bulk. He takes it outside in the stone-fenced backyard and plunks it beside a weeping willow tree. He unties the opening, pulls it open and is greeted by a jumbled, rumpled plethora of odds and ends. The mixed smells of dust and coffee and musty paper meet his nostrils. He rummages through the bag, and various items come to light. Care package foods—Lipton soup, Spam, malted milk tablets, pouches of powdered hot chocolate, coffee, chocolate bars, pouches full of teabags. Books: Dante's *Inferno,* Homer's *Iliad* as translated by Alexander Pope. Neither of which he's read in a bid to improve himself while on down time. Magazines: *The Maple Leaf Italy Dispatches, Life, Macleans, Time.* Bundles of letters. Pictures. His duty roster, his officer's field manual. Spare underwear, spare socks, spare undershirts. A tin of boot polish, and a soft cloth bunched up and blotched with deep black polish stains. Wrinkled dress uniforms for different occasions, wrapped in shaped and wrinkled garment bags. A yellow and black kilt, wrinkled and pleated. A sweater. His cobeen. A beret. An iron. A box of paper tissues. A half-used metal tin of Brylcreem. A bottle of Benzedrine pills, given to all soldiers. A brass picture frame, taken from a blasted house in the ruins of Pesaro not two weeks ago. A shoulder patch torn off a sullen German *hauptmann* in the 29th Panzer Grenadier Division, one of a hundred and twenty prisoners taken from the heights of Montecchio. Another German officer's Luger, taken during a nighttime patrol back at Cassino. A silver goblet, liberated from a shelled-out farmhouse in Ceprano in the spring offensive, the Road to Rome as the newsreels and newspapers pegged it. The evening program from Christmas dinner in Aldershot, England, 1942. Two bottles of Canadian Club whiskey. All these things and more beckon for attention. You are what you collect, he thinks. The contents of your pockets are the accoutrements of who you are. I am a packrat and a scrounging thief, he muses with a twinkle of glee. He adds to the pile the letters from Barrett and his father, as well as most of the packets of cigarettes from his carton. With some minutes to spare, he leafs through his pictures and his letters from home. The first item he looks at is a picture of himself and Marianne smiling in front of her family furniture store, smiling the day of their engagement in celebration of the life on which they were embarking, in front of the store that they would perhaps own and manage. He usually does not carry such pictures save for the thumbworn one of Marianne in his wallet, not wanting them to fall into the hands of the enemy and be scoffed at and belittled, should he be killed and his pockets picked.

He thumbs across an opened envelope stamped with 'SALVAGED FROM AIR CRASH' that triggers a vertiginous feeling of sadness, a letter from the mother of the first soldier killed under his command, felled by a sniper during a patrol on the Arielli Line last winter:

To Lt. James McFarlane, C.O. No. 8 Pltn, 'A' Coy, 1CIR.

Dear Jim,

Thank you for taking the time to write me about my son, Ryan. You are very thoughtful. Telegrams are so impersonal—it was nice to have someone who knew him send a personal letter. I will miss him and there is nothing I can do to bring him back, but at least I know he died doing his duty under the command of a fine officer such as yourself.

There are some things that I was compiling to send Ryan—cigarettes, socks, snacks, etc. They will go to waste if I don't send them. So, I have sent them for you. You take these things; he doesn't need them anymore. I have included for you four pairs of wool socks, ten packets of Lipton's onion soup mix, two tins of Klik, ten Hershey chocolate bars, a carton of Players' cigarettes and a box of Red Rose orange pekoe tea.

Again, thank you very much for the letter. I continue to pray for you and the men of your battalion and I pray that this war will end sometime soon. Take care and come home to your loved ones safely—

Take care,

Mrs. Doreen Harrigan

The padre, Father Maitland, told Jim when he received a reply from her to his own next-of-kin letter that Harrigan was her only child. Jim had lifted some of what he'd written to her from a sermon from church parade with the padre about a hundred yards from the front line, behind the cover of a blasted pile of stones that was once an ancient farmhouse, a sermon wherein Father Maitland quoted Ecclesiastes: "To everything there is a season." A nearby storm of combat, mortar shells plopping in the mud in the valley not a hundred yards away. The rocks on which he had stood vibrated faintly traces of artillery in a faint wireless dispatch from the front, as though in Morse Code. To everything there is a season. Jim had turned the words over in his mind as the padre continued: "There is a time for war, a time for peace." To everything there is a season. If not a reason. I was in charge of your son, and he died. Many people have died in units under my command, and I remember every one, will always remember every single one of them, oh God, I never forget a face … and I wish I could.

XVI

After lunch, and after a film viewing during which he fell almost instantly asleep, Jim shuffles papers and handles mundane clerical tasks at a desk in a room in a house serving as his company headquarters. Soldiers come and go with questions as he pores halfheartedly over rosters and orders and reports: Sir, could I apply for a leave-pass? Sir, we need a kit inspection. What time would be suitable? Sir, could you help me with a letter to my girlfriend back in England? Never much good at writing, sir, left school when I was nine.

As he puts out a cigarette in an old wine bottle standing on his desk, he hears a flurry of activity outside. Reinforcements arrive in a rumble of trucks outside his window and are dispersed into various platoons and companies. They are pep talked and drilled by their new sergeants and corporals, and they are paraded through the serpentine streets and lanes and along the castle walls to skirl of pipes and beat of drum, along the rows of townhouses, by the churches, by the farmhouses and alongside the rows of vines in the late afternoon sunshine, the mature late summer sun, the last days of summer in its glory, the light pouring down from between the puff-white clouds and between the branches of roadside trees and sun-speckling the heads and shoulders and faces of marching soldiers. As they march they hear incongruous thunder, to the west, to the south, to the north, as at the front mere miles away men fight and die; and they are inspected by the RSM standing on the street side, swagger stick in hand, and as they march by, their shadows lengthen and sharpen into spearpoints in the late afternoon sun, the advance guard of the coming of the night. As the march concludes back in the main piazza where Jim stands after his office duties, many are dismissed and sent to their mess for dinner. Those who are NCOs are sent into the officers' mess, now crowding with officers and sergeants and warrant officers, to receive the colonel's orders.

Jim joins the tide of sergeants and warrant officers dismissed from the parade, and he enters the crowded mess for the third time today, accompanied by Witchewski, and by Warrant Officer Albert, Regimental Sergeant Major and senior NCO of the entire battalion. The floor trembles from the concussion of a German shell. Lieutenant Colonel Hobson sits at a dining room table with other officers, including Major Gordon and Battalion Adjutant Major Reynolds, Major Wyler and Captain Van Der Hecke of Dog Company, Captain McCambridge, Major Rowlands and Captain Alward of Charlie Company, and Lieutenant Sachs of the mortar platoon.

"Hello, McFarlane," says Hobson, shooting a grey-eyed wink at Jim, looking up from his map as Jim steps into the dining room. Mr. and Mrs. Ceci are nowhere to be seen.

"Good evening, Colonel," Jim answers with a salute, returned by Hobson.

"Grab yourself a seat and help yourself to a cup of tea." Hobson stuffs a straight-backed pipe with tobacco from a pouch in his pocket, and lights it, puffing sweet, moist roils of smoke into the room like unwinding strands of scented cotton. He moves the portable chalkboard and stand, where would normally be written the daily special, closer to him, and he picks up a well-used piece of white chalk.

"Thank you." Jim helps himself to a tin cup full of tea from one of several large thermoses set up on the serving table, grabs a broken-backed wooden chair and pulls up to a crowded table. He stirs his tea with the butt-end of a dirty fork as others make their way into the room and take their seats.

Hobson scans the room a moment and says, "I think everyone's here who needs to be here. Good." His face becomes serious and he addresses the officers and NCOs gathered in the mess: "Gentlemen: orders. We're planning our next moves, as you can probably determine." Jim takes a huge gulp of tea and it kindles a welcome fire within.

Hobson continues, drawing on his pipe, its ember glowing with the promise of victory: "This is the moment we have been waiting for. The offensive in this section, as I am sure you are all aware, will continue." He scans the gaze of his audience with his eyes, intense and steely with confidence and a studied ruthlessness. "That damned ridge that has held up this advance is going to fall. That damned ridge that held us up and shelled us for several days straight while we waited for it to fall, that held off a major British attack, has been assigned to us to take. And take it we will."

There is a cheer, a loud fists-in-the air "Aye aye!" After the cheering abates, Hobson scans the collected soldiers again, and continues in the ensuing silence. "We will march out and form up once again behind the San Mateo ridge tomorrow night. Not to worry; we will not be sticking around long enough for Jerry to shell the wits out of us this time." There is a rueful, knowing laugh from some of the men. "The artillery's going to hammer the hell out of Jerry all night. The gift exchange will start at precisely 2100 hours," he says, chug-chug-chugging away on his pipe as if he were a locomotive, and he continues: "There will also be massive, and I mean massive, airstrikes on and behind the Jerry lines, carrying on throughout the entire operation. "When the guns go off, company and support platoon commanders in battle rotation will meet me at TAC, the location of which is yet to be determined, for any last orders or possible changes. Starting at 1100 hours, the British 1st Armoured is moving in far to our left to secure the southern end of the ridge. At 0100, our brigade goes into action to secure the village of Coriano itself. The Sydney Highlanders will move into the valley and up the ridge to cut the town off from the north. The Stratford Regiment will move across and cut it off from the south." He draws a map of the battleground, complete with the arrows of the battalions' movements. The stony scrape and squeak of chalk grates against the silence. "We will move up into the Sydneys' positions once they have departed."

There is an expectant silence as the men await the revelation of their role, however unpleasant it may be. "As for us," eyes darting right to left, left to right, "we've been assigned the role of janitors. We pass through afterward to mop up and clear whatever resistance is left in the village itself." There is some murmuring, both excited and nervous.

"It'll be a little Ortona," says Lieutenant Muller. "Won't it?"

"Silence, please. Dog Company—" He glances at Captain Van Der Hecke, young and baby-faced with a wide Dutch farmer's face and a protuberant nose, who stiffens up in expected pride in expectation of success, and at Major Wyler, equally young, though tempered with a cool confidence exemplified by his Errol Flynn moustache. "You will be in reserve and protect sappers from the 11th Field Squadron as they bridge the Besanigo River. The Besanigo Creek, more like, but it will likely seem an imposing crossing at the time. This will allow tanks from the Lucky Sevens to cross the river and support us in our endeavour. You will move before dawn, at 0500. Beware German fire from here." With his swagger stick Hobson points out a map feature. "From this hill on the southwest corner of the village, the Castella, the Germans enjoy an exceptionally fine view. Able, Baker and Charlie companies will move in once the bridging gets underway." He glances at Jim, and at McCambridge, Rowlands and Alward, to emphasize the responsibility inherent in his order. "Able will move up first and enter the town from the north, followed later by Baker. Charlie will cover the flank from the west and engage with the Castella. After the bridging, Dog must be ready to exploit any successes, and Support Company will be ready to dispatch any possible reinforcements by vehicle as needed. Each company will be supported by representatives from both the mortar platoon and the AT platoon."

He looks at the congregation of officers and NCOs and meets their eyes, holding his gaze a moment for emphasis in unspoken expectation of success and trust. "Of course you realize, this will probably be a dirty scrap, a hand-to-hand affair. Unless, of course, they've retreated or surrendered by then, which is doubtful." There are small twitters of laughter. In an instant Jim reads the room, looking at his fellow officers, both senior and junior, and wonders what they think behind their masks of professionalism. Sees the relationship these men have with one another, and with where they are, why they are there. All part of a bureaucratic network, a great machine whose purpose is to kill and destroy, passing decisions down, rank by rank, couched in jargon that washes away the bloodshed and suffering that many of these decisions entail. He is chilled by his thoughts.

"Be warned: we expect medium to heavy resistance. By now, I'm sure you know that when you are told to expect medium resistance from the Germans, expect heavy, and when someone tells you to expect heavy resistance from them, expect to be fighting the devil's own legion. We expect them to have a little of everything, from anti-tank nests to machine-gun bunkers to Tiger tanks, so we're making good use of our friends in the RAF. Fighter-bombers are supposed to knock out any reinforcements coming our way, especially tanks. Also, they're going to hit any known minefields on the way to set off the mines to clear paths. Notice I said 'known minefields.' Watch where you step, regardless. Any questions so far?" Hobson scans the faces of his officers with his eyes, and sees that there are no questions. He continues.

"I'm going to stay behind and wait for Able, Baker and Charlie to secure a position. Reynolds, it's up to you to oversee the advance and coordinate the companies in action. I'll move in along with Dog once these initial objectives are exploited; then, Gordon, you will relieve me. And while we're all busy removing this thorn from the side of Eighth Army's advance, 1st Division is going to make a break for it across the Marano. Just like we intended to do days ago. So, the Germans have plenty to keep them awake over the next night and day. The British 4th will pass through us when our objectives are taken." A shell thuds in the distance to punctuate his sentence.

"Also, you may have noticed if you looked up in the last few days or so, the autumn rain has started. The real fall rain. The terrain may become awfully muddy over the next few days for all we know, and it could become slow-going and uncomfortable, especially in regards to getting tanks across the river. Any questions?" Hobson asks.

"Yes," Jim pipes up. "When during all this can I get some sleep?" The officers laugh, Hobson included. That was only half funny, Jim thinks. There are no further questions.

"Good. Company commanders, I leave to your discretion who will lead and who will be left out of battle. Rest up—tomorrow night we head out and hopefully send those Panzer-Grenadiers just a little closer to Austria. You are dismissed. Help yourself to dinner, the kitchen ought to send us in some chow within the next few minutes before the evening's festivities."

Jim sips his tea and looks out the ornate picture window facing east toward the Adriatic, out of sight beyond a medieval-looking jumble of buildings built of mortar and stone. The sea. How I long to see the sea again right now. Put a note in a bottle: Dear Marianne, Mom, Dad: SOS.

"This meeting is adjourned, gentlemen," concludes Hobson with a salute, which is returned by all the others. The meeting over, a hubbub of voices closes over the silence like the breaking of a wave. The NCOs leave to their own mess elsewhere, leaving the dining room to the officers. His stomach growling, Jim awaits dinner. In the wake of the departed sergeants and warrant officers, he now finds himself sitting with a new officer, who by the brass stars on his collar and the name sewn into his shirt, is named Captain Riley.

"Good evening," says Riley, young, well built for football or rugby, floppy dark brown hair parted over the ears, refreshingly free of an officer's moustache, nervously and tepidly trying to introduce and ingratiate himself to Jim.

"Good evening." Jim lights a cigarette. About to put away his silver cigarette case, he checks his impending rudeness. "Smoke?"

"Sure," says Riley. "Thank you." Jim lights their cigarettes with his overworked Zippo. Awkward silence. Riley clears his throat to herald words that die on his tongue, and the silence continues.

"Dinner is served!" yells the chief steward, Sergeant Greiner. At the announcement of dinner, Father Maitland stands and leads the congregation in the saying of grace, and then soldiers detailed as mess orderlies, as well as the Ceci's, serve the awaiting officers their meals. The servers deliver mess tins and bowls with beef and vegetable stew, and plates with rolls and butter and margarine, and they bring the the officers cups with coffee, tea, juice. The crowded dining room fills with a savoury, stewy aroma of food, and the sounds of over two dozen men chewing and talking and scratching their forks and spoons against plates and bowls and tins.

"Hm. Not bad for being so close to the action, I guess, eh?" muses Riley after trying his stew.

"Could be worse." Jim takes a bite out of his buttered roll. The roll is warm and spongy, and he has to choke back the hiccups for trying to swallow too big a bite.

"Hey, Jim! Are you in for a round of poker with the Lucky Sevens tonight?" shouts McCambridge from the next table.

"Maybe, we'll see." Goddamn all these people and their demands, I just want to go home now. He takes a forkful of beef stew. It is passably good, hearty, if a little bland.

"Well Christ a'mighty, that was the funniest damn thing I ever witnessed here!" shouts someone, a Lieutenant Farrell from Dog Company.

"Nah, for me it was when Schneider let off a T-flash to scare Radic when he was napping. You shoulda seen him! He jumped like a flea in a frying pan. Leapt out of his cot, and when he sees Schneider, he chases him down for five full minutes in his shorts and boots! Went right by the officers' mess tent while we were all gathering for breakfast. Hilarious."

"This guy Lessage transferred to us from the Van Doos for some reason, I remember he really fancied himself a ladies' man with his French moustache and all, and back in England he got the clap on I think the only night he was successful outta many attempts. Got it again, and ended up with the name Lovesick."

"Ha ha! Vinci. Vidi. VD."

Much uproarious laughter from several tables. Spirits are high tonight. With their meals come one complimentary quart sized bottle of Molson Export Ale, and two bottles are parked at their tables by Private Chalmers, who bows and winks at them, saying, "Enjoy, sirs."

"Oh, we will," says Jim, and Chalmers departs.

"Sounds like a tight unit," observes Riley, between forkfuls. "You guys've been through thick and thin together, haven't you?"

"Some of us have. Some are newer."

Riley takes the hint, goes back to eating a moment. He tries again. "So, it's a big show tomorrow night, eh?"

"That's what the colonel said." After a time, Jim feels guilty, and he raises his bottle up and proposes a toast: "Here's to a successful venture with our regiment."

"Thank you." They both take a sudsy, bitter gulp of beer. "By the way, my first name's Albert, everyone calls me Al."

"Sure Al, I'm Jim."

"Nice to meet you."

"Uh huh." More chewing. "The last time I took it upon myself to introduce myself to an officer, I sent him out to his death."

"I'm sorry to hear that." A contemplative moment of silence, and then Riley asks, choosing his words carefully, "He was a good man?"

"I wouldn't know one way or another. Only met him the once. I know he's a dead man."

"I'm sorry to hear that."

"So was I." Another slug of beer. He looks into the distance, eyes unfocused. "Of course, it's not my fault, you see. It's just the way things work over here. It's all just mathematics in the end, isn't it?" He turns his head, and moves his eyes to focus on Riley, his face tensed. "Isn't it?"

Riley shifts, and with a blink and a nasal exhalation, he responds, "Yes, I suppose it is. Mathematics." This last word he utters thoughtfully after a pause, and muses on it as though he were looking at it, as if it were floating in front of him, freed from his mouth.

"To Lieutenant Blake." Jim raises his bottle, and Riley follows. A clink of bottles, a slug of beer. Cold and bitter, fizzy and filling. A glow, a warm thrumming about the temples. He raises his bottle again. "And to Lance Corporal Fitzpatrick. I can't get his face out of my mind."

"What happened to him, if you don't mind me asking?"

"Wounded in the stomach by artillery fire. Didn't make it past the aid post. They carried him right by me in a stretcher and I knew he was a dead man."

"I'm sorry to hear about that, too."

"I was sorry to see it." Neither of them speaks for a moment, and they surrender their attention to the hubbub of the mess, the sounds of slurping and chewing, the screech of utensils on plates, the chatter and laughter and clink of bottles. Jim looks at Riley, watches him eat uneasily, fitting in awkwardly, trying to make his way through his meal. After a lengthy silence, Jim makes an announcement: "Let's get drunk tonight, as tomorrow we fight."

"Okay, sounds good." More beer. "So, tomorrow we fight, eh?" Riley looks nervous, uncertain, ill-at-ease but eager to please by way of conversation.

"Yes. This rest town is the first time we've really been off the line since the last week of August. Pretty much two straight weeks of battle. My CO is out of commission, so I'm running the show alone for some time." Jim drains his bottle in a long, gassy gulp that reemerges in the form of a deep belch. "Pardon me, *Kamerad.*"

The two of them are served seconds by Private Chalmers, who heaps their plates and tins with food, and who pours them each a generous splash of diluted army rum in their cups. The two officers greedily gobble up all of their food before beginning their conversation anew.

Riley begins: "You know, I'm a bit nervous about tomorrow."

"So am I." Am I ever. Don't tell me this now, please, I'm just trying to get myself back together today! The two of them are silent for about ten seconds. Then Jim pipes up: "Look at it this way. They're losing. They really are. We're winning. The writing's on the wall. We still have a home to go to. They might not."

"True."

"Anyway, just keep focused. Enough horror happens around here to drive you mad if you dwell on it. Save it for Father Maitland. Empathy's his game. Ours is doing whatever it takes to carry out the mission." A sip of rum. "Whatever the cost, I guess."

"Yes, I suppose it is."

"To the mission!" Clink of glasses, the syrupy sugarcane burn of rum down the throat.

"Gentlemen, attention please!" shouts a voice over the convivial noise of eating and drinking and talking. All are silent as Colonel

Hobson stands at his table and addresses the seated crowd. "I would like to propose a toast to all of you seated here tonight on the eve before battle. I have served with most of you before, and I trust every single one of you to see the mission through. Final victory is in sight, gentlemen; it is in sight and it is due to the strength and sacrifice of officers and men such as yourselves, and it can only come through so many battles and campaigns such as the one we are engaged in now—so, let us raise a glass to our success tomorrow night!"

"Here here!" Jim and Riley raise their glasses, clink them and drink along with all the others.

"And now, let's enjoy some airs played by Pipe Major Mullen. Enjoy, gentlemen!" There are some cheers as Hobson sits down. Mullen, kilted and cobeened in full ceremonial regalia, makes his way to the front of the room with his pipes and begins skirling the airs of "Danny Boy," and men sing along, some in key, others not, singing the slow, swaying, mournful and longing notes of the song in a deep despairing tone, a sombre soul-laid-baritone, and others sway to the slow rhythm and think of their own loved ones so far away, so long ago last seen:

"Oh Danny boy, the pipes, the pipes are calling
From glen to glen, and down the mountain side
The summer's gone, and all the flowers are dying
'Tis you, 'tis you must go and I must bide.
But come ye back when summer's in the meadow
Or when the valley's hushed and white with snow
'Tis I'll be here in sunshine or in shadow
Oh Danny boy, oh Danny boy, I love you so ..."

And they finish the song verse by swaying verse, followed by "Tipperary" and others. By this time, Italian wine has made its way to various tables, and Jim and Riley find themselves halfway through a bottle of particularly strong and rough, slightly vinegary red, their temples humming, their voices singing along ...

After half an hour, Mullen abandons the centre stage. The drinking and conversing and spontaneous singing continues, along with card games. Gordon, Father Maitland, and others who do not drink abandon the party, and the conversation becomes louder and ruder. Maitland and Gordon leave precisely as a group of tipsy officers begin a rowdy rendition of "Sing Us Another One":

"There once was a hermit named Dave,
Who kept a dead whore in his cave.
He said, "I'll admit I'm a bit of shit,
But look at the money I've saved!

That was a great little rhyme.
Sing us another one.
Just like the other one,
Sing us another one, do . . . "

And on it continues, getting dirtier and dirtier as men recall the bluest of limericks from a long compiled list. Jim finds himself playing cards with Riley and Therrien and Major Riordan and Captain McCambridge, slurping wine and smoking cigarettes and losing game after game, by now too drunk to concentrate on his cards, missing opportunities, failing to recognize the winning patterns oft held in his hands.

"Jesus Christ McFarlane, how'd ya let a full house get by you like that?" laughs McCambridge in a loud, booming, booze-hoarsened voice, as he scoops up the aftermath of a hand of five card stud and deftly shuffles the cards like a fan and redistributes them with scarcely a glance.

"Well, I figured I had to let others win for a change," he slurs, butting out a cigarette as he does so. "Congratulations, Therrien."

"Thank you, Captain." Therrien smiles briefly and uncomfortably, and looks down at his cards, all business. Uncertain with his words, comfortable only in action. Young. Tough. Scarred, look at the scar running down his face, bloody shrapnel, ours no less. Misdirected fire knows neither friend nor foe. Poor fellow's old lady in England upped and left him for a destroyer captain when we shipped out for Naples.

Still can't believe that one. He's not the only one, though. Lieutenant Therrien, 1st Battalion, Royal Canadian Cuckoldry. In a helmet with cuckold horns. More than a few men have gotten their transfers to that unit since coming here. Dear John. Dear Joe. Dear Jim—not yet, thank God.

Riordan lights a cigar, and a rich, resinous scent of tobacco rises in blue tendrils of smoke.

"Smells good," says Jim. "I don't suppose Private Breen gave you that, did he?"

"As a matter of fact, he did. Would you like one?"

Jim laughs ruefully, without a trace of humour. "No, thank you. I can't smoke a dead man's cigar. Any more than I can walk in his shoes. My luck is bad enough as it is, this evening." He finishes his sentence with a burp. "I'll stick with these." He slides open his silver cigarette case, and removes a cigarette as though it were a loose tooth from a gapped smile. "I wonder who will next enjoy this case as a trophy," he ponders dramatically, holding the case out as though it were the skull of Yorick. "Cigarette, anyone?"

"McFarlane, you're sick," says McCambridge. "Alright, let's go. Starting with me. Two rounds, and you can sub up to three at a time. I'll take two." He puts down two cards and replaces them with two others from the deck.

"Pass," says Therrien, looking slit-eyed and suspicious.

"Hit me for one," says Riordan, replacing a card.

"Two," says Riley, acting accordingly.

"Three," says Jim randomly, and he replaces three cards. What do I have here? Three of a kind? A flush? Ah, what do I care anyway. I'm drunk.

"So, Riley, you're in charge of Support now?" asks McCambridge, making conversation.

"Yes, that's right."

"You have big boots to fill."

"Literally," adds Riordan. He winks at McCambridge. "Turcott was a size thirteen! You're stuck with them, supply shortages in this theatre and all. Bunch up some newspaper in the toe and they'll fit like gloves!" Much laughter. Riley looks nonplussed. Though, this is short lived: after the next round, upon the revelation of everyone's cards, Riley assumes the mantle of victory.

"Welcome aboard," says McCambridge, whistling at Riley's flush. "You'll do well around here—I'm sticking by you tomorrow night!"

After more wine and another lost round, Jim staggers out of the dining room just as a group of officers from the Lucky Sevens arrive to join in the evening's activities. He nearly trips over one of them.

"Oops, careful there, sir," says a young lieutenant with a familiar face, as he steadies Jim with his hand. In the cramped lobby, Gordon sits playing a game of cribbage with Father Maitland and Lieutenant Voorhees. All are sober. Mr. Ceci joins in, sipping a glass of wine.

"How are you, Jim?" asks Father Maitland.

"Never better, Padre. Yourself?"

"Care to join us for a hand?"

"Yes, come, *Capitano*, play a hand, have-a some wine," entreats Mr. Ceci.

"I think that he has had quite enough of that," says Gordon sniffingly, though not without a trace of humour.

"I think that you could use some of that, Gordon. It would loosen you up."

"Careful now, McFarlane. Let us settle this like gentlemen. I think that in your state I could clean you out handily. What do you think, Padre?"

"I think Major Gordon has a bone to pick with you. Join us for a game, if you will."

"No thank you Padre, I think I'd like to get out for a bit."

"Understood."

After a moment's pause, Jim dismisses himself with a perfunctory, "Gentlemen." Out into the street. Soldiers mill around in the darkness, shining flashlights to get around, bumping into each other, joking, drinking, smoking. A flash in the sky from distant artillery. The wine is going straight to his head.

"Sir, that's quite a story."

"What? What'sss quite a story?" Leaning over on the curb, he feels nauseous. He tries to stand on rubbery legs, but his legs give out as though he were a foal trying to take its first steps and he teeters over into the arms of the two men.

"Careful, sir, I think we'll have to help you back."

"What? What'sss wrong?"

"You've been drinking with us for too long, it's time to go back to your billet. You can hardly stand."

"Huh?"

"And you smoked all of our cigarettes, too. We need to cadge some more."

"No fucking way! I'm ssstaying here!" He tries to stand again, and he wobbles about on bandied legs, breaking free from their grasp. "You hear me? I'm staying put, right here!" he shouts in the ragged ends of his voice. "Wanna go home! Wanna fuck my wife! Make loooove! My cock is limp, I cannot fuck! The nitrate it has changed my luck!"

"Sir, come with us." One of their hands reaches out to hold him, and he spins around and lands a punch square in the man's cheekbone. The soldier drops down, out cold.

"Hey!" yells the other, who takes a swing at Jim.

"What's going on!" The blast of a whistle. "Halt!" Two shadowy figures emerge from down the winding lane. Provosts.

"Everything here okay?" one of them asks.

"This captain here's been with us for over an hour. Drunk out of his skull. Crying over his wife who doesn't write him letters or something. We tried to get him back to his billet, then he knocked my buddy out cold, just like that!" He emphasizes the force of Jim's punch with a click of the tongue.

Jim sits down, knees up, and puts his hands on the side of his head.

"Right, okay, I see what's happening here. Come on with us Captain, let's dry you out."

"Sir? Sir, is that you?" Another voice, a familiar voice. "Sir? I've been looking for you." A hand on his shoulder. He turns wanly to see Cooley looking over him.

"You know him?" asks one of the military policemen.

"Yes, he's my CO. I'm his batman."

"He just hit a soldier, and he's publicly drunk. He's in for a bit of a wakeup call. A drunken officer punching an enlisted man … makes for an interesting night."

At this, Jim moans into his hands. "What have I done? Christ … " he whimpers. "I'm sorry, I'm sorry, I'm sorry … " He looks up to see Cooley speaking quietly with the provosts, lots of nodding, gesturing, bargaining. The irate soldier has calmed somewhat, and is slapping his comrade in the face lightly and is shaking him, trying to revive him. The unconscious man comes to, eyes fluttering and then focusing, and he props himself up onto his elbows, looking about with a dazed and groggy expression on his face.

"Can you get your buddy back okay?" asks one of the provosts.

"Yeah, I think so."

"We can handle it from here." The provost goes back to speaking with Cooley. The two soldiers leave, and Jim mutters "Sorry," to them, though it is doubtful that they hear him. After about ten seconds, the provosts leave, and one of them says over his shoulder, "You take care of yourself, Captain."

Cooley approaches and pulls him to his feet. "Come on, let's get you back to the mess. As you are a wreck, sir."

"What did you do?" he asks in a slur punctuated by a hiccup.

"I offered them your last two bottles of rye from your kitbag. They'll meet me back at the kit storage in about twenty minutes. Sorry, sir. I had to do something."

"Ss' okay," he says, staggering, supported by Cooley.

"Now, I think you owe *me* a favour for once."

XVII

"No. 12 Platoon, slope... ARMS! No. 12 Platoon, open or-DER ... MARCH!"

Selected as an officer candidate, he found himself polishing boots and buttons, pressing tunics and pants, marching and doing drill, and on training weekends, making and remaking beds, as the training sergeants barked ragged orders into his ears. Every night he marched back home to Marianne, now looking trim and fit in his uniform, and he would take her out on pay day for a steak dinner and maybe some dancing. She did like the uniform—that at least partly won her over, the first time he went home in it—"Well Jim McFarlane, if by joining up you meant you'd be wearing this I might've had an easier time with it! Come here, soldier, let me help you loosen that belt ... " But damn it all if there wasn't still tension under the surface. He was going to be shipped out and she knew it.

One day, a month after being selected for officer training, he received a letter from his university buddy and football teammate, John Barrett, in response to one he sent a month earlier:

Dear Jim—

Good to hear you've signed up! Me, I'm now in the First Battalion of the Canadian Irish Rifles. Currently I live in the Fort York Armoury in Toronto, not too far from the waterfront. All is fine and dandy here, and with training and the like, my days are quite busy. I was commissioned not too long ago—I must say I like being an officer. I'm not sure

> *if I qualify as a gentleman yet, but I bought a spiffy new suit from the Tip Top tailor factory near the armoury after my last pay day, and that should help make up for my myriad shortcomings. I'll be damned if I don't wow the ladies with that or my dress uniform. You know, this is a fine regiment that I am in. The spirit is high, the laughs are many, and everybody is itching to get over there and get their licks in before it's all over and done with. You know, I may be able to put a word into our CO or the recruiting officer to see if maybe you could get transferred. People get changed between units all the time, I'm sure we could think of something …*

Jim wasted no time in putting in a request for a transfer, going so far as to bribe his colonel with his liquor ration before he even mentioned to Marianne that he was mulling over the possibility of switching units. And so, by virtue of a bureaucratic stroke of the pen, ink being the lifeblood of governmental decisions, he was transferred to the 2nd Battalion of the Canadian Irish Rifles, based out of Toronto. After a month there, he was transferred to the 1st Battalion stationed at Camp Borden north of Toronto, and from here, everywhere—Alberta, Quebec, Newfoundland, Nova Scotia, England, Italy.

On the eve of his departure to Toronto, they walked down the street from the movie theatre toward the parked car outlined among others along the curb in the streetlamp glow, silent save for their steps; his, hushed and soft-soled, hers a standoffish clicking of heels. The movie was *Gaslight* starring Anton Wallbrook and Diana Wynyard, about a British heiress under the menacing thrall of her husband. That rough plot sketch was about all he'd gotten from it; he had been too distracted the whole time, twitching in his seat, mulling over his leaving tomorrow. She, too, had seemed distracted, but she'd stayed still much of the time, her index finger pressed pensively in the hollow of her lower lip, chin rested on the rest of her fingers, elbow propped up on the armrest of her chair, holding her poise as she often did when perturbed.

She was the first to speak. "So, I guess this is it then, isn't it. You're out of here tomorrow, and I won't see you for a long time."

"Well, that's not exactly true." He reached out and touched her shoulder.

"Oh?" She stopped and turned to him. "I won't be seeing you very often. With you stationed over there and wherever else afterward, I'll see you maybe once a month. That's going to be very, very hard, you know that."

"Look, it's not going to be too hard for me to wrangle a forty-eight or seventy-two hour furlough every once in a while. Occasionally, I'll probably get a week. And as we discussed before, you can also come visit me. I can get you discount tickets, no problem. I'm told one of the guys in the new unit, his brother works for the railway. I'll bet we can see each other every other weekend if work at it."

After a moment of simmering silence: "Let's just go, shall we?" Her voice was mumbly, weighted down with an irritable resignation. "It's late, and I have to wake up early tomorrow." They made their way to the car and drove home, barely speaking all the way. Later, in bed, after another loaded silence, after he had turned the bedside lamp out, she leaned over to him and whispered very tenderly into his ear, "I still love you, you know. I love you, I hope you know that I do … despite all this." She put her hand softly on his shoulder, and he turned to her and looked into her wide and watery eyes. He stroked her hair, moved a spiral strand out of the way of her face and softly rubbed her temple. She cooed softly as he did so.

"I promise I will be true to you. And the moment I get leave, I will be back here to visit you, I assure you. I will visit every chance I get."

"You'd better, Jim McFarlane, because if you don't, I'm coming to your base to give you a stern dressing down in front of all your men." She smiled, albeit sadly. "I assure you *that.*"

"Oh, really? A dressing down? I think that we've both dressed down after a fashion, and it's incumbent on us to make the most of it."

"Not now," she said, softly touching the side of his face to gently keep him away. "Not just yet. Let's just talk awhile."

"Okay," he said, disappointed and uncertain as how to handle the moment. "What should we talk about?"

"Something else." She smiled. It was a deep, warm smile. She reached out and put her hand in his, squeezing softly and then allowing his fingers to surround hers, letting herself be taken into the firm embrace of his grasp. "We got married a number of months ago," she started, leading into her thoughts. "Just over a year. We got married at a very bleak time … for the world, I mean. And now you're going off to war, and I understand that, I really do, and … "

"And … ?"

"Well, remember when we used to have those long talks when walking along the river?"

"I remember," he said with a light chuckle. "What's on your mind?"

"Well, on a few of those walks we discussed having children. We agreed to wait a bit, to try to have maybe a couple years for ourselves, if possible, and, well … "

"I think I know where this is going," he said.

She winced slightly, hurt. "Where did you think I was going with that?"

"I think that you were going to ask if we could try to have a baby now."

She looked at him long and hard. "Yes, as a matter of fact, I was. But not quite, Jim. It's not the right time. Literally." She sounded sarcastic.

"Sorry, I didn't mean to offend you." He looked her in the eyes and carefully considered his words. "But do you think it's wise to try and have a baby whenever I'm on leave and the timing's right? Really? I mean, with me gone, how can I be of any help?"

"Well, you can help by sending money home," she said. "That would be a start."

"It is a good idea, Marianne. Just not yet."

She was silent a minute. "We used to plan together a lot on those walks," she said softly. "We did a lot of things together." She lay awhile, collecting her thoughts in the silence as he held her hand and stroked her fingers, and she looked him in the eyes. "But you've seemed really restless since we got married."

"Hm? How so?"

"You suddenly seemed put everything into question. Right up till we married, you and I seemed to really see the world in the same way, to act in unison. You're a number of years older than me; I would have figured you'd have gotten some of that restlessness out of you by the time we met. Hadn't you?" She fixed her gaze on his, her eyes tender yet probing.

He hesitated before speaking. "Well, yes," he answered in a near whisper. "Yes and no, I guess. When I left university I really didn't know what I was supposed to do. I didn't follow my dad into medical school because I really have no interest in it. So I dabbled here, I dabbled there. I got the job at Ashton, and it's gone well enough, I guess … I guess … but, in the army I feel I have found my place, my purpose. I really do." He smiled.

"I just worry for your safety."

"As do I."

"If we started trying for a baby before you left for good … "

"Again, Marianne, it's not a good idea. Not yet." He continued. "If, and I mean *if,* the worst happens to me when I go, I would leave you unsupported with a baby. Think of it that way. Just think of it that way, please."

Her reply was long in coming. He continued stroking her hand as she composed her response in contemplative silence. "I understand," is all she said after awhile, a tear streaking down her cheek. "I understand."

XVIII

Too many cigarettes last night. Jesus. He breathes in and his lungs reluctantly inflate themselves with a laboured sighing wheeze, glued together as they are with his own sooty phlegm. His air passages feel burnt, as though a frayed rope were pulled up from his lungs and out through his mouth, rubbing raw the sensitive tissues of his mucous membranes all the way up. Phlegm pools in the back of his throat, having risen like watery slag from the bituminous catacombs of his lungs. He clears his throat and spits a grey-green sooty wad into a tissue, and examines the clot of sputum, flecked and streaked with blood, and he compresses the tissue and stuffs it into the bedside wine bottle, now requisitioned not only as an ashtray, but also a spittoon. The ingenuity of the modern fighting man. Mom would not be very pleased, Marianne less so. Goddamn, my knuckles hurt. Must've hit something last night—or someone? After a slug of water from his bedside canteen, he feels ready to confront the task at hand: appearing not to be too hungover at breakfast. Good as new. Time for a cig. He lights up a smoke. With his first deep caustic inspiration of smoke, he paradoxically feels clearer, aided by a rush of nicotine-triggered euphoria. He complements the drag with a slurp from the bottle of Canadian Club standing at attention by his bedside. It is already a quarter drunk. Thank you Dad for the prescription. Well, onward Christian soldier—

Breakfast is a veritable feast: bacon, ham, scrambled eggs, toast with jam, hash browns, orange juice, tea, coffee, as much as you want, sir, eat up, enjoy, tonight we're going in, this is it, back in to take the damn ridge that's held up our otherwise textbook advance, the Brits couldn't do it so it's up to us, yes, should be a piece of cake once the arty and air force flatten it all and leave us with nothing to do, yessiree, just picking through the rubble, sounds good to me, I hate it when they shoot back. As he eats in the mess, he finds himself for awhile talking to no one, the bleary morning chatter about him largely banal, last night's festivities casting a heavy hangover shadow over the morning: slurp, chew, looks like it's gonna be a warm one today, yuh, yuh, let's get in a couple hands of poker before we roll, are you in Riordan? We move in at what time again exactly? I hope the newbies are up to it, hope the RSM whupped them into shape, hope I'll have time to visit Chelsea at the hospital today before we go and give her a goodbye kiss, she gets so bloody worried, can you blame her? Only the padre and Gordon seem bright, teetotallers that they are, chatting together in a considerably more buoyant manner than most of the others—

"The eggs are rubbery."

"The eggs are always rubbery," answers Barrett, pensively examining the yellowed clot of scrambled egg on the end of the fork, turning it, face set in mock suspicion. "That's where the army puts its surplus rubber—they just mix it in with the eggs, stretch 'em out as far as they'll go."

"Wouldn't be surprised if they did."

"You should see what they do to the meat."

"I'd rather not, thank you, Barrett."

"These eggs, they are shit," Leprenniere adds with his customary trace of an accent. "How they feed such rubbish to us sometimes is a mystery. Cannot Riordan get his hands on anything better than this crap?" A breeze billows the flaps of the mess tent, bringing with it a damp swampy odour of rotting vegetation and mud. The damn rains. Falling on the plains. Not only in Spain, he thinks. The rain has been pouring hard on their bivouac area for two days straight now, has turned the fields into muck. The sodden training exercises yesterday, slithering through the chilly muck, splashed by that goddamn tank full of laughing jackasses, the treads turning up muck like a water wheel,

Christ almighty, who'd a' thought that Italy could be this miserable? Clearly the elements have been sympathizing with the Fascists.

"It's not the eggs, it's the preparation," Barrett corrects Leprenniere. "Shoot the cook, not the provider, perhaps some poor Eyetie farmer in need of a buck or two. Or your good old stout Canadian farmer, producing for victory."

"Hear hear!" Leprenniere slams his fist on the table in hearty agreement. "Are you two in for a game tonight?"

"Sure, why not," offers Jim with a genial yawn. "Around here?"

"No, wit' the MO from the RCR. He challenged me at a medical seminar yesterday, so I told him I will bring some men to play a group of their officers led by him."

"Count me in." Barrett is adamant. "Damn those RCRs lording their bloody record over us, just because we're new around here. We oughta show them."

"May I step in here, gentlemen?" It is Captain Bly, holding a mess tin full of breakfast and a steaming cup of tea.

"Well that depends, sir," Barrett stipulates. "Will you help stand for the honour of the Canadian Irish Rifles tonight in a card game against a vain group of officers from the RCR about to have their sorry arses handed to them on a plate?"

"Well, I do suppose that *could* be arranged." Bly looms with mock menace over the perpetual smartass Barrett, moving his face closer as though he were a stern headmaster at a school noted for its iron discipline. "After you do shit detail for your insolence, Barrett, I'll do anything to celebrate your humiliation!" There is laughter, and Bly joins them, lowering his wide-framed bulk beside Leprenniere. As soon as he sits down he tucks into his scrambled eggs.

"Damn, the eggs are really off today, aren't they?" he complains in mid-chew. "We should stuff them in shells and fire them at Jerry, for Chri—for You-know-who's sake." He winks at Jim and Barrett and Leprenniere, and nods toward the padre nearby. The four of them chortle over their beverages.

"I think the decision on eggs around here this morning is damned bloody unanimous." Barrett has taken on the persona of a union boss leading a meeting to strike.

"Agreed. That's why you have to get yourself a good batman to scrounge up your own meals around here," Jim advises. "Though if it weren't for these sorts of issues, we'd have little to bitch and joke about, now would we?"

"Pardon, sir?" Jim looks into the uncomprehending eyes of Lieutenant Muller, innocent in his misunderstanding.

"Nothing, really. I said, 'a good batman could've coughed up better eggs than these.' Just once again giving Cooley his due."

"Agreed. They're always terrible, aren't they?" Muller returns to his own conversation with Olczyk and Lieutenant Flaherty, about a game of poker today with the MO from the battalion and officers from the Lucky Sevens before the move to the start line. Bly and Leprenniere and Barrett. Dead, dead, and invalided out, respectively. He has fallen into reimagining old conversations anew.

Riley takes a seat beside him, having arrived to breakfast late.

"Good morning," Jim croaks.

"Hello, Jim. How are you today?"

"Oh, been better. Yourself?"

"The same. Woke up late and caught hell from Gordon. Say, what happened to you last night after you left our game?"

"Not sure. Ended up with a sore knuckle, though." He then resumes eating, uninterested in any further conversation with anyone, and Riley takes this cue and eats his breakfast in silence.

After his third cup of grainy and bitter black coffee and a mountainous helping of breakfast, the highlights of which were the unctuous shrivels of chewy bacon and the crispy cakes of hash browns, the lowlight of which, as always, was the eggs, he feels sufficiently awakened to meet the day's challenge, neurons lighting up one by one like the lights on a telephone switchboard at the start of a business day, relaying calls from the disconnected departments of his mind, building the coherence with which he can face the demands of the day, and more particularly, the demands of the night. He listens to

Gordon dispense the orders of the day, which until dinner amount to not much other than company and battalion inspections in the late afternoon. A highlight of the day is his announcement that Father Maitland is organizing a swim parade at the nearby coast precisely an hour and a half after breakfast, and that interested men are to report to the trucks at the maintenance area. Upon dismissal he makes his way to his headquarters down the road.

Hmm. He shuffles papers in his hands, fidgets with his fountain pen, turning it in his hands, twisting and untwisting the segments of its cylinder. Careful with that or you'll leak it all over yourself like you bloody well did in Caiazzo. There are now fifteen sodden and swollen cigarette butts in the wine bottle on his desk, the green glass of which is now smoked dark and murky. A gun rumbles in the distance. Or was it thunder? The hard wood of the church pew against his back, the flicker of the bottle candle as he turned the pen in his hand, the shells erupting on the roof and outside in the ruins, all over the ridge. Can't get much sleep with all this gunder. Said something like that to Cooley up there, didn't I. Barrett's wit rubbed off on me. Still have to address those greenhorns. They're in your hands now. The minutes pass.

He walks about, into the streets, alongside big blocky slant-roofed houses with colourful shutters and window boxes, along palisades of cypress trees like folded green umbrellas, along winding cobble streets of pastel townhouses and little shops, a pleasing warren of doll-house domesticity pressed into service as a collective barracks for yet another invading army in Italy. The shadow of the arch under which he marched two nights ago falls under him. Laundry flaps out of windows, mostly of a military nature—boxer shorts, white undershirts, green wool socks, khaki overshirts, wool khaki pants. Soldiers mill about, many displaying a breezy informality in the form of wedge caps or berets cocked at funny angles on their heads. He checks out the sights—a sergeant from the Lucky Sevens tank battalion getting his boots shined by a local boy while chatting to him and a couple of his comrades, a rude and rudimentary exchange of English and Italian with the boy, lots of laughter. The boy, scrawny, underfed, with a long, narrow nose, tousled dark brown hair and sunken eyes, who cannot be older than twelve, smokes cigarettes along with them. “Pietro, how d’ya say fuck?” Along a narrow street canyoned with the façades of ancient townhouses, he half expects to have the contents of a chamber pot dumped on his head, or for a newlywed husband to hang a bed sheet out the window decorated with the florid proof of his wife’s previous virginity while all those about him whoop and holler and beat on pots and pans with merry approval, as he witnessed once near Caiazzo in the summer while the battalion was on training manoeuvres.

He makes his way to a small stone bridge over a creek and looks down, his view garlanded by the drooping leafy branches of gnarled oaks and the droopy curtains of willows. He stares out over the water awhile, at the houses and sheds along the leafy bank. He recalls having marched over this bridge, too, upon entering town by way of a weaving weary march in the rain from the front, the shells streaking over, the clouds galvanized from within by sheet lightning and bruised in the flare of the guns—the weather of war, the spirit of the age, or as the Germans say, the Zeitgeist. And the knowledge that he will be part of it again tonight, exemplified by the distant guns he hears now.

XIX

The padre forms up the swim parade and about a hundred men head off to the seaside to nearby Cattolica in trucks provided by the transport officer, Lieutenant Phipps, who himself declines the opportunity out of busyness. Jim avails himself of this opportunity and enjoys the brief drive with Cooley in his jeep. They follow trucks packed with men, the canvas canopies removed, the sun melting through a milky haze of overcast, the wind blowing through their hair as they drive in the procession to the seaside over a road lined with vineyards and willows and the coned minarets of cypress trees. Lush grapes, nearly bursting with juice, cluster on untended vines, powdered with dust. A withered willow weeps over the road and brushes the ribbed backs of the trucks, and is whipped by the radio antennas of a troop of tanks from the 2nd New Zealand Division passing the other way, their turrets shaded with stolen beach umbrellas, and the antennas bend and snap back from under branches. A mule brays bucktoothed annoyance at them from across the roadside gully in a tangled thicket of untended roadside weeds, its sandy honk of discontent ringing familiar to Jim as he and Cooley approach it, their jeep crawling behind the lumbering army trucks. He salutes the mule in passing. Another soldier chucks a half-eaten apple as a gift in its general direction from the truck in front of Jim and Cooley, and the mule bends over to claim its prize.

"Just trying to win the favour of the locals, sir!"

"Damned stubborn they are!"

From beside him in the driver's seat Cooley asks, "Hey Captain, how's your hand?"

"Huh?" Jim asks, bewildered.

"Your hand. Do you remember last night when I found you?"

"Uh, no. What happened?"

"You hit a soldier. Hard, I might add. I had to smooth things over with the MPs to get you out of shit, and then I got you back to barracks. Sir."

"My God," Jim reflects. "Thank you for that."

"No problem. Just doing my job, sir." For a moment both are silent as Jim is at a loss for what to say. Perhaps this is best forgotten?

"Hey, by the way," he says in order to change the subject. "How's Briggs faring?"

"Nice of you to ask," Cooley says, glancing at him as he drives, a kind look of acknowledgement on his face. "He's gonna make it, Father Maitland said. I'm going to visit him before we move out in the evening. Father Maitland is taking some soldiers to visit our wounded."

"Good to hear. Give him my regards."

They pass the crumpled, twisted mass of a wrecked jeep beside a hole in a side road at a 'T' junction to the side near a whitewashed stucco farmhouse. Two engineers stalk ahead of the wreckage and slowly sweep the poles of their metal detectors left to right and right to left again, and attempt to divine from the earth wellsprings of death that screech and scratch from below the surface and into their headphones, fighting a war of concentration and nerves, of sweat beading on brows, of careful, balletic movement and pause around unseen and sudden sources of death, around the calculated consummation of murderous wills since moved on.

They make their way through the partially ruined southern reaches of the town of Cattolica nearby, seeing their reflections in the shopfronts and hotels and bistros, under red and white striped dirty awnings, behind wrought-iron railings, and they drive along the desolate rows of townhouses and businesses, and, heralded by the shrill honky cries of circling greedy gulls, on to the beach, the seemingly endless expanse of white sand beach, drifting with dunes and tufted here and there with weeds; and they bask in the sun in front of abandoned hotels and beach resorts while sappers de-mine the cordoned off perimeters, and they swim and watch as northward in the distance, far up the sandy and shifting border of land and sea, out in the water near the misty haze of horizon, a lone British destroyer lobs desultory shells at unseen German coastal defences further north in Rimini, weaving about, here and there obscured by smokescreens fired from its guns. A fresh sea breeze blows in from the rippled turquoise surface of the Adriatic, and up above parts the milky clouds as though it were curdling them in its sharp solution. Waves roll lazily ashore and break into foam as they lap the beach, sssshhhhhhh sssshhhhhhh, retreating outward and exposing in their lathery wake seashells and bits of seaweed and slick and newly sifted sand, to be replaced again by another wave in the patient and ageless massaging of the water, the erosion of the land.

"Captain, you coming swimming?" It is Cooley.

"Yes, of course, Cooley, I'll be right there."

The two of them make for the water, splashing ankle, knee, waist deep, diving into and parting the concave, rolling surface tension of an incoming wave. The water is cool and refreshing, its incoming, outgoing currents washing over and under and about him in his near weightless suspension. He dives in headfirst into another wave and opens his eyes into the brackish murk, the salty water scouring his body. As he bobs in the waves, he contemplates wordlessly for a few moments the ephemeral nature of human movements—migrations and invasions mocked and mirrored above by the clouds that swirl, storm, crash and dissipate in a constant current and eddy and boil of vapourous thunder and rain. Like the sea on the emetic voyage to England, the ship nosing into and upward upon the gently rolling mountains of water, stomach juices and inner ear fluid sloshing within, his head oft hanging over the rail, returning unto the sea that which came from the sea. Yet, the sight of the bucking, rolling sea in its rises and falls, the folding of mountains that then crashed back into the sea. The sight of it! Rough Andean foothills, surf-crested Himalayan peaks, deep Grand Canyons between the mighty ripples of unseen properties driving through and playing with sublime force and supercilious indifference the medium of water; the rippling, torsioned musculature of the changing world under a tensile skin of water, heaving and pushing endlessly at the land, shaping it through the ebb and flow of its inscrutable and tempestuous will. Borne aloft on another wave and the wave of his own exhilaration, being dashed back to the beach in gleeful surrender to the power of physics, the broken wave washing over him, the grit and pelt of disturbed sand. Ah, water, run over me, baptize me anew, wash off the ravages of experience … The waves break over him as he lies on the beach, and he is soothed by the slow and rhythmic strokes of water that wash over and gently push and pull at his body, the grit and grate of the sand underneath.

Later, back on the beach, he feels ready to head back to await the inevitable battle, but in need of distraction until departure time, he joins listlessly in a card game with Riley, Muller, the padre, and Sergeant Kerr from the anti-tank platoon, making small card talk in an atavism of earlier games.

"I'm feeling the luck this afternoon, gentlemen," says the pockmarked Muller, whistling through his teeth as he deftly parts and shuffles the cards together with hands well practised in games of chance such as craps, blackjack, poker and warfare. Poker it is, this time, five card stud. "Here's to victory." Jim always did like cards; perhaps it was his love of chance that got him into this mess. He wins the first round with a full house, getting twenty army-issue lire in banknotes in the bargain.

"Ooh whee, the luck favours Captain McFarlane today, does it not!" Muller laughs as Jim claims his winnings.

"More than last night, eh, Jim?" Riley grins and nudges Jim with his shoulder.

"Indeed." Smell of smoke on the wind as the breeze changes direction, the industrial reek of paint and rubber and fuel, the smell of the industrial world aflame. The carrier is still burning from the mine that blew it up twenty minutes ago, the mine that killed Cedarville and Trebb. They look up from their card game at the trail of black smoke dissolving on the breeze, kitted up and awaiting movement, the breeze blowing the acrid smell of metal burning in their faces as they sit clustered about a stone wall separating farmers' fields. Behind them, about them, are dead turrets of the Adolph Hitler Line, pierced by the Eighth Army, tank turrets and concrete gun emplacements embedded in the ground, many of which have been destroyed, all of which are now abandoned. From the valley beyond echo the sounds of battle, the distant crump of shells. A squad of sappers stalk along the road for further mines with their metal detectors. Two are busily and very carefully dismantling a disc-shaped Teller anti-tank mine that they have unearthed from the chalky white fine road dust, gingerly sweeping and blowing the dirt off it as though it were some ancient artifact. The resting soldiers are semi-covered by trees and the wall, and therefore the forward companies of the battalion, waiting in reserve and held up by mines in their approach to the front, have largely eschewed the order to dig in, abandoning their half-dug shellscrapes to the more immediate problem of killing time. Other parties of men sit and lie about in their gaggles, sleeping, joking, chatting, reading, writing letters, gambling.

"Christ, get a load of that smell." He chokes as he says this, as if for emphasis. "It's your deal, Barrett."

"My deal it is." Barrett wrinkles his nose and shuffles and hands out the allotted number of cards to all involved—Jim, Bly, Davis, himself. The wind changes direction and relieves them of the reek of the smoldering hull of the nearby carrier. There is a throbbing drone above as a squadron of Hurricane fighter-bombers buzzes ahead in the sunny sky that belies the carnage underneath, heading into enemy territory presumably to deal death to any advancing reinforcements. Captain Bly looks up over the wall, cards in hand, looking at the horizon, undulating with hills and framed by the mountains of Lazio, and veiled in the smoke of battle.

"I wouldn't mind moving soon," he says to no one in particular. No one responds. Jim replaces two cards, comes up lucky in the exchange. He draws heavily on his cigarette and puts down his hand.

"Two aces, you bastard!" Barrett throws down his hand of cards in disgust. They fan out in the weeds. Jim rakes in his allotted lire and cigarettes.

"What can I say, I'm a lucky fellow," Jim grins. By now they have started to draw a crowd, a handful of soldiers from nearby.

"I'll follow the luckiest officer into battle," says Private Cook, a signalman currently attached to Barrett's platoon. "If you keep losing sir, can I transfer to Lieutenant McFarlane's platoon?" There is scattered laughter.

"That depends on the outcome of the court martial I'm about to bring out on you due to lack of confidence in your commanding officer, Private," Barrett sneers with just enough humour to show that he is joking. "Another hand, shall we?"

"I think that's in order," concurs Davis. "Your deal, Jim." Cigarette set in mouth, bluish wisps of smoke dissolving in the warm breeze, dappled in sunlight dripping from between the shuttering leaves of the oak tree above, Jim begins dispensing his cards. There is a commotion, and he looks over at the wall. The engineers have moved aside, having removed the Teller mine. A long line of soldiers are marching up the road toward them, kicking up a cloud of white chalky road dust, about fifty German prisoners with their hands on their heads, sullen, shuffling listlessly, driven onward by a handful of Canadian soldiers wielding their bayonet-spiked rifles like medieval pikes. Jim and the others get a good look at the parade of passing faces, the Germans looking out at them, some old, some young, some thin, some strong-looking, faces wan, their grey-green Wehrmacht uniforms tattered, some with their badges ripped off, dusty, some wearing long-brimmed sun caps, few if any looking anything like the Aryan ideals painted on propaganda posters and touted in the blustery speeches of the Führer that Jim had seen in countless newsreels. A few of them help wounded Canadian soldiers walk, or carry stretchers, pressed into service as medical aides. A soldier yells out from the sidelines, "Not lookin' so tough now, eh, Fritzy?" Another bellows out the German anthem with mock beerhall brio—"*Deutschland, Deutschland, über alles, über alles in der Welt!*" A few others accompany him by singing or by humming loudly and raggedly along. But most just watch the sad spectacle, put off slightly by the sight of men shorn of their fighting pride, official enemy or not. If the winds of fortune change, that could be us, says this scrolling display of bedraggled defeat on exhausted, shuffling, dusty feet.

From the rear a Tommy-gun-toting Canadian sergeant abruptly barks, "*Schnell! Schnell!* Move it, move it!" Jim looks at this ragtag river, this grey and dispirited moving menagerie of discomfiture flowing by, these castoffs of combat, and feels more sorry than triumphant, almost embarrassed. Jim meets eyes with one of the prisoners, dark oily hair parted like a schoolboy, his thin, fine-featured almond-shaped face too fragile seeming for the rigours of combat, impossibly young, looking not a day over seventeen. The soldier holds his watery brown-eyed gaze for a moment then looks back ahead, resignedly shuffling up the road to eventually end up in some prisoner of war camp in Britain or Canada or America. Jim nods at him. The boy nods back. The sergeant at the rear blows a bent-belled trumpet, a loud, sour, brassy note that pierces the air unpleasantly like the wheezy protest of a dyspeptic elephant, likely a prize captured from the Germans, and barks again, and the prisoners pick up the pace, shambling off to whatever geographic fate awaits them down the road. A series of muffled concussions rumble out from beyond the horizon, bombs from the Hurricanes that flew overhead earlier.

"Damn, that must've been loud as hell," muses Riley. "If you were there, I mean." He looks uncertain, nervous, not quite up to the task awaiting him tonight. The distant concussions of a British air raid on Rimini have settled, have vibrated through the air and through the sand under their buttocks and spent their energy, their sonic imprint washed away as though by the ceaseless lapping of the sea.

"Oh, it gets much louder, sir," Muller says. "Much, much louder." Riley looks ashen. He looks like me, Jim thinks. I hope he doesn't want to talk to me again, Jim thinks, I have no idea what advice I can give him. Talk to the padre. That's his job.

Father Maitland attempts to soothe Riley's jittery nerves. "When you get down to it, on the field, it is mostly noise to put you off. It is ninety percent noise and ten percent effect, so long as you dig in when required and you keep alert when you move. Always remember that. So, take your mind off it now and let's keep this game going, shall we? And McFarlane," he looks at Jim, "are you going to let anyone else win?"

Jim grins out of the corner of his mouth as he meets the eye of the padre. "Hey, I just had to make up for last night's losing streak." He yawns, and is suddenly overcome by an agreeable lethargy. I could go to sleep here and never wake up and that would be just fine by me, just lie back and let the wind blow the sand over me and sift it through my fingers and toes and cover me ... He finds himself in yet another hand of poker and this time loses all his money to the padre, who wins with a royal flush. I don't know these people, he thinks to himself. I don't know them and I doubt I ever will. He thinks again of Bly, of Barrett, of Leprenniere, of Davis, of others that he served with, served under and commanded, and realizes that he no longer really has any friends. He is too withdrawn into himself. Too tender to handle the stress and horror of combat, too distant to befriend anyone and risk losing them to war's callous arithmetic. He eats his meals and plays cards and as he does so, he layers these experiences to earlier ones, shared experiences with those no longer with the world. Riley wants to be his friend, wants to be somebody's friend, he's green as the buds of spring and wants somebody to talk to ... Witchewski would have insulted him were he here at the beach, would have torn him a new asshole, like when he took on some newbies before the Liri Valley battles, when that greenhorn Private Wilkes almost buckled from a case of nerves on the eve of his first battle when the guns opened up with their crash and frightening, unearthly wail—

"What if I'm wounded?"

"Well, that's why we have medics, son."

"What if I'm killed?"

"That's why we have shovels. Now fall in."

The only person I want as my friend around here is Mark, wherever he is right now, braving the skies of Europe or chasing skirts in a saloon in England. He misses the times they met together while in England, drinking in Aldershot, then in Nottingham, then a trip to Edinburgh and a stay in an inn on the coast of Wales near Swansea. He resolves to read Mark's letters, and others from home, before marching back out into the fray tonight. One more taste of home. Mark, Mark, the only person I know from home who understands my experience fully.

More soldiers come out onto the beach, soldiers from other units billeted in Cattolica proper. The mine-free corridors of the beach are now choked with men lounging and milling about. A group of soldiers Jim recognizes as being from 1st Division set up a volleyball net nearby and begin a game of beach volleyball, leaping and twisting and arching about and knocking about a soccer ball commandeered for this game. One of the soldiers, a tall, young, muscled blonde man, is adorned with tattooes, his military experiences recorded for posterity for all to see. Emblazoned into the very vellum of his back is tattooed in blue-black ink a map of Italy, with arrows marking his advance from the shore of Sicily inland, over the Straits of Messina and upward, up the Appenine ridges of his vertebrae. The arrows terminate in the north-east near Rimini, where he is now.

It is time to leave. Father Maitland assumes the manner of a high school football coach and pierces the air with a whistle, the whistle's sharpness out-shrilling even the seagulls. He assembles the men together and they remount their vehicles and head back to the rest village, retracing their route. Jim peers over his shoulder from the passenger seat of the jeep and watches as the beach recedes through the dingy corridors of Cattolica, soldiers and townspeople waving from laundry-draped windows, and the town itself disappears from view as the convoy rounds a hillside along the snaking country road.

XX

It's 1400 hours. Seven hours till showtime, seven hours to curtain call. Seven hours till the thunderous overture of hundreds of guns blasting in unison like a mighty crash of cymbals, rather than the haphazard shelling going on now like the testing and tuning of instruments. Nine hours till Act One, the first stage of the assault. Sixteen hours till Act Two, his cue to strut upon the stage. Act Three is anybody's guess. This springs to mind as he awaits his turn at mail call again.

Private Glasser and Lance Corporal Coutts stand each with a sack of recently arrived mail at their feet, calling out the names of those lucky enough to receive letters and parcels. Coutts is a bearish, strong-looking man with curly hair, thick lips turned into a permanent scowl, a fleshy face, broken nose replete with the ruddiness of burst capillaries, and the bellicose, brim-browed look of a boxer. It is a wonder he is not in the infantry, Jim thinks, and then sees that Coutts can only walk with the aid of a cane. Wounded, transferred here out of his platoon, doing light duties. Ah. It all makes sense. Glasser hands out letters and Coutts hands out parcels.

"Captain McFarlane!" shouts Glasser. "Here. A letter for you!" He hands Jim a letter. Jim's heart pounds in anticipation.

"I've been popular these last couple days, haven't I," he says without looking at the writing on the envelope. Save that for later. I hope it's Marianne. I hope. I hope. He is almost dizzy with excitement and a gnawing nervousness. "Thank you, gentlemen."

"Our pleasure, sir," responds Coutts. "Next! Lieutenant Therrien!" Jim marches briskly back down the street to the hotel and up to his room. He shuts the door and sits on his bed. He holds the letter in his hand without looking at it. Time to smoke. He has a cigarette, smoking it nervously with shallow breaths, snuffing the butt out in the smoky wine bottle. It dies with a faint hiss. Holding the letter in both hands, he finally looks down and reads the handwritten address:

To Captain James McFarlane
'A' Coy, 1 CIR

He recognizes the handwriting immediately and he becomes light-headed with anticipation. To verify, he looks at the return address in the corner:

Marianne McFarlane
Ottawa, Ontario,
Canada

Finally! He tears open the letter carefully with this hand and pulls out two pieces of paper, neatly folded together three times over so as to fit into the envelope. His heart skips a beat. There is naught in the world but this. He reads:

Dear Jim,

I hope this letter finds you well. It is not an easy one to have to write to you—in fact, finding the right words in this instance for me is very difficult.

His heart sinks at this, and he resumes reading with a dread fatalism:

When I married you, I married you because I was deeply in love with you and you were deeply in love with me.

I couldn't agree more.

Love is something that you have to act on instead of just say. I'm sorry Jim, but 'I love you,' and a kiss on the lips is just not enough when it is the only thing that you do. Yes, we've had some passionate times. But you haven't proven to me that you can always be there for me. Eleven months into our marriage and you run off and join the army. Two months later you skip town and transfer to another regiment. Why? Were you that afraid of commitment to our marriage? Is it because you couldn't live up to the duties of being a husband? You could have done something else to support this war effort. You could have joined the reserves and still answered the call of duty. Remember our arguments over this? Look at me. I joined the civil service and I didn't have to go far away and risk life and limb to do it.

Ouch. The sting of it.

Eleven months in and you left me—you chose love of country over love of wife. I haven't seen you in over two years, Jim. I go through every day walking on knifepoints. At night I can't sleep for worry. When I read the headlines or hear Lorne Greene's doom reports on the radio, I fret. You picked one of the most dangerous possible jobs in this bloody war right AFTER YOU MARRIED ME. *That cut me, Jim, cut me more than I think you realize. Had we discussed this before marrying, had you at all indicated that you were thinking of serving, we could have planned differently, could have accommodated this differently. And yet, I supported you. Reluctantly, of course, but I've supported you, allowing you to carry on, to live out this sense of duty or this need for boyhood adventure to prove yourself. Do you know what I asked myself when you finally upped and did it, when you went to the Cartier Armoury and signed up? I asked, 'Does he even love me anymore? Did he ever really love me?' I know that sounds hard, and I think you really do love me, but you must understand how your decision made me feel at the time.*

You send such passionate letters, Jim, that I'm afraid of loving you anymore. You're more in love with the idea of being married to me than you are with me. When we were at home those last couple months before you signed up, we argued, argued, argued. When you came home on leave, we argued. All the plans we made together fell by the wayside. And now I'm afraid, because I fear that the whole horrible danger you willfully put yourself into when you didn't have to will get you killed, or worse—maimed and made an invalid. I don't want you to end up like my father. Sweet man, but missing something upstairs on account of a war that he too volunteered to fight. If you wanted to go, you should never have married me.

I am sorry. I am so sorry to bring you this news. I have no doubts that you are the fine officer that you had wanted so much to become. Wanted to become more than you wanted to be my husband. Maybe you are doing the right thing. But it was not the right thing at the right time, given my part in your life, and vice versa. You chose this path when I think you had another priority: us. And the life we were beginning to build together. I probably sound like a bitch right now to you, a heartless bitch. But you must understand me. I am leaving, I am finished with this. If it makes you feel any better, I have not found anyone else yet. That would be unfair to you if I did so without telling you. I hope that in your absence you have also remained celibate, but given your desire to run away so far from home, I cannot be so sure.

A twinge of guilt pangs through him, and he recalls for a moment the fragment of a dream he had while under the church pew at San Mateo, of waking up beside Marianne in some hotel room, yes that dream, but it wasn't really Marianne, was it … no it wasn't Marianne at all, that night on leave in Naples, or was it Jesi or Sorrento, that night, that nurse, Carolyn was her name, and John Barleycorn united us for a night and I was so drunk I scarcely remember … He winces from shame at this transgression and continues reading:

I feel terrible, but I can go on like this no longer. The stress of your situation is too much to bear, I am afraid.

I am sorry, I am sorry, I am sorry, I am so sorry, writing this letter is tearing me apart. Waiting for you has been tearing me apart. Jim, I sincerely wish you all the best, and I want this war to end, and I want you to come home safely.

Marianne

The papers waver in his trembling hands. Tears burn hot down his face. He is seized with rage and sorrow. He picks up the wine bottle ashtray and dashes it against the stucco wall. It explodes in crystalline chaos, scattering glass and sodden ash and water on the wall and swollen cigarette butts on the floor. He glances at the letter again. There is a bitter smell of soot. He looks back at the thin, tissue-like pages of the letter clamped tight in his white-boned hand. A phrase leaps out at him:

Does he even love me anymore? Did he ever really love me?

Questions each pulled upward by the hook of a question mark. He reads the questions over again, disbelieving the words:

Does he even love me anymore? Did he ever really love me?

He can hear her voice through the medium of her pen, through tonal vibrations of squiggles of ink. She berates him in his ear as though she were in the room, stalking about, arms crossed. "Do you still love me anymore? Have you ever really loved me?" He can hear her, reserved, no-nonsense, though with a touch of plaintiveness in her voice, a plaintiveness he neglected to consider when he enlisted. Reflected in her handwriting, orderly, precise, though canted to the right in a slight romantic slant and reaching outward with a curl, bringing to mind the curlicued locks of her sumptuous hair hanging over him as she kissed him from above in their bed, oft the prelude to making love. He sits on the bed. He can smell her perfume, the fruity fragrance of her freshly shampooed hair. Potpourri on the windowsill by the kitchen sink. He can smell bacon and eggs frying, he rubs her shoulders while she is stirring a pot, he is kissing her, he is taking her to bed for the first time, they are arguing, they are flirting, speaking in phrases remembered and half-remembered, half-formed and morphing impressions bubbling up from his subconscious, disremembered and re-remembered, a sensual broth formed of the sum of their experience together. Mostly, they are arguing. He avails himself of a giant, burning gulp of whiskey from the bottle from his bedside and fills his flask, along with his canteen, with more, spilling some as he does so. He finds himself walking, and as he exits the hotel into the streets clogged with men and the honking of jeep horns, he produces from his pocket again the thumb-smudged sepia-toned picture of Marianne.

XXI

"Damn it Jim, you really did it, didn't you?" She looked at him through fiery eyes. They were at the kitchen table again. The kitchen had become the Kitchen Front, a line drawn through the centre of the table. He had just made a bold gambit, creeping forth across the line with his hand and snatching up the saltshaker, a bold prize, the contents of which he lightly sprinkled on his pork chops and gravy and mashed potatoes and green beans, the light of the kitchen catching the facets of the tiny granules in gemlike translucence, a score of little diamonds taken as spoils of war, the reparations of repast. She had countered, liberating a napkin from his clutches, the napkins being set roughly seventy percent on his side, at an angle. An escalating of tensions, from Sitzkrieg to Blitzkrieg, as each crossed the Imaginot Line drawn between them on the table, right through their marriage. She raised the white napkin, as if to surrender ... and then promptly sniffled into it before lowering it, bunched in a ball, to the table. A feint.

"I did indeed, didn't I?" He was wearing his service dress uniform, wool khakis smartly pressed and correctly creased in the legs, buttons polished, and the badges of his regiment sewn into each shoulder underneath his brass officer's stars, his wedge cap hung on an angle on the hat rack at the door along with her pillbox hat. He cleared his throat, and the grumbly sound rolled like distant artillery.

The atmosphere was so charged; the situation was such a cliché, like one of the many movies about going off to war that had been hurriedly released in recent months. "I went and did it. I had an idea and

I ran through with it. I joined the army and became an officer and now I'm shipping out." After a moment's pause: "You know, I thought we crossed this bridge already, I thought these damned arguments were all in the past. For God's sake Marianne, I know I'm shipping out soon and I know I'll be gone a goodly long while, but damn it, I got this embarkation leave and we have the next five days to do as we please. Look, it's back to Halifax for me on Wednesday, and then it's off overseas sometime soon after that, I don't know exactly when or where because they don't tell us anything because it's a war and loose lips sink ships, as they say—"

"Jim, it's not that I don't appreciate this time we have." Her expressions softened somewhat, aided by her voice, modulated in tactfully chosen words tendered with emotion, "and it's not that I don't support you on this venture—it's just that I don't appreciate all the time we don't have anymore. I've seen you a total of twenty days this last year. My visit to you in Halifax two months ago was the last time I saw you. The last time before that was when we met your family in Sudbury two months before that. And now ... " Her voice trailed off into silence, absent words defining absence.

"And now ... " he refrained. "And now, let's make this last weekend count, darling." The choice of the word *darling* jarred like a bad note or a snapped string during a violin solo. It seemed so gratuitous after this gradual parting over the two years, since he'd joined the service and been moved all over the bloody country on various postings with his unit. Darling—did that word even apply anymore?

She was right about the lack of time spent together, and the implications for their marriage. She had every right to feel the way she did, her true feelings breaking through time and time again like stress fractures in a poorly built bridge, demonstrating in actuality what he tried to forget, tried to convince himself was not really the case, that he was just taking a leave of absence and all would be the same again, he would be home with new stories to tell, new scars to show. She was right, she was right; boy, was she right about a great many things, some that he refused to believe.

"Let's eat before our dinner gets cold." She looked back down to her plate, stirred the beans around into the gravy, and dragged the tines of her fork screechingly across her plate as she did so before nibbling halfheartedly. He cut into a sinewy chop with his steak knife and chewed, every chew ringing out loudly into the silence.

"Mrs. Wright dropped off some flowers today for us—more African violets. I put them on the windowsill. Sweet old lady, don't you think?"

"Uh huh." He looked up at the kitchen windowsill. Indeed, a pot of primly arranged African violets called for attention from the kitchen windowsill. He sipped his root beer, licking the excess froth from his lips.

"She comes by often, you know, for tea and whatnot."

"That's very nice of her."

"I think it's because her own kids all left the nest." A mouthful of mashed potatoes.

"That would make sense." Another mouthful of pork.

"And I think because I'm alone so often."

He rolled his eyes. "Yes, well, you know, it could all be ... " He thought better about finishing his sentence.

She picked up on this thread he had left her. "Could be what, Jim? Could be what? Over before you know it, all over and it's back to normal and you're back teaching at Ashton and I'm typing in the office and maybe we can take over the furniture store later? Have a couple kids, grow old and all those boring things a married couple do together?"

"Sorry," he said with a sigh, and ran his hand through his hair. He felt awful and stupid about leading the conversation in this direction, as if it wouldn't have gone this way later anyway as it had so often in the past. "I'm sorry. Let's ... just eat, then."

"You know, it wouldn't have been so bad if you didn't take your damn friend John's advice."

"John who? Barrett?"

"Yeah, him, John Barrett. It's one thing to sign up. You could have stayed with the Camerons, for crying out loud, then you'd be training nearby and you could see me more often. You could've switched to the

2nd Battalion and had a job training other officers who volunteered for overseas service. You would still be involved, and would have an important job. Instead, you have to go carouse with your old buddy and jump ship to another regiment all the way in goddamned Toronto!" Her voice began steady, wavered in the middle, and broke into crying by the end. "You went away before they even stationed you anywhere else! You left me then because you wanted to, not because you had to, Jim!"

"Damn it Marianne, goddamn it, I get my embarkation leave and it may be my last weekend here and you drag out this fucking argument yet again!" He was up and pacing throughout the kitchen, gesturing with his hands. "Look—it really doesn't matter what happened and why anymore. What matters is that I'm here. And please, for God's sake, please don't make me feel I wasted this leave pass on you when I could maybe have seen my parents instead, if you're going to be this way."

"Maybe you should have." She too was standing now, arms folded in a protective, combative stance.

"You know, I do what I can to wrangle these extra leaves. I've tutored Colonel Brophy's son, I've traded all my liquor rations with others for leaves, used what connections I have."

"That doesn't sound too difficult, you know." She circled about the table, pausing to continue. "You hardly drink much as it is."

"Well, you know Marianne, there isn't much to do after hours on some of these postings, a stiff drink now and again is just what the doctor ordered, do you hear me?"

"It's a pretty small sacrifice."

"Yeah, well, whatever works to bring me to you." For dramatic emphasis, he made his way into the cramped front hall and grabbed his wedge cap and his duffel bag. "I could leave, if that's what you'd prefer. And go where I'm welcome. I'll take the first train to Montreal, have myself a gay old time, spend my leave enjoying myself, for Christ's sake!"

"This isn't ..." she began, then stopped herself, averting her eyes.

"Isn't what?" he snapped back as he made it to the hat rack, looking behind his shoulder for emphasis.

"This isn't all because you've had doubts about marrying me?"

"Come again?" A look of bafflement. "Pardon?"

"This isn't ... I mean, all of your wanting to quit your job and walk out on me and prove yourself at some epic venture, all this isn't because you've had your doubts about me, is it? Or doubts about tying yourself down and settling and raising a family when you felt you had accomplished nothing of your own merit yet? Because you felt that you'd wasted a lot of time up till now? That you had yet to grow up yourself? That you felt upstaged by your younger brother when he joined the air force? That me and us and our plans together just weren't good enough for you?"

"Why in hell would you think that? What on earth would any of that have to do with this? And why do you think that I think these things?" He fumbled a moment for extra words. "This—this decision of mine—this call of duty as it were, is just that—a call of duty. I feel it incumbent upon me to do something for my country. We are at war, Marianne. Wars don't just fight themselves, you know. And they don't go away until you fight them, and until you win them."

"I think that you're just fighting yourself, Jim. And I am the one being left out in the cold."

"Whatever you say," he mumbled into his hand.

"Well, I think that all of that certainly does play a role, anyway."

"I already told you why I joined."

She looked at him from the entrance to the kitchen, leaning against the doorway in moody resignation. She turned her head slightly and the hall light caught a flash of tear streaks running down her cheeks. He stood in the doorway, poised to leave, cap under arm and bag clasped in hand, riding out this charged moment. Then he looked down and was greeted by black socked feet, and he felt ridiculous, his polished patent leather shoes parked several feet away on a mat beside her two-toned Mary Janes. He smiled foolishly. She looked at him and he surrendered to her watery gaze, her sad, longing watery gaze.

"I'm sorry," he said sheepishly, and he felt the water welling in his own eyes, all defences down, tenseness subsiding, and he put the bag down and the hat upon the rack, and he stepped toward her, and she lifted her head, and her head flashed tearshine in the light again in an angle of sadness, a glinting of bodies in space drifting slowly apart.

"I'm sorry," he uttered again, pulling her close, and she surrendered to his arms, a sad surrender, and she placed his arms around his waist and rested her head upon his shoulder, and they held this position for awhile, rocking gently, uncertain of who was the prime mover, a pendular equilibrium marking time and riding out the waves of uncertainty.

"Should we finish our meal?" he asked softly into her ear.

"I'm not hungry anymore."

"Neither am I. Shall we go upstairs?"

"I'm not feeling that either."

"Well goddamn it Marianne, make up your bloody mind what you want to do."

A stinging slap across the face, and an expression of outrage on her face. He rubbed his hand over his enflamed, burning cheek. "Ouch! For the love of God, what was that for?"

"You watch your mouth around me. You're swearing at me like you would with your soldier buddies. Don't 'goddamn' this and 'bloody' that and 'fucking this' with me."

"Sorry."

"You know, I'm not some prude, and I'm not a shrew, but I feel that you could talk to me a little better than you would your comrades in the officers' mess."

"Sorry." He stood longer in front of the door, and she stood looking at him, eyes burning, and they both glared and glowered until the embers of their eyes cooled in the thoughtful silence, blood pressure subsiding, reason reasserting itself heartbeat by slowing heartbeat. "I'm so sorry."

"Me, too."

"So sorry," he blubbered as he dissolved into tears, against the wall by the door, sliding down to the floor, sobbing into his hands, his knees curled up, and Marianne went to him and enveloped him in a hug, whispering into his ears, "It's okay, baby, it's okay, cry if you have to, go ahead and cry," all the while crying herself, rocking him, and he rocking her, the two of them rocking and swaying like a pendulum ticking away the last of their time together.

XXII

Drunk on a hill at the outskirts of the village, among the vineyards and the copses of trees and the hills; standing beside an ancient church, overlooking the town and its spires and the brownstone medieval walls encapsulating the old town centre, wandering walls jutting into a promontory here, indenting there, baring their crenellated teeth at ancient enemies; and looking at the clusters of pup tents in surrounding fields, the parked lines of vehicles, the massed and concentrated assembly of force. His flask and canteen are now empty. He has no idea how long he has been out here, he has been in a blur, neither here nor there, really, avoiding company, especially his own. A gaggle of British truck drivers brew up tea in a bucket in a vineyard with a gasoline fire and offer him some, and they make cursory conversation with him" "'Ello Canada! Want a spot of tea, sir? We don't 'ave scones, you'll 'ave to make do with only tea, it's teatime here at the front you see, sure, thank you, not a bad brew at all considering."

Soldiers come and go in their small bands. Flashes in the nearby woods; guns crump from their positions, hurling shells here and there toward the German lines. He takes his tea in a tin cup they've offered him and sits on an edge of the vineyard wall, made of loosely fit stone laid down and replaced over the ages, mottled with lichens, the aged liver spots of stones. Mosquitoes buzz about him, and one buzzes him in the ear with its high-pitched whine, and he swats absently at it before it flies off and tries its luck with one of the truckers. Over yonder the drivers sit cross-legged on the ground by a high wall entangled with withering sunbeaten ivy, and they smoke cigarettes and chatter and drink their tea, filmy as it is with a touch of oil, and the wind changes direction and the smoke blows into Jim's eyes and they burn and sting.

"Goddamnit!" he grunts, choking, and he slides a little further down the wall. A mosquito follows him to smokeless sanctuary and he is pestered about the ears again.

"Sorry, sir! Bloody wind is Jerry's Fifth Column!" shouts one of the four drivers with good cheer and in a Cockney accent, a rough-cut man with a sunburned face and a deep scar in his cheek. The others laugh.

"You enjoyin' your-r-r tea, sir?" another asks, a smaller, gaunt and wiry man with a brown moustache, who with his thick brogue and upward-turned inflections proves to be Scottish, likely from Glasgow.

"Yes, thank you," he answers loudly with a forced smile. "Very much so."

"You wan' in a round o' craps, sir? We're playin' for fags."

"No thank you, I'll just drink my tea here, okay?"

"R-r-right, sir!" And with that they deal out cards and dice, rolling the dice in a frying pan procured from their truck parked nearby. He sits in a silence broken by the clattery dice rolls and the shouts and laughter of the drivers. After awhile, he stands up and surveys the scene about him, tin cup in hand. He looks into the sky. Clouds conspire against the last of the late summer sun in the sky above, and they fill up with the autumn rain that that will start and build to a torrential crescendo, turning the fields into muck, swelling the dry, trickling riverbeds to varicose versions of their summer selves, creating further obstacles to an already grinding advance, as what happened the previous autumn to the long-suffering 1st Division and 1st Canadian Armoured Brigade, as happened for a few days while he held the church, a preliminary taste of the autumn rains. The rains will come and churn the fields and gulleys into cold porridge. Cold porridge, he thinks, like a bowl of soggy-sweet Red River for breakfast on a prairie farm. Red river, he continues, pensively turning the words in the hand of his mind, examining them, musing on them. A horrible metaphor comes to him. Yes, red river indeed. The rivers will run red when we cross them. Like at the Melfa. And the Foglia. The near-parched riverbeds fed and made torrential with the lifeblood of youth.

The air cools a little, just a little, as a cold front moves in and tangles with the warm, nature locked in its eternal struggle with no thought toward the man-made one that litters the ground below and poisons the air around and above. A casual breeze, a slight change in pressure, a twitch of planetary muscle more powerful than all of man's engines of war put together. Still, he takes in this scene, this pastoral painting of rural northern Italy, this postcard intruded upon by military men and vehicles. However, even the men and the vehicles add something, are part of it: as little is happening, the soldiers are just part of the scene around him. Surface details, ephemeral details in a world of great and subtle changes millions of years in the making—the seasons, the erosion of sea against shore, the formation and destruction of mountains, the quick-change costume pageant of human history atop all that and aware of little of it, like microbes on the skin of a great animal, living out their lives and purposes with little perception of the nature of their environment. Here and there, the stone walls separating the fields and orchards, the stone and stucco and cinderblock walls of houses, and the wooden slats of barns and toolsheds are pitted with bullet holes or broken by shells; but there is a strange, still beauty in that, too. Below the hill, in the valley, the village of San Giovanni, the centuries mixed together in mortar and stone and wood, still standing after centuries, changing hands like the moving of seasons—Romans, Byzantines, Malatestas, Venetians, Austrians, French, Germans, Anglos. Pitted in the walls of many such towns are chiselled experience, architectural memories, the seismic buckling and volcanic change of the human landscape.

My, Jim thinks after his wordless survey of the world about him. A moment. No one is trying to kill you right now. Your wife just left you but you are still standing. Tottering, but standing. And your head is beginning to hurt, because you are drunk now. The sun is still shining—take it in. If I were commissioned as a war artist, I'd paint one of those houses with holes in it. I'd call it *The Endurance of Everyday Life.* That sounds like an artist's title for something, like something Arthur

Lismer would paint, I imagine. He recalls a detail from last night's overview of the battle plan, that the Germans may use the castle on the outskirts of Coriano during the upcoming attack as a firing position or an observation post, a castle still malattestant to human conflict. Fulfilling its martial purposes centuries again after it was used for such purposes. He takes a deep breath: invigoration.

He stares ahead and around him and lets the scene envelop him within its frame of escape, letting his eyes paint his mind with what he sees before him. Supply trucks rumble behind him. A shell sizzles overhead forward through the sky, but he does not really care. It's not aimed at me. It's aimed beyond this scene, beyond the scope of his eyes. In the distance, a plumed row of smoky puffs, followed moments later by the succession of reports like the rolling of distant thunder. The sun cuts through parts in the gathering clouds with shafts of light that suggest to him, optimism. So what if it's going to rain. The sun will still shine. So what if there's a war on. There's no war without peace to compare it to. And peace will return. And the sooner you wake up, the sooner you clear your bloody head and take your charge and lead, the sooner that peace will return. There is a time for everything, war and peace. In the meantime, take in beauty where and when you can find it. Like the smashed bits of stained glass in the church, beautiful in a broken way, teasing the eyes, the mind sketching what it sees. The smell of olive oil, suggesting comfort, home-cooked meals, a grateful family serving up what little they have to someone they feel is a liberator, who acknowledges the hardship. Or the sun-gilded surface of the Adriatic, the miles of beaches of fine sand, broken down over millions of years. Sea at dawn, lapping molten at the beach. But don't swim lest you lose your legs and your balls to an unfound mine! *Achtung! Minen! Attenzione! Minatos!* Danger! Mines! proclaim the signs, or yell frantic seaside dwellers when they see someone absently milling about in such a situation. But you can still look at the beach and at the sun rising from the sea, and that is good enough.

A motorcycle snarls up behind him and stops. Fuck. Orders, I'm sure.

"Captain McFarlane?" asks a voice from behind.

"Yes?" Jim answers vacantly as he is propelled back into the world of action and decision.

"Lieutenant Colonel Hobson wants to see you at Battalion HQ." Jim turns around to see a young lance corporal, a despatch rider sitting on his motorbike.

"Yes. Thank you, Lance Corporal," Jim says as he collects himself with a smile. "I don't suppose you can give me a lift there, could you?" His mouth is dry and an awful flavour of previously drunken whiskey wells up from deep within, the beginning of a painful purging, a late afternoon hangover.

"I can, sir. Hop on."

"Hold on a moment." He walks over to the drivers and hands the wiry Scotsman the tin cup they have leant him. "Thanks for the tea, boys," he says. "I must be off."

"No problem, sir, take care sir!" With a collective salute, they go back to their game.

Jim turns to the rider and says, "Let's be off."

"Yes, sir." Jim hops onto the bike behind the lance corporal and clasps his arms to the younger man's waist. The lance corporal spins the bike around and it roars up the rutted road from which it came. They bounce over a hilltop and veer around a tight corner. It's exciting, liberating, fun, though his guts slosh a little and he has to choke back a light wave of nausea. In the distance, between trees and houses, Jim sees a convoy of trucks, either Canadian or British, pulling artillery pieces. A bearded, incensed-looking billy goat bleats at them from the upper branches of an unattended olive tree in an abandoned grove. They pass a whiskered and shoeless and muttering old woman with a deeply wrinkled face, skin hanging like waddles off her chin, pushing a handcart full of broken sewing machines, and she yells something at them in Italian as they roar by, and Jim looks back and sees her go back to her palsied muttering. They swerve to avoid a family of white farm geese waddling on the road; the mother, too, cranes her arched neck and hisses at them as they pass. They are overcome by the rotten, gassy stench of decay as they whisk by the bloated, flyblown carcass of an ox lying just off the road in the weeds of a cratered field. Perhaps five minutes after the ride commenced, the lance corporal slows down, putt-putting through the winding streets of San Giovanni, up to the mustard-yellow stone house with red-shuttered box windows that serves as the battalion headquarters. Beside, on the grass, are parked several jeeps and Colonel Hobson's tracked carrier, all under camouflaged netting and a canopy of poplar and oak trees.

"Thank you for the ride. You ought to race these things for a living when all is said and done!"

"There's no better practice than being shot at, sir. See you later!" They salute one another and the rider races off to another destination, further behind the lines. Hope he didn't realize I'm drunk. Oh boy, I'm drunk and I'm about to be addressed by the colonel, oh damn you idiot your wife left you and you're about to get an earful of winnowing words from Colonel Hobson for something, you're getting a reprimand I'm sure of it wandering off like that in a daze ... Stuck to the door is a wooden sign plate with Bn HQ, 1st Irish, stencilled on it. A sentry stands alert outside at the doorway, rifle at the ready. They nod at one another as Jim enters the house, heart thudding, feeling suddenly six years old and glumly awaiting a spanking from his father for harassing his mother, legs crossed Indian-style on the rug in the upstairs hall, driving a toy locomotive back and forth in repetitive, listless arcs, as his mother whispers to his father downstairs at the front door as he comes in from work, bringing into the house with him a frosty breath of winter air that adds to the foreboding—

"Uh huh, okay, I'll go talk to him." That calm voice, and then the tramping steps and extending shadow up the stairs, the weight of inevitability, pangs of fear ranging up from his behind in bodily expectance of being hit, an antsy tightening of scrotum and loosening of bowels ... Inside the headquarters is a bustle of activity. The intelligence officer, Lieutenant McGann, is marking features on a map spread out on the kitchen table, corresponding the map to the features recorded in a group of black and white aerial reconnaissance photos. A couple of clerks type orders and reports. The colonel's radio set, a large bulky monstrosity of wires and hoses and dials, chatters staticky transmissions from all over the Eighth Army's front. A signaller, a corporal he does not recognize, turns a knob and there is an accompanying screech, as though he picked up the signal of a banshee foretelling and announcing on its supernal frequency the deaths of distant soldiers. The sound makes Jim wince. Jesus Christ, those bloody radios and their awful racket.

"Is Colonel Hobson around?" he asks. McGann looks up from his task. "He's up at Brigade, should be back any time." McGann has dark, almost black hair, a pencil-thin moustache, and intense brown eyes that together make him look older than his twenty-odd years. "There's tea ready if you want some."

If I want some. If I need some, you mean, if only to mask the stench of alcohol. "Sounds great." He helps himself to a cup from a pot on the kitchen stove, feeling nervous, unable to sit down, feeling he has to urinate and urinate desperately; out the back door he goes and into the enclosed backyard canopied with willow trees, to the outhouse against the stone wall veined and fringed with wisteria at the very back of the yard, next to an outdoor stone oven for summer cooking. He steps inside and realizes he has to relieve himself in every way, and he feels a sudden nervous buildup, an uncomfortable stewing, brewing pressure in his bowels, an urgent weight on his rectum; and he bumbles around in the dusty reeking dark, a sweetish meaty stench of shit and a heavy yellow ammoniac rot of old piss hanging in the air, and he yanks at his pants, desperately pulling them to his ankles, and he sits on the rough and grainy wooden bench, cheeks bracketed by the round wooden hole. He releases the pressure he has accumulated, and it empties in a sputtery, wet, gaseous outgoing tide, and he exhales along with it in profound relief, face dewed in sweat. A moist, bacterial reek of shit follows, rising upward from the bucket below, swampy, and he pisses all over the stinking mess he has made, a torrential tide of urine like rainwater through an overworked eavestrough, relief continuing as he empties his bladder of whiskey and tea and anxiety. Hoo Hoo! he thinks, like the horn of a tugboat, like Steamboat Willie, saluting the late afternoon. At least no one tried shelling me while I did this, as has been experienced by so many others, squatting over hastily assembled bench latrines in the midst of a barrage ... He wipes the muck from his behind with tissues from his pocket from his pants heaped at his ankles, and drops them into the stinking, pestilential abyss one by one. His hands shake as he stands, and a wave of nausea overtakes him, a woozy lurching of his stomach, Steamboat Willie is caught in an ocean swell; and he turns around, overcome by revulsion, by fear, by drink, and seasick with this combined experience, he buttresses himself against the bench with his hands, pants still twisted around his ankles, and he sees outlined in darkness the swampy mess below, a shine of sunlight through the hole in the door trapped and reflected in urine, a hanging haze of attendant flies; and he retches and he belches and he throws up, sour whiskey and tea and coffee and mashed sandwich and soup and bacon and eggs and bile. One more gurgly belch and it is over—the world stops turning, the ocean swells subside, and Steamboat Willie once again steams upon a sea of calm, ready to face the great liners and tankers all round in the harbour peering down at him from mighty stacks, haughty superstructures and leering bows, Hoo Hoo!

He wipes his mouth and pulls up his pants and does up his belt, and he dumps his tea into the hole, one final act, a coup de grace, and he emerges from the outhouse into the yard on rubbery legs, and he makes his way along the stone path set in tall grass to the well around which the yard is centred. Gotta rinse, he thinks, gotta rinse, I taste and smell like puke. He is about to hoist up a bucket of water when a skinny young private in a borsalino hat tells him, "Don't drink that water, sir. The owner dropped a couple dead chickens, and Lord knows what else, in there to poison it on the way out." Jim peers down the well and sees the dirty white fluff of chicken feathers, hanging just under the water's surface. A few stray ones, along with a used wad of tissue dropped in by a soldier, lily the surface. There is a damp whiff of spoiled meat. Jesus Christ. What a fucking waste. The private snickers and imparts, "Don't worry. He was found hanging from a tree in the neighbouring orchard. Partisans got 'im before we got here. Serves that bastard right, eh, Captain?" Yeah, serves them right. C'mon, Canada! Lick 'Em Over There!

"I suppose." Jim steps away from the well and enters the house again. All thoughts of poisoned water and a poisoned world exit his mind as he makes his way back through the house, back to the dining room and kitchen, to his appointment with the colonel; back to the clickety clatter of typewriters and staticky radio chatter of Battalion HQ, cigarette in hand, in mouth, masking the smells of alcohol and vomit and fear.

The dry, rattling engine of a jeep, a perfunctory skid of tires. Moving the locomotive back and forth in listless arcs. Waiting, waiting. Into the kitchen comes Lieutenant Colonel Hobson, face firm, the wheels of his mind turning with plans and worries.

"McFarlane, hello," he says upon his brisk entrance, out of the side of his mouth, taking off his cobeen and stowing it smartly underarm, the pom-pom bobbing with each step, "Come along with me, please."

"Yes, sir." They walk through the dining room with its grandfather clock, its long mahogany table marred with a spike-tipped bayonet protruding upward from it, clerks typing away in mahogany chairs, one of the chairs with a broken back, a smashed china cabinet and shards of broken chinaware in the corner, and through the dining room, gutted and graffittied with German insults and expletives, into a hall and through a door into what serves as the colonel's office, his bedroom with a four-poster bed and a small writing desk. The colonel shuts the door.

"Sit down, please."

"Yes, sir." Jim takes a seat in a wooden chair in front of Colonel Hobson's desk, pulled out to face the chair in which Jim sits. He butts his cigarette into a metal ashtray on the bureau.

"Do you have any idea why I called you here, Jim?"

A light and tickly queasiness in the pit of his stomach. "I might, sir."

"Do you know what time it is?"

"Yes, sir." A quick look at his watch. "It is 1705 hours."

"You missed your company inspection. You have ten new guys in your company, and you missed your company inspection. In turn, and more importantly, you missed the battalion inspection and parade afterward. I had to send a goddamn despatch rider to find you, as the last you were seen you were wandering through the streets. You didn't tell anyone where you were going. That is just unacceptable, do you understand?" His voice is curt and sharp and stabs Jim right in the conscience.

"Yes, sir." Waves of shame.

Hobson pulls out his pouch of tobacco, and when he unfolds it open, it releases a rich, moist, sweet aroma of cherry-tinged tobacco. He stuffs an earthy plug of it into his pipe, lights it, and continues: "Lieutenant Doyle covered for you. Gordon was livid, absolutely livid about the whole thing, broke his swagger stick over his knee and tossed the pieces into the street. The Italian street cleaner picked them up right after him on his rounds, to much laughter, and not a little embarrassment, from the spectators."

At the suggestion of this image, Jim suppresses with all his might a smirk. "I'm sorry, sir."

"Embarrassing is what this is. Downright unacceptable is what this is. I promoted you to captain last spring, now what the hell is the matter with you?" He puffs angrily on his pipe, the glowing coal lighting up an angry, intense orange at each drawing of his breath. "What on earth made you miss this parade? It was clearly outlined in the morning orders in the mess according to Gordon, for Christ's sake. What do you have to say for yourself? Hmm?" Before Jim can answer, Hobson picks up on his rant, standing up and pacing about, gesturing with his pipe. "Drill, parades, inspections, these prepare everyone for the real thing. If you can't show up for a dress rehearsal, then are you fit to go in when it's real? Are you? You know what I could do to you? I can revoke your commission, bust you back down to the ranks. How about becoming an infantry private? Or I can have you transferred to some lighter duty, something less important. How would that be for your pride?" He shoots a steely glance at Jim for emphasis and says, slowly and thoughtfully, revealing each syllable with slow deliberation, "Or, I can have you court-martialled. How about breaking rocks in a quarry? Would military prison suit you?" He pauses and stands behind his chair, holding the wooden back with his hands. He leans in a little: "Before I dispense any judgements, I want to hear what excuse you possibly have for this dereliction of duty. This had better be good."

Jim finds himself tongue-tied for a moment. He exhales slowly, and says simply and honestly, "Sir, I'm sorry. Nothing can excuse what I did. It was conduct unbefitting an officer, I know."

"Mm hmm, on with it." Hobson is now back in his chair, eyeing Jim angrily, yet with a certain patience and concern, a willingness to hear the other side of the story.

Jim runs his fingers through his hair. He feels that he is in the headmaster's office, about to be strapped or expelled from a prestigious boarding school for which his parents saved up for years to send him. "Sir, I'm sorry, when I went to get mail today I got a letter from my wife. She's leaving me." He throws his hands into the air and shrugs at the injustice, or the justice, of it all. "I'm sorry ... When I read that I kind of left the planet ... I just lost all track of time, sir, found myself up by the church on the hill outside of town. That's where the despatch rider found me on his bike, having tea with some British truck drivers."

"I'm sorry to hear that. But it's hardly a first around here. Father Maitland has his hands full talking with men whose wives and girlfriends flew the coop. That does not excuse your missing two inspections and a parade."

"No sir, it doesn't." Jim looks Colonel Hobson in the eye to demonstrate a manly willingness to confess and face the consequences. "It doesn't, I know. I submit to whatever punishment you feel fit to give me." Stand me in front of a wall and shoot me without ceremony for all I care.

"It's just not like you to do something like this. I promoted you for God's sake. I promoted you and put you in as 2IC of Able. We took a hell of a shaking in the spring, and I promoted you because I thought you could handle company command, and I didn't have to look outside for some greenhorn. And until this moment, I feel that you've done a fine job. These last weeks haven't been easy, but this is what we do. This is our job. It is a very public duty. And nothing from your private life can get in the way of it."

"Yes, sir." But sir, he thinks, it is my private life that got me into this in the first place.

"I ought to have you busted down or court-martialled. I really ought to. To have such concerns springing up the eve before battle creates undue stress when I have more than enough concerns to keep me occupied, have you considered that?"

"Yes, I can imagine, sir."

"What's private is private, and it has to remain thus. You are commissioned to be an officer, and as such, your job is to follow orders given to you by your superiors, and to give orders to those under you, so that together we can win this war. That means that you must never disregard or disobey any order. Your private life cannot get in the way of your commission, do you hear me?"

"Yes, Colonel."

"I am sending an understrength battalion into action again after only two days' rest. You're lucky in that regard; I can't afford to sack you right now."

"Thank you, sir."

"The new captain we've picked up, Riley, is too green to take a rifle company into action yet I think, I'm putting him in charge of Support for now to learn the ropes. Goldberg won't be fit to return for some time yet, so I have little choice but to let you stay right where you are. You will keep your appointment, as your field record has been exemplary up to this point. You will, however, have all leave revoked for two months. And you will have a black mark on your file, and this will seriously impinge on any future considerations for promotion. Am I understood?"

Relief washes over him. "Yes, I understand you, Colonel. Thank you for your leniency." Embarrassed, head aching, he resumes: "I guarantee that this will not happen again, and I am ashamed to have done it ... and I will do my best to bring out the honour of myself and this regiment from this point forward, sir."

"You are dismissed. Now get out of my face."

"Yes, sir." He stands at attention, salutes, and leaves the office.

XXIII

It is announced by Colonel Hobson that for the final dinner before marching into battle, the battalion officers will be hosting the officers of the nearby-stationed British London Irish Rifles at the mess, and to this end men arrive and file into the hotel dining room, extra chairs, tables and benches having been dragged in; some even dine in the small lobby at the low table, in the winged chairs and on the sofa. The officers eat together and share stories and laughter and offer words of encouragement to one another, and after dinner, after plates and mess tins have been cleared away, the pipe majors of both regiments stand and play their pipes, blowing into the pipe-stems, cheeks red and puffing, elbows pumping the baggy bellows, skirling boldly airs and ballads to much hearty and merry approval.

Riley and Jim and a Captain Gibson from the London Irish, a droll, mustachioed young man with lively green eyes and a habit of hitting the table with his hands to punctuate every point, listen to the music and clap along, carried away for the moment by the moment's escape. Jim sips just enough wine to get rid of his mounting headache and clarify his dull and hungover mind for a time.

He looks at Riley, tapping his foot, and at Gibson, tapping his hand; and he remains in the moment, swaying his body and tapping his hand to the beat until the dinner is adjourned, until it is time to go, to quit waiting, to go back into the fray, back across the Stygian Conca into the land of the dead beyond, helped along by an extra tot of rum on the colonel: "Gentlemen, bottoms up! You are dismissed!"

At this, the officers promptly exit the mess and make their way through the streets in the evening darkness to their companies now assembling in a field.

"Hello, sir," Witchewski says to Jim at his arrival. Able Company stands milling about in the field, kitted up in helmets and battle-dress and webbing and boots, smoking and kidding and ribbing one another. Witchewski looks at Jim, his usually hard eyes sparkling with relief and unalloyed joy. "It's good to see you again sir, whatever the hell happened to you today."

"I'll tell you about it later sometime," assures Jim, "But not now." Not now indeed.

"Shall I call roll?"

"Indeed, whenever you're ready."

"I'm ready." Witchewski steps up in front of the company gaggled about and barks: "Able Company, by platoons, in three ranks, fall—IN!" The soldiers fall into their ranks and stamp their right feet in unison and stand rigid.

"Calling roll." He looks at a clipboard he is carrying and calls out the names one by one, answered with an exclamatory "Here!" for all. "At ease! Stand easy, relax!" At this, the soldiers physically relax, standing comfortably with their legs far apart. "All right, we're moving! We'll be going into battle again. You all know your parts to play, and you will be briefed once again by your platoon commanders before we move into the staging area. Expect anything and everything. When we move into the valley, expect bombardments, mines, you name it. When we move through the Sydneys' positions into the town, it's anybody's damn guess. Expect more of the same, plus snipers, machine guns, hand-to-hand combat, ambushes, you name it! Many of you are vets now, you know what to do when the shit hits! If you're new, watch what the old-timers are doing, and do what they do! Let me say this once, and let me say it clearly: WATCH AND LEARN FROM THE MEN AROUND YOU. LISTEN TO THEM. I don't want any goddamn greenhorn mistakes. I don't want anyone blowing themselves and their comrades up with their own grenades. I don't want anyone firing on their own side. And I don't want any goddamn insubordination of any kind. I feel I can trust you, and together we will defeat the enemy, we will carry out our orders. Watch each other's backs, help each other out, do what it is you are supposed to do. And remember, if you run out of bullets and grenades, you can always offer Jerry your rations! *Fior go bas!*"

"*Fior go bas!*" they yell in unison.

"Alright, gentlemen, here is Captain McFarlane." He moves off to the side as Jim steps up to the ranks of men standing in front of him. Ninety-four pairs of eyes are fixed on him in the deepening gloom, ninety-four pairs of eyes of ninety-four men expecting an inspiring address of some kind, at least some kind of assurance that they will not be led into battle by a coward who shirks his parade duties. If he shirks his parade duties, how will he be in combat?

"Good evening, gentlemen," he begins, voice hesitant, uncertain. He feels awkward and ashamed to be addressing his company on this evening; his head aches, it is as though pins are poking into the backs of his eyes, and his mouth is dry, his tongue hardened into a slab of cured ham from all the smoking and drinking these last couple days. He cannot find the right words. He scans from one side to the other, the men looking right back at him, and he feels much the same way as he did in the orchard behind San Mateo days ago, his lieutenants looking up at him awaiting orders, awaiting orders that he'd momentarily forgotten. "Welcome to all the new members of our company. Welcome back to all others. Tonight we go back into action, to take the Coriano Ridge. For four nights we were shelled by their gunners up there; in the early hours tomorrow we will go into that village and silence those guns once and for all. I have faith in all of you that we will meet our objectives. To the reinforcement soldiers among you: follow Warrant Officer Witchewski's advice, and watch your more experienced comrades. Listen to them. Listen to your section and platoon leaders. They have experience that you do not yet have. Keep your heads down and your fists up. By doing so, man by man, section by section, platoon by platoon, company by company, we can once again demonstrate that the Irish are the best damn battalion in this Corps, if not in the whole Eighth Army!"

"Hurrah!"

"Be alert to any dangers, and listen for any commands or changes in orders from myself if I'm near you, or your platoon commanders, or anyone above you. When we get to the forming up point, you are to dig in; many of you were up at San Mateo, you know what to expect. The enemy will likely not spare us his shells. Remember, once we move, the battle is on. Don't take any unnecessary risks. We relieve the Sydneys in their trenches up on the ridge top once they attack, after midnight. We occupy those trenches until we get moving ourselves before dawn. Your platoon commanders will brief you on the particulars if they have not already. I'm terribly sorry, gentlemen, but we're not getting a lift this time—we're on foot. We move in precisely five minutes." Bolstered by his own improvised speech, he reviews the ranks with a sweeping glance to the right, and to the left and right again, a slow, emphatically held gaze; and then after this dramatic pause, dismisses them with a perfunctory, "Able Company, you are hereby dismissed."

"Not bad," says Witchewski from beside him, having approached just as Jim was concluding. "For someone who reeks like old whiskey."

"Thank you, Witchewski."

"You're welcome." Witchewski turns to the assembled men and shouts, "Get ready to move, check your equipment one last time, you have one minute to make sure you have what you need!" The platoon commanders emerge from off to the side, where they have been waiting, and call out, "No. 7 Platoon, with me over here!" "8 Platoon, with me!" "No. 9 Platoon, follow me!"

Each assembled with his platoon and briefed by his commander, the platoons assemble into a full company once again and are marshalled into place with the rest of the battalion. From near the head of the column of men standing single file in the charged and awaiting night, Lieutenant Colonel Hobson shouts: "Battalion, by the left, quick ... MARCH!"

XXIV

"Left ... Left ... Left, Right, Left!"

And they march into the night, kitted, spades clanking against packs, rifles slung over shoulders, shallow helmets strapped to chins and sliding askew, left right left right down the road, the stomping boots of soldiers kicking up dust as white the puttees that cover them. Whump, whump, whump, whump, whump, the rhythmic march of hundreds of feet in single file compacting the dirt of the road, a spectacle to all who witness it, men arrayed into fighting formation, a concentration of will passed down rank to rank, unit to unit; a regimented, organized force of human nature, a concentrated column of will.

They pass scenes of desolation chalked into the night. Dead cows, lying bloated in their fields. A farmer, wearing a black fedora and with a weed in his mouth, waves at the passing troops by the roadside, keen to see what is the nature of the commotion passing his house. He has no shoes on. Jim waves back. The farmer's house has no roof. Overhead, the buzzing propeller drone of bombers. Alongside, on the road, the grumbling, trundling column of the battalion's support troops, carriers and trucks and jeeps towing or laden with heavy support weapons, ammunition, water, food, equipment, medical supplies. And they sing:

"If you want to find the sergeant,
I know where he is, I know where he is, I know where he is.
If you want to find the sergeant, I know where he is,

He's hangin' on the old barbed wire,
I've seen him, I've seen him, he's hangin' on the ol' barbed wire,
I've seen him, I've seen him, he's hangin' on the ol' barbed wire!"

Through the Toronto streets they marched, from the horse stables and field at the Canadian National Exhibition out into the streets, sporrans flapping, a breeze up under the orange and black pleats of their kilts, oh my. The novice piper piped out the laboured, piercing strains of "Garryowen," and people lined the sidewalks: men, women, children in their Sunday best, in hats and caps and long coats, in dresses and suits and sweaters and bloomers, the children in knickers and breeches—

"Left, right, left, right, left, right, left!"

Across the parade square at Borden they marched in celebration of an eagerly awaited change in command, the possibility that they would move out finally, and under cover of night and without any senior officer supervising them, they sang an ode to an outgoing and unloved commander:

"I am the very model of anti-productivity,
For malingering avoidance I have quite a great proclivity.
For parade ground pomp and orders shrill there is no other officer,
I like to snooze and sip and tipple in this little office, sir.

Regarding matters martial I am really uninformative,
And this is something at my rank that not at all is normative.
Still, I'm very well-acquainted with matters real and corporeal:
There's a rumour that I buggered a very young lance corporal.

There's a rumour that he buggered a very young lance corporal
There's a rumour that he buggered a very young lance corporal
There's a rumour that he buggered a very young lance corporal … "

Through the empty streets of a town in Quebec on a recruiting march, faces staring out sullenly, voices calling out, "*Maudits anglais!*"

The pool hall scuffles between soldier and lumberjack, Englishman and Habitant.

And on to the streets of Halifax, the harbour teeming with a hundred ships: freighters and tankers with stack-topped white superstructures perched amidships, framed by masts at either end of the raised bows and sterns; and destroyers and corvettes weaving between them, preparing to lead them out into the Atlantic, to be haunted by unseen submarines like dark and dangerous thoughts lurking in the subconscious. And they boarded the troopship, a great liner stripped of its finery, sauntering up the gangplanks and cheering and waving, hundreds of men waving from the decks, caps in hand, waving from the promenades, from every bollard and davit and vent and porthole and window, waving to the cheering crowd; and they left in a paper flurry of ticker tape out into the storm-whipped spray of the North Atlantic, iron grey skies leering down on iron grey seas, where ticker tape turned to blowing swirls of snow, and subconscious fears to submarine threats, until they made landfall in England, and the snow turned back to ticker tape, the wind moaning between the ice-encrusted wires to cheering crowds again. And they marched—

" Left ... Left ... Left, Right, Left!"

Through winding lanes along ivied stone walls, layers of green upon green, moist velvety verdure exhaling mist; along rows of old houses and cottages, the wooden signs of pubs hanging overhead with homey, inviting names: The Fox and Pheasant, The Old Spotted Dog, The Huntsman's Hearth. And they marched along country roads, alongside the undulating patchwork of farmers' fields, and over little stone bridges over burbling creaks, while farmers in brown suits and grey caps and green Wellington boots up to the knees waved at them from their fields, from the seats of high tractors, from haystacked wagons pulled by teams of mighty Clydesdale horses—nostrils snorting mist, heads bobbing, bells jingling, mighty knobby-kneed legs bent at the ankles and condensing into a chorus of clopping hooves, tails sweeping haughtily from side to side as they deposited cairns of steamy, grassy round turds in their wake.

And they marched aboard ships once again, out into the sea, a great armed convoy, troopships and transports and warships, through the Straits of Gibraltar, into the Mediterranean, the coast of Africa off to starboard, fabled Deepest Darkest Africa; they crowded the rail and looked at the ghostly sliver of land between sea and sky rising into a greyish hill here and there, reaching upward from one abyss into another; and they steamed on in the knowledge that they would arrive in some zone of contention, perhaps Africa, perhaps Italy, perhaps Greece and the Balkans.

And they disembarked at Naples and marched through the streets, and they marched along country roads choked with tired and bedraggled refugees, the refugees hauling their possessions on foot, or in limbers and wagons pulled by mules or sick, skeletal horses; and they moved day by day, week by week to their first combat posting.

And now marching back along this road, alongside which is strewn ruin and destruction, he feels like he did that first time he marched to the front. As they marched through the shattered ruins of Ortona, marching upward to the front for the first time, their nostrils were greeted to a ripe wet smell of char, the rains having extinguished the last of the fires of the great battle and left in their wake a match-stink of old burning, the scorched and bitter essence of incendiary decay. Along the ghostly streets of the port city, rubble bulldozed aside, were the gutted shells of shops, the tottering façades of blasted townhouses, the chinked and chipped and pitted edifice and shattered basilica of the medieval San Tommaso Cathedral, the city's centerpiece; the broken beams and piles of brick and stone, the advertising signs, the marquees, the morbid little details—a ruined ladies' wear store, wooden mannequins lying heaped in the street like artists' studies for bodies, one of them missing a head, having been heaved out of the display window by an explosion or by the vandalism of soldiers, the store bereft of goods—there were likely men from the 1st Canadian Infantry Division who had fought the battle with trophy brassieres, skirts, dresses, stockings and elegant hats for comic mementoes.

Moving ahead to where war had moved its season, to the front, at night into position, digging in while awaiting the exposure of a flare, the sweep of a machine gun or the crash of artillery and mortars. Observing from his position on the eve of his first patrol, looking out over the sandbags, preparing to step out into the darkness. Distant crackle of machine-gun fire followed by the thud of a mortar, a conversation of weaponry. A staccato sentence of lead, of death, punctuated with an exclamatory explosion. The knife edge, the sharp end, the front.

"Left, Right, Left, Right, Left, Right, Left! Left! Left, Right, Left!"

And now, here and now, marching back into battle under the cloak of the fallen night, he finds himself unable to march of his own free will, bonded to his officers' oaths, beckoned by the voices of General Hoffman, Colonel Hobson, and even Gordon, that fusspot; moving ahead if only to prove his mettle to his fellow officers and men; pushed ahead by the expectations of others and the pride of the regiment; urged onward by a grumble of tanks from behind.

To the side, as they march, he sees Lance Corporal Fitzpatrick lying on the ground clutching his stomach, the blood flowering out from between his fingers; Fitzpatrick looks at him and meets his eye in passing, and nearby are Blake and Schneider and Kelly and Leprenniere and Bly and Big John, Big John clutching his bleeding gut, the dead tank crewman hung slack over his shoulder, for Christ's sake; and all are looking at him with their pale revenant faces as if awaiting him to join their ranks, as if in death they see the future and are seen only by those who will soon join them. What the hell are they doing here, they're dead, they're gone, they stand guard at the gates of eternity, now they're in white robes in the meadows of heaven with Grandma and Grandpa or so you conjure as you cry into your pillow and muse on eternity forever and evering its way into the vortex of itself—there is thunder and his mother is nowhere near, he cannot dash into her bed or slide under a church pew. The images of the dead soldiers, so vivid for a moment, so real, are now gone. Get it together, man! You're an officer! Smarten up, for Christ's sake and straighten up by God you have a job yes you have a job here a commission—

"Battalion—HALT! By the right, break—OFF!" The soldiers break ranks and are marshalled in the ensuing commotion by their company commanders.

"Able Company, dig in!" shouts Jim as the soldiers disperse from the road. They chip away in the darkness at the earth with their spades by the roadside, obscured by trees, hacking, digging, grunting, sweating. Witchewski barks at them, as do all their section leaders, encouraging them, bantering with them, digging along with them, nearly a hundred men in a small glade digging into the earth for what protection it can offer. Here and there, shells fall, mostly in the distance.

His scalp itches. The stress of awaiting action has brought on dandruff. He removes his helmet and scratches the top of his head to the accompaniment of a cathartic sigh. The scratching triggers a snowfall of yellowy white flakes. Too much living, lived too quickly, and another layer of life is shed, now food for microbes. The earth is content with shed hair and skin in the knowledge that after these dainty hors d'oeuvres, these appetizers, will indeed come the main course.

XXV

In the roomy cinderblock barn now serving as his headquarters, he ticks down the minutes till the attack, cigarette by cigarette, the burning fuse of time. Twenty minutes. Ten minutes. Soldiers come and go.

"Tea or coffee, sir?" He looks up to see Cooley.

"Coffee, please. Or tea. Actually I don't care which, whichever you can serve me the quickest."

"Yes, sir." Awaiting his beverage, Jim opens his cylindrical map case and produces his copy of the battle area map and his typewritten orders, now dog-eared and oiled by the nervous thumbing of his fingers. Time to look like an officer again. There is a poke on his shoulder. Jim looks up and sees Cooley hovering over him: "Tea, sir?"

"Please." Cooley hands him a china teacup full of steaming orange pekoe tea.

"Where'd you get a cup like that?"

"The ruins of the adjoining house. There was a perfectly preserved English tea set in there."

"Good work, as always," commends Jim.

Cooley smiles, salutes, and walks away. Jim tries the tea. It is surprisingly good, sugary and tempered with milk presumably bartered for from a local farmer. Real milk, not powdered milk—sometimes behind the lines miracles are worked, particularly by batmen, the de facto miracle workers of the army. Jim lights one last cigarette to go with his tea. He drinks the tea too quickly, and his stomach contracts and curdles. His cigarette, burning in his hand, is suddenly off-putting, and he snuffs it out in his teacup and it hisses with one final protest before dying, a sodden cork-tipped butt floating in a cup of half-drunk tea. God, not again ...

He steps outside for air. A moment later, the attack announces itself suddenly. Seven hundred guns erupt in earth-shattering unison, a fugue of thunder. Stunned, he blocks his ears, falls to his knees. He looks up. The sky is lit by the fireworks of muzzle flashes and the consequent trajectories of hundreds of shells. The fillings in his teeth rattle. He looks above at the streaking shells as they hiss and moan and whistle through the sky, and he looks back down to his watch. It is 2101, one minute past the point of no return. The attack is on.

With the sudden discharge of artillery comes a strange elation: at last, after a week of waiting under fire for his next attack orders, he can finally consummate his fear, get it over and done with, sally forth and seek his prey, take it to the enemy, for a time his nerves no longer frittering away but their tension concentrated into trained soldier's instincts, to be transmuted into action, correct action and reaction, a Newtonian ballet of bodies and bullets. Become your orders, carry them out, make the men instruments to carry them out, and lead bravely by example. Be an officer and all that that entails. The day he received his commission, he burned with pride. Even Marianne looked proud of him. She probably was, then. He cut an impressive figure, holding the signed scroll and wearing his dress uniform with peaked cap, posing in front of the mirror, his image as an officer rhyming back at him in a heroic couplet, compound glory, twice the man.

He absorbs the pounding pyrotechnic display about him. The sky is streaked in trajectories. The earth rumbles underfoot and the horizon flares with countless muzzle flashes that bruise the clouds in their flicker. An overbearing overture of power, the prelude to every major offensive in which he has taken part. There is a pounding in his ears, and he tears two pieces from a Kleenex tissue, wets them with his spit and plugs his ears to what little avail they can offer, the bombardment pounding at his eardrums like a battering ram at the gates of a beleaguered castle, rippling through his bones, shaking his teeth like chinaware, echoing through his head, the shrapnel of noise shearing and snapping the frail filaments bonding his thoughts, reducing the interior of his head to a crashing, jangling catastrophe of noise disrupting all possibility of coherent thought. Here and there, flash by flash, are illumined trees, houses, hills, recoiling guns and men in action, captured in flared snapshots, yellow and orange flicker, red glow, a purple bruise of clouds.

The bombardment underway, Jim realizes that it is time to meet with his fellow officers, and he makes his way to Tactical Headquarters, now situated in a dilapidated, gutted stone farmhouse. An upper corner of the house has been bitten out by a shell, exposing the gaping maw of the attic. Inside, Hobson addresses them in the scanty, wavering half light of an oil lamp, all the company and support platoon commanders, as well as Lieutenant McGann and RSM Albert and other officers and NCOs attached to HQ, and the artillery and heavy mortar officers from Division, some seventeen men in all huddled round a wooden table in the kitchen upon which is spread an operational map. About them is the usual hubbub of busy clerks and signallers.

"Get on with the tea, will you, Olafson?" asks the colonel in a commanding question to his batman.

"Yes, sir."

"Now where were we ... Okay, gentlemen, final orders for this evening. You all know your movements. There is no change in the general plan thus far." The phone rings, a piercing jangle, and a clerk answers it in the next room.

"Sir, it's for you, it's General Hoffman."

"Goddamn it. Alright." He steps away from the table and answers the phone, his free hand blocking his other ear, and he speaks over the muffled thunder of the barrage. "Uh huh, yessir ... Yes, sir, everything is going well ... I contacted Colonel Christie earlier, and all targets have been marked and coded, yes sir ... You too, sir, thank you." With a click he hangs the receiver upon its cradle and reemerges into the dimly lit kitchen, the features of which are suggested in shadowy relief: a hanging pot, a wooden spoon, a large wood-fired oven which Olafson stokes for tea, the flare of the paper and kindling in the oven's mouth briefly lighting the room more, bringing it into a sharper focus flickered with shifting flame shadows until he shuts with a rusty groan the metal oven door.

Hunched or leaning over the table, the men all pore over the map, McGann's map, and Hobson dictates to them their specific movements, their specific times, and McGann briefs them on the various features they are likely to encounter as identified on the map. Tea is served, and they sip out of tin cups and cups found in the nearly bare cupboards of the ravaged house. The positions of mortars and machine guns are outlined, the names for artillery targets and unit objectives are coded by the colonel and the artillery and heavy mortar observers, the areas for supply dumps as arranged by the quartermasters are pointed out. Each company is thus prepared.

An ashtray is heaped with a felled forest of cigarette butts. As the men are consumed in their plotting, they smoke and smoke and smoke, spinning into cinereal being ghostly spirals of smoke like a dead galaxy of burnt-out and exploded suns, particulate matter drifting apart, breaking loose orbits and caught in casual drafts, caustic smoke adrift, a brief, imperfect gnostic universe born of the happenstance of nervous unrest, dissipating and untwisting and displaced by the opening of the door when a runner comes in to announce the arrival of tanks to their jump-off positions.

"Are there any questions?" asks Hobson, his face in the lamplight a flickering orange, half shadow and half light, his moustache a dark line, his eyes scanning through the semi-darkness. There are none. "Then stay around here until it's almost time to move up to the start line to monitor any developments. This meeting is adjourned." The men relax and finish their tea, and some of them begin a poker game to the ambient radio and telephone chatter. Jim joins the game and wordlessly plays awhile, to the coded reports of troop movements repeated and transcribed by the signallers, and to the steady pounding of artillery shuddering the floor and making those reports all too real, winning and losing hand by hand according to the vagaries of fate as dealt and dealing in fate himself when it is his turn to shuffle the deck.

"Alright gentlemen, it's time to move!" Hobson commands, looming over them, having emerged from the shadows of his plotting. "Get back to your units and give them any last briefings you might have. We move up in precisely half an hour. You know your places. You are dismissed!" Captain Van Der Hecke of Dog gathers his cards into a deck and stuffs them back into the package. Everyone gets moving in a bustle. As they're all exiting, Colonel Hobson stops Jim, last, with a hand on his shoulder:

"And Jim—"

"Yes?"

"I'm sorry about what happened between you and your wife. It's a real sonofabitch when these things happen."

"Yessir."

Hobson looks him in the eye and holds his gaze a moment. "Keep it together, McFarlane, this is a big night, I need all my officers in shipshape, you understand?"

"Yessir, I do."

"You are dismissed."

Jim stamps his right foot at attention, salutes, spins on his heel in a right turn and marches out into the night toward his headquarters, stumbling and groping in the dark amid the roar and flicker of the bombardment. He arrives at the open door of the barn from inside of which trickles soft, milky lanternlight, his arrival heralded by the bleating of a goat chained just outside.

Back into the barn where it is somewhat quieter, the walls shuddering, the earth quaking, the lanterns wavering and throwing shadows about every uneven surface: jugs, bales of hay, equipment, bodies, faces. Cavanagh, the signalman now detailed to him to operate the company radio, sits in the straw with his radio set, his headphones on and his hands upon the headphones, pressing them to the cups of his ears, a look of strained thoughtfulness on his face as he listens intently for any transmissions worth noting. Beside him four medical runners await their duties, their stretchers leaning against the wall.

"What do you hear?" Jim asks. The spell is broken. Cavanagh looks up at Jim. "Nothing. Not a damn thing but static, sir," he answers, taking the phones off and placing them upon the bulky set.

"Don't sweat it. We'll hear anything we need to hear from TAC. Just wait out the storm, and we'll be on our not-so-merry way in no time."

"Yes, sir."

A moment later, Staff Sergeant Nichols enters the barn and hollers over the noise, "Any outgoing mail? If you have any letters you want to send before we go, give 'em to me now!" Various men hand him envelopes which he puts into an already half-filled sack he is carrying, and he then turns his attention to Jim with a look of contempt, his mailbag sagging under the weight of letters. "Hey, Captain! How was the parade?"

"Not now, Nichols."

Nichols comes close to him and fixes him in his gaze and says, "Allow me to speak freely."

"Go on, let's hear it."

"I'm not sure why you're leading us tonight. One of the others could be made acting captain tonight and you should sit it out with the rest of the LOBs. You look like you could use some rest. That is just my opinion, sir."

"And you should mind your duties. That is my opinion." Jim tries to change the subject. "Just keep the ammo and food coming, Nichols, and we'll accomplish the mission. Okay?"

Nichols looks him deep in the eye and says, "Yes, sir. Good luck."

"You too." Then, after a moment, he says, "You are dismissed, Staff Sergeant." Nichols' brows furrow deeply and his face reddens with anger for a moment.

"Yes, sir," he grumbles, each word squeezed reluctantly out of lips pressed thin, and turns away. As he does so, he chews out a new reinforcement posted to Jim's HQ section, Private Neidhart, Briggs' replacement, whose No. 38 radio chest pack lies in disarray at his feet, and who is nervously loading and unloading his rifle as the shells crash about outside.

"Goddamnit, Neidhart! Look at that radio of yours! And don't be messing with your cartridge, for Christ's sake! You could let one off in here by accident! Get your shit together!" He approaches Jim again after a moment, after Neidhart's mumbly apologies and fumbly handling of his radio, and hisses, "Captain, don't you notice anything around here?"

Jim forgives Nichols this bit of insubordination: "I said, you are dis*missed,* Nichols."

"Aye, sir. See you in action." He departs in a huff. Jim looks around to certify that none of the others in the barn with him have witnessed his tongue-lashing.

Another look at his watch. The Sydneys should be making their move soon. And soon after, the soldiers of the battalion will occupy their abandoned positions on the reverse slope of the ridge. Three cigarettes later, it is about time. He stands up and addresses the men in the barn.

"It is now time to go. Get yourselves ready! Move!" The men pull themselves upward and move out of the barn into the shrieking maelstrom. Jim leaves last. "Come on, Able Company! Up and at 'em, let's go!" Jim barks above the blast and wail of guns and shells. "Form up in your squads and platoons and follow me up the hill on the double!" Cavanagh is beside him with his radio set now mounted on his back; Cooley is at his other side, rifle slung.

"Move, move, move!" yells Sergeant Stringer raggedly to his platoon dug into a copse of trees, he standing in for Olczyk who has been left in reserve. They leap out of their holes, donning packs and slinging weapons. Therrien's men emerge from theirs on the other side of the path on which Jim stands, and Doyle's emerge from around the barn Jim occupied. Just as they are about to depart they are joined by a Corporal Tillman, who wears a No. 38 radio pack slung over his chest.

"Here I am, sir," he says to Jim with a wink. "Mortar Platoon at your service."

"Nice to see you, Tillman. Stick by me and I'm sure we'll find you some targets before long."

Down the road march Dog Company who jeer them for being late—"Hey there's a war on!" yells a cheeky sergeant, "You guys thinking of joining?" Others whistle as if at attractive women.

Captain Van Der Hecke winks at Jim as he marches by, and Jim nods at him and says, "Have your boys dig us some fine holes up there for us!"

"In your dreams, McFarlane."

"Alright Able, let's move! Move, move, move!" As he says this, the sky flares up, and the light bathes the world about in a glowing yellow orange; turning his head to look at the source, he is suddenly buffeted by a tremendous thunderclap, and he squats to his knees, watching as a great roiling ball of orange fire and black smoke rises into the sky upon a stalk of flame, consuming itself as it does so, fissures of black smoke expanding as the fireball is spent on itself in its brief flowering. An ammunition truck or a fuel truck has been hit, likely. Flames hiss and crack and lash the sky red. Awestruck soldiers stand around as the fire roars like the inside of a furnace and then makes the noise of a flag flapping in a furious wind, tugged by the vacuum of the wind and snapping—standards and banners and pennants, great tatters of flame pulled up into the sky, the resultant smoke dissipating into the darkness. A filmy, fumy smell of burning fuel permeates the nostrils. The goat, chained up outside the nearby barn, is cowering and trembling, folded up on its haunches, making a whimpering sound—

In the glow of the fire he is back at Cassino, on a steep hillside, making his way up to the line with the carrier platoon, his charge for the month in a rotation of duties, moving ammunition up to the forward companies at night along a winding path while watching the night bombardment before a Polish attack, the members of the platoon slowly making their way in the darkness pulling a train of pack mules laden with ammunition and supplies. The mules are both led and ridden by soldiers, and a few of them bray restlessly, their heehawing like the swinging of a rusty gate, and they chew at the bits in their mouths and yank at their reins, twitching their ears in aggravation, unaccepting of their role as slave animals. The mules give off a barnyard smell of manure and leather and oily hair, earthy and sweetish, no doubt triggering homey farm memories from more than a few of the men leading them by their snouts. Together they are silhouetted in the flash of the guns, in orange and red and yellow and purple. Explosions ring their rhymes and terzias of terror off the mountains and are distorted and amplified by the rocks and the ruins. There is an off-kilter whirring sound and a short round comes sizzling and wobbling out of the sky, trailed by smoke like the curled shreds of the air through which it rips. It crashes nearby, sending him and the others to the ground with the shock of its impact. He looks back up and sees a mule combust, flaring up and blazing bright like a torch in a great hiss of phosphorus flame as an incendiary grenade on its back ignites, and he hears its agonized braying, a sandy honk mixed with a shrieking piggish squeal, stark animal terror, and there is the oily rug-reek of burning hair, the sweet pork smell of burning flesh, the unearthly raving of an animal on fire and leaping about in throes of incendiary agony as twisting, hissing snakes of flame uncoil from its body. The other mules leap backward out of the way, braying with a primal fear of fire and scarred by the pain of one of their own, and they pull at their reins and shake their heads and snort at the air in an attempt to get away, the soldiers clutching the reins from their prostrate positions like trainee rodeo clowns, trying not to get dragged through the dirt. The sharp cracks of his own pistol as he empties his clip into the blazing beast, into the centre of its tormented mass. Its legs buckle out from underneath as it collapses to the side, its tongue lolling out from its mouth stupidly like that of a dazed cartoon character.

"Stay down!" he shouts needlessly to his men as they wait for the explosion of ammunition, which occurs a moment later as banana clips full of machine-gun rounds crackle and burst and spark like so many fireworks, erupting from the burning mule, a hundred starbursts flickering off crouched helmets and rocks and faces under a sky rent by the howling of the shells, wayward bullets pinging off stones and chucking into the bark of skeletal trees.

"Any casualties?" he hears himself say after the surreal display has burned itself out, and he stands up, choking greasy smoke roiling up from the charred, steaming remains of the mule, its yellowed buckteeth bared in a burnt and lipless sneer—

"Casualties?" Jim asks louder. "Are there any casualties?"

"No, sir." It is Doyle, hand on his shoulder. "Not that I can tell. One hell of a bang that was, eh? Jesus!" He looks shaken, the sharp features of his angular face changing and shifting in the firelight. "So, are we moving or what, Captain?"

"Yes, yes, we're moving, Lieutenant, we're moving. Sorry, just a little stunned from the fuel truck." God almighty, I don't belong here anymore. The goat continues to cower amid the noise and is shushed and patted by a concerned young soldier, a trembling new reinforcement who looks at a glance to be about eighteen.

"None from our battalion, I don't think," says Doyle, surveying the fire one last time over his shoulder. "Shall we, Captain?"

"We shall." Jim turns away from this scene, and from the roaring fuel fire, and he moves up to near the front of the company and shouts a marching order, and Able Company marches up the slope of the ridge and into slit trenches that have been previously dug, shoddy half-dug trenches, and the men dig themselves in deeper into the reverse slope as the shells streak across the sky and the return fire from the Germans increases, and they sit and wait, many trying to sleep, helmets over faces, arms crossed over knees folded up, huddled up under gas capes or blankets, and others ride out the waiting hours by talking, by smoking, by playing cards; a few read by the firelight of small gasoline fires at the base of the ridge, brewing tea and chatting and risking the bombardments.

Later in the night, between bouts of fitful sleep, he gets reports that the first attack has broken through the German outpost positions in the valley, and that the first companies are engaged in a bitter melee on the ridge, fighting against dug-in positions, fortified farmhouses, tanks and self-propelled guns. There are German counterattacks. He raises his head. Slanted coils of razor wire scrawl across his view, the very signature of suspicion. Peering over the sandbagged lip of the trench, between the scribbles of wire, he experiences a phantasmagoria of sight and sound, awesome and unearthly—tracers of machine-gun and cannon fire unseam the sky in thudding stitches; overhead streak and sparkle whistling, shrieking, moaning, howling, roaring shells; guns flash and explosions effloresce in concussive thunder, and the earth bucks and trembles. The glow of fires here and there outlines and wreathes the profile of the ridge as buildings and positions burn from incendiary shells and bombs. Oh Marianne, if only you could see this, he thinks, if only you could hear this, if only you could smell this … if only I could relate all this to you someday. Wish I could send you a postcard now from Sunny Italy. Wish you were here. He laughs to himself, but can scarcely hear his laughter for the din of destruction. He sips water from his canteen and the last of his hangover headache is gone at last, and he crouches down into the corner of his small trench, his pack beside him, Cavanagh's No. 18 radio set at his feet, Cavanagh sitting knees up to his chest, Cooley beside him, three men huddled up against themselves in a hole as the world tears itself apart over their heads. There is a spectral wash of light overhead as a parachute flare bursts over their position, followed by several others. They crouch lower into the hole as shells come crashing in nearby, about thirty yards away, atop the ridge. No one speaks, three silent men, unknowable, riding out the storm. He stops laughing, and his eyes well up, and he feels tears coming on, he feels devastated about the letter, the letter, the letter. Do you love me anymore? Do you? Over, finally over. She had left him. She had left him shivering and huddling in a hole in the north of Italy, left him to call out to his mother in the night, amid the thunder and lightning and its terrible spectacle. How on earth did you not see this coming? You idiot. Of course she left you. You left her two, three years ago, you selfish fool, you goddamn idiot, of course she left you! She finished what you started! *Comprenez-vous?* He sobs into his hands, his helmet over his face, oily and rubbery smelling, he sobs and he snivels and feels very much alone at the edge of the world, at the edge of reason, perched uneasily upon the shaking precipice of the present.

"Smoke?" he offers after a time, helmet pushed aside, silver cigarette case open, and the three of them take a cigarette each, and he lights them one by one, three on a match. The sweet herbal smell of cigarettes mingles with the dry, caked smell of dirt.

"Are we having fun yet?" he shouts over the noise.

"Pardon, sir?" yells Cavanagh. Cooley turns his head toward him.

"I said, are we having fun yet?" he shouts louder.

"Yes, we're having a grand old time!" barks Cooley, huddling himself in his corner of the trench, wrapped in his gas cape, fervidly smoking his cigarette.

"Good to hear, gentlemen!"

The barrage builds in intensity and abates, and builds again, waxing and waning through the midnight hours, the unearthly wail of shellfire and the relentless explosions entering dreams, becoming thunderstorms, volcanoes, freight trains, brass bands and carnivals; and eyes flutter open and the furnace roar of combat becomes what it is again, reality asserts itself with the stony, earthy smell of dirt, the overbearing noise, the smell of smoke, of cordite. In and out of sleep moment by moment, hours become minutes, and minutes become hours.

Jim chews his cheeks and counts down again until it is time to move. In the distance Coriano becomes vaguely visible. Smoke and mist are intermingled; the horizon is dewed in water and blood, a dawn of day and of death. Still, the guns pound; machine guns and rifles crackle and rattle in the distance, airy and light sounding between the bigger bangs of shells and bombs.

XXVI

H-Hour. Forward, into the waiting jaws of the enemy. The first company to march out is Dog, under Captain Van Der Hecke, and they leave their holes and trenches alongside the men of Able and disappear into the darkness of the valley in the blue-grey of the predawn, to cover the engineers bridging the stream fording the valley, a bridge for the supporting tanks to cross. Cavanagh picks up radio signals from his set, scratchy coded transmissions of progress; shells fall amid Dog as they cover the bridging operation, and the soldiers trade fire with German forces overlooking them from their heights.

Jim is ordered to advance, and the men of Able Company shed their haversacks and move slowly and alertly from their slit trenches after a hot breakfast delivered to them under fire. They cautiously creep ahead down the grassy slopes, heads up, hunched over, tensely meeting the day's arraignment; first Therrien's platoon, then Doyle's, then Stringer's, Jim in the middle along with Cooley, Cavanagh, Neidhart, Lafontaine, Tillman and Witchewski; and they make their way to the river, marching briskly and silently over a Stygian land of destruction, mist and smoke hanging over the ground in a vapourous shroud. They pass a dead Canadian soldier lying on his back, one leg bent under the other, arms upraised as if in supplication to some deaf god, blood staining dark around him like old spilled wine in the dust of the roadside. Shell craters here and there. A freshly tilled field gently sloping upward into the smoke and the mist, pocked with holes. Blasted trees. A battered rock pile where a house stood, only a single wall remaining, a wall with a window upon the sill of which there stands an empty vase. Ahead, the dusty rattle of a small engine, and a jeep drives toward them from a distance, two stretchers laden with men lashed across the hood, two others in the back, four pairs of splayed feet whisking across their gaze as the jeep passes by. One of the men is writhing, moaning, whimpering. The medics nod grimly at the passing line of soldiers making their way to the front. Heading the opposite direction further in the distance, a troop of carriers, small and open, their two-man crews sitting tall in the cockpits, ferrying mortar crews and anti-tank gun crews, the men flinching from the bursts and the shrapnel, the passengers hunkered low and clinging to the metal sides of the hulls. Two of the carriers tow two-wheeled 6-pounder anti-tank guns, and the grooved rubber tires of the guns bounce over the ruts and potholes in the road, and the hitches that bind them to the carriers bend at the joints, and the segmented assemblies, vaguely insectoid in their construction, grumble and creep past. Onward. Beyond them, the ridge is plumed with covering artillery fire, a constant, wailing, rolling, rumbling curtain of sound, a driving, pounding metal rain. Ahead is a stream, the Torrente di Besanigo, a small flowing brook cutting between two ravaged farmers' fields. They slosh through the water and muck, weapons held overhead, and it soaks into their boots and through their pants. As he emerges back on the ground, he thinks as he trudges with soaked boots, Jesus Christ, another water obstacle, here we go into the fray and we get a bath first, a wee bath and—

An impossibly loud, unnatural and unnerving moan bearing down from the sky, a tailed meteor of flame. A moment of frozen terror. As he throws himself to the earth, there is a mighty impact to the side. A jarring crash. Deafness. Like a punch in the face. Vacuum. Push-pull. A furnace blast of heat. Dirt stinging the eyes, a pelting rain of matchsticks and clots of earth.

"Take cover!" Before the order is fully out of his mouth, he has rolled himself into a roadside depression as the earth pounds and palsies under another impact, and another and another, beside, behind, ahead, along with the howl of metal through sky. He looks up a moment to a scene of destruction, of blasting columns of flame and dirt and black smoke, showers of sparks, flying debris, rockets crashing all about right next to Able Company. The noise is absolute, all-encompassing, a sonic totality of consciousness. Then, nothing. The sudden silence is as deafening as the noise it replaced.

Before he can catch his breath, another volley of rockets dives in with the frightening sound of inverted air raid sirens, intoning upward their frightening, deafening, blaring wail before erupting this time nearer. Blast by blast, shock by shock, concussion by concussion. Trees splinter and crash, branches fly. There is a plunk next to him and he is shoved aside. He looks over his shoulder to see Sergeant Stringer, his jowly cheeks pulled back in a rictus as he grimaces through clenched teeth and closed eyes, as he always does during bombardments. The bombardment stops again for a moment and then restarts, now in the form of shells, shrapnel raking through the grass and singing over his head. He faces downward again and he hugs the dirt his mother's knee in a flower-print dress in church under a pew a helmet on his face, explosions ricocheting off the hills the trees the walls and floor and pews of the church and he can taste the dust and the cordite and feel the shellfire rippling underneath in waves, primal waves of discord and decay shaking the bonds between man and man, atom and atom. Hail Mary full of grace the Lord is with thee blessed is the fruit of thy womb Jesus Holy Mary mother of God pray for us sinners now and at the hour of our death Amen. Amen more than ever more than ever just stop the fire—and with that it is over.

Sand in his mouth, a lingering ringing in the ears, tintinnabulations so loud that outside of the clanging echo chamber of his own head all is silent, a thick cottony silence as though his head were swaddled in bandages. A desire to break and run, to desert, to hide under hay and avoid the provosts, to pay a farmer to hide in his flatbed truck and take him to Ancona, and then jump a train to Rome, to melt away into the underground of deserters there, to hitch a ride out on a tramp steamer to somewhere, anywhere where there is no one around, no one to fight: the North Pole, Antarctica, Deepest Darkest Africa, El Dorado, the edge of the world. Malingering ringing in his soul, oh why do you dwell on these things? Get on with your command!

He pulls himself to his feet in the cratered, upturned, smoking earth to the sounds of moaning penetrating through the thick haze of his perception. There are, it appears to his surprise, only four casualties, the bombardment having been inaccurate. In the distance, shells continue to fall, flashing in the smoke ahead and erupting like beacons of destruction. The medical runners tend to the wounded.

He attempts to rally his men to move. "Able Company! We must keep going!" There is a waver in his voice. "We have to get moving or they'll do it again. Every approach is marked for shells, got it? Come on, get together, fall back into your sections, let's go!" Platoon and section leaders shout as they gather their men back together in their small groups and continue their advance. Ahead, a line of explosions along the ridge. And ahead they continue, Jim again in the middle, now with Stringer's platoon. Alongside is Cavanagh, looking dazed, his radio set babbling away, hissing and popping coded reports, fading out here and there with the distortion of battle and the ruggedness of the landscape. Jim grabs the microphone and dons the spare headphones attached to Cavanagh's set and calls in smoke from the artillery to obscure their advance, and in moments lines of phosphorous smoke shells burst in front of and beside them, and it covers the area in a heavy pall of noxious yellow smoke through which the company marches. More German shells fall, but in looser concentrations, here, there, a steady peppering of artillery fire as the company advances ahead, ahead toward the shadowy profiled rise of the ridge emerging from the smoke and the mist, the smokescreen through which they march heavy and yellowy and clinging to and crawling along the ground like the feelers of some phantom intelligence; and they advance ahead toward the houses of the town amid the trees, through the smoke and mist, ahead to their objective. Behind them, to the east, the first milky light of the sun's spectral reconnaissance, weak probing beams feeling their way through mist and smoke and the reluctant rearguard of the retreating darkness. The sharp crack and rattle of small arms combat become louder, nearer; the artillery continues to fall, and the riflemen of Able Company bow over in a quick march, rifles in their hands or strapped loosely to their shoulders, teeth clenched, eyes wide, single-minded on their objective, the thunder beside them, behind them, ahead of them, over them, and they move, move, move, up the tilled and cratered and blasted slope of the hill to form a base of attack; and as they trot ahead he finds himself whistling the dogged, tired strain of "When Johnny Comes Marching Home," the fatigue and melancholy of which is so perfectly captured in its slow, swaying melody and dragging rhythm. Stringer joins him, as do others, and he can hear their voices between the bursts of shells both far and near, giving expression to the tautness of their nerves.

Up the slope, they pass blasted-out slit trenches and dugouts, the remains of a German soldier lying in a shallow weapons pit, perforated with bullets, grey uniform caked and stained with dried blood, lying with his legs sticking upward over the edge of the hole, shrivelled mismatched socks on his feet, one green, one navy, his boots having been removed as spoil; his wallet lies discarded on the ground, pilfered from for valuables, a string of family photographs shivering naked in the breeze. Another weapons pit, revetted by torn sandbags, with a broken black machine-gun barrel hanging limply on its tripod, and the two operators, dead in frozen frenzy and heaped on top of each other, partially buried in sand and dirt dumped on them from a blast. One of them is draped over shoulders and chest with heavy belts of bullets like strings of teeth, as though mummified in the chain-linked aggression of his trade. A burning barn, smoke spiralling and twisting into the sky as if sucked into an atmospheric maelstrom. Piles of rubble that were very recently occupied houses. Past a German Panzer IV tank, severe black iron crosses painted on its sides, still burning after an hour or more, its turret lopsided and canted at an angle, fire hissing up like that of a blowtorch and swirling in translucent streamers of funnelled flame from the turret hatch, fire that culminates in a noxious pillar of roiling, sooty black smoke; beside it are littered the bodies of two of the crew, one still wearing a radio headset, both of them gunned down as they tried to escape their knocked-out vehicle. Alongside, a ruined copse of trees, trees blasted to ragged stumps and split kindling in the battle to secure the hill during the night, and in the shelling this morning. Around are strewn bits of human viscera, blotches and smears of blood on the grass and on the road. From the branch of a lone sycamore tree hangs a length of intestine, like ivy or garland or a vine.

Behind them as they march, silently and with increasing apprehension, the sky turns from a milky greyish white and brightens into a soft rosy hue in anticipation of sunrise. Above, a drone of fighter-bombers, a squadron of single-engine Spitfires, their deep throaty growl loudening, throbbing the ground underfoot as they swoop in over the horizon, lower, lower, out of sight, and there follows a series of deep, rippling, overlapping booms, vibrating underfoot, as yet another German position is doused with bombs. A shell lands mere yards away. Soldiers duck. Another explosion, and a pelting of grapes.

"Keep it up, keep on ahead!" His left ear is still cottony and fuzzy and stunned with ringing from the Moaning Minny stonk, and he can scarcely hear with it and his thoughts are scattered; he is unable to focus. A particularly intense volley of artillery on the horizon, sprouting up in great black columns of dust and smoke and debris. Judging by the direction of the moan of shells overhead, it is an Allied volley, a covering barrage for an advance ahead of them. From the radio, updates from Dog Company's adventure covering the bridging. They are taking fire not only from artillery, but also from machine guns and snipers ensconced in the castle overlooking the valley, now behind and to their left, deeper into the waning blue-grey remnants of the night. They make it to the staging point.

XXVII

"Give me the radio," he says to Cavanagh.

"Yes, sir." They squat by the roadside and Jim takes the extra set of headphones from Cavanagh's set. He grabs the handheld microphone and says into it, "This is Sunray Victor 1. Victor 1 is leaping at Tango 7, Victor 1 is leaping at Tango 7, do you read? Over."

"Roger Sunray Victor 1, you are leaping at Tango 7, over. Dance to Hotel 3-0 and check in. Repeat, dance to Hotel 3-0 and check in. Over."

"Will comply. Dancing to Hotel 3-0 for check-in. Over and out." He stands, and shouts at the men, "Move ahead, the Sydneys are just ahead of us!" And they trudge onward, briskly now, and they come upon a cluster of collapsed houses and scraggly hedges and shattered trees, and all about are shell craters, bomb craters, and ruin—blasted trench complexes, twisted wire, a smoking Bren carrier abandoned and upended front first out of a crater, its thin armour casing bent and warped, a track broken and hanging off the metal bogie wheels; a German halftrack troop carrier, part truck, part caterpillar-treaded armoured vehicle, burns yards away from it. A slight breeze, and the sooty smoke from both vehicles blows into their faces, bringing with it a noxious, acrid, oily reek. Soldiers dug into slit trenches wave at the men of Able Company as they approach their staging point, and they yell out from their holes, "Took yez long enough!" "Glad yeh made it!" "Give 'em hell, yeh Irish bastards!" "We leftcha some Jerries there in the village, we didn't wanna take all the credit!"

As Jim awaits his tank support, the soldiers occupy craters and abandoned slit trenches or dig their own shallow holes for protection, platoon and section leaders urging them to dig in with their shrill commands. He turns to Corporal Tillman, crouching nearby, chewing bubblegum and blowing balloon after pink balloon with his mouth from nervousness, and asks, "Are the mortar crews on schedule?"

"Yes, sir," Tillman says as a bubble breaks with a wet smack. "They should deploy just as the tanks get here. They'll set up in the woods on the Sydneys' flank, as planned."

"Okay, good."

"Sir, message from TAC," says Cavanagh from beside him, his set dismounted in front of him and its aerial extended, his hands cupping his earphones as if with them he could better hold onto the words pulled from the ether. "Charlie is crossing the river now and is proceeding to our flank."

"Good to hear," Jim answers, bemused and unnerved by the weighted momentum assembling behind him and urging him to spearhead the attack.

Awhile later, there is the squeaking, grumbling tremor of tanks. He turns his head and sees, behind, a squadron of Sherman tanks trundling toward them, high-profiled, the fronts of their hulls steeply sloped and capped by the turrets, side runners packed with pickaxes and spades and spare fuel cans, segmented lengths of spare treads laid out on their fronts for extra armour like medieval chainmail, barrels pointing this way and that. The commanders protrude from the turret hatches, the commander of the lead tank scanning with field glasses, the heads of the two drivers protruding from their hatches in the forward hull, the tanks trundling forward, fourteen in all, moving at a cautious, creeping pace. Just in time. The bridging was successful, thanks be to God.

They park, their passive engines grumbling as if impatient of waiting. The oily reek of diesel and gasoline fumes funnels up Jim's nose, courtesy of a smog-bearing breeze. Pflagh! It calls to mind for a moment the smog of London. How the German airmen managed to pinpoint anything through that murk is beyond me. Like walking on the London sidewalk with rows of double deckers idling at the bus stops, with their black oily puff-puffing piston farts grunting away—

"Good to see you!" yells Jim up at the commander of the leading tank as it halts beside him, projecting his voice over the shudder of the idling engine.

"You too!" replies Major Marchand, the commander of the squadron.

"It sounds like the crossing was hairy!"

"It was! We traded a lot of fire with the enemy while waiting, that's for sure."

"Good to hear. If you're ready, we're ready, sir."

"By all means—Brigade gave the go ahead." Major Marchand is an older man, moustachioed, skin crinkled at the corners of his eyes. He wears a radio headset over his black beret. More droning of planes, more thunder of bombs.

They move ahead, the men and half of the tanks together, dug-in or passing soldiers from the Sydneys cheering them on or making jokes, or just looking at them, dazed and tired and awaiting the end of the battle, and as they approach the Sydneys' flank, they become more cautious, crouching, ducking, compacted by instinct.

"I'll call in a covering barrage!" Jim calls out into a telephone wired to the back of Marchand's tank, which lumbers along in front of him.

"We'll give you smoke cover."

Here, they pause at Jim's command at the bottom of a small incline and everyone crouches and hunches into squads. Jim dons his headphones and grabs his radio microphone again, and calls out the coordinates while crouching with Cavanagh behind a hedge, riflemen crouched about him, weapons raised at the ready, soldiers from the Sydneys amid them in their holes and ditches and depressions. "This is Sunray Victor 1, Sunray Victor 1, requesting creeping barrage before Tango 9-0, repeat, creeping barrage before Tango 9-0. Over."

"Will comply Sunray Victor 1, creeping barrage before Tango 9-0. Over and out."

"Heads up for our guns!" he barks. Here it comes, he thinks, here it comes and I'll never hear again. A metallic whine above, and a line of explosions, one after another in quick succession, black Vesuvian eruptions of shellfire, their splitting bangs ringing off the trees, barns, contours of the land; and they get up and move, platoon by platoon, walking slowly behind the curtain of continuous shellfire exploding upward in rows like a budding bounty of crops sown and grown in an instant from seedpods of destruction, to supplant the crops they uproot in a rain of debris.

As they pass through the dug-in positions of the Highlanders' flank to shouts of "Give 'em hell!", they approach the serrated ruin of the town itself jutting up from the trees across an open field. Beside them, just beyond the roadside thickets, on either side, are untended overgrown vines, powdery with white dust and dirt kicked up by the guns; the vineyards are a cratered, upturned ruin, deep shellholes gouged out of the rich earth, many grapes harvested by the rough means of shellfire. They approach the outskirts ahead, the blocky houses of which are seen in silhouette through the smoke of the bombardment and the trees on the outskirts, against the dark and hazy blue of the predawn, the rear of the retreating of the night. Before this ... what? What lies before this? Surely some German position ...

Jim leads, chewing his cheeks, his stomach boiling with fear. He refuses to draw his pistol, keeping it hidden in his holster under his pants for fear of being identified as an officer and shot. Beside him is the soft-spoken Private Cavanagh, radio on his back, rifle in hand. Cavanagh, like all the other riflemen in the company, spread out in squads and platoons, has his bayonet-tipped Lee Enfield rifle cocked at the ready. Into the unknown they weave their careful way. Squad by squad they move, the screen of exploding shells banging and pluming just ahead of them, throwing up great clouds and clods and chunks of earth. Another squadron of fighters overhead swoops in low in the distance far beside them and rakes the land below with a daggered spray of automatic cannon fire, following with the deep, rolling concussion of bombs, a seismic rumble underfoot, a shudder of the air. Closer, there is the wall of noise, the screaming, crashing cacophony of the creeping barrage. Close-up, there is the sound of boots in the dust of the road, boots in the grass. The air ahead is misted with creeping white smoke like incense from a priest's censer as the tanks fire smoke rounds from their turrets, spreading white tendrils of heavy smoke that hang like curtains of mist. As they wade into the stinging miasma of smoke, there is a wobbly whine overhead, the eccentric path of a short round.

"Take cover!" someone yells, and all nearby hit the ground. The resultant explosion is to the side, and Jim is lashed by twigs and showered by grapes. Before he picks himself up, German return fire comes in the form of a clutch of mortars, diving in from high up in the air, pounding the earth about them in a brief, sharp concentration. He squints, hands on helmet, prostrate in the grass as earth pours down about them in a gritty shower. He picks up a handful of dusty, powdery grapes, and pockets them as he picks himself up to his feet a moment later. He surveys his company, the men weaving their way behind the protective bombardment, surveys for casualties as he himself moves forward, dragged ahead by the immediate demands of duty, pushed ahead and held together by the invisible but very tangible bonds of personal honour and regimental honour and national honour, bound in a web of expectations stretched between the king and the lowest and greenest of his privates, and threaded within his insignias and within the very values and fears and qualities of himself. There are, it appears at a sweeping, squinty glance in the smoke, three casualties.

They continue advancing, spread out in a hunched, brisk trot. Heavier German shells dive in and explode near them, among them, on them, and the soldiers fan out, the shrapnel singing and whirring by them and over them, and ripping through them. The shells part the air and pound the earth, throwing up great fountains of smoke and dirt and debris, crashing, deafening, sucking up the air around the men, buffeting them about in their conflicting crosswinds. Our Father who art in heaven hallowed be thy name thy kingdom come thy will be done ... Past the moaning, writhing form of a soldier reaching out and grabbing his ankle, leaving a bloody handprint smudged on his dusty puttees as the hand slides off ... Give us this day our daily bread, and forgive us our trespasses. Deep inside, somewhere, he is sorry for all wrongs done by him. Another terrific impact in front, and he finds himself squatting amid the push-pull displacement of dust, coughing and gagging.

"Keep going!" he yells, his voice hoarse about the explosions. He spits a gob of dirty saliva. Talons of shrapnel slash the air in angry red arcs. A pebble pings off his helmet, and it is knocked askew, a new etching in its hieroglyphs of experience. The line of shellfire creeps ahead in coordination with the infantry, and they find themselves at the entrance of the town, the shells hitting buildings, pounding roofs, blasting the streets, splintering trees, wrecking gardens, gouging out walls. He turns behind him and sees the land cratered, numerous men lying on the ground in the dissipating smoke cover, the lifting shroud of which reveals a wake of ruination. The stretcher-bearers tend to the wounded and try to whisk them off to an aid post; the dead are left for the men of grave details. Very grave details indeed. Behind them, the tanks approach. As they approach the first houses, Tango 9-0 according to the codes given to him, the protective shelling stops with an abrupt silence. Everyone hits the ground in anticipation of enemy bullets. The German shellfire continues, albeit sporadically.

XXVIII

"Everything okay?" he asks Cavanagh as he warily stands, bent over as he does so.

"I think so. Not sure about my equipment. Heard some shrapnel whirring over me, sir, when we dove for cover."

Jim inspects the radio. He looks and sees that the radio set is cracked and broken. There is a deep fissure inside which a smoking twist of shrapnel has embedded itself.

"The wireless is broken. Goddamnit. Well, you might as well dump that thing; it's just dead weight now. You're a rifleman now, like everyone else."

"Yes, sir."

Ahead, he shouts, "8 Platoon, lead the way! 7 and 9, covering positions! Ready your mortars with smoke!" His commands are relayed down the line by others. "Speaking of mortars, Tillman, do you reckon your 3-inchers are in place yet?" He turns behind to Tillman, who is nervously looking around, the earphones of his radio plugged into his ears and tuned for messages from his comrades.

"They're getting into place, sir," Tillman answers, "now that the bridge is up and the tanks are across. They'll send me a message when they're ready."

"Good." He turns around to observe his men moving in. The first German positions are a smoking, upturned, cratered ruin, with broken equipment, shredded barbed wire, blasted stumps, torn sandbags, and blasted-out slit trenches on the edge of the village. There is no one around. The squads of No. 8 Platoon pick through this abandoned ruin, covered by those behind crouched and crunched into firing positions, looking for any sign of the enemy; but as of yet, there is none.

Among the exploding shells, the tanks trundle up, steering around the dead and wounded, around the medical runners dashing off with bleeding men, and they make their way to Jim's position. Major Marchand inquires about Able's next moves.

"We're sending in No. 8 Platoon first to probe and we'll secure the way in."

"We have you covered." Into his microphone he commands, "Ready rounds, HE." He holds onto the trigger of the turret-mounted machine gun, keeping at the ready. Squinting, his eye watering from a damnable piece of grit lodged in it from the bombardment, Jim envies Marchand his goggles, though they are pushed up over his beret.

"Our radio's done with," Jim says to Marchand.

"Sorry to hear."

Jim signals Lieutenant Therrien, who has been looking back at him for directions, to go on ahead. Therrien nods, a knowing nod, the grim nod of a man accustomed to carrying out and ordering violent acts. With pounding heart Jim watches the twenty-five men of the platoon dash ahead in sections, covered by other sections, watched over by the rest of the company and the tanks. Soldiers kick in a door, run inside a house, and emerge, again. Others root through a backyard garden. Others disappear down a lane between battered houses. They do this again and again, down the street, house by house, getting smaller, disappearing into alleys. Sweat beads on Jim's brow, sweat beads and time stands still in the eternities between heartbeats; the ambient artillery of the surrounding battle is a dull roar in the back of his mind as he focuses all his energy ahead, waiting for the eruption of gunfire, the ripping sound of a machine gun. There is nothing.

"I don't believe it. They buggered off," observes Sergeant Stringer from nearby, incredulous at the Germans' disappearance. "Just buggered off and fell back."

The day crowns itself with a shimmering diadem of sunlight—dawn.

"Let's move," commands Jim. "9 Platoon, go. 7 Platoon, cover and hold. Witchewski, Tillman, Cooley and Lafontaine, stay here and maintain a skeletal HQ. Cavanagh and Neidhart, you come in with me." He looks up at the uncertain, suspicious-looking Major Marchand, who has his hands on the trigger of the mounted machine gun, his lower lip subsumed beneath his moustache and likely being chewed by his front teeth, a tableau of controlled fear.

"Are you coming in with us, sir?"

Marchand breaks his pose. "*Oui.* Yes, we'll move in now." He relays a command into his microphone for the other tanks to follow. Into the ghostly, empty streets they creep ahead, Jim with Stringer's platoon. Sergeant Stringer is yards ahead, scanning left to right, appraising the situation, his Thompson submachine gun held at the ready. Behind Jim are Cooley and Neidhart. Other soldiers are fanned out in their squads. All is silent inside the town save for their boots and for the kicking in of doors, the dashing up the stairs of houses, the surrounding battle reduced to a dull echoing roar refracting off the façades of the buildings. The cobblestone street goes up at an angle, and is strewn with broken masonry and glass. Shattered windows gape down at them through their empty sockets. In the growing morning breeze groan on their hinges a pair of open red shutters. A half-painted whitewashed wall, pitted and peppered, a sign leaning against it—*Vernice fresca!* Fresh Paint! The interruption of daily life, the sudden onset of disaster. Like the set tables in Pompeii, petrified figs and bread laid out for a last supper never eaten, and the ancient Roman election signs seen when on leave back to Naples in the midsummer so many eons ago, the ragged stump of Vesuvius steaming, brooding in a vapourous, sulphurous haze in the background.

Hunched over at an intersection, the road bisected by a winding lane lined with an ivied stone wall, topped by a wrought-iron fence, trees peering down from an embankment above it. The ivy triggers a momentary longing for the safety of England … Above, a buzzing drone as a squadron of two-engine Mitchell bombers returns from a raid, rumbling in the sky, dozens of them soaring like great birds of prey, one of them trailing a line of black smoke from a burning engine. Out of a large house with a shelled-out roof emerges a squad of soldiers from No. 9 Platoon. Their leader, Corporal McLeod, shrugs, one hand on his Tommy gun, and he says, "Nothing, sir. No one. Not a trace." Nearby, a soldier kicks in the door of a wooden shed, rifle projecting from the hip at the ready. The door squeaks on its hinges. No yell of surprise, no eruption of fire. Nobody emerges. No prisoner is yanked out of a furtive hiding place. Behind, the tanks creep down the street, barrels sniffing this way and that with the mechanical whine of turning turrets.

"Nothing, nothing at all so far. This area is secured," Jim calls up to Marchand from the field telephone wired to his tank, his tank now second in line.

Marchand mulls this intelligence over for a moment, and decides, "We'll move on ahead." And so the tanks do, picking up the pace, their engines grunting, one after another, outpacing the infantry who now are less cautious, walking casually down this street and that, still sweeping for activity, but seeming to be no longer very convinced of any.

XXIX

The two platoons continue snaking their way through the streets, securing the town and awaiting the arrival of both Baker and Charlie. Ahead, to the right, a white Romanesque church perched on a knoll and smashed by shellfire, steeple blasted away, the large ragged holes in the walls and the shattered windows revealing within shifted rows of pews covered in stones and plaster. A flash of San Mateo, of Lieutenant Blake. From out the corner of his eye, to the right, in a shard of a broken window, a glance of Fitzpatrick, wan and white and staring back at him. A shudder, and he sees his own reflection. Christ, I'm tired. Pompeii. Plaster cast corpses strewn about. *Vernice fresca!* A row of townhouses, packed close together, with their roofs blown off or their façades blasted wide open, spilling their guts of furniture, bricks, framework and decorations. A wrought-iron fence, a line of wrecked houses and an arch leading into the main piazza, and beyond, the smashed clock tower of the post office and municipal office, another possible vantage point destroyed by the air force and artillery and a midnight barrage from tanks.

The tanks press on, farther and farther ahead, the weighted squeaking trundle of their treads and the rasping rumble of their engines receding, and the first one passes under the arch leading into the central piazza. He turns his head from the line of tanks heading up the street to a flurry of motion in the corner of his eye—he looks down at a street cat peering up at him through suspicious yellow eyes from between two wrecked buildings, a mangy-looking black tabby, flanks ridged in ribs. It pours its form into one soft-pawed step after another. The cat pauses and hisses as he passes, along with Cavanagh and Neidhart, and it withdraws a step and condenses its lithe form low to the ground, shaped to pounce. Or to run. Get away, get away, all of you, it seems to say with its shifting, yellow, suspicious eyes, this is my trash heap. Animals made destitute by war, like the stunned three-legged dog at Pesaro, stumbling about in a shell-stupor, or the goat, compressed and terrified by the exploding truck during the long hours of the night.

Jim's tongue is parched. Sweat beads on his brow, coaxed to the surface of his skin in the intensifying sun, and a drop tickles its way down his cheek. He wipes his brow with his hand as the morning sun beats down and bathes the world golden, morning shadows huddled in corners, at the bases of trees and buildings, and at the feet of patrolling soldiers, straggling and deserted in the wake of the retreated night; and he unscrews the cap from his canteen as he pulls it from his webbing, yessiree, not a bad morning for yourself, you're taking your objective without a bloody shot—

A rifle crack. Explosions, an exchange of shells, a banging of tank guns, muffled and refracted by the buildings. Alarmed, Jim looks down the road, turning his attention away from the cat, which flees into the shadows, and looks toward the arch, the piazza, and sees a column of black smoke rising up from beyond. Another exchange of tank fire, and an orange ball of fire rises up above the rooftops and dissolves into smoke, followed by a sky-high shower of whistling, popping ammunition.

"Jesus Christ!" someone yells. Another flurry of explosions, and the nearly solid ripping sound of a German machine gun.

"8 Platoon, follow me! 9, cover and then follow!" Dashing down the lane toward the fire and smoke, toward the spraying of machine guns. As he approaches, he sees the column of tanks jammed up, and there is a grunting of engines as one of them moves ahead and shoves the burning lead tank into the piazza, and then fires its own turret at some unseen target. It is answered by a German turret. The remaining tanks grumble into reverse, backing up toward 8 Platoon.

"There's a goddamn Panther in the square!" yells the commander of the tank closest, as his vehicle backs toward Jim's men. "Took out the leader!" The angry scour of a machine gun from behind, and the crack of rifles. Bullets snap about and chip into the cobblestone lane, pluming in white puffs of dust and smoke. Men lie prone or crouch in doorways, or huddle beside and behind trees and hedges and walls. Jim finds himself kneeling beside the segmented treads of the bogie wheels of the tank, the smells of dirt and grease in his nostrils, the ground vibrating to the loose shudder of the engine, bullets cracking about overhead. The thud of a grenade. From another street, a loud explosion. There is the ragged yelling of German commands, the frantic shouting of Canadian soldiers caught in an ambush.

The tanks continue reversing, and the wheels squeal and the treads crawl along, buckling here and there in Jim's close view, one tank, then the next, then the next, leaving the first one a burning wreck in their wake, smoke and fire twisting upward from the scorched chassis, the German tank in the piazza looming over it, turning its turret and blasting with a recoil toward another street or building, then turning again and blasting elsewhere, and there are machine guns and rifles and grenades, and all about the clatter and bang of a melee—

Hands on his lapels, shaking him. "Sir! Sir! Are you wounded?" It is Stringer.

"No, no, I'm okay!" He can scarcely hear himself for the noise. "Just stunned!" He gathers himself. "Pull back to the approaches and let's regroup with the tanks!" He pulls himself to his feet and falls back, gesturing wildly to his soldiers and yelling, "Fall back and regroup, fall back and regroup!" His commands are relayed by the sharp barks and shouts of his subordinates, and soldiers withdraw when they can in a slow and piecemeal fighting retreat, dashing through lanes and alleys, gardens and orchards; others are pinned down by the sweep of machine guns or the murderous accuracy of snipers.

Back at the entrance to the village, soldiers occupy the abandoned slit trenches and dig shellscrapes while trading fire with enemy soldiers shooting from windows and breached roofs and walls. The tanks have made their way to the edge of town as well, and Marchand, his nose bloodied and his face scratched and blackened with soot, dismounts from his tank and confers with Jim and his platoon commanders as they, along with many others, huddle in a trench behind a hedge. Marchand's eyes are wild, scared, angry, yet focused.

"In you go, house to house," orders Marchand. "We will provide covering fire. Once you've secured the way in, we move in and assist you in small groups—understand?"

"Yes."

"Be damn sure you nail any AT positions you see, got it?"

"Yes, sir," Jim answers.

"Good. *Bonne chance!*" At this, Marchand leaps out of the trench and climbs aboard his awaiting tank.

"Mortars!" Jim yells. "We need mortars on those first houses! Get those mortars into action!" He turns to Corporal Tillman, crouched near him in the trench, chewing his wad of gum ever more quickly and forcefully. "Get your mortars firing!"

"Yes, sir!" Tillman calls orders and coordinates into the microphone of his small radio set, repeating them loudly over the noise of combat. The mortar crews respond from out of sight, the bulbous, finned projectiles of their weapons diving down onto the buildings from on high after a number of seconds. Jim signals for Doyle to lead in his platoon first, and the others to fire. In they move again, squad by squad, under a fusillade of supporting tank shells and mortar bombs and the supporting fire of their comrades, that further chip and chunk and chomp away at the shattered buildings. A rifle shot from a house, and a man goes down, hand on his hip. Someone scurries out from the hedge to save him, but he is turned away by another shot, and then there is the sweep of a machine gun, the strobe flicker of its muzzle pulsing in the broken window of a house and illuminating the helmets of its two operators. The machine gun knocks down several of the attacking men in Doyle's platoon in its scything arc. The whine of a turret, and the window is blasted away into a shapeless hole by a tank shell. A tank rumbles ahead to better cover the advancing men, when a rocket slices the air and erupts against the sloped front of its hull with a sharp report. The crew, now hunkered down under the hatches, throw the tank into reverse, and it pulls away, its sloping front ablaze with burning paint. The other tanks sensibly remain out of range.

Moments later, another machine gun snarls to life from another vantage point and scours the air and the ground, bullets shearing the hedges above Jim's head. Mortar bombs and artillery shells crash about them. Jim peers over the hedge with his field glasses as the bullets snap overhead, and in the shaky frame of his magnified view he sees a section of Doyle's men kick in a doorway, one of their own writhing on the street and bleeding, and they charge into the doorway. He sees the flash of gunfire and grenades in the house, and he scans by and sees others dash through a large hole in the wall of another house, and moments later he watches as a German soldier falls headfirst from an upstairs window, limp and dangly as a doll, his helmet tumbling from his head as he does so. His hands tremble and his view trembles, and he feels a rush of air as a mortar explodes nearby, and he hits the ground and is covered with dust and earth, and he looks about himself, dazed, at Cavanagh, and Cavanagh looks at Jim as he loads a magazine into his rifle and pulls himself back up into a firing crouch, and Jim looks at Cooley, and Cooley looks back at him and smiles and nods as he too changes his cartridge, and all about is the din of combat, the shouts of men: "Jesus, Selk, watch out there, keep yer head down!" "More fire on that first house there, get that machine gun!" "Where's that sniper, where is he firing from?" "I'm hit, I'm hit, I'm hit!" "Hold your fire, save a little ammo, will you!" "They seem to pop up everywhere and vanish!"

"Where? Where is he?" Another crack from the unseen sniper.

"Witchewski!" barks Jim.

"Yes, sir!"

"Go up there and find out what the hell is going on and come back with a report!"

"Right sir, I'm going!" And with that, Witchewski scrambles out of the trench and back toward the perimeter of the town. There is another nearby mortar blast, and Jim is yanked about in the push-pull vacuum of the concussion, and his bad ear is once again ravaged by the noise. He turns his head to see a soldier, whom he recognizes as Private Schneider, a black soldier from Hamilton, gagging and gurgling and shaking, bright red arterial blood spurting from his neck, blood pooling in his chest and soaking through his uniform. Jim yells for a medic, and caught in the moment finds himself trying to apply a field dressing of sorts, feverishly ripping a shell dressing from Schneider's own belt. As he rips open Schneider's shirt he sees a mangled meaty mass of torn flesh and exposed innards, the glistening slats of ribs, one broken, yes, one broken he notes, snapped like the twig of a tree, and he hears a whistling, a gurgly sighing whistling from the ragged pulpy hole, and Jim gags and burps in his mouth and tastes the sourness of his own bile, and he puts gauze on Schneider's chest. Schneider's eyes are wide open, elsewhere, gazing at the gates of mortality, and the blood coats Jim's hands and it soaks the gauze, making the gauze useless, and a medic crawls over and takes over, pouring sulfa powder on his chest and saying, "It's okay there buddy just hang in there, you're going to be okay buddy just good as new, that's right, there, there, you'll be good as new and you'll be back at Blighty with the nurses in no time," gently calming him like a parent would a frightened child. As Jim turns away to mind his command, to pull himself away from this horrible morale-draining scene, Schneider's hand darts out and grabs his, bloody hand clasping bloody hand, and Jim turns his head a moment, and Schneider looks pleadingly, imploringly, deeply, into his eyes, his own eyes wide and terrified, irises and pupils bordered in bright and infinite white. Jim meets his gaze a moment with sad, wide eyes, a reluctant shrug that says in an instant, I'm sorry, I have to go, I have more important things to do, that is the way war works, I have to go; and the lights go out from Schneider's eyes and his agony is over.

Jim feels the world withdraw away from him, or he from it, the world whitening as his heart begins to pound, Schneider dead beside him, bleeding from the neck and the chest, spurting bright freshets now reduced to a trickle congealing into and dying the fabric of his uniform and slicked onto Jim's hands and soaking into the earth, a metallic odour of iron-rich blood, of raw meat, his face gone a greenish white, his hand gone cold in Jim's, eyes deadlit under the early morning sun that filters indistinct through the smoke, the bullets shearing the hedge, sshk sshk, cracking and snapping to the side and overhead. Jesus, Jesus, Jim thinks in a hurry, oh fuck what to do where's the colonel where's the colonel or where's Reynolds I don't know what to do anymore I'm not fit for this anymore get me off the line I've cracked I'm not good I'm just going to get everyone killed. He hears behind him the grumble and squealing treads of a Bren carrier. Turning his head, he sees the carrier silhouetted low to the ground and, obscured in the pall of smoke, the crouched silhouette of the battle adjutant, Major Reynolds, and lower, his batman and his driver and his radioman. The cocky young major, with his black tapered moustache, and wearing his beret and goggles, observes calmly the scene about him with his field glasses. The madness of those in command! How I long for such control! Jim releases Schneider's cooling hand and shimmies over the backs and legs of Smith and Hauser, crouching from the storm of bullets and shrapnel.

"Jesus Christ, train that machine gun up on that house over there!" he shouts as he regains his composure. "Get that thing into action, boys, don't just lie there or we'll be pinned down here forever!" This bolsters the gunners and they train their Bren machine gun, mounted on a bipod and with a banana-shaped magazine jammed into the top, up at a house being used as a machine-gun post, and they open fire in deep thudding volleys. The clatter of the gun in its proximity to him assaults his eardrums. Others, he can see, are aiming their rifles, discharging them with their pops and cracks and puffs of smoke, joining the exchange of metal, and he shimmies over legs and backs back to Reynolds' carrier.

"McFarlane!" Reynolds shouts over the noise.

"Sir!" Jim responds, looking up.

"What's the situation?"

"We moved in and were ambushed! We had to fall back! I've sent Doyle in to secure us the entrance before we move back in with the tanks! Our 18 set is broken, too!"

"Okay, good work Jim, just get a move on when the coast is clear! The aid post is up and the 6-pounders are on the way!"

"Yes, sir!"

"When you get the perimeter secure, I'll send Charlie into action, and Baker is forming up in reserve behind you!"

"Thank you!"

At this, the carrier backs up. Jim scurries back to his position, field glasses hanging from his neck and bumping against his chest, and he picks them up in his hands and resumes his shaky, magnified survey of the carnage ahead of him, the muscles of his arms burning as he holds them rigid. There is a fierce melee, the silhouettes of men in smoke, a house ablaze. Suddenly, in his view is blocked and he is knocked backward and whipped by the leafy branches of the hedge as someone heavy tumbles into him. It is Witchewski.

"Sorry for that!" he shouts, as he picks himself up into a crouch. "Nearly got a mortar there! We have secured several houses. They come out here and there with machine guns, rockets and snipers! The whole place is booby-trapped and ready for defence!"

"Thank you Witchewski, go back and tell them we're coming!" Witchewski does as ordered, and Jim shouts out to advance, 9 Platoon covered and then followed by 8, let's move, out and on with it, out out out, come on, move it like you mean it and let's get in there and take this town, yes, that's it, do it, go go go, and he watches with his field glasses as they dash out of the shallow trenches and back out into the field into a noisome haze, a smokescreen fired by the artillery and tanks to hide them, a smokescreen that has mixed with the dust and earth kicked up by boots and treads, and artillery and mortar fire. There is blood on his hands, Schneider's blood, sticky, syrupy. As he joins them, trotting out into the open, dust cakes on Schneider's blood on his hand. In the acrid haze, Jim retches, his passages choked. A thin stream of bile lurches upward into his mouth, and he tastes the sourness of his own stomach contents, feels the acidic burn on the roof of his mouth, his membranes scorched. With the stimulus of an explosion, instinct picks him up and throws him to the earth. Just ahead of him a bullet rips into the earth in a mushroom-shaped puff. Lead by example Jim, expose yourself running down the road, go straight, there's no hiding in the fields for the threat of mines, get the hell moving, get rolling, there is no time to dawdle, to lose your nerve, just move, just move on will you, Jesus Christ! The remainder of the company advances ahead, ahead into the livid, roaring inferno of combat, into the arena of its ruthless and anonymous causality, the riflemen of Able Company bowed over in a quick march, rifles in their hands or hanging loosely from their shoulders, teeth clenched, eyes wide, a unity of cells, a body of men.

XXX

Upon reentering the town, he ducks into one of the first houses, one taken by Doyle's men. There, in the shattered roofless interior, a ragged, splintery hole in the ceiling above him, the floor heaped in masonry and wood, he finds Doyle with a number of his men, and he congratulates them on their job securing the outskirts. Doyle thanks him while trying to stage an attack on another house, acting and reacting, pointing here, barking there, responding fluidly to the needs of the battle. Jim ascends the stairway with Tillman and Cavanagh and Neidhart to what remains of the above floor, surveying the efforts of his company through a breach in the upper wall. Witchewski, Cooley and Lafontaine remain downstairs with Doyle. For a long while much of the company hides out in or around several captured houses, trading fire with Germans perched in windows and holes, and Jim and Tillman direct mortar fire to aid with the ongoing attack.

Eventually, the tanks return to the outer edges of the town, one by one, and grumbling down the road and crunching over rubble, they fire at a house occupied by a machine gun and several riflemen, several turrets pounding away into the windows and at the walls until the edifice disintegrates and collapses into a dusty heap, exposing the interior of the house like a multistoried play set or the cutaway of a dollhouse, the edges of the upper floor leaning downward, poised to fall. The silencing of this fortress frees up a section of men to dash off to another objective, running exposed down the road, though Jim can see one of them slump forward and fall limply onto the street like a sack of grain.

"Huh?" Doyle reacts, bewildered, shouting from below. "That came from behind!" Jim looks out from the hole in the wall of the house they occupy.

"Didn't you take out that house there?"

"We did!" shouts Doyle from the bottom of the stairs.

"Well, how the hell could they be in it again? We secured the perimeter!"

Other men shout from their positions: "Sniper, somewhere behind!"

"Draw his fire and flush him out!" Jim yells through the hole. "Gutch and Daniels, do it! When you identify, Pitwanikwat, line up your shot and try to take him out!" He shouts out to Neidhart. "Neidhart, get on the radio and get us the services of a tank!"

"Yes, sir!" comes the answer. Gutch and Daniels do as ordered, running into the street, and they are pursued by one, then another, and another shot, bullets nipping at their heels. Pitwanikwat crouches and identifies the source of fire, and the source is indeed a previously captured house. He fires a shot, and the sniper fires again. Minutes later, there is the grunting of an approaching tank; it raises its turret and fires into the sniper's window, blasting inside the house. Doyle dispatches a squad of men to charge through the door and clear the house of any remaining men. Other shots come from another supposedly captured house, including a rocket that narrowly misses the tank, exploding beside it with a terrific report. The tank's turret turns in the direction of the rocket, and blasts again. It dawns on Jim that they are under fire from all directions. A terrific clamour coming from the west announces that Charlie Company is now engaged in battle. The term 'front' loses all meaning as the village and its surroundings become fogged in a shapeless, directionless, cacophonous turmoil that erupts from everywhere all at once, small battles flaring up here and there as small parties of men attempt to extinguish other small parties of men. Another rocket from another window, and with a clang the tank is hit in the wheels, its tread snapping, its lumbering bulk now immobilized in the street. Still, the crew fires shell after shell into the building, bolstering the fire of Jim's own company.

"Take that house, Therrien!" shouts Jim across the street to the building now occupied by much of Therrien's platoon. Therrien readies a group of men for the task. Under the impact of another high-velocity tank shell, the corner of the house gives way in a pall of dust and smoke.

"In we go!" is Therrien's battle cry, and into the yawning hole pours a section led by him, and there are the echoing reports of grenades and gunfire from inside. Out they come from another side, baffled, and then they are pinned down by rifle shots from another nearby house. Jim can see the sloping outline of a German soldier's helmet and, in another window, the ruffling of curtains. What is going on? Jim frets as his perimeter dissolves, what is going on? Anger and fatigue consume him all at once; he throws his helmet to the floor in disgust and paces along the tilted floor, and he spits out of the hole in the wall into the rubble below. His thoughts are unclear; he has no idea what is going on, how to act. He begins to tremble. Where is that bottle? Where is that bottle? he thinks. I need liquor to steady my nerves, where is my whiskey, where is my whiskey! He rummages through his pack and discovers to his dismay no whiskey. None at all. He is filled with a sudden, crawling dread, seized by a feverish confusion. His hands continue trembling, and he feels a prickly, tickly sensation on his skin as he begins to sweat from nerves. Craving a drink, as if he could escape this situation with one in hand.

"Cooley!" he shouts amid the noise of battle. "Cooley!"

"Yes, sir!" comes Cooley's response from below. Cooley runs up the stairs to where Jim is, the contents of his pack strewn out in front of him. "What's wrong?" Cooley looks concerned.

"Don't broadcast this too loudly, but I need a shot of something to steady my nerves." He glances over his shoulder to ensure that Tillman, crouched and looking out the hole in the wall, and Cavanagh and Neidhart, aiming and firing their rifles from a window, have not heard his words.

"Sir?" Cooley takes a moment to digest what Jim has said. "Sir, there's a battle on!"

"I know, I know, but I can't concentrate without a fucking drink, do you understand? Our whole perimeter's melted, I'm exhausted and I have no idea what the fuck to do. Do you have any whiskey?"

"No. And I had to trade yours away."

"Why?" Jim is incredulous.

"That's how I got you out of hot water with the provosts. Don't you remember?" After a pause: "I guess you wouldn't remember."

"Damn it." There is an explosion. "What about rum?"

"Sir, not now for Christ's sake! We're in a battle!"

"Cooley, I'm telling you now, get me one or two shots of rum and I'm back in the game; without it, I'm good for nothing. Go!" Cooley looks at him wide-eyed and unbelieving. "GO!" Cooley goes back the way he came. Jim wonders if he is going to bring back someone to relieve him of his command. He hardly cares.

A messenger runs upstairs; it is Witchewski. "Sir, Therrien's boys got to the bottom of it. The Jerries have tunnels between buildings; they pop up, shoot, disappear, pop up somewhere else! They had a hell of a fight in there, and tossed some grenades down their hidey hole!"

"Then we're just going to destroy this town, building by building. I can't call in the artillery; my radio's busted. We'll have to use the tanks and mortars, and we have to get in some AT guns. Get some 6-pounders in here to help take this town apart!"

"Okay, sir, I'm on it!" Jim is dazzled by his own semblance of courage, though as Witchewski departs in search of heavy support weapons, the house is hit by a mortar bomb, and Jim hits the floor, the floor that slopes into a sagging hole wreathed in splinters, and his leg hangs over the hole and his pants are torn and his skin is scratched by a jagged spear of wood, and he feels that tingling, senses the world whiten at the corners, hears all sounds recede into the distance, into the echoey corridors of faintness, and he feels his heart pound, his mind frozen, his breath shallow and heaving; and he reaches to pick up the helmet he has tossed onto the floor, and he picks it up and puts it back on his head and refastens the chinstrap just to focus his mind on something. Fatigue and fear and despair have finally claimed him, have marked him as unfit, have rendered him a shellshocked malingering coward, a failure, a jittering nervous wreck. Someone is now shouting at him, and he looks up and sees Doyle shouting, imploring him for information, for orders, for something.

"Permission to move up the street from Tom and capture Dick and Harry! We will move up with a tank and we will blow our way through those houses!"

"Yes, go ahead," Jim says, picking himself up, addressing Doyle with dazed eyes and withdrawn voice. "Go ahead, you have my permission. Sorry, I'm just stunned is all, just stunned." Doyle pierces him with a barbed and lingering glance before dismissing himself to undertake the task of advancing up the road; he can clearly see that Jim is wobbling, that his command over his own faculties, and therefore the company, is uncertain. Another mortar round impacts nearby, called in, in all likelihood, from the heights of the nearby castle, and Jim feels an electrical charge surge through his nerves, an involuntary contraction of muscles, a zap of fear. Get it together Jim, get it together. He hums with a trembling voice, rock a bye baby on the treetops, when the wind blows the cradle will rock, when the bough breaks, rocking and swaying gently—

"Here you go, sir," Cooley says to Jim, putting a metal flask of rum up to his nose, the fumes of alcohol wafting upward into his nostrils, "Drink up." He takes two large gulps of strong, syrupy rum, and as it burns its way down his gullet it kindles a strength within him that brings with it both focus and a deadening of awareness, and he hands the flask to Cooley to share a sip and thanks him for his effort. Down the creaking steps piled with dust he goes, into the main room, shouting orders: "Okay, Doyle, up you go, that's it, go, go, all others provide covering fire! Let's kick these Jerries out of town! Let's go!"

Members of Doyle's platoon charge out, a tank lumbering its way down the street to cover them, crunching over rubble, and the tank blasts into a house again and again, blasting the bombed-out ruin into a shell of itself, and the infantrymen charge into the house in search of defenders holed up in the basement. Other members of the company fire from windows of captured houses, from slit trenches in yards, from ragged roof holes. After a brief shootout the house is in company hands, and two dazed prisoners are whisked out, one of them a stunned blonde boy with dusty, floppy hair and a bloodied face, and the other a shorter, wider man shaved bald and a look of resolute hatred on his face; they are waved off by a corporal and fall into the hands of men in Therrien's platoon, and they are marched off to the rear. As they stumble by, someone whistles as if whistling to a comely woman.

XXXI

All about small battles rage, small fires blending into one monstrous inferno. Two companies and numerous tanks are now engaged in the battle for the town, shooting their way through the bombed-out streets, blasted gardens and shells of shops and houses, and fighting on the outskirts, trading fire with the defenders of the surrounding farms and the Malatesta castle holding sway over all. Overhead is the drone of airplanes, vast swarms of buzzing, rumbling planes that bomb and strafe German positions and German reinforcements, and go back to land, reload, and do it again and again and again, an aerial highway of obliteration and liquidation. Through tunnels German soldiers scramble and emerge into buildings, firing and disappearing, and houses cave in consequently under the blasting of tanks and mortars. A pall of dust and smoke obscures the town, fires burn, guns and mortars pound, small arms crackle, grenades concuss, and men yell and swear and scream in English and German; others groan unheard, holding in their innards, praying and trembling and cursing in the midst of the chaos around them.

Into the town grumble a small troop of open carriers towing 6-pounder anti-tank guns and carrying their crews. Into the acrid fog they arrive, and the crews dismount and pull their guns into positions and join the fray, gun crews ducking behind the blast shields of their long-nosed guns, jamming in shells and aiming and firing and breaching the walls of houses and gardens, giving close and accurate supporting fire to the beleaguered infantry. Into the yawning holes and broken doors of buildings blasted open by the guns and tanks, into the heaps of rubble and broken furniture move small parties of anxious infantrymen, guns at the hip at the ready, to engage in ruthless hand-to-hand combat in those houses where the defenders decide to make a stand; a melee of grenades and submachine guns, riflebutts and spades, fists and teeth and knives and bayonets; of snarling shouting spitting naked violence, the stubborn bluntness of different countries' policies toward one another, a hot and fevered intercourse, an explosive consummation of the rising tension of suspicion and threats.

As Able Company fights its way deeper into the town, Jim finds himself charging into the fray and into the broken shell of another house, its roof gone, the second floor completely collapsed, cleared moments ago by soldiers in his company just ahead of him after being holed numerous times by two tanks and a 6-pounder gun. He steps over the mound of rubble in the centre of the house and avoids the plaster- and dust-covered corpse of a German soldier, the head flattened by a swing from a shovel, like a squashed pumpkin, black blood soaking through the surrounding plaster dust, a failed infusion of life into clay. Beside the body lies the disused metal tube of a *faustpatrone*, an anti-tank rocket launcher. Soldiers comb through the wreckage, room to room, to see if there are any others lying in wait. A tall, bewildered-looking soldier with jug ears and a beret instead of a helmet, a new recruit, stands with his spade, stunned and impressed by his own handiwork.

"Come on! Outcha come, outcha come!" come the hoarse commands of Witchewski from the doorway leading down into the darkness of the cellar. "Let's go, let's go, outcha come!"

"Don't shoot, don't shoot, we are coming!" exhorts a ragged, exhausted-sounding voice from the cellar. Three prisoners stagger out of the basement, two of them supporting another, helping him walk; the legs of the wounded one are badly mangled, blood soaking through the shredded tatters of his pantleg. Witchewski grabs the lead German by his lapels and yanks him through the doorway, and the others are yanked along with him, almost losing their grip, and the wounded one winces in pain, eyes squeezed shut; and they are shoved into the street to be herded along to a prisoners' cage somewhere in the rear. Pistol drawn, Jim stalks through the ravaged interior and out the back door into the untended and overgrown garden, and he can see through a blasted break in the wall of the yard men pushing a 6-pounder along on its rubber tires, grunting and sweating and heaving and shouting as they do so, the axle of the wheels squeaking. Another German emerges from the mouth of a tunnel in the garden in an attempt to escape; as Jim catches sight of him the man is promptly shot in the back and falls forward, doubled over, his legs still in the hole from which he tried to crawl to safety; blood blooms through his shirt, patterned into and dying its dusty fibres. His Schmeisser machine pistol lies discarded beside him. Another shot to the head, and a final electric twitch through the arm, a final shiver of life.

"Got 'im!" yells out a voice from behind, that of a man impressed with himself. There is a loud bang and a shudder in the earth, from under the centre of the house, as engineers detonate the cellar, and the remainder of the house falls in on itself into a rock pile in a great shroud of dust, no longer usable as an enemy strongpoint. Jim is reminded of the mining blasts underfoot from his childhood, many years ago.

The house effectively silenced, Jim ducks in the garden to plan his next moves. There is a momentary lull in his sector; most of the fighting he can hear now comes from beyond, where Charlie Company, under the command of Major Rowlands, is fighting. Overhead streak shells, a barrage from behind the lines onward to German positions elsewhere in the massive battle in which he plays a small part. Jim takes another slurp from the flask of rum and surveys the town through the break in the wall, the jagged stalagmites of ruin that jut up from the ground, the swirls and roils of smoke. He can hear little out of his damaged ear; its hearing has been muffled, the sounds all sounding as though from far away. He sensibly chases the slurp of rum with one of water from his canteen, and water runs down his face, and he wipes the water from his face with his forearm and puts the canteen away, and he suddenly finds himself at a loss for what to do. He sees the waver of his fevered, adrenal pulse beat at the corner of his gaze; he longs for a cigarette but knows that the curl of smoke could send a signal to an awaiting sniper, and that he could end up caught in a stranger's sights ... and this for the moment does not bother him. Not at all. He considers lighting up a cigarette, considers pulling out his pistol and raising it high, revealing himself beyond all doubt to be an officer, and yelling "Charge!" and advancing toward the central piazza, where a German tank holds sway, into the booby-trapped centre of the enemy's defensive works, into the sights of any and every weapon that could be brought to bear on him. He would be at least assured an honourable memory. Doyle or Therrien could take command of the company, or they could hand it over to Olczyk, left out of battle and sitting and waiting in reserve. This whole thought occurs to him in a visual sequence, with almost no words, a dumb show prologue of the action to come.

A muffled shout from the side of his buzzing left ear. He turns to face Cooley.

"Huh? I can't hear out of that ear, Cooley, you have to speak up!"

"Sir, Staff Sergeant Nichols' been wounded. Covered in shrapnel from a mortar round trying to get us ammo."

"Did the ammo manage to arrive?"

"Yes sir, it's on its way into town."

"Okay, thanks Cooley."

"Sir, how're you faring?" A hint of a concerned smile.

"I'm okay, thanks Cooley, just catching my breath." Jim tries to clear his head, to focus on the action at hand, though the rum is starting to dull not only his sensations, but also his thoughts. Other soldiers rally together and await Jim's order, the house now taken, the strongpoint destroyed. Where to, sir? What next, Captain? Expectant eyes stare upon him. He realizes that they must halt their forward advance toward the central piazza, where the German tank reigns supreme, and try to link up with Charlie Company, engaged in furious combat on Able's flank and under fire from the battlements of the medieval castle, to try to bridge the gulf between them, to try to cut the German defence in two, to seal as many of the defenders off in a pocket as is possible and destroy them thus. He relates all this in words he barely registers as he speaks them.

To this end, Doyle holds his position on the company's front. Members of Therrien's platoon veer right to draw out and engage a sniper who has opened up from the window of a house; mortars are summoned by Tillman to augment this attack. Therrien then sends another section to comb down an adjacent street to draw fire, so that Jim, with the aid of Tillman and Neidhart, can relay orders to nearby tanks and mortars to destroy any enemy positions that reveal themselves. Jim sticks by Stringer's platoon, and together they take positions to provide covering fire and direct the fire of nearby mortar and tank crews. Sure enough, a sniper shot cracks and a soldier is felled. Soldiers scramble to cover, and there is another shot. The source is located, the roof of a house, and soldiers begin cracking away with their rifles and letting loose with machine guns. Mortar rounds bear down on the sniper's house, called in by Tillman who is by Jim's side. Another house-clearing struggle ensues. It is time to for he himself to move forward, to try to close the gap between companies.

Jim shouts and waves men onward, and as they crouch and move ahead to catch up with their compatriots, into a leafy lane lined with trees and the walls of closely packed backyard gardens, overlooked by tall houses eyed with windows and blast holes, there is a shot from behind, another sniper. Perhaps the one who was just firing at them from another house. As they dash ahead into the smoke, he sees ahead of him two medical runners carrying a stretcher laden with a wounded soldier toward them. The wounded man contorts in agony, grasping at the sheet as if to life itself. A pair of mortar rounds crash down into the lane, and there is a correspondent rain of debris. The medics fall to their knees, the stretcher and the wounded soldier falling to the ground. Jim can see that the wounded man has no legs below the knees; there is only a bloody mass of ragged bandages. One of the medics himself has his head swaddled in a dressing. The stretcher-bearers pick up their gravely wounded charge and continue their trot to the aid post beyond the perimeter of the town. More mortar rounds dive in and crash about the houses and the streets.

The platoon makes a break for it down the lane, into the smoke, section by section, quickened by the sudden bombardment, dashing in a low hunch, weapons in hand, followed by Jim and his small entourage. A distant machine gun pronounces upon them from on high a rapid and staccato death sentence. Two soldiers, Carson and Symic, are caught by the sweep of the machine gun and crumple over as if punched by the air itself. Carson lies still, unconscious or dead, while Symic writhes in agony, clutching his gut and his pelvis, and bullets beat and disrupt the earth all round. Nearby, a grenade bursts, flung from a window; the rest of the platoon duck from the shower of debris, crouching by the wall, protected partly by it and by the staccato hail of covering fire from their comrades.

"Fire into that fucking window!" shouts Stringer from behind a broken wall. Rifles and a Bren gun are trained on the window in a furious clatter, bullets chipping away at the masonry and window frame, cutting through the curtain. "Get the PIAT on there!" In response to this order, two soldiers crouching beside him fumble about loading and cocking a spring-loaded anti-tank projector. One of them then braces the weapon against a broken section of the wall and, resting the tube on his shoulder, squeezes the trigger. There is an explosion up inside the window of the house. "Corporal Tomlinson! Lead your section in and clear that house! Move!" and the soldiers of Corporal Tomlinson's section leap to their feet as Tomlinson relays to them a signal, protected by the fire of their comrades now banging away with their rifles. In minutes the house is silenced, and the rest of the lane seems for the moment clear.

"Advance to the end of the street!" shouts Jim.

They leap into the fray, covered by Corporal Tomlinson's section, now holding the house they have just stormed. An eternity of a moment. Bullets snap by from beyond, impossibly fast, knifing through the air. He feels as though he is running through water, through molasses, through quicksand, as though he cannot move fast enough. He feels at the random mercy of fate. If he is hit, he is hit, that's just the way it is, there is no escaping from such speed, such force. Past Carson, his blood pouring onto the stones, channelled into and streaming through the cracks between them and irrigating the weeds from a half-dozen holes, eyes bugged white. Past Symic, who reaches out to grab onto someone, anyone, legs and pelvis soaked in blood. Behind, another loud bang. He dives to the ground, to a smell of dirt and cordite mingled with the lactic taste of his own exertion. As he stands up again and resumes his run to the façade of the house at the end of the street, there is the mechanical grunting of an approaching engine, and the long barrel of a self-propelled gun protrudes through what was once the window of a building. He can scarcely formulate the words to command those about him to take cover when the gun belches a tongue of flame, and there is a whooshing vacuum beside him, a sharp bang behind. Another machine gun erupts, and there are the harsh shouts of German commands: "*Schnell! Schnell!*" The vehicle crashes through the remains of the wall, fully visible, its long barrel set in the slopes of its armour, its engine grunting and rumbling. The engine labours and the tracks squeal and grind as the vehicle pivots to aim at another target. Another shot, and behind, a Bren carrier that has just unloaded spare ammunition is hit, bursting into flames. The driver leaps out of the blazing and crumpled wreck, clothing aflame, shrieking and rolling in the street, until another soldier smothers the flames by dropping a gas cape on him. Soldiers scatter and run backward. Jim cannot help but to join the retreat, which is hastened by the bark of the machine gun, the crackle of rifle fire on the heels. Another shell tears by and blasts away the corner of a house held by men in Jim's company. Jim dives into a deep slit trench dug into a garden, one of the Germans' defensive works now in Allied hands. Members of the company regroup in similar positions and in houses now held by them. Under a protective hail of artillery and mortar and machine-gun fire, German soldiers race in to occupy a deep trench dug in front of the gun. Several fall as they do so, shot by members of Able.

There is the sound of approaching men in the distance, of boot-steps marching from their distant right. They are from Baker, coming to mop up resistance in Able's wake and push beyond. Neidhart's radio, tuned in to the same frequency as those of the tanks, has been broken and discarded in the retreat, and Jim fires a red flare into the sky from a Verey pistol to warn the tanks of the mobile gun; and the soldiers of Baker's leading platoon are pinned down, unable to do anything as German mortars and artillery shells begin to rain down them as well. It is unthinkable for the tanks to penetrate this far into town, with so many anti-tank boobytraps and such weapons as the self-propelled gun and the German tank holding the central piazza. The attack has stalled.

XXXII

Over a hastily eaten midmorning breakfast of rations, of dry scones and hard bread and saccharine jam, Jim is able to centre himself a little and think up a way to deal with the gun impeding their advance.

"Cooley, I don't suppose you've been able to scrounge up anything better than this in our journeys this morning?" he jokingly asks as he bolts a scone with jam.

"'Fraid not, sir. It's hairy out here." A grin as he takes a drink from his canteen.

"I can't believe we've been fighting in this town for over four hours."

"Time flies when you're having fun."

Jim guffaws. "True enough, true enough." Now it is time for business, he thinks. "Okay, we need to get this gun out of the picture before we link up with Charlie. Stringer!"

"Yes, sir!" responds Sergeant Stringer from his neighbouring hole, keeping hidden from the bombardment.

"I'll round up all the company PIATs, and then we will attack their position head-on. I will go in with you. I will get Doyle to hold our main line of advance and cover those machine guns and snipers, and Therrien to cover our attack. Got it?"

"Yes, sir!"

"Hey, Cooley," he says, looking beside him at Cooley, who is nervously holding his rifle upright in his lap.

"Yes, sir, what?"

"Come with me to Therrien's command post. I need you to help carry some ammunition." Cooley follows Jim back to Therrien's position behind the sole remaining wall of a house, and as they scramble to this position, they are harried by machine-gun fire.

"Sir!" exclaims Therrien with surprise at their arrival, huddling at the base of the wall under its only window with several of his soldiers, one of them wounded in the side and shivering.

"We need to rush that gun." An explosion from the gun pulverizes the earth nearby as the German gun crew tries to methodically smoke out the attackers, giving impetus to Jim's words. Mortar rounds pepper the area as well, keeping the men further pinned down. "We need to rush that gun," he repeats. "Therrien, you will stand by in reserve and provide fire support for us when we move in. Once we take out the gun and consolidate our position, you will push ahead to link up with Charlie—understand?"

"Okay sir, no problem."

"Also, give us your PIAT."

"Okay, sir, it's yours." Jim takes the platoon's anti-tank projector from one of Doyle's soldiers, Lance Corporal Snell, and Cooley takes a satchel of ammunition. The two of them scurry back to his trench with the heavy and cumbersome weapon and its accompanying ammunition, risking incoming mortar rounds and machine-gun volleys as they do so, and they give it and the ammo to Stringer to delegate who in his platoon will carry it.

"Witchewski!" Jim shouts into the fray. "Witchewski!"

"Yes!" responds Witchewski from a nearby trench.

"I want you to make a break for Doyle's position and tell him to cover those high buildings on our front with the machine guns and the snipers. Round up a 6-pounder or two to give them more punch. Have them flush out any snipers and destroy them if possible. They can hold the line at least until Baker gets there. Take Lafontaine and Cavanagh with you and send them back here with their PIAT, so that we can better deal with the gun. Once we take out the gun, we can send in tanks with Baker to finish those positions off!"

"Yes, sir, I'm on it!" Witchewski assures him. "Lafontaine, Cavanagh, come with me!" At Witchewski's command, Lafontaine and Cavanagh shimmy out from their positions and the three of them scramble under fire to Doyle's more distant position.

The soldiers wait in their positions for Doyle to engage the machine guns and snipers harassing them, and enemy mortar bombs dive in among them, the concussions pummelling the earth and reverberating off the walls. After what seems an eternity, as Jim sweats in his earthy trench and huddles from the incessant mortar blasts, he hears a cacophony of gunfire from Doyle's direction, complete with the banging of two 6-pounders. They have received Witchewski's message, thank God. Moments later, Cavanagh, weighted down with a PIAT and ammunition satchel, struggles back under the weight of his load amid the exploding mortar bombs and plunks back into his trench, sweating from strain and fright.

"Here's the PIAT," he huffs. "Lafontaine got wounded on the way back. Shrapnel."

"Thanks, Cavanagh, glad you made it back okay. Give it to Stringer." Jim then shouts out, "Platoon mortars at the ready with smoke! Get ready to lay down a smokescreen on their position and keep it up until we're on them! Alternate with high explosive as well to keep them down! And Tillman, get a fix on those trenches and be ready to call in the coordinates to your mortars to stonk them! Platoon mortars, when the 3-inchers come in, fire your smoke rounds!"

"I've called in the shots!" shouts Tillman from a nearby trench. "They're on their way!"

"Be ready, Stringer," advises Jim. Moments later, two mortar rounds crash in near the trench. Tillman calls in again to adjust the range, and then more come crashing in about the Germans' defences. Smoke rounds from the company's own small 2-inch mortars burst amid the defenders as well, obfuscating the view in an acrid haze. More enemy mortar rounds crash in, again, and again and again.

Jim rallies his men and yells, "8 Platoon, ready with covering fire! 9 Platoon, advance!" This they do, covered by men from Therrien's platoon. From the lip of the trench he leaps, moving ahead in a low crouch, and the men make their way up the slight incline of the lane, and a round from the big gun lands nearby, felling a tree; mortar bombs explode in their midst. As they get closer, bullets whip past in a swarm. Closer, he can now see the barrel of the gun. The vehicle turns on its axis to point straight at them. Everyone has made it, except Private Smith, who is clutching his foot and clenching his teeth. He has been wounded by the gun, or by the mortars. The stretcher-bearers will get him. Jim looks ahead and the barrel of the German gun recoils, spitting a dragon's breath of flame. The shell explodes close by, felling several men.

Jim's men trade fire, firing their rifles and submachine guns and their light machine guns from the hip, and bullets ring off the armoured hull and casemate of the gun, and men firing from trenches around the gun and from houses in the distance return fire at them. They charge at the soldiers in front of and around the gun position, German soldiers frantically firing and reloading and pitching stick grenades at them. The grenades explode among them. Several fall from enemy bullets and shrapnel, wounded. Men lob grenades into the trenches and fire down on them, killing and maiming the defenders. In the fever of the melee, Jim dodges a swing from a shovel. The wild-eyed German soldier swinging the shovel hits someone else in the head before being gunned down in a blaze of bullets from a Bren machine gun fired from an advancing soldier's hip, and he slumps into his trench. Able Company overwhelms the position, and realizing this, the crew of the self-propelled gun throw their vehicle into reverse, but it is knocked out by projectiles fired from the three PIATS carried by soldiers in Stringer's platoon. The crew attempt to surrender, to run out the top hatch of their now-burning vehicle, but they are cut down to a man in a fusillade of rifle fire, their bodies tumbling off the casemate onto the pile of stones below them.

Jim observes this last coup de grace in a half daze, nodding to his men, bells born of noise tolling in his head this recent forfeiture of life. Men begin combing through the belongings of the dead Germans. One of them tosses aside an empty wallet; another peels the boots off from another. Someone kicks away a coal scuttle helmet. Jim's soldiers begin occupying the slit trenches and the ruins of adjacent buildings, and men from Therrien's platoon and from Baker Company move ahead in the push to link with Charlie Company. In his newly taken trench, over which looms the imposing wreck of the gun, Jim attempts to catch his breath. Cooley and Neidhart are with him, and they deepen the trench with their spades in this lull in the battle, the action for the most part having moved beyond where Baker has joined the fight. Jim surveys the decimated ranks of his company, ordering them to fortify, to dig in and hold, and as he does so, another clutch of mortars comes raining down on them. He huddles against the side of the trench, and he joins in the digging, hacking into the earth and heaving a shovelful of dirt out onto the ground. There is the crack of a rifle. Neidhart whimpers in pain. Jim presses himself to the dirt wall of his trench, against the hairy root endings, and he turns to face Neidhart, who is holding his face and rocking himself back and forth, blood in his hands, and he sees as Neidhart moves his hands that he is missing his four upper teeth, and there is a hole through each of his cheeks, his mouth a sobbing, blubbering, bloody hole; as well, there is a bloody gash in his forehead from him hitting his head against a rock when he was shot.

"Neidhart!" Jim addresses him in a harsh whisper. There is another crack of a rifle shot amid the shelling and mortaring. Neidhart whimpers and shouts and sobs. Neidhart's war is finished; he will never again regain his nerve, he has what they call combat exhaustion, what is more accurately described as shellshock. Jim at once feels sorry for him and loathes him, and he looks at this simpering coward, this stout and muscular farmboy reduced to a trembling child with a mouthful of broken teeth and a bleeding forehead, and he wants to shake him, and he wants to punch him, and he wants to toss him aside, and he wants to comfort him, and he hates what he sees because it makes him uncomfortable, and he wants to look away, to avert his eyes from what he may well himself become, what he feels welling up inside him. "Neidhart!"

Neidhart is moaning, rocking himself, "Uh-uh, uh-uh-uh," he is shaking, and his voice is shaking, a fragile whimper, and he puts his hands over the holes of his cheeks.

"Neidhart!" Neidhart tightens into a ball at the bottom of the trench, elbows pressed against his knees, hands blocking the holes in his cheeks, and he rocks himself back and forth, rocking himself in place of his mother whose lap he would crawl into now if he could, momentarily shorn of manhood and dignity. There is a dark patch in the crotch of his khaki woollen pants, the sharp ammonia tinge of urine. "Get yourself together! Here, let me try to clean you up! Cooley, I need some bandages!"

He turns to face Cooley—and he is greeted by sight of Cooley lying dead against the opposite side of the trench, his eyes closed and his face gone a waxy white, blood pouring down his cheek from a bullet in the temple. He is still holding his spade. Coldly murdered in a sniper's sights. Jim registers this sight unbelievingly. His hands begin to tremble. He turns to look at Neidhart again, Neidhart sobbing, bloody hands over his face, whimpering and blubbering like a child. A third shot from the sniper grazes his own shoulder, shredding his maroon divisional patch. He sinks lower into the trench. He feels tears welling in his eyes, tears of sadness, tears of rage. He looks again at Cooley and touches his hand, the hand growing cold in his own, growing cold as the warmth of his life, its thermal register, dissipates into the air, growing cold like the stones and the rocks and the timeworn erosion of the earth that line the walls and floor of the trench.

"Cooley," he whimpers, his own whimpering joining that of Neidhart. He feels ready to stand down, to admit that he has battle exhaustion, to malinger. A tear burns hot down his cheek. "Cooley, I'm sorry Cooley, I'm so sorry, oh God Cooley, why you for Christ's sake why you and not me if it weren't for you I'd be in the stockade right now, oh God Cooley, oh God." He sniffles and his nose runs. He feels rage burn within him, a white-hot rage competing with his anguish, and it begins to focus into a compressed tautness, a controlled and focused anger.

"We need to take out this sniper!" he shouts, tears drying on his cheek. "Flush him out! Where is that goddamn sniper! We need to draw him out!" Another shot lands near another trench; the source seems to be from off to the side, from a house yet untaken, or previously taken and reoccupied by way of the tunnels. A tank approaches, supporting tanks having made their way back into the secured areas of the town as engineers and the platoons from Baker take out remaining anti-tank emplacements and remove anti-tank mines in the northern areas of the town. As the tank approaches, Jim shouts to the commander and the drivers to watch out, batten down the hatches, there is a sniper, we are going to draw him out, and we need you to fire at him. He orders a soldier to leap up and run, and as the soldier does so his actions are answered by a clatter of rifle fire from a row of several houses, and the tank begins shelling the houses, its shells biting away at the walls and at the roofs, blasting and blasting. Jim shouts to Sergeant Stringer to ready members of his platoon, we're going in, and together they surge toward the central house, the one from which the most fire is coming, and they charge to the front door, bullets snapping past them. Bullets crack all about him, and he charges, emboldened by his anger and contemptuous of the vagaries of fate.

Into the gutted, blasted interior of the house they surge. Three soldiers charge upstairs to search amid the broken furniture and gaping shellholes and sagging roof, finding only one body buried in rubble. Jim and Sergeant Stringer and another storm into the kitchen, hearing frantic footfalls in that direction, the tromping of fleeing enemies, Sergeant Stringer spraying bullets from his Tommy gun as they do so. They face the closed wooden cellar door in the floor. Jim pulls open the doors, stone steps leading down into the darkness of the root cellar. All three of them unpin grenades, and in unison they throw them down the stairs, and the grenades clatter and roll down the steps. They crouch to the floor in anticipation of the earsplitting triple bang that erupts smoke and plaster debris up into the room. There is a rush of air, a loss of pressure, a sudden and instant storm. Dust and smoke choke the kitchen. They get up and charge down the steps, Jim in the lead with his pistol drawn, Sergeant Stringer close behind with his Tommy gun. Stringer unloads a drumroll burst from his Tommy gun into the dusty darkness. They look about in the root cellar. There is a jumble of broken furniture, gardening tools, canned goods, a workbench, handsaws and hammers, a smashed table, broken chair legs, all heaped about. The walls are sooty and pitted and sprayed and splashed with dollops of blood. One German is propped against the wall, legs splayed, covered in dust. His midsection is black with dirty blood, centred by his crossed blood-syrupy palms trying to hold in a twisting slither of intestines, as if he were trying to divine his fate from his own entrails. He breathes shallow, gurgly breaths, looks up with wide and pleading eyes. Another is dead across the room, head hanging to the side from a neck sinew like a broken lollipop or candy apple. The last is crumpled amid the jumbled heap of household items, missing a forearm, the splintered white couplings of ulna and radius exposed, stunned surprise on the misting deadlights of his eyes. His torso is a raw and mangled meatscape of perforated flesh. A broken cask spouts airily from a score of ragged holes red wine gone to vinegar, the wine mixing in the dirt with the blood of the dead and dying in base communion, a false transubstantiation of the sacrifice done in this cellar. The air stinks with the sulfurous burn of cordite mixed with the earthy smell of the dirt cellar floor, undercut with the syrupy richness of blood, the humid sickly rot of excrement, the sharp sourness of vinegar. The smoke settles into a greyish pall, like trapped and bitter ghosts. Nausea queases through him as his stomach curdles at the sights and smells he is registering, but he holds his instinct to vomit.

"*Kamerad*," a weak, gasping voice intones, scarcely above a whisper, "*ein wenig Wasser?*" He looks at the quivering man holding in his stinking entrails, sitting against the wall, and he meets his gaze for a moment, and in his eyes he sees the wan and grimacing face of Fitzpatrick all those days ago at the church; in his eyes he sees the man, the boy, who possibly killed Cooley; in his eyes he sees the mirror of his own fear, his own resignation, his own desire to just quit it all and yet frightful of the void, of eternity all about the cracked and tottering precipice on which he sits.

"*Ein wenig Wasser, Kamerad? Eine … eine Zigarette?*" A wan smile. He raises his pistol and shoots the wounded German soldier in the forehead, the sharp crack of his pistol resounding off the walls, the flash of its muzzle flaring into a moment's focus the destruction strewn about. The soldier's head slides sideways, eyes still open, a trickle of blood running down from the perfectly round hole. Most of his blood, it appears, is in his lap and soaking into the thirsty earth of the cellar floor.

"All dead here," he says, turning to face Sergeant Stringer. Stringer looks impassive, his face stern, and he rigidly holds his submachine gun against his chest. "Let's move out." Up the stairs they go and they exit the way they came in; upon exiting, Jim tells Stringer to get the tank, and any other tank that can be mustered, to raze the house to the ground with their turrets, to wreck it as a possible strongpoint, to entomb the dead in their cellar vault. He exits the house back into the garden, and as he does so he hears the clattery roll of a grenade on the concrete walkway behind him, yes the roll of a grenade his spinal column wordlessly knows, and he is about to dive, his muscles reacting with adrenal clarity to his spinal instinct; and the world goes white and becomes noise, noise so loud and all-encompassing white that it becomes silence itself, so sudden that it is eternal, ongoing like the dying of the crash of a gong; and he is airborne, and then there is darkness.

XXXIII

Sssshhhhhh ... Ssssssshhhhh ... Skis gliding through soft drifts of snow. A slow-change of mountains cresting white over valleys bristling with pine and spruce and cedar, a storm-tossed sea slowed to stone in a snapshot instant of perception; liquid earth, the clay of creation, destruction, cremation. Lives inhabiting a single frame see only a frozen storm, a time-lapse moment of earth in action, an increment of its own changing definition, a molten sea to ageless eyes that oversee, if such eyes there be. Mountains crested by snowcaps, the whitecapped surf of great waves congealed into curds in the slowtime of experience.

Sssssshhhhhh ... Sssssshhhhhhhh ... The waves roll in and roll out, and the lathery foam on the beach subsides into the slick wet sand; clumps of seaweed move this way and that in the slow, seething push-pull of the sea; and the waves of the sea are mountains, and the mountains are the sea, and the wind through the wheat makes a wave, the force seen only in its effect. A hundred thousand arms saluting in the air, a hundred thousand sheaves of wheat waving in the oratorical ranting wind, a harvest of souls: "Heil Hitler!" The wind through the wheat like a wave through water, a rippling of the elements like a fold through a rug, a tremor through earth. The mountains are boiling seas and the seas are chains of mountains, force running through the anger of the voice, the swing of the hammer, the pull of the trigger. The sig heil rallies, the newsreels of marching goose-stepping Nazis, the banners snapping in the wind, the tatters of flame, the burning of books, of flags, of nations; conflagration, conflagnation, birth, death, the moving and shaking, the storms and volcanic fury and fire of history. Fascination: fascist nation. A jackbooted puppet of failure and envy and vengeance. We fight a small fool with a huge vendetta. Vendetta: fascisti. Il Duce! A rallying cry ending on the noose of the hanged fascist swinging from a tree in the neighbouring orchard. A marionette made and played by the theatre of conflict, creaking in the breeze this way and that way, head swollen and purple and blackening, eyes bugged out, tongue hanging limply from dry and cracked lips. Puppet of a greater puppet, ventriloquized by Hitler. At this, the breezy rippling of tent flaps become the rally at Nuremburg, thousands of arms waving, voices raving.

Far from this at home on an October morning. The trees are alight like candelabras, each leaf a flame burning yellow, orange, red in the slow, cold fire of autumn, to be consumed into a dry crinkled brown, holocaust of summer. Youth to the fire. Sunk in the mire. Situation most dire. Fire of time, mire of place, set in clay we live our days. Too many images, too many thoughts and few words to name them, to make them thoughts entire. And the waves roll in and the waves roll out, and he is bathed in his own sweat, and the waves roll in and the waves roll out and the waves are mountains and the mountains are waves, and he is nauseous swimming in the sheets, and the creased and rumpled sheets are waves, the waves of oily seas breaking over him as he lies on the beach, the tide coming in, the world shifting and turning and shifting and turning and redefining itself before he can interpret any freeze in its mutations. In a moment of clarity he notices that he is cold and he is sweaty and he needs a glass of water, if only he could say that he needs a glass of water, if only …

"It is okay, McFarlane, you will have your turn, you are in good hands now." Leprenniere smiles at him from the shadows of the tent. "I will fix you up good as new! Then we can play cribbage, you can help me against Doc Allenby from the Strats, we have a bottle of scotch riding on this one, so you just hang in there, McFarlane, I need you." That bushy moustache, that avuncular smile …

"Sir!"

Jim ignores the voice, running down the dusty lane with a section of men, bullets pelting about him. He makes it to his destination, a shallow Jerry trench alongside a hedge, abandoned, and the others leap in along with him.

"Okay, Charbonneau, you take out that Spandau with your PIAT. Everyone else, covering fire."

"Sir!" yells the voice again, right in his ear. It is Charbonneau himself, pressed up against him in the trench, loading a bomb into the muzzle trough of the platoon PIAT. "You're wounded in the arm!" Jim looks down at his arm as Charbonneau cocks the weapon and takes aim, the metal cone of the projectile sticking outward like an Industrial Age arrowhead, and the others fire into the basement window of the house with the machine gun sputtering away, and Charbonneau fires his PIAT, the projectile springing forth and hitting the corner of the window with a blast and a crash of masonry; and all this is distant, distant, as Jim feels a cold faintness about him, a cold faintness and a whitening, spots in front of his eyes like black holes in his consciousness as his blood pressure drops, blood soaking his khakis, and he clutches the hole, yes the hole in me my God you've been hit hope it's not bad don't pass out it doesn't hurt but my, the blood—then the pain begins, a hot burning throbbing pain, a deep aching bone pain, then his breathing becomes shallow and rapid and he feels shock take over, a cold numbing distance from all about him.

He barks some more commands, but Corporal Hendrick will hear none of it, his lieutenant is down, is wounded and he has to get him out of here, and he helps him up and guides him, stunned, to a carrier. The carrier crew drives him back to the aid post, and dirty blood from a dozen men sloshes on the floor of the carrier like fetid water in a swaying bucket as they trundle over bumps and holes in the field outside the smoking ruins of the small hamlet, past a smoking Sherman tank and a burned-out German bunker, all this destruction. They lead him out of the carrier and he finds himself at the aid post, smoking a cigarette on the floor, propped up against the wall, Father Maitland delivering last rites to a man so badly burned he can scarcely be recognized, a tank crewman or a gunner or a downed airman perhaps; beside him is Private Tarnowicz, a Ukrainian and a fellow Sudburian, looking like raw hamburger all chopped up from a shell and sucking wetly air from a hole that was once a mouth based on its location; and on the other side is a captured German paratrooper muttering to himself in German, leg outstretched and bleeding through gauzy field dressings, shivering and muttering and sharing a cigarette with another man beside him; and they sip water, and some others sip rum, he can smell the boozy waft of alcohol.

"*Leutnant*," says the German wanly in the two-syllable German pronunciation of that rank, turning his head to him, buttressed against the wall, "Smoke?"

"Thank you," Jim accepts in a dizzy half whisper, and he takes a long drag and hands it back to the wounded paratrooper, who nods a polite affirmative nod and has a drag and passes it to the wounded soldier beside him.

The medics bring in another, medics smeared in the blood of others, pigmented in the sap of friend and foe alike, a mingling of blood types; and this man has no legs, gauze and bandages wrapped around sickening bloody stumps, the man pallid, the man shivering, let him go before me for God's sake thinks Jim, and he wants to be sick but he holds it in, yes holds it in and rocks against the wall, rocking, about to break, for the first time truly about to break, oh God just get me out of here now now now please, just get me out of here, and he looks to the right as Leprenniere pours sulfa powder into somebody's wound, his face lined with concentration, saying little and doing a lot, humming as he does an old Quebec folksong, and Jim buries his head in his arms as he awaits his turn.

"Hey, Jim, hang in there!" That smile again, as he calmly resuscitates a wounded soldier with fresh blood, the plasma bag suspended from a pole, and Jim feels an unease creep over him, crawl over him, a terrible sinking feeling; he wants to reach out and shout to Leprenniere to get down but the words are caught in his throat—something is going to happen, he knows it, something is going to happen—and he shakes and he jitters and there is a great quaking of the earth as a fusillade of artillery bears down upon them, and the window blows in and the blood bag bursts, and Leprenniere is killed where he stands, shredded by shrapnel and glass, and Jim screams, why, why, oh why didn't I tell him? Why? Why? You knew what was going to happen, you knew, you knew, you knew!

Shaking, twitching, muttering in the sheets.

A shell like a siren. A gate wrought of iron, streaked with rust the rot of iron, adorned at the handle with agate. No poor man's home this is: but whose? Yes yes that's it that mansion in The Glebe some magnate's social magnet. Walked by it once. Spired, looming black behind manicured oaks like the House of Usher. Lumber tycoon methinks, lumber the lumbar of old Ottawa. A spine made of wood, eh? Supporting the head, the government. Wooden spine: blockhead. Built on the back of many a lumberjack. The logs bobbing down the river, vast floating rafts nudged by puffing tugboats. Hoo Hoo! Boozy waft in the air, though cleaner. Rubbing alcohol that is. Some poor bastard's getting a needle. Needle and thread. Takes more than that to sew on the head. Lead. Dead. Buried: to the earth, fed. Dead! Dead! The finality of that word. Dead! Dead! He feels his heart pounding, feverish, feeding the delirium in which he swims bedbound, the trees waving in the breeze, ssssshhhhhh, ssssshhhhhh, the rustle of trees, too windy to swim shall we all head in?

Home at last! He stands in the bathroom of his childhood and turns the faucet and runs a bath. There is a basin of hot water for his disposal. He looks down at his uniform, his sweaty, stinking battledress worn for days and weeks on end. God, but the filth of me. He peels it off and pours into the tub the basin of hot water, and steps in, one leg and then the other, and lowers himself in. In the bathtub a wave, a circle of disturbed water radiating outward as he puts his hand underwater to scratch an itch in his thigh. The hot water pricks his skin like a thousand tiny needles undoing the damage done, threading the frayed ends of nerves back together, knitting skin ravaged and rubbed raw by a week in the stinking, grimy rags of his uniform. His skin is marbled, flushed red, suffused in the heat of the water with his blood, his blood contained in his body in its proper role as sustainer of life.

His penis floats in its nest of hair like a deadhead timber protruding upward from the seaweed depths at an angle, terminating in a mash of wrinkled foreskin. He hugs his legs and cowers from the world—embowered in this copse of trees in a hole in the dying light of dusk amid the rumble of the guns, the ceaseless drumming rumble of the guns, the rubble from the guns, the crumble of buildings under the pounding of the guns, the guns beyond the hills; cowering in his hole, worrying on his fate amid the chlorophyllic freshness of the leafy emanations, contrasted with the sourness of his sweaty Gethsemenations, sharp and skunky, the stinking, clinging grime of his own fear as he hugs his legs and pulls himself tight—

Shifting machinescapes of moving parts: cogs, wheels, gears and pistons grumbling and churning and turning and whirring, wheels within gears within cogs, an infinitely detailed mechanoid monstrosity infernal in its workings, intricate and infinite in scope and scape and ongoing, encompassing and unfolding, a passing digestion through the churning vortices of machinery, a dizzying kaleidoscope of sight and sound folding in on itself and inescapable in its geometric permutations—

Crump! Crump! Tremors underneath. The lamps flicker. Where am I? I'm everywhere. Everywhen. My, I think I'm losing my mind … losing my mind. Mouth muttering the mad meanderings of his mind—Jesus it's like a fever when I was a child when I was a child oh Mommy.

"Mommy? Mommy? It hurts, Mommy."

"It's alright pet, it's alright." Soft moist breath on the back of his neck. She wraps him in a maternal hug, enfolding him in placid sanctuary … the gentle timeless rocking of the chair, hushed calm rocking in the nightmare world of the unknown beyond, primal solace, sssssshhhhhh …

"Hush little baby don't say a word,
Momma's gonna buy you a mockingbird,"

Clinging to her nightgown, to the worn warm smell of sanctuary, soft whispery lullaby tones breathed over him in a wash of tender images that softly illuminate the darkness—

"And if that mockingbird don't sing,
Momma's gonna buy you a diamond ring—"

"I'm going to be sick," he says weakly, thinly, in a tiny voice, mind hot and febrile, a halo around the bathroom light. Halo: Grandma said we all have guardian angels.

"It's okay honey, it's okay." She pulls his hair up from his eyes, his sweaty matted hair, and she holds him as he leans weak over the toilet bowl, bonewhite hands on cold smooth porcelain enamel, and he burps a gurgly nauseous burp and he thinks it's funny the way it sounded, BRRRRRP! And he feels the hot lurch of his stomach, the bubble of burning juices queasing, squeezing their way up, and he tastes and feels the hot burning sourness in his mouth, and he vomits into the bowl, belching all the while, stomach muscles tensing in painful contractions, tugging, tugging, and he heaves again, muscles seized and lungs deflated, and the world turns about him, and the room thumps with a pulse and spots form and dance in front of his eyes and the world goes small and his skin crawls and tingles in this distention of a moment as he heaves again in oxygen debt and past the very limits of his straining stomach muscles; a bilious yellow stream projects from his mouth, and he can't yet catch his breath; it tugs, tugs, tugs, God the colonel's gonna kill me I'm drunk about to be rebuked by the colonel oh God just kill me now and get it over with I should be shot at dawn or break rocks in the quarry for this, and Mother soothes with her hand his shoulder and ruffles again his sweaty hair now, and she says, "There now, there now it's over, let's get some water and some rest," as the tenseness subsides, the world returning to its proper proportions, the vertigo ebbing, the swaying revolutions of the world about him slowing, his stomach settling, and he spits out little chunks and bits caught in his teeth, ridding his mouth of the pungent sour taste, Mother so soothing, so soft, like when she sat him in the chair in the basement and rubbed stinking heavy coal grease into his hair which made him smell like tar; sssshk sssshk went the comb, nits gritting against the teeth of the fine-toothed comb dragging backward along his scalp and furrowing the greasy mat of hair into waxy rows, ssshk ssshk, long and careful strokes scraping his scalp, a cool and satisfying feeling, though it hurt a little, though his hair was being pulled backward; he could see the bluing of the clothes soaking in the laundry tub by the stairs, could smell the heavy creosote smell of tar-gelled hair, could feel its waxy weight upon his head, could still feel safe, safe, yes safe, safe, safe from the schoolyard taunts, the chanting of "You have li-ice! You have li-ice!" I got it from Tommy Bowden I know I did he's the poor kid never bathed always wore old clothes his Daddy beat him yes that's what they say, his Daddy got home from the mine and drank and beat him with his belt, he gave me lice, he probably works in the mine and comes home and drinks and beats his son now too, sssshk sssshk sssshk went the comb, and the heavy brownish grease made him smell of sunbeaten tarsweaty railway ties—walking along the tracks with a fishing rod slung over shoulder, the tarry smell of ties in the air; ear to the rail and he could feel the vibration of an approaching train telegraphing its presence through the conducive strands of metal, the chugging rumble of an approaching freight train—blustering black locomotive bearing down, reciprocating rods turning great iron wheels, a flash of sparks, stack unspooling thick sooty smoke into the sky. With each chug and piston turned there was spiritual release, fossil fulfillment, ancient fossil spirits released through the medium of the steam engine and its rhythmic chugging mantra. The smile and wave of the coveralled engineer from the cab as it roared by with its coaltender car in tow and piled high with coal, followed by the weighted rhythmic gallopy clatter of railcars, a hundred of them that time it seemed, the train shuddering the latticed beams of the trestle underneath it; boxcars closed and stuffed with goods or riding empty, both doors open, framing the passing scenery; flatcars stacked and bound with timbers or steel 'I' beams or newfangled farm machinery and Massey-Harris tractors; slag-heaping ore hoppers and oblong black gleaming oil tanker cars; slit-windowed and wood-panelled cattle cars packed with livestock and trailing their barnyard scents; followed by the caboose, a little house with chimney on screeching metal wheels. Impressed by the power of modern machinery, the sound of it, the weight and speed of it, the squealing of metal wheels on metal rails, the bucking of wheels from rail-length to rail-length, the roar and the tremor underfoot; yes, yes, I remember that, caught two sunfish after, too, caught two sunfish at the creek and threw them back, not good eating, too bony Dad said, not good eating but fun all the same to catch; the nibble-bent nudging of the rod, the tugging, the rush of excitement in pulling them in and holding them by their mouths and unhooking them, tiny teeth in rubbery maws picky on the fingers, slitted silvery fishgills fanning their red razor rows as they tried to wring oxygen from the air; tarsweaty hair creosoaked in grease, and his mother combed those lice out of his hair by the steel laundry tub with a black fine-toothed comb, and it went sssshk sssshk sssshk sssshk sssshk, gritting against and collecting the nits in his hair, the voice soothing, saying, "Now you'll be clean, you'll be lice-free, you can go back to school now, get these bad little bugs out of here where they don't belong"; sssshk sssshk went the comb the razor on his face, harvesting whiskers, shaving behind the lines before the battle while the shells crumped harmlessy in the distance, muffled through the walls, the floor; savouring the razor's scrape, a civilized cutting of weeds, a gardening of the self, a morale-boosting ablution, man rising from the animal within, from the overgrowth, oh God that feels good it does I feel like a gentleman now feel like sssshk sssshk the bullets shearing through the hedge all about and overhead as Schneider reached out to a stranger and died alone beside him clasped hand in hand ...

Get a grip on yourself man, breathe, you're a man now, you're in the army, you're in the hospital. Sweating dreams into the sheets in expiatory fever. Head cupped in the hands of a woman.

"There, it's over, take a rest," says the soothing voice, the nurse holding him up over the metal pan he has just puked in. The hospital rumbles as a convoy of military traffic passes by. "It's okay Captain, just relax, you're alright now, just relax." He feels shaky, jittery, his hands are flushed and clammy, images and sounds mix and mash. "I think maybe you're not handling the morphine too well."

"Am I okay?"

"You're doing great." She smiles a professional smile.

"I thought you were my mother," he says weakly, smiling wanly. "I'm really out of it." His voice is wavering. He catches a sharp, sour whiff of his own vomit.

"I know you did," replies the nurse, and she looks at him, her eyes kind and sad. "And you thought you were fishing, and you thought you were watching a train, and you thought you were shaving, too." She looks young, no older than twenty-five, with pert auburn hair cut in a bob that accentuates her youth. Seen her before I'm sure of it, think her name's Gwen, yes seen her before when laid up before with my arm my throbbing arm, sure I saw her after Leprenniere bought it at his post, RIP in the RAP, when they sent me back to the aid post wasn't I just there now again yes I know I was I know I was. Shoulda warned him, shoulda told him. Coulda warned him. She picks up the pan and is about to carry on, when Jim interrupts her with question.

"Are you a mother?" he asks, gathering himself and clinging to the conversation to pull himself together, out of the fever-dream world which will surely kill him.

"No, I'm not, I'm not even married," she answers with a soft and thoughtful laugh, a little taken aback by the question. "Hmmm." She smiles close-mouthed at him, and lets him be, leaving.

"Nurse?"

"Yes?" She looks over her shoulder, paused in mid-stride, puke-filled pan in hand.

"Am I okay?"

"You're doing great." Form-letter response. Like a government telegram. She continues on her way and returns with a glass of water a minute or a thousand years later, it is hard to tell which. "Drink this, Captain, it will make you feel better."

"Thank you." He sips the water. It soaks into his parched and pasty mouth, into his thick and swollen tongue. The lantern above shines a dull orange, haloed in its own light, and the world about him thuds with a pulse and the walls of the tent shimmer in vivid shadow-play as they billow gently in the breeze. "Thank you."

"You're welcome." She is wearing a long brown felt coat and her black pillbox hat that he loves so much. "I'm glad you like it." He takes his new wallet and inserts his money and his driving license and birth certificate into it after emptying his old one, his old tattered wallet, splitting at the seams, frayed threads sticking out raggedly from the hole in the corner, tattered and battered beyond repair; and he throws the old one in the wastebasket.

"Happy birthday. I tolerated that one for too long—so shabby!" She laughs at him, and he shrugs and smiles sheepishly. And they walk, and the tent walls billow in shadow-play, and the clouds move through the sky, the halo of the lantern the rays of an evening sun, the orange glow of a harvest moon, and why oh why did you do it really why did you do it why did you leave what is the reason really?

She asks him this, toe tapping rhythmically on the floor in the kitchen, toe in silk stocking want to crawl under the table and put it in my mouth just unroll that stocking and take it out of the stocking and suck, suck her toe under the table it makes me feel so dirty my dirty little mind like Miss Klein in school wanted to take off her black heels and just suck, suck, suck her toes lick in between them and purse my lips over the webbing and suckle yes, oh yes, want to smell her shoes the worn leather lived-in smell like my helmet I suppose but so much more appealing not the smell of a dirty man with dirty thoughts want to lick her pussy want to crawl up between her legs kissing up her leg, kissing up her leg oh yes her stockings rolled up in my hand, want to lick her pussy just put my tongue inside and lick oh my God what haven't I done what haven't I done I'm so inexperienced I'm so sorry for these dirty thoughts right now my darling I haven't seen you in two years darling I have a mind like a French postcard darling rings out rather falsely now doesn't it after all we've been through after all I've put you through I'm sorry I have these dirty thoughts these dirty perverted thoughts like masturbation, pulling the pud, cranking the shaft, choking the chicken, stroking the sceptre, the shame of it when I did it, the Christ staring down from the cross hanging over the dining-room doorway bloody shame of it, the hair on my palms shame of it, the wasteful messy sticky milky shame of it, when I did it I thought something broke inside, the whole squalid shame of it; forgive me Father for I have sinned, the dusty pleated curtain of the confessional like the pleats of his dress kilt worn proudly on the march, I'm sorry Father the shame of it, I've done so many things I've thought so many things and I'm sorry, I didn't study, I just thought of Miss Klein, the shame of it, hands and knees against stones scurrying under the church pew to hide from the bombardment and hide your shellshock from the men rather than try to rally their morale while they were shelled time and time again, leaving your wife why so you look elsewhere to create your legacy and you add more bodies to this war how many people have you killed or had killed because of what private demons oh the bloody shame, shame, shame of it!

How many have you killed? How many that you have seen with your own eyes? One. Between the eyes, in the basement, bang with his pistol like the mule put out of burning misery, the man with splayed legs and his guts in his hands yes his guts in his hands his sticky slithering guts in his hands and the blood between his fingers and black in his clothes, the sticky syrupy meaty raw steak in butcher's paper smell of it, mixed with shit, stinking shit spilling out of intestines mixed with the smell of smoke, of plaster, of broken stone and splintered wood, of spilled vinegar, of destruction, of deconstruction; those eyes, those young schoolboy eyes, those stunned eyes, understanding eyes, the eyes of a man who knows this is it, it's over, this is the final moment ... watching inevitability playing itself out, watching gravity assert itself, the laws of a moment reaching their verdict, their capital sentence, an eternity between those final heartbeats that beat like the beating of a gavel, the tolling of the bell to your own funeral; those eyes in the crack of the pistol frozen, last sight and every memory like a roll of film ripped from the camera, exposed, a flash of white, blinding exposure to the light.

A shadow hunches over him, the shadow of a man in the flickering half light of the tent, and he tries to avert his eyes, and he hides his face in his pillow for a moment, buries himself in his sheet, the monster has emerged from his closet from behind the coal pile behind the furnace in the basement, from the shifting labial shadows of the tent wall, and is now looming over him, and he looks again and the shadow is closer, and he can see now the face of the man standing over him, can see the wan greyish bloodless face and the bullet hole between the eyes, can smell the rotting meat stench of his breath, and a hand reaches out to touch him, and the hand touches his arm, cold, clammy, moist and blistered with putrefaction, and the lips mouth, "Come with me ... "

The approach to the front was tedious, a long march down the country road, and his head was sore from all that Dago wine with Schneider and Weiszack the night before; he could still taste the alcohol two hours after awakening. His head sweat under his cap in the beating of the sun. His tongue was thick and dry. *Mein Gott,* he thought, my God it's hot out here and Decker has smoked my last damned cigarette. Thoughts turned to Elsa, back to Hamburg, if only he could call her and she could answer from the switchboards— oh Elsa I miss you, when you sent me your panties in the mail I nearly creamed myself, and Reinhardt offered me his schnapps ration for them! Obviously, his luck at the brothels has been nil. Must be that he's circumcised, yes he has the mark of the Jew about him, or so says Fricker. This is the sort of knowledge that Fricker would possess; I caught him glancing at Braun and Schneider when we were swimming. Oh Elsa, Elsa, Elsa!

Boots in the road dust, beating up a white pall of chalky grit, the sun in his eyes. Ahead, an even bigger cloud of dust, and as the company caught up he heard the braying of mules or donkeys, and they passed a convoy of field guns and ammunition trailers being towed by mules. Mules—are we really to win when we are reduced to these means, when the enemy has all the fuel and trucks he needs at his disposal? Never mind that we are better fighters than them—they have all the materiel. And where the hell is our transport? Damn logistical messups! Tromp, tromp, tromp, tromp, the monotonous stamp of boots to the front, and the clatter of carts and braying and snorting of mules.

And they marched and marched and marched, over the fields, the sunbaked fields, and over a ridge, and over more fields, and up another slope to a town, a small town on a hill and they passed the townsfolk who were wisely leaving, poor Italian townsfolk smelling a battle in the air, knowing it in their bones and conveying this ancient wearied wisdom in their passing glances, sizing up these latest invaders in a long history of them. Into the alleys they marched, and no sooner did they catch their breath and drink from their canteens and listen to the rolling thunder of the Allied advance beyond the valley before them than they were ordered to dig, and dig they did, into the perimeter of the town and underneath the town, slit trenches and fortifications and tunnels. They dug and they dug; inside the hole they dug and they passed dirt toward the mouth, and they sweated and they stank, hacking away into the chalky dirt with picks and spades in the dim lamplit darkness, hacking with spades and hawking gobs of dirty saliva from their mouths, and the earth shuddered as the bombs fell above them, and they dug and they dug, and the bombs crashed upon them, and they sang "Lilli Marlene" and passed the bottles of wine and smoked cigarettes, and they slept in their trenches and in the cellars and the tunnels.

And they waited in the ruins of the town, knowing that an attack would surely come, the Canadians amassed on the hill ahead of them hunkering down and preparing to attack despite all the artillery that could be brought to bear on them, and they dug and they dug, and they smoked and they talked and they slept when they could, and the bombs continued to fall, and in the lanternlight he read a letter:

Dear Helmut,

I hope that you are holding up well over there. I was doing laundry today and I thought of you, how I used to always wash your clothes. And all you kids making such a racket as I tried to work! I admit I cried a little as I did this. Your father and I and all your sisters miss you so much! But we are proud of your service to the Fatherland. Speaking of which, I hate to be the bearer of bad news, but your cousin Thomas was killed on the Eastern front recently. We are told that he was killed instantly. We can only pray that it was so, and that now he is at peace. Your Uncle Oskar's family's house was destroyed in an air raid—thankfully, they were out of town at the time.

These are hard times. But keep up the fight and come home in one piece. One day, we can all share coffee and cake in the afternoon as a family again, this war behind us like a bad dream. Missing you—

With love,

Mother

And then a tremendous bombardment, a shattering crashing totality of destruction, and the expected attack came in the night, and they fought on the hill in the shell-shattered darkness and fell back, back into the town, and they waited as the enemy soldiers arrived at the town and combed through the streets and lanes and searched through buildings; and then they fired the first shots and the struggle for the town was on, yes, on, and house by house his friends were killed in the melee, and they fell back through the tunnels or dashed through the yards; and then as they fired through the windows and blast holes of a house near where an SP gun got overwhelmed, they attracted a wave of enemy soldiers, and tank shells crashed into the house—one, then another, buffeting the room. A crash of debris. A wall blew inward and he was buried in debris, bleeding from the arms. He picked himself up from the floor in a daze, and he and Kaufman and Braun raced down the stairs as another shell smashed into the house; down the stairs they went as the upstairs was rocked by another hit, and they ran through the parlour, and then enemy soldiers were upon the house, shouting in their coarse barks, and there was a tromping of boots up the stairs, the thud of a grenade, the stutter of rifles and tear of a submachine gun. They made it to the kitchen, and they heaved open the cellar door and leapt down the stairs, pulling it shut behind them, and no sooner did they do this, fumbling through the dark for the mouth of the tunnel, than the door was flung open and there was a shaft of dusty light and the clatter of grenades rolling down the stairs—they all leapt away in different directions, and he tripped backward over some heavy object as he tried to avoid the explosions, and there was a stunning bang … a shivering, shuddering coldness. Ears abuzz. He found himself against the wall, stunned, and he looked down to see his own guts in his lap, and in his dazed state he tried to sensibly hold them in. He almost laughed, with what little energy he had left, almost laughed at this incongruous and ghastly sight, this slither of gore, this indecent outing of innards … out of the smoke approached three figures hunched in the clutter, enemy soldiers, one with a Tommy gun, one with a rifle, one with a pistol. The basement flickered as the soldier with the Tommy gun let loose a thudding volley. He shuddered and shivered; he was growing cold. He was thirsty, wanted to drink water, could drink Lake Constance dry, oh for a sip of water, just need some water, and as the man with the pistol approached, he managed to summon the fortitude to whisper the words, comrade, a little water, comrade, a cigarette, to the man standing before him; and he felt the darkness closing in, and his hands were cold and he shivered, and all he needed was a sip of water and a drag from a cigarette, just send me off with a sip and a smoke, please; and he stared into those eyes and into the mouth of the gun upraised to his own face, and he knew this is the end, this is it. A calm moment of reckoning. A crash, a reverberating crash, and an infinitude of experiences all at once exploded in a flash of white light—childhood, adolescence, adulthood, first steps first day at school first communion first kiss first day on the front, a million voices, a million questions answered and unanswered, memories colliding with memories, pushed aside as a bullet ripped through his mind—and forever and ever ring, foreverandeverandeverring …

A furious clanging within the belfry of his head. Shaking and cluching his pillow. I'm dead, he thinks, I'm dead, and who am I. Who am I. He hears the sound of breathing, another person's breathing, the soft and sensual breathing of a woman.

"Sssssshhhhhhhh, sssssshhhhhhhh," she says from beside him, brushing his face with her hand, and the long twirls of her hair brush lightly against his cheeks as she looks down at him tenderly, "Sssssshhhhhhh, sssssshhhhhhhh, it's okay darling, it's just a dream," and she wipes the sweat off his face and her lips meet his and they form one mouth over a long and deep and tender kiss, soft as his tongue caresses the velvet chamber of her mouth, and there is a stirring and a tickly throbbing tightening in his shorts, ahh, it works, this is what it's like again, it's wonderful so wonderful to kiss you again I want to make love to you, "I love you," he says, "I will always love you … "

Bump! A stir of delirium. Their embrace dissolves into a haze of fragmentary impressions, the dissipation of dream. Eyes squint open to the shadowy bedroom jumble of the predawn. The wardrobe and mirror take shape in the gathering ghostly light. A sighing exhalation. A strange tingling warmth in the loins, a cool breath of air from the window. A draft, the flap of the curtain, the steady murmured whisper of cars. I must have left the window open a crack. Must've left it open yes I left the window open. You'll catch a chill, as Mother says. You'll catch a chill now close your window, dear, words told a thousand times in childhood. Hand on the white-painted window frame, enamelled in old paint cracking, a congealed drop of it forming a bump under finger; a little oomph and the reluctant window groans shut on its dusty cobwebby runner. I've got to do some cleaning. I've been too busy lately. Back into bed, a sliding under covers, a cocooning, sheets pulled up to face and enwombing her in nestled comfort, her own soft bed odours. What was that dream? So vivid, the kiss … that floating kiss, a floodgate of feeling. The smell of cigarettes, the smell of sweat and leather and earth. I love you, he said, I love you and I will always love you. Her eyes well up, her heart beats light and feathery, and her breasts pang, oh God I love you too ... A tear runs hot down her cheek in a twisting course, following the vagaries of gravity and contour. She sits up and breaks into tears, stomach muscles contracting in sobs, tears streaming down, lips blubbering, voice shuddering. She dons the rumpled nightgown in the skeletal wooden chair beside the bed. To the closet. The floor is cool on her bare feet. She opens the sliding closet door and is greeted by hanging rows of clothing in collapsed and unworn profile—dresses, skirts, blouses, bloomers on one side, and pants, shirts, undershirts, a blazer and a suit on the other. She sniffs a white button-up cotton shirt, sniffs it, the last civilian shirt he wore before going … when later they parted at the train platform, he looked so handsome in his uniform, oh God he did, didn't he, he looked so handsome as though he were really meant to be doing what he was doing, but what about the life we were working toward ourselves, what about those dreams we had of starting a family? We would have a child by now if he stayed, yes, a child in a world run amok with death, she thinks as she holds the sleeve, limp, unfilled, cast off like a snakeskin, shed from an earlier time, a time now lost to memory and slipping irrevocably into the past, into its dark erosive depths; and she tries to fill it with her mind, but the images that come are just images, just imaginings; she is here, she is now, holding a hanging sleeve and crying into the breast pocket. It doesn't even smell like him anymore, it smells like cloth and dust, the gently sifting accumulation of time, domestic decay.

It is two hours until she has to wake up for work. She finds herself in the kitchen boiling water for tea, filling the mesh globe with flaked leaves of orange pekoe and sinking it into the teapot, steeping tea at the kitchen table in the greyish predawn murk, melancholy, eyes wide open, gently rocking herself in the kitchen chair. She pours herself some in a favourite cup with a floral design and a chipped and gilded rim, and adds milk, watching it cloud and diffuse as she stirs it with a tiny spoon, and she takes a sip and opens up a box of letters that she has brought with her from the bedroom upstairs. She pulls out a letter:

Somewhere in Italy, July 20th, 1944

Dear Marianne,

Well, not much new to report around here other than that my arm is healing up fairly quickly. Given all of what I've seen bullets can do, I feel I've gotten off rather lucky. I am told I will be able to undertake full duties again soon. This makes me feel good. It's funny—when you're up at the sharp end you think a trip to Blighty is exactly what you need, and when you are at rest you can't wait to go back in. I guess we always want what we can't have, or want to be where we are not now.

Thank you again for sending me treats after you heard that I was wounded—my recuperation has been so much more pleasurable than it may have been without. I should send you more letters telling you that I've been wounded! (minus the wounds)

My convalescence and the loss of friends in battle recently has led me to ruminate a lot on the meaning of what we're all doing over here. It's made me really appreciate what I've got, and it's made me reflect on the value of each inch of ground taken, each drop of blood spilled.

It's also made me reflect on just how much I love you, Marianne, and how alone I am without you over here. I love you every bit as much as I told you I did on our wedding day. When I get back let's have a baby. I wish I had agreed when you suggested the idea that night. With you a mother and I a father we can together create a legacy that will outlast us, a legacy that will be a testament to the better days ahead, the better days after victory. I know this may sound a bit grandiose, Marianne, but hear me out—I long to be with you again.

Please give everyone my regards, in particular your parents. You are always in my thoughts and are a beacon of hope to me. I will see you someday soon—

Love Jim

She had missed him so much. She had feared for him so much. She had loved him, loved him, loved making love to him, like when they made love on their wedding night, the rest of their lives supposedly sealed, she secure and happy and satisfied in his hold, his arms around her as he fell asleep, her eyes starry, the soft whisper of their plans echoed in the early autumn breeze blowing through the trees outside the window—this is the man I will spend the rest of my life with, she said to herself, and a lightness percolated up through her—this is the man whose children I will bear, will happily and lovingly bear. This is the man who will give me the stability I have so always wanted, she thought, her mind turning to the failing family store and her father's spendthrift and intemperate ways, borne as they were at least in part by his purgatorial stint in the trenches in the blood and bonemeal welter of Passchendaele, leaving her mother stoically and unsmilingly in charge of keeping up appearances with her thrift and savvy as her father slowly decayed, gambling and drinking and wandering and rambling and lending money he did not really have anymore to broken-down old comrades even more down on their luck than he was, who came knocking and asking like in the song oft heard on the radio in the lean and hungry years before the blood-red opportunity of war beckoned again, "Brother, can you spare me a dime?"

When Jim had embarked on the same path and enlisted she had been proud of him, in a way, worried that she would lose him one way or another, in a flash and a bang or in a change so horrific as to make him a different person, a stranger returning home whom she would have to learn to love, and oh, the guilt she has felt from this thought, and the fear she felt and still feels about his safety during these lonely hours of the night gnaws away at her own health, her own wellbeing, magnified by the headlines and movie newsreels and sobering radio reports; and she wonders if he has yet received her letter, and in the kitchen, over tea, over the same table where many an argument had erupted, over a letter, in the gathering ghostly light of the predawn, she starts to sob and tremble. She knows what needs to be done, what can only be done.

She puts the letter away in the box and carries the box to the hearth. She crinkles a section of newspaper and places it in the fireplace, surrounding it with a small teepee of split kindling, and lights it with a match struck on the stones, watching the paper contract and crumple as it feeds the growing flame. She puts in the letter she has just read and watches it, too, crumple as it is set alight. In goes another, and then another, and another. One by one she sets fire to every letter he has ever sent her, and as she does so, as each letter is consumed in the pyre of their marriage, her heart lightens. She knows that she will have to leave, that she will be held to scarlet-letter shame for her abandonment, but that is the price she is willing to pay, and as the flames burn higher and higher in the fever of their consumption, she feels a feeling of peace come over her. It's over, she thinks. God bless him wherever he is, but it's over.

Waiting, waiting, waiting. Did you never stop to think that she was waiting for you, too?

Guilt courses through him. I was there, I was just there I was just there oh my God I was where am I really what is going on I am swimming my head is swimming I am swimming in the sheets I must be near the end.

"Well? Do you have an answer?" Standing at the front of his fourth grade class, Miss Ward imposing over him, brandishing a yardstick. She glowers in highly studied disapproval at his failure to correctly recite his twelfth timestable. He bungled twelve times eleven, and now has been singled out for public punishment and humiliation. The nervous and expectant silence of his classmates rings loudly and dumbly across the years, and he can still smell the woolly sop of wet mittens baking crustily on the classroom radiator. The windows rattle under a blizzard beating of wet snow. His hands are stretched out in front of him, and he is awaiting the sharp strike of the yardstick across his palms, with which Miss Ward hits those who fail to measure up. She brings it down and it raps his knuckles with a stinging, burning snap. Tears of shame burn down his face, prompted by the stinging of his hands. For the rest of the day, he keeps to himself, on the verge of tears, ashamed of his ignorance and his humiliation at the front of the class. On the way home, bag over his shoulder, crunching through the weighty drifts of wet March snow, he breaks down and punches a snowman in someone's yard until the head rolls off and splats into the snow like the top of a melting ice cream cone, superimposing an image of himself on the pebble grin, carrot nose and coal eyes as he does so; not knowing what you were supposed to know, taking out your frustrations on something else, something you never made—the shame of it! But he resolved to never again cry in public like that, never again; he would be a man from now on. That was weak! Weak! Weak! You little weakling! Never again! And he projected fanciful dreams of strength from then on. He would be like Louis Cyr the weightlifter and strongman! He would lean down over those who would try to tell him what to do, those who would try to make him cry in shame in front of everybody like that! And cry he never did after that, cry would he never do in public like that ever again until the curbside in San Giovanni, crying into his hands drunk alone at the edge of the world, at the edge of reason so many years later—

"Well? Did you never?" Colonel Hobson looks him up and looks him down, and then booms, "Answer me McFarlane, tell me *something*! Damn you, McFarlane!" Colonel Hobson shouts curtly down upon him as he huddles broken in spirit rocking himself on the floor of the slit trench, arms wrapped round his knees, hands over his face, the ammonia tinge of urine in the air, the demeaning warm flood in his pants, down his legs, the growing dark stain on his trousers, oh how he hated himself just now, crying and crying, I thought I never cried again—

"You malingering coward, McFarlane! I ought to strike you across the face with my hand, McFarlane! You simpering baby! I ought to have you court-martialled and drummed out for cowardice, McFarlane! Remember when they drummed out Stradwick for buggery? That should have been *you* we drummed out! Stradwick might have been a sodomite, but you are a malingering coward! You are good for nothing, McFarlane! Nothing!" Next to him a dead man propped against the side of the trench, staring at nothing, eyes unfocused, hole in his forehead, guts in his lap, a twisted slither of intestines turning into worms, into slithering coils of fattening, feeding worms, and the hands move and pinch the worms that they hold, and there is a wan smile and a wink, and a centipede, armoured and segmented and many-legged, emerges from the lips—

"Hey, sir." A hand, cold and clammy, reaches out and grabs his shoulder. "Come on, sir." He removes his hands from his face and looks up from the trench corner in which he is huddled. It is Lieutenant Blake, squatting on the lip of the trench, reaching in to pull him out into the inferno with him. He has a jaded and furious look on his pale and greenish face. Jim shudders and tries to withdraw, loosening dirt from the side of the trench, exposing the mucosal sheen of a fat, slithering earthworm. Worms everywhere, slithering in wriggling piles, dozens, hundreds, and he can feel their hunger, and he feels the earth wants to claim him, and he is to be devoured by worms and maggots, the prying, wriggling fingers, the digestive intestines of the claimant earth. There is a choking, gassy stench of decay. He gasps and recoils, kicking at the writhing and slithering stew of worms as he does so.

"Come on, sir! You can't scuttle away under a church pew this time or go and hug Mommy's leg! Come and face the music with the rest of us!" Blake yanks his shoulder hard, pulling Jim up to his knees. Blake glowers as he looks Jim deep in the eyes, and he spits, "Don't send me anywhere you're too afraid to go to yourself—sir. If you outrank me, then show me the way yourself! Prove your worth!"

"That's right, you coward, follow this man!" barks Hobson. "He's a hero! Died for King and Country he did, right at his post. If you have the balls to call yourself captain, then you should do the same!"

Kicking at the worms again as they inch toward him in his hole, his grave.

The thunder of the shells pounding the earth. The bullets cracking overhead. A sudden desire to charge into this maelstrom, to consummate his fear into action. Out of the trench and into the ruined streets. Volcanic ash rains down upon them in hot sifting winds; pumice falls like hailstones. A dog lies gagging, curled up, chained to a post. A sign on a newly painted house shouts out, *Vernice fresca!* A fuel truck burns; flames hiss and crack and lash the sky red. All the soldiers around him charge into the fray, into the red and black glowing volcanic roar, the crackling inferno; and to a man, they fall, gagging on the ash, the dust, the earth that claims them; they fall to their knees, onto their faces, onto their backs, and they curl onto their sides in their death throes and are buried in the ash, and he can see their faces, every one; among others he sees Fitzpatrick, Bly, Leprenniere, Peltier, Harrigan, Kelly, Blake, Schneider, Symic, Cooley, all frozen in their final postures, eyes squeezed shut and hands over mouths and noses; and he tastes the bitter ashes and the ashes lash and sting his eyes and choke his throat and rake his air passages, and he peers down upon his fallen comrades, and the air is thick and sulphurous hot and acrid poison, and he gags and his throat begins to close and he falls to his knees to take his place among them and he feels his body stiffen as he too is buried in ash and pumice, and his essence dissipates into nothing, the void breaking the bonds between molecules and between atoms, the void expanding as his form dissipates like particles of smoke into the moonless blackness of the night sky, bonds broken, matter inert, energy released ... and the ash is blown away and the sun is shining, the storm is over, and he hovers above this scene and sees all of them, himself included, reduced to petrified plaster casts of their final agonies on the stones of the street, grey and twisted, filled in from the hollows formed through the centuries of their bodies' dissolution, the ruined façades on either side of them, the faded sign still shouting out *Vernice fresca!*, weeds protruding from between the stones and the sun shining over all; and his bed of ashes is a bed of snow, and he is lying on his back in the snow of childhood, making a snow angel as the flakes sift softly down from the sky, and he exhales a crystalline smoke of frost, a million perfect symmetries, just close your eyes and catch a snowflake on your tongue and then it's homeward with your sled in tow for hot chocolate and a hug and a kiss oh yes, just close your eyes and float into the sky, a restful release … He hovers above the bed, above his own form, his eyes closed, his face an ashen grey turning white, ashes to ashes, dust to dust, and he feels an unspoken understanding commingling with all those who have died recently in all the recent battles and those who have expired in the hospital, and he feels the world leave and himself leave the world, sounds and images fading, a wordless understanding, and there is a tunnel and a pinprick of light at the end of it, a compression of white flowing light, eternity compressed in a diamond, and is this the heavenly meadow of forever he wonders as he wondered once in his mother's lap in church and in his bed during the childhood nightmare storms and under a pew as another storm raged, a storm not of innocence but of experience, a storm of men and their fury, and he lets that go, he lets it all go and lets himself bathe in the soft white approaching light and he feels himself freed and floating toward the light peace beyond words an acceptance, and I the pillar of the ego melts like a candle in the approaching of the light, and he is dissolving in the light enfolded in the night, understanding and expanding and truth at once unsequenced and ungrammared in the arrival of the light—

No! No! Pulled back, dragged away from the light through the cold cosmos, centred and solidified back into the supine form of his own broken self. Eyes flutter open to shapes and shadows and a muddle of noise. Shapes sharpen into doctors and medical instruments, noise articulates into voices; and he sees himself being transfused, blood from another running from a Coca-Cola bottle into his arm in a new tributary from the ongoing stream of life, of consciousness, opened up and carried along from anonymous others into and through his veins. Two masked doctors brace him, one with spectacles and furrowed brow staring intently at him, what can be seen of his face defined sharply by the demands of the urgent task at hand. No! He cannot form the words; he can scarcely move and his mouth is dry. If only he could just ask for a sip of water.

XXXIV

Dear Jim,

Thank God to hear you're alive. When I heard about your being wounded, I nearly collapsed. Your father had to console me in the front hallway, along with the Western Union man. I am just relieved that the worst did not happen. This is the second time you've been wounded and I understand it's much worse than the first time. You know, I feel it in my gut when there's something wrong, and I felt bad for about a week before. I knew there was something wrong with you, that either something was going to happen or had happened already. I felt this when you were shot in the arm in the spring, you know. I felt it when your brother crash-landed in England and lost his co-pilot. I have had many dreams about you lately. Call it mother-sense, or something like that. I don't know. Call me crazy if you want to, but I'm just glad you're safe, so glad you're safe, my big brave boy is safe and will be coming home.

Your father tries to keep my spirits up about all this—I am proud of you, Jim, I'm proud of both of you, I really am—but I am so tired from worry. I suppose the best consolation I get from your being so wounded is that you will recover and you will come home. There will be no more fighting for you. One of my boys, my daring and adventurous boys, has been pulled out of the fire and will come home.

I cannot wait till I see you again.

I remember rocking you when you couldn't sleep in the middle of the night, I remember helping you when you were sick, I remember disinfecting your bloody knees when you came in from roughhousing with

Mark or your school friends. You always were an active one! I will do whatever I need to do for you, Jim—the work of a mother is never done.

Let me tell you something else. You will walk again. It might take weeks, it might take months, it might take years—but you WILL walk again. Never give up. Don't let your spirits drag you down. So much depends on your attitude, your resolve.

I will now write to you about what is happening around here, but there is not much to report. Things are going fine here, the mines are booming, and since the mines are booming from the war effort, so is the city. Your father has been busy lately, and I have gotten involved with the Victory Bond drives to spend my nervous energy. It has been going well. The neighbours are always asking after Mark and you, and I often have to answer, "I don't know, I hope they are doing fine, I don't hear from them too often, especially Mark." Well, I know you are okay now; at least you will be okay over time.

I miss you Jim, my little Jimmy, miss you so much and I will see you sometime in the coming months, I am sure of it. At church, the priest led the congregation in a prayer for local boys who have been wounded. Your name was mentioned. In like fashion, I continue to pray for your recovery.

Take care, and once again, I cannot wait to see you—

Love Mom

Dear Jim,

Al Riley here. I hope you're on the mend—that's quite a wound you took there at Coriano. One hell of a battle that was. My real baptism of fire, as it were. I went in after you to relieve your command and had to finish the battle as commander of Able Company. It raged on until the wee hours the next morning. It took forever to clear the Germans out of the castle and out of every last damn house. There wasn't much of the town left afterward, let me tell you.

Well, after the battle we had ourselves a proper rest and reorganization back in San Giovanni for over a week. Though, I can tell you that reinforcements are getting thin around here—we are fighting on a forgotten front, as they say. Some of the reinforcements aren't even fit for combat—we have truck drivers and cooks pressed into the infantry. It would be nice if they sent us conscripts to get the job done, but that doesn't seem to be happening. The conscripts just get to sit around and hold the fort against imaginary invaders. The damn government keeps waffling on this conscription thing. But we manage! Over and onward, river by river, we are doing it.

Since our rest after Coriano, we have seen lots of action lately. I hate to be the bearer of bad news, but I feel that I should tell you about some recent casualties. Captain Van Der Hecke's company found themselves cut off north of a river, having pushed too far without support. After a short battle, they surrendered en masse. The padre led a search party for information a few days later, and they found scattered webgear and abandoned weapons, along with several bodies.

As well, and this pains me the most—Warrant Officer Witchewski was killed by a sniper while in action near San Mauro. He was leading a platoon to capture a fortified house in a mucky field. The bastard got him at three hundred yards! I know that he thought very highly of you. I'm sorry to bring you this news. But that is war, I guess.

I want to thank you again for making my introduction to the front line easier for me. It's hard to make friends among hardened veterans—everyone seems to keep their distance. You gave me the confidence boost I needed the night before my first action. Anyway, I hope you are recovering well from your wounds. We are in a pleasant medieval city right now on rotation off the line, and I will raise a glass to your recovery with some of the boys tonight. Take care, Jim, and I hope to catch up with you some time when all this mess is over (judging by the morale of some of the enemy we have taken prisoner lately, that hopefully shouldn't be too long from now.)

Over and out,

Al Riley

Dear Jim,

I'm sorry to hear that you were wounded, but I know that you will pull through. You're my big brother and I look up to you. Always have, always will. I am sorry to hear about you and Marianne, by the way—hardly the first time that that has happened among us fighting men. I thought that you two were very good together. Oh, well—plenty more fish in the sea, right? There are plenty of beautiful and available nurses in the service, let me tell you …

It's been awfully busy here. We've been on lots of raids, and some of them have been really hairy. I've lost a lot of friends over the last while, but thankfully we have been flying light duty assignments lately to rest and rebuild the squadron—laying sonar buoys in the ocean, that sort of thing. We did one raid over Cologne awhile back that really tore us up bad. The night fighters really had their way with us on that one. Our plane limped back on three engines and with a huge hole in the fuselage. We had a dead gunner and a wounded navigator. Our plane was all shot to hell—Thank God Almighty the landing gear deployed well enough!

It's about time this war ended. I've had about enough of Mom's fretting and Dad's "I'm so proud of my fighting son," all that sort of stuff. Boy, we have sure been over here for a long time, haven't we?

I really enjoyed those times that we met up while in England—I'm so glad that we were able to spend time together before you got shipped off to Sunny Italy. Well, pull through, big brother, and I can't wait to see you when all this is over. Take care over there—

Mark

Dear Jim,

I am sorry to hear about what happened to you. I wished the timing wasn't so bad—I feel guilty now, I feel horrible pangs of guilt. I sometimes wonder if the receipt of the letter led to your wounding. Whatever has come between us, I want you to know that I worry about your well-being. I am not sure that these words will find you well, but you know that none of your words in recent months have found me well. I had been in an increasing funk over our separation. You can understand that I feel that you chose duty to country over me; I would certainly understand your decision were you a bachelor, but the fact is that you were not one. I have thought long and hard about the decision that I made in consequence of yours, and I feel that it is the correct decision.

We had some good times, we made some good memories, but now we must together make our separate ways. I hope that over there maybe you found the meaning you were looking for in life. I would like to think that I was fulfilling to you, that I satisfied you, that the two of us together made you genuinely happy. I always thought that you were man enough, that there was nothing that you really needed to prove.

When you come home I will have gone. Where, I do not yet know. People can be very judging and when word gets out I think that I will find myself under very unpleasant scrutiny. I think I will be going far from here, and I cannot be certain that I will be leaving a forwarding address.

I wish you the best, Jim. I really do. I wish for you to find your own way, to achieve all it is that you want to achieve, to bloom where you are planted. Take care, Jim. Whatever it is you do in the future, wherever you go, take care. I hope you find happiness and contentment in any future venture. All the best—

Yours truly,

Marianne

XXXV

Up, down, up, down, the lulling swells of the sea, the shifting mailed coat of the sea, the overlapping scaled armour of the sea, wind-flexed and rippling; a gunmetal sea under a gunmetal sky. The corvettes and destroyers that dive into the troughs and climb upon the swells, and sweep this way and that on patrol, their sticks and stacks protruding above the waves and the spray that break over their decks, the casemates of their deck guns pointed askew; the corvettes and destroyers that dive and sweep and arc are currents perched upon larger, deeper, subtler currents, like disturbed swirls water in the wake of an insect swimming on the waves; the troopships and merchant ships in their charge are slower and more plodding, a steady westward current, a weighted momentum of men and materiel, lumbering through the water like lazily swimming beavers.

Push, pull, push, pull ... The air is cold and damp and the wind is biting, but the sun now winks through the rolling grey clouds, the tatters of clouds that scroll through the sky, the winking sun like a semaphore message from the heavens, a Morse Code signal to hold steady, relief is on the way, there has been a breakthrough. The clouds are breaking apart in the sharpness of the wind. He shivers as a faint sunray makes its vague contact, the filtered light of the sun having made its ninety-three million mile journey through cosmic radiation, through the gases and water vapors of the atmosphere, reflected and refracted and trapped in transparent prison by countless droplets of moisture, the billowing and vaporous fortifications of the atmosphere that now crumble under the persistent bombardment of its radiant columns, aided now by the capricious winds that strip away the clouds, sometimes friend and sometimes foe, always switching sides; and the clouds loosen and whiten into tattered banners of surrender, and on this occasion, the sun has won the day and occupies the sky and the sea below it with its luminous legions, firmly set in its dominion of the day, turning the sea a sparkling blue as it glints off the calming ripples of the ocean in countless rows like shields upraised in victory; and as the sun hits his face, as the warmth of the sun caresses his face, he sighs almost inaudibly. He is the only one on the promenade right now save for the nurse who is blowing on her hands as she surveys the sunlit ocean scene. His head is humming, and he feels dreamy. The screaming pain in his legs and back has been reduced to distant background noise; it comes in waves, and he is riding the crest of one now. The slide down into the next trough will be as the codeine wears off. He wheels up closer to the deck railing, pushing the wheels of the chair with his hands, the metal turn-wheels of the chair cold to his hands. The chair squeaks ahead to the railing of the promenade deck. He can hear the swish of the sea as the converted liner cuts through the waves, and the ship rocks gently, wave by wave. He is not seasick; in fact, he has not been at all on this journey, however long it has been in the opiated haze in which he has been, sitting, sleeping, being tended by doctors and nurses, eating small meals with what little appetite he has had, and listlessly watching films and playing cards with other wounded servicemen on their way home, hailing from all the battlefields of Europe, from every corner of Canada.

Overhead, a buzz of planes, Liberator bombers covering the sea lanes, on the watch for submarines. It must be getting on to winter now. Of course it's always winter on the North Atlantic; it is a wintry place, a snowy windswept storm-tossed prairie of water. At home it is cold, cold, cold, the front windows of houses straining their gaze through their cataracts of frost upon the denuded branches of the trees and the frosted blades of grass like hair gone white in the dawning old age of winter.

Ssshhhhh ... ssshhhhh ... ssshhhh, the lulling sound of the water against the hull, the sibilant swell of ocean waves ... ssshhhhh ...

ssshhhhh … a temptation to become part of that sound, to immerse himself in the soft sibilance of the sea, the womb, the saltwater sea of origin; it would be cold at first, yes, so cold it would be like a million burning needles of heat, but sleep would come quickly and there would be no more pain to run from, no more pain at all. He would be dead before they could rescue him. The nurse would alert the crew, and the officer of the watch would yell, "Man overboard!" And that would be his eulogy. After awhile, the pain intensifies a little from the vague throb it has been for the last hour, intensifies, heats up, becomes more acute. This is the time to do it.

"I'm going to try," he says weakly to the nurse.

"Don't hurt yourself, Captain. Just rest, and tell me when you want to go back inside into the saloon." Her voice is patient, calm, caring.

"No—I want to." He braces his arms against the turn-wheels and tries to lift himself out of his chair. As some of his weight shifts to his feet, there is a horrible, grinding pain all the way up his legs, up into his back. It takes his breath away, bright lights dance in front of his eyes, and he winces and gnashes his teeth together. His arms, weak from disuse, tremble and burn with exertion.

"Captain, let me help you," the nurse enjoins from somewhere at the end of a tunnel.

"No—leave me alone, please," he commands with teeth bared against the pain. He puts one hand and then the other on the railing. He focuses his concentration into throwing all his might into his arms so that he can hoist himself over the railing into the sea below, just concentrate, yes, concentrate, just concentrate, sssssshhhhhh … sssssshhhhhh; and as he begins to flex, to lift, he stops for a moment. Breathes a minute. Still grasping the railing, still weakly standing, he reaches into his pocket for his pillbox, and without any further thought casts it into the ocean where it disappears amid the foamy wash alongside the ship, amid the subsiding waves that lap and break against the parting of the hull. He settles with a thump back into his chair, and relief washes over him. Throw out the pills, not the pain, he thinks. The pain will subside on its own.

"I'm ready to go in now."

Acknowledgements

I wish to thank, in no particular order, the following people and organizations for their help and encouragement during the writing of this novel. They are as follows: Adam Boyle, for his hands-on help with the extensive historical research needed to make the story authentic, and for the endless late-night discussions about the subject matter; my sister Patti Murphy, for her early support and editorial encouragement; Rick Dubé, for his feedback and advice; Mary Sutton, for her expert critical faculties as applied in the first full draft edit; my wife Lia Roy, for her narrative advice and eagle-eyed copyediting, as well as her expert promotional savvy and overall encouragement; my parents, Lou and Sheila Murphy, for their ongoing encouragement; and the National Library and Archives of Canada, for the endless fund of resources that were made available to me in my research. Thanks also to all those who contributed to the Indiegogo fundraising campaign that helped me to publish this book. You know who you are, and I could not have done this without you.